A Fly Has a Hundred Eyes

A FLY HAS A HUNDRED EYES

AILEEN G. BARON

Academy Chicago Publishers

Published in 2007 by
Academy Chicago Publishers
363 West Erie Street
Chicago, Illinois 60610

Hardcover edition printed in 2002

© 2002 by Aileen G. Baron

Printed in the U.S.A.

**Library of Congress Cataloging-in-Publication Data
on file with the publisher**

To
DAVID, BOB, ERIC AND JIMMY

ONE

LATER, LILY WOULD REMEMBER the early morning quiet, the shuttered shops in the narrow lanes of the Old City. She would remember that few people were in the streets—bearded Hassidim in fur-trimmed hats and prayer shawls over long black cloaks returning from morning prayer at the Wailing Wall, an occasional shopkeeper sweeping worn cobbles still damp with dew.

She would remember the empty bazaar, remember that the peddler who usually sold round Greek bread from his cart near Jaffa Gate was gone.

She would remember the crowd of young Arabs, their heads covered with checkered black and white *kefiyas*, waiting in the shade of the Grand New Hotel, leaning against the façade, sitting on window ledges near the entrance; remember them crowded under Jaffa Gate in a space barely wide enough to drive through with a cart, standing beneath the medieval arches and crenellated ramparts, faces glum, arms crossed against their chests, rifles slung across their backs, revolvers jammed into their belts. One wore a Bedouin knife, its tin scabbard encrusted with bright bits of broken glass.

Only their eyes moved as they watched her pass. Lily remembered holding her breath, pushing her way through, feeling their body heat, snaking this way and that to avoid touching the damp sweat on their clothing. No one stepped out of her way.

She would remember the bright Jerusalem air, fresh with the smell of pines and coffee and the faint tang of sheep from the fields near the city wall; the empty fruit market, usually crowded with loaded camels and donkey carts and turbaned *fellahin* unloading produce, deserted and silent. Vendor's stalls, looking like boarded shops on a forlorn winter boardwalk, shut; cabs and carriages gone from the taxi stand.

She would remember the pool at the YMCA, warm as tea and green with algae, and the ladies gliding slowly through the water, wearing shower caps and corsets under their bathing suits, scooping water onto their ample bosoms, gathering to gossip at the shallow end. She would remember swimming around them with steady strokes, her legs kicking rhythmically, and the terrible tempered Mrs. Klein, blowing like a whale, ordering Lily to stop splashing. A tiny lady holding onto the side of the pool and dunking herself up and down like a tea bag nodded in agreement; Elsa Stern, the little round pediatrician with curly gray hair, gave Lily a conspiratorial wink and kept swimming laps.

She would remember it all. Everything about that day would haunt her.

Lily Sampson was on her way to the new YMCA on Julian's Way that morning, to catalogue pottery from the Clarke collection in the little museum being built in the Observation Tower.

She had stayed at the YMCA four years ago when it first opened in 1934 and reveled in its splendor, in its graceful proportions, in its arches and tiled decoration, its tennis courts and gardens, and the grand Moorish lobby paved with Spanish tiles. It had a restaurant, an auditorium where Toscanini played, and a swimming pool—the only one in Jerusalem. Tourists came to ooh and ah and told her this was the most beautiful YMCA in the world. They would climb the Observation Tower for a view of the city and look through telescopes into windows of apartments on Mamilla Street and Jaffa Road.

Lily went there to swim three times a week when she was in Jerusalem, walking from the American School through the quiet lanes of the Musrarra quarter, or cutting through the Old City.

At five minutes to nine, her hair still damp against her ears, her eyes stinging from chlorine, Lily climbed the six flights to the little museum.

Sheets of glass and wooden shelving for cases were stacked against the wall in the corner of a large, bare room that held only an old table, two wooden chairs, pottery wrapped in newspapers and stowed on the floor in old grocery cartons, and a wall clock that said four minutes before nine.

Eastbourne had said he would be here around nine o'clock. Lily suspected that if Eastbourne agreed to help her today, he had reasons of his own. She was grateful that he recommended her for this job, grateful for the small windfall from cataloguing pottery during the short break in excavations at Tel al-Kharub.

Lily stepped onto the balcony that opened off the museum, holding her breath at the sight of Jerusalem, creamy gold in the morning brightness. The great gilded cupola of the Dome of the Rock glinted in the sun. The Old City—its stone walls adorned with towers and battlements, steeples and minarets—loomed behind the King David Hotel.

She could see the grim-faced young Arabs she had passed this morning at Jaffa Gate, the crowd now grown to two hundred or more. The tops of their heads bobbed like so many black-and-white checkered beach balls.

Smoke twisted from small fires in the Valley of Hinnom. Lily looked through the telescope toward Government House on the crest of the Hill of Evil Council. She could just make out the Union Jack, flopping limply from its tower.

On the street, a dapper American tourist in a Panama hat and seersucker suit came out of the King David across the way.

The ladies left the YMCA one by one—Mrs. Klein, still frowning, her hair pulled back tightly in a bun, marched down the street. Dr. Stern walked toward the corner.

Lily heard Eastbourne enter the museum. "Let's get to work." He looked at his watch. "I don't have much time."

Full of his usual charm this morning, she thought. "I was watching for you. I didn't see you in the street."

"I had breakfast downstairs."

"You actually ate here?"

"I was hungry for some good English cooking and a real breakfast."

Of course you were, Lily thought. Good British housewives get up early every morning to cool the toast and put lumps in the porridge.

"You don't have a cook at the British School?"

"He's an Arab. This morning I had ham and eggs."

Lily noticed the newspaper under his arm and twisted her head to read the headlines.

Eastbourne folded it into a small packet and put it in his pocket. "I haven't finished with the paper." He looked out at the street and checked his watch again.

On the wall clock, it was exactly 9:00 a.m.

An explosion somewhere in west Jerusalem rocked the air.

After a tick of silence, a shout of "Allah Akbar" erupted in a full-throated roar from the crowd gathered at Jaffa Gate.

Lily rushed to the balcony, Eastbourne close behind. A mob spewed out of the Old City, propelled by the rhythmic chant, onto Mamilla, around the King David Hotel, spreading in a torrent toward west Jerusalem. Five or six men carrying rifles ran down Julian's Way. They encircled a truck, rocking it back and forth until it turned over.

At first the impassioned madness and destruction seemed strangely distant to Lily, choreographed and rehearsed, like a slow-moving pageant. She watched three men rush from the gas station at the turn of the road with full jerry cans, spilling gasoline on the street as they ran.

Waving fists, brandishing rifles, kefiyas flying in the wind, the horde swarmed into the warren of back streets with old Jewish shops and houses, down Jaffa Road toward Zion Circus. A blare of sirens, scattered shouts and screams carried from the direction of west Jerusalem on wind heavy with smoke.

Lily heard the crash of shattering glass. Looking toward Mamilla she saw a man with a jerry can splash gasoline through a shop window. A rumble of flames erupted and danced in the currents of heat from the rush of the blaze.

"It's that bloody Grand Mufti, al-Husseini," Eastbourne's nostrils dilated with anger and he wiped his hand across his mouth. "You can't trust him. He's orchestrating this from Syria, with the backing of Hitler and his crowd."

The tourist from the King David, his back arched in a posture of fear, stood in the middle of the street now, tilted this way and that by rioters who swirled around him as if he were a lamppost.

Eastbourne watched from the doorway, looking toward the tourist in the Panama hat, and glanced at his watch again.

Mrs. Klein advanced on the rabble like a tank, shouting and flailing her arms. The mob surrounded her while she punched and kicked and screamed. They pressed against her, pushing her back onto the road. She floated to her knees, her skirt billowing around her, falling to the asphalt, her hair undone and sticky with blood that began to puddle on the pavement.

Dr. Stern turned back, hurrying toward her friend splayed on the sidewalk. A man careened to face Dr. Stern. He stepped into her path, thrust a fist in her direction as if to greet her. Her eyes widened, her mouth opened. She staggered against him. He pushed her away and slowly, carefully, she plummeted straight down, silent, onto the sidewalk.

Benumbed, Lily reached over the balcony railing as if to help. Trembling, she closed her eyes in horror and Eastbourne pulled her back, back to the notebook on the table, back to the comfort of the past to count clay lamps, juglets, burnished bowls with turned-back rims. She picked up a lamp, the nozzle smudged with ancient soot, and put it down again, drawn back to the balcony with a horrified fascination.

The tourist in the seersucker suit, without his Panama hat, disappeared into the revolving door of the hotel.

"Get inside," Eastbourne said. "This isn't a peep show." He looked at the street. "When this is over, they'll cover the bodies, take them away, and hose down the streets."

What will be left in two thousand years, Lily wondered? Just a thin layer of charcoal, without memory, without skeletons to mark the day, just one more level in the stratigraphy of Jerusalem?

People hung out of the windows of the King David Hotel, one man with field glasses, others leaning against balcony railings, some aghast, some curious. A father led his small daughter inside, shut the door and pulled down the blinds.

The tourist in the seersucker suit was gone.

Dr. Stern lay on her side in the street. Little rivulets of blood seeped from beneath her, flowing downhill and staining the pale blue cloth of her skirt. The little tea bag lady lay on the steps of the YMCA as if asleep in the wrong place.

Mrs. Klein lay in a widening dark pool, her hair, beginning to mat with blood, loose and wild against the asphalt. She looked oddly peaceful, her frown gone, her jaw fallen open in death.

False teeth lay beside her softened cheek. A man stopped, looked at the teeth on the sticky pavement, picked them up, wiped the blood on his sleeve, and put them in his pocket. He pulled a knife from his belt. Brandishing the knife, he ran on toward Mamilla.

"The name Jerusalem means City of Peace, you know," Eastbourne said.

Shuddering, Lily edged back to the table. The haze of smoke from the fires, the blare of fire trucks, the sounds of sirens from ambulances, of sobs, of wounded and mourners, of shutters ringing down with a clatter, penetrated the room. Lily was drawn to the balcony, and back inside to the table, too mesmerized to stop, too terrified to watch, mourning for the ladies who would never again skim across the green water, for Canaanites and Jebusites, for Israelites and Judeans, for Crusaders and Mamelukes who fought in this city with its twisted streets, its strange mystique and power, its heritage of blood and vengeance.

"Go downstairs and get me a packet of Players," Eastbourne said, reaching into his pocket. "Here are fifty mils. Bring me the change."

Lily dropped the money when he held it out. Her fingers numb and shaking, she picked it up slowly. "Sorry. I wasn't looking." She turned toward the door.

In the lobby, the desk clerk looked at her dumbly, his eyes glazed, his face pale. A bushy mustache hid his mouth and quivered when he spoke.

"Rioting in the streets and you ask for cigarettes," he said in a hushed monotone. "Cigarettes? Are you mad?"

"Players," Lily repeated.

"I don't sell them here. In the dining room."

Lily trudged into the dining room. The desk clerk followed and placed himself behind the bar.

"Players," Lily said again and put the money on the counter. He counted it and pushed back the change. "You cold-blooded English. You have no feelings. Here are your cigarettes."

"I'm American."

"Crazy American. You're all the same."

She climbed the stairs, catching her breath at the landings, looking down empty halls at laundry carts stacked with fresh linens for unmade beds. She felt heat from hidden pipes radiate through the whitewashed walls, heard the elevator knock and clatter as it moved from floor to floor.

On the sixth floor, the museum was silent. The notebook was still open on the table. The clay lamp was where she had put it down.

And Eastbourne was gone.

TWO

LILY PUT THE CIGARETTES and change on the table and waited for Eastbourne. She wavered back and forth between the table and the balcony, picking up a black juglet and putting it down. "He's a grown man," she said aloud and sat down at the table. "He can take care of himself."

She pulled the pottery registry toward her and turned a page. He's probably down the hall. Maybe downstairs.

She dipped the pen in India ink to write a registration number on the juglet. Maybe he was out strolling down Julian's Way with a gentlemanly swagger, scorning the brouhaha with his usual bravado. Register the juglet. What number? What comes after two hundred forty-seven?

She imagined Eastbourne trying to shout down a clutch of angry rioters, lying on the pavement in their wake, his white Bermuda shorts and knee socks bright with blood.

Is it two hundred fifty?

Oh, God.

She put down the pen and started toward the balcony. The elevator door clanged open and shut. Steps sounded in the hall. For a moment, she was relieved. But it wasn't Eastbourne—the gait was faster and heavier. Lily moved toward the far side of the table as the footfalls came closer, clicking and reverberating on the tiled floor.

The tourist in the seersucker suit, his Panama hat gone, faced Lily from the doorway. He stared at her, his eyes deep-set, a distracting electric blue. He glared at the notebook on the table, the pen, the bowl, the juglet in Lily's hand.

"Can I help you?" she asked.

He hesitated. "Beg your pardon." His voice was deep and resonant. He watched her come around the table and waited, his expression blank, his fists clenched.

"You're looking for Eastbourne? He was here a minute ago," Lily told him.

The eyes of the man in the seersucker suit traced her movements. She went to the balcony, and he followed.

"He might have gone out," she added.

His jaw protruded and the side of his face twitched. The man leaned over the rail. "I don't know anyone named Eastbourne." His eyes continued to search up and down the street.

If not Eastbourne, who was he looking for?

"You lost your hat."

"Beg pardon?" He worked his jaw again. His eyes glinted at her, hard and angry. "Sorry to bother you." He went back through the museum, pausing at the table, eyeing the cardboard boxes on the floor, turning a page of the notebook.

"Something you wanted?" she asked.

"Just curious."

Lily followed him into the hall. The elevator had remained at the sixth floor. She watched the man get in and close the glass door. She waited for the light from the car to descend, then returned to the balcony to scan the street.

Where in hell could Eastbourne have gone on a day like this?

Smoke swirled around the lower floors of the old stone Windmill, almost obscuring the squat rows of Montefiore cottages nestled against it. Looters, their kefiyas flapping and nodding as they ran, dragged a dazed old man into the street and flogged him with a heavy stick in rhythmic blows, like a housewife beating a rug. One gang of men brandishing rifles converged on Barclays' Bank on Mamilla just past the Palace Hotel, another moved toward the new Post Office on Jaffa Road.

In front of the YMCA, only pigeons strutted and pecked on the grimy sidewalk. The dead women, silent and desolate, lay uncovered on the pavement, open to the sky.

Lily shuddered.

She started down the stairs, closing the door behind her. She stopped at a landing to gather sheets from the linen cart. In the lobby, the sheets hidden in her bag, she passed the clerk, still pale behind his bushy mustache. He sat at the desk, holding a sandwich, his fingers shaking.

"Can't go outside," he said, without looking at her. "Too dangerous."

"It's all right," she told him. "I have an errand. I'll be right back."

He came around the desk to stand in front of her and block her way. A crumb hanging from his mustache fluttered with each breath. "You can't go. Door is locked. I summoned police. They arrive soon."

She moved around him toward the women's locker room. He called after her, and she kept going, past the showers and dressing room, out to the tennis courts, and around to the front of the building where the ladies lay, their blood crusted and brown on the street and buzzing with flies.

Stepping carefully, first she covered Dr. Stern. The sheet whipped in the wind and spread over the silent corpse, drifting and sagging like a blanket over a restless sleeper. Then, eyes averted, she hid Mrs. Klein's bruised face and bloody hair. Next Lily covered the little tea bag lady as though she were tucking her in for the night.

Lily's legs began to tremble. Hardly aware of what she was doing, she started to run toward East Jerusalem, away from the sounds of screams and sirens that carried toward her from Zion Circus, away from the smoke that caught at her throat.

Heart pounding, breath burning, she ran—away from Julian's Way toward Princess Mary, away from the relentless sight of the ladies on the sidewalk with their staring eyes, to the safety of home at the American School, to the familiar world beyond its iron gate, behind its green-shuttered windows.

Stay away from banks and post offices, she remembered. That's what they hit first.

Not that way.

She zigzagged through the streets, still running, gasping for breath, toward the Musrarra quarter, her legs moving automatically, her sandals hammering the street.

She hurried past houses with locked gates and empty gardens. Panting, she slowed when she reached Musrarra. Her footsteps echoed along the deserted alley. Gunfire crackled from somewhere in west Jerusalem. She began to run again. Winded, she paused at the top of a narrow road, the sound of her pulse beating in her ears, and ran again.

Across the field on Nablus Road, the high walls of the École Biblique hid the serene compound, with its tombs and chapels, its library and hostel, and the ruins of the ancient church of Saint Stephen. Almost home, she thought. Almost home.

Four young men, dark and thin, with pinched chests and narrow shoulders, their shirts hanging open and creased with soot, turned the corner. Street punks, Lily thought. They carried heavy sticks and sauntered toward her, four abreast, a gang of hoodlums on the prowl, slashing at the air.

"Hello, darling," the shortest called out. He had a knife in his belt.

Lily ran toward the École. Her sandal slipped on a stone. She lost her balance, threw out her arms to steady herself, and kept running.

They were closer now. "Darling, I love you," the short one said. A cigarette was propped behind his ear.

Lily pressed the bell next to the small door in the wall of the École. The explosive ring echoed through the street. The two on the right flourished their sticks and sniggered.

"You know you want me, darling," the one with the cigarette called out.

Lily pressed the bell again.

The one on the right brandished the stick up and down "You waiting for me, darling?" He leered at her while he licked the downy moustache above his upper lip. His nose was running.

The door opened just wide enough for Lily to see dark eyes and the tilted head of the guard. "Library is closed," he said.

"I have an appointment with Pere de Vaux," she told him.

The guard started to close the door. "He's not here. He's at En-Feshka."

The thugs were closing in. Lily jammed her bag into the door to keep it open.

The tallest one had a cracked front tooth and the beginning of a pimple on his chin. He waggled the stick at her and whipped the air with it, close enough for Lily to feel the rush of wind when it passed. She grabbed the end, pulled it toward her, and jabbed it back into his chest. He fell backward against the one with the knife.

Before they could regain their balance, Lily shoved against the door with her shoulder, forced it open, and pushed her way inside, knocking the guard aside. She slammed the door behind her and the lock clicked shut.

The guard gawked at her, then bent down to pick up the pencils and keys that had fallen from her bag. Lily leaned against the wall to catch her breath. Outside, the hoodlums banged against the door, cursing in guttural Arabic.

The guard handed Lily her bag and peeked through a peephole at the street. "You stay," he said and motioned toward a chair in the small guardhouse next to the gate.

He poured coffee into a small cup from a battered *finjan* and brought it to her. "Rest here." His voice was almost drowned by the pounding at the door.

Still gasping for breath, Lily tried to sip the sticky-sweet coffee in the steaming cup. The hot liquid spilled over her fingers and onto her skirt. She stared at her shaking hands, put the cup on the ground, and rubbed at the warm brown stain in her lap, rocking back and forth with the motion of her arm.

The clamor at the door gradually subsided, first curses, then mutters, and finally silence. Lily leaned back in the chair and cradled both hands around the warm cup.

She breathed the aroma of the coffee laced with cardamom, of the pine needles that carpeted the remains of the ancient Byzantine church of Saint Stephen. Vestiges of columns from the atrium stood open to the sky, seeming to grow among the trees. A monk in a light summer robe glided from the chapel toward the library, his sandals crunching on the gravel.

The guard searched through the peephole again, then unlocked the door. He held it ajar and inspected the street.

"Safe," he said. "You go now."

She hurried through the rocky field across from the American School, snaking around stones from ancient walls scattered on the ground, avoiding remains of old excavation trenches now overgrown with weeds.

The dogs in the yard at Sinbad's Taxi on the corner threatened and growled, straining at the ends of their chains. They never got used to her, no matter how often she passed.

They snarled. Lily tried a smile. Behind the closed gate, across Salah-edh-Din Street, was home. Lily read the sign, *American School of Archaeological Research,* attached to the iron fence.

A large American flag fluttered on the railing of the balcony of the room next to hers, like bedding set out to air.

She lifted the hidden latch in the fence, stepped through the gate, and took the path around the building toward the refuge of the garden.

A shrill din of at least fifty people mulled about. They clustered on the sandstone walk, sat on the ledge of the fountain, stood in the rose beds. They talked in high-pitched American voices about hotels, restaurants, the cost of taxis, the riots in the streets outside.

Sir William and Lady Fendley sat in a corner behind posts of the portico, rigid in their chairs. Lady Fendley had once told Lily that they had retired to Jerusalem for the mild climate and because expenses were one-third of what they were in England. "In Jerusalem, the air is like champagne," Lady Fendley had said and told Lily shamefacedly that they chose to live at the American School instead of one of the other archaeological missions for the creature comforts, for ". . . the beds with springs instead of those horrid straw mattresses. We wanted hot water and steam heat in winter."

Lily walked toward Sir William. "Who are all these people?" She gestured in the direction of the Americans thronged in the garden.

Lady Fendley, her back straight, her elbows close to her body, eyed the crowd as if they were rabble. "They're refugees from some sort of madness in the street." She stood up and helped Sir William from his chair.

"Come inside to the Common Room," she said to Lily. "Less noise in there."

Lady Fendley led Sir William, holding him by the arm, guiding his steps. Lily never knew how he was going to behave, or how to speak to him. Some days he was his old self, the genius of Near Eastern archaeology, blunt and brilliant, with a nimble-witted sparkle in his eyes. At other times he was dithering and helpless, losing the thread of conversation, asking foolish questions. Lady Fendley hung over him like a nesting bird, arranging his collar, smoothing his long white beard, pushing hair from his eyes.

Lily paused at the door, adjusting to the incongruous peace of the Common Room, the dimmed stillness, shadows and silence hovering over woven hangings and heavy leather furniture. Only the drawn blinds rattled with gusts of explosions and gunfire. Small and frail in the large black chair, Sir William smiled at Lily.

"What's going on out there?" Lady Fendley asked.

"A riot." The heavy tick of the wall clock was the loudest sound in the room behind the shelter of the closed drapes.

"They've been rioting for the past two years. Never been such a fuss before." Lady Fendley looked offended. "This is the time we take our walk. Why are you shaking like that?"

"It's worse now," Lily said. "People are dead in the streets." She pointed vaguely toward west Jerusalem and saw her arm shaking, her fists tightly clenched. She sat down in the nearest chair, consciously opening her fists, resting her wrists against her thighs to steady her hands.

"They behave like savages," Lady Fendley said. "No one uses restraint nowadays."

Lily tried to picture Lady Fendley somewhere in the misty rain of the English countryside tending a rose garden.

"It will be all right," Sir William said in a quiet voice. "When I got off the boat in Alexandria in '82, smoke filled the air. Sounds of guns and screams were everywhere. Europeans lined the wharves in wagons, their household goods piled in carts behind them, ready to flee to safer refuge."

Lady Fendley brushed some hair behind his ears. "That was a long time ago, my dear, over fifty years. This is a different matter." She patted his arm. "It's the Mufti, you know. He called for this insurrection. Because of the influx of Jews."

"All the same." Sir William looked up at her. "It's about Suez. Makes us look bad."

"We brought it on ourselves, you know," Lady Fendley said to Lily. "Promising Palestine to the Jews and independence to the Arabs. Ned Lawrence's work. I never did like that young man. Not after that dreadful slaughter in Damascus."

"Lawrence of Arabia?" Lily asked.

"Lawrence of Arabia indeed. Prostituted archaeology for politics. His Negev survey in 1914 was just an excuse to stir up the Bedouin."

Sir William smiled at her. "Has a flair for the dramatic." He wagged his finger. "Without young men like him, we can't win the war."

"The war is over." Lady Fendley gave a sigh of impatience. "Enough about Lawrence. Speak no ill of the dead."

"Ned Lawrence is dead?" Sir William clutched the arms of his chair and leaned forward. "Killed in the line of duty?"

"In Cambridge. Three years ago. I told you then."

Sir William closed his eyes and tilted back his head. "They're all dead. Cairo, Khartoum, Damascus."

"That was all a long time ago."

He screwed up his face as if he were caught in a nightmare. "Nothing is the past. It's always with us. Everyone who died left the ghosts of their unborn children." A tear appeared in the corner of his left eye.

Lady Fendley wiped it away with the back of her hand. "It's all right, my dear." She stroked his cheek and smoothed his hair. "It's all right."

Lily looked away self-consciously, at the window, at the clock, at the newspaper on the table behind the sofa.

She heard Sir William's voice again, coming from the depths of the chair. "So you work with Eastbourne and Kate. They were my students, you know. With me in Egypt. Did I tell you they were Fendley's Foals?"

Many times, Lily thought. Each time she saw him he would babble about Kate Hale and Eastbourne and their student days in Egypt. Sir William kept talking, words spilling out of him in a scatter from a repository of disconnected facts, like bits and pieces from a torn encyclopedia. Now and then there were glints of lucidity. He talked about Egypt in 1882, the plunder and burning of Alexandria, his innovations in archaeology, a toothache at Tel al-Hesi.

Lily glanced down at her hands. Her curled fingers still quivered. Sir William Fendley was the greatest genius archaeology had ever produced. That must be remembered, Lily thought, while his voice went on. Fifty years ago he developed the technique of dating pottery that still bears his name. Visiting scholars come to tea at the American School just to see him and pay him homage.

"Kate's brighter than Eastbourne," he was saying. "But she has a harder time because she's a woman. She should be the director of the dig. They were lovers, you know."

Lady Fendley leaned over and wiped the corner of his mouth with a handkerchief. "Now, now," she said, "we mustn't repeat naughty tales."

Lily looked away again, embarrassed, in the direction of the newspaper. From this distance, the picture on the front page looked like the American in the Panama hat who was in front of the King David Hotel.

"That's an old paper, a *Paris Tribune* from last week," said Lady Fendley. "Someone left it."

Lily went around the sofa to pick it up. The man from Julian's Way had the same powerful jaw and deep-set eyes.

"Whose picture is this?" she asked.

"Konrad Henlein. Leader of the Nazi party in Czechoslovakia," Lady Fendley told her. "Where have you been? He's the Pooh-Bah of the crisis in Sudetenland."

"On the tel I never catch up with the news," Lily said. "We only have an old *Liberty* magazine. Last I heard, Hitler took over Austria."

"The *Anschluss* was months ago. You should keep up, my dear," said Lady Fendley. "Henlein is agitating for German autonomy in Bohemia, wants the Nazis to control Czechoslovakia."

Sir William stirred in his chair. "I met him, you know. In Prague. He came to my lecture and interrupted with questions about Indo-Europeans. Aryans, he called them." He smiled and wiped the side of his mouth with the back of his hand. "And his brother Karl." He shook his head and gazed at a spot on the carpet. "Bismarck says that whoever controls Bohemia, controls Europe," he began, and launched into another series of disjointed recollections. He listed every brick and tile in his schoolroom, the grain of wood on every desk. And Lady Fendley answered "Yes, dear . . . I know, my dear . . ." as she stroked his hand.

Lily became drowsy from the drone of his voice and the still air of the room. Sir William paused, looking at her expectantly, and she realized that he had asked a question that she hadn't heard.

"Eastbourne had the paper with him this morning," Lily said into the silence, "but he wouldn't let me look at it."

"Ha!" said Sir William. "He's so stingy he's afraid you'll wear off the print." He shook his head and wagged his finger. "He may have a lonely-hearts notice in the personal column he doesn't want you to see. I could tell you stories—"

"But you won't," Lady Fendley told him, leaning toward him gently, her hand on his arm.

Lily shifted in her chair and gazed at her hands again. "I'm worried about Eastbourne. He disappeared from the YMCA this morning in the midst of the riots."

"You ought to ring the British School," said Lady Fendley. "He may be there."

In the hall alcove, Lily picked up the telephone receiver and waited. She jiggled the hook impatiently, but still no operator came on the line.

"Try again later," said Lady Fendley. "Nothing works in this fool country. Go upstairs and lie down. You look tired."

As Lily left, she could hear Sir William saying, "When I was a boy, before there were telephones, you could send a street urchin with a message for a ha' penny . . ."

* * *

Upstairs in her room, Lily stared out the window at the street and the empty field across the way, where *fellahin* from Isawiya usually grazed sheep. She sat at the desk, conscious of the smell of smoke, the distant sounds of chaos in the New City, and fingered the coffee stain on her skirt.

She sat, numb, until the noon call to prayer from the distant mosques in the Old City. The call echoed from the minaret on Nablus road, from a mosque in the Sheik Jarrah quarter, as muezzin after muezzin chanted in unmatched cadence. The gun-

fire and shouting in west Jerusalem stopped, and one by one
the rioters returned from the New City, crossing the field and
trudging through the street in their stained clothing, their faces
heavy with exhaustion, their backs loaded with carpets, stacks
of dishes, a European gas range. A bearded man carried a satin
evening gown, still on its hanger. It caught the wind and billowed behind him like a sail. They were going home to wash, to
take lunch, to take afternoon siestas, Lily thought. And in west
Jerusalem, children will return from school through empty streets
to find their homes looted and gutted, their parents dead, lying
in the wreckage with their throats slit.

*   *   *

A week ago, someone shot at Eastbourne as he drove down
Bethlehem Road. Lily could think of a thousand reasons why
someone would take a potshot at him. But as long as she was
on the staff of his dig at Tel al-Kharub she could overlook his
stinginess, his sour moods, his bouts of petty malice.

Four years ago, Lily's dissertation advisor at the Oriental
Institute in Chicago had told her in the tangle-tongued jargon
of academia that "mixed groups of men and women are not
compatible in a field situation." That was in 1934. Everyone
was out of money then except for Rockefeller, who sponsored
excavations at Megiddo.

"I'll work with a team of women," she had said.

"I don't think you'll get funding, Miss Sampson. You can
work on jewelry. There's some in the storeroom, left over from
Breasted's excavations in Egypt. Jewelry, Miss Sampson, jewelry."

Her advisor always called her Miss Sampson. Male graduate students were Chuck and Hank and Flip, and they drank
beer together in a saloon on the other side of the Midway.

But ladies didn't. Ladies didn't go south of Sixty Third Street, or sit around in saloons. Ladies didn't dig up ancient skeletons and get dust in their hair. Ladies married field archaeologists, followed their husbands to excavations, slept in their tents, wore rubber gloves to wash pottery, and said, "Yes, dear. Of course, dear. Don't forget your lunch, dear."

Eastbourne wasn't like that. Women were the same as men to him—he was condescending to everyone.

* * *

At three o'clock, Lily went around the corner to the British School on Azarah Street to see if Eastbourne was there. Tony Something-or-other, who was working on Crusader Churches, answered the door.

"He was here earlier today, but he's gone back to Kharub," Tony told her.

She had already started home when he called after her. "He said to tell you to get down to the dig as soon as you can."

THREE

AT TEL AL-KHARUB, Lily awoke every morning still tired, to shake out her shoes for scorpions and dress in the dark. The tent flap, snapping in the wind, barked like rifle shots and woke her from another fitful sleep. Since the riots two weeks earlier, her dreams had been haunted by frenzied pigeons hovering over the lifeless face of Dr. Stern, the slack-jawed stare of Mrs. Klein, hollow-voiced inside a mask of tragedy, intoning the words of Antigone "... unwept, unsepulchered, a welcome store for birds to feast upon ..."

Soon it would be first light and time to be on the tel, to clamber up the slope, avoiding scattered clumps of thorny weeds, skitter around fallen ashlars and tread on the broad stone walls that rimmed the remnants of ancient pavements.

I must be crazy to live in a tent with a cracked mirror on a peg, with clothes strung on a rope across my cot, with only a bucket of water and a sponge for a shower, she thought. There was a *hamsin* in the making. It was hot; it was windy; dirt blew in her face; her skin itched; her tent veered ominously. And to-morrow, more blasts of dusty hot wind would feel like an oven and smell of turkeys from the kibbutz over the hill.

It was her third season at Tel al-Kharub, and every year, she cursed the weariness of mornings like this. But during dark Chicago winters at the Oriental Institute, she missed the clean heat and the blue sky, the romance of tension and curiosity, the release of mindless physical labor. Then she longed to be here, to see the sunset from the tel reflected in the dappled gold of the distant sea, to watch cars and wagons moving in the dusk along the self-same road that had been the ancient King's Highway.

She yearned for the excitement of mysterious streets, the pleasurable shock of the exotic. She hungered for the whispers of the past that swirled in the remains of ancient houses and echoed in broken and discarded jugs—messages from long-buried cobblestones and old footsteps in the dust, shadows of laughter eddying in cooking pots and jars filled with the dried remnants of pomegranates.

But today she was so tired that she envied the Bedouin, in spite of their waterless days and tents that smelled like goats. She watched them in the field below the tel, sitting around a campfire in the shelter of a rock, drinking their morning coffee. Jamal had left the kitchen and sat with them, nodding and talking, cradling a small coffee cup in his hands.

They were probably gossiping about Eastbourne again, how stingy he was, how mean and unfeeling, how poorly he paid them. Yesterday a wheelbarrow ran over the toes of one of the workmen, who screamed, pointing to his bleeding foot. Eastbourne told him to shut up. When Lily ran to help, he waved her back to the pottery shed.

"They always complain," Eastbourne had said. "They do anything to get out of work."

She tried to right the tent, pulling the rope taut and hitting the tent peg with a rock. Eastbourne swaggered toward her with his sandy-haired, horse-faced British elegance, his shining boots and white linen breeches, carrying plans and sections, ready for the day.

"What do you think you are doing?" Always immaculate, even the dust was afraid to settle on him. "We have workmen for that," he said. He spread the plans on the ground, positioning rocks on the corners to hold them down in the wind. He marked where they would dig that day and told her what they would find.

Lily listened and nodded and said I know, I see, I understand. When he finished, she asked for a ride up to Jerusalem for the opening of the Rockefeller Museum the next day.

Old John D. Rockefeller had been an endless font, funding the University of Chicago, the excavations at Megiddo, her fellowship, and now the museum. Praise John, from whom oil blessings flowed. She met him once in the Oriental Institute at the fellowship awards. They had cleared a path for the old man's wheelchair and he congratulated her, his eyes rheumy, his nose pointed with age.

"It's called the *Palestine* Museum," Eastbourne said. He rolled up the map and stood over her. "You were invited?"

The wind furled the tent flap over the rope again, and he watched her struggle with it.

"There's a bus stop not two miles up the road," he said, and walked away to get his tea.

She pounded the tent peg until the rock broke. The flake scars on the stone and the small pieces of flint-shatter looked like a Paleolithic hammerstone and debitage, and she was tempted to put it on the shelf in the dig house to fool Eastbourne. Not likely. He would say it was unprovenienced and throw it away.

He was a nitpicker on the tel, and ran the camp with military discipline, but his digs had the cleanest squares, the straightest balks, the most meticulous plans and records in all of Palestine.

Eastbourne had an instinct for archaeology. Two seasons ago he found *ostraka*—messages of fear scratched with burnt sticks on broken pieces of pottery—mingled with arrowheads and missiles, buried beneath a pile of burnt bricks in the guardroom of the city gate. The scrawls called out unanswered cries for help: "May Yahweh cause my lord to bear the tidings of peace this very day. . . . Nedebiah has fled to the mountains . . . Let my lord send help . . . We are watching for the signal fires of Lachish . . . We can no longer see Azekah."

And last year, on the side of the tel, down toward the wadi, Eastbourne had merely brushed a stand of wild mustard back and forth with his shoe before he called the surveyor. They put in a trench and uncovered a mass grave.

Lily had looked down at a disordered sea of bones, and Eastbourne pointed out the organically darkened soil, the blood-shadowed remnants of humans, and reminded her of the Assyrian stele in the British Museum with an inscription commemorating the conquest of the site. He described scenes on the column—defenders crawling through the debris of battle; the walls above them breached and in flames, the refugees fleeing the city. These are their bodies, he told her. She was fortunate, he said. Few people had the chance to excavate skeletal material.

She learned to work with bones, to identify the rounded surface of a patella, differentiate cervical from thoracic vertebrae, to separate earth matrix gently from bones and place each one in a box on a cushion of tissue paper. The first time she lifted a femur, she was surprised by its heft, and for a moment a shock of intimacy and the phantom life that had once surged through the leg made her skin prickle. That season, she recovered remains of over 1,500 men, women, and children.

A week ago, Lily had found the ancient skeleton of a young woman in the remains of the storeroom near the gate—the bones of the feet charred, arms across the chest embracing a spectral memory. Near the sternum some baby teeth were all that was left of an infant. Lily imagined how the woman had run, trapped and cowering into the storeroom, flames catching at her long gown. She had fallen, clutching the infant, and was buried for over 2,500 years under a tumble of burnt and calcined mud brick.

In the ruins of a house along the casemate wall at the back of the site, Lily had found part of an arm, hacked off by a heavy blade, next to the remains of an oven. Lily envisioned the victim, alone in the courtyard where women once had spun and woven and dyed coarse woolen cloth. Others already had fled the deserted town, leaving the soup still on the table. The lone woman stood before the attackers, trying to shield her face with her forearm before the blow came.

This week, Lily was working on the steep eastern slope of the tel where Iron Age tombs were hewn into the weathering limestone bedrock. Yesterday she had seen a glint of blue through the dust, and brushing carefully, exposed a glass amphoriskos, dark as lapis lazuli—a perfect little pear-shaped vial with a long neck and delicate handles.

It fit into the palm of her hand. She brushed at it gently, moved into the light and turned it. As a child, she held one like this. She had taken it from the shelf in her father's study, stood at the window, and rubbed her finger along the smooth surface, shaded and glowing in the sun. Her father had come into the room and taken it from her hand. "We mustn't break it," he had said. "It's from long ago. Such things were rare and coveted, and belonged to princes."

That was before the day that she had opened the dark wooden door and saw the terrible sight in the closet under the stairs.

* * *

Lily slid through the entrance to the Iron Age tomb, through the small opening that had been cut into the hillside. Inside the sepulcher, a tangle of bones and pottery lay on the floor and on stone benches hewn into the walls of the man-made cave.

What would she look like in three thousand years, she wondered? Would someone dig her up and say, "Ah yes, there's Lily. I recognize her from the shape of her eye sockets and her nasal aperture. I'd know her anywhere."

She spent the morning carefully freeing one bone after another from the compacted mass with dental picks and sculptor's spatulas, with camel's hair brushes and pouf bulbs that emitted soft puffs of air when she squeezed them to blow away the dust. The anthropologist in London told her she was the first to recover the delicate nasal bones of the face, and she dug carefully, proud of her expertise.

Lily knew she had to finish the tomb quickly, before the Bedouin looted it. Jewelry, figurines, whole pots from tombs were the handiest source of revenue they could wrest from the dry, impoverished Palestine soil.

Especially since Eastbourne refused to pay them enough to guard the site.

*   *   *

By noon, the heat of the sun penetrated inside the tomb. White limestone powder from the walls of the cave dusted her arms and clothing. She brought the morning's finds up to the pottery shed—the bones wrapped, labeled and boxed; the pots in tagged buckets. From this height, she could see the coastal plain shimmering in the heat. Eastbourne was below in the Bedouin camp, waving his arms and shouting at the foreman. Jamal had turned away and had started up to the tel.

She saw Kate, with her wide-brimmed hat and her gardener's gloves, clambering to the pottery shed. Kate had been working on the ramp the Assyrians had built when they laid siege to the city. Lily thought of what Sir William said about Kate and Eastbourne and tried to imagine a pimple-faced Kate and a callow Eastbourne as lovers in each other's arms.

Jamal came up the hill from the Bedouin camp. His dark eyes always followed her, like those on a recruiting poster. "You are very beautiful," he whispered as he passed through the pottery shed on his way to the kitchen. It was barely audible, and Lily wasn't sure what she had heard.

She looked into the spotted mirror above the sink. Her face and the scarf on her head were blanketed with limestone dust, little rivulets of sweat ran down her cheeks, and her lashes and eyebrows were covered with white powder. Only her eyes, gleaming bright blue in the mask of dirt, were visible. She laughed. "I look like a clown."

Jamal had already disappeared into the kitchen. Kate, flush-faced and sweating, carried a bucket into the pottery shed, the tag, attached to the handle with a string, swinging back and forth as she walked. Her boots were covered with dust, her white linen breeches were wrinkled and soiled, and she wore an expression of jubilant satisfaction.

"Look, look," she said, "part of a bronze helmet from the last defenders of the city. From the ramp, stuck into the city wall. It was covered with ash, hard as a rock, and buried in mud brick. Digging through that mess wasn't easy." Kate hugged the bucket with one arm and ran a finger along the crest of the helmet.

For a instant, Lily felt the chill of the moment when a blow had sent the broken helmet tumbling into the fallen wall, now only a green fragment of corroded metal, gnawed by time.

* * *

Lily awoke from the afternoon siesta to the clatter of the cooks preparing tea in the kitchen. She had been asleep in the shade of the pottery shed, exhausted from the heat, dozing in a rickety beach chair with torn canvas that Jamal's Samaritan helper, Abu Musa, presented with a flourish after lunch. Wind had scattered a fine dust over everything—store jars, boxes of figurines, cooking pots, even the carton that held the small blue glass amphoriskos.

She blew the dust off the outside of the box, opened it, and took out the amphoriskos. She held it up to the light, ran her fingers along the edge, and placed it gently back into the container. She could feel her father's hand softly on her shoulder and the ghost of his kiss waft against her cheek. He didn't mean to leave you, the amphoriskos told her. He sends you this as a message of love.

She lovingly replaced boxes that had blown off the shelf and assured the long-gone owners of the artifacts that they would be remembered. She shielded the boxes with a tarp, weighting it down against the wind with a heavy rock.

A jar handle, with the impression of a fingerprint where the clay had been pressed into the body of the vessel, had fallen. Lily picked it up. She fit her own finger into the depression, and felt as if she spoke to a potter across 2500 years.

Abu Musa, with his silent steps and subservient manner, startled her when he came into the pottery shed. "Jamal wants to see you in the kitchen." He gave her his brown, gap-toothed grin. "He has something important to tell you."

In the kitchen, there was dust on the teacups and saucepans, and even a fine film on the dishwater where Jamal rinsed the tea things.

"Don't ride to Jerusalem with Eastbourne tomorrow." His voice was low and secretive. "And don't let him see you leave here."

FOUR

⁂

ONLY A MUD-SPATTERED LORRY was parked on the gravel behind the dining shed. Both cars—the camp station wagon that Eastbourne used and Kate's sun-streaked Austin—were gone. Kate and Eastbourne would not be at tea again. Lily imagined their assignation in some dusty pensione on the outskirts of Ashkelon, where they sweated and groaned in the afternoon heat on a straw mattress with creaking springs. She smiled at the ludicrous picture and continued toward the dining shed.

Avi, the boy from the kibbutz on the other side of the hill, sat at a table, his red hair and freckled face shining in the dappled shade. She could dimly make out snatches of an argument between him and Jamal.

When she came into sight, they stopped. Avi smiled and jumped up to greet her. Jamal, arms crossed, legs straddling the threshold, still glowered from the kitchen door.

"I was waiting for you," Avi said. He picked up a crate from the bench beside him and planted it on top of the table. "I brought grapefruit."

Jamal leaned against the doorjamb, his arms still crossed over his chest. "We don't need them. We're closing camp."

Avi turned to Lily. "You're leaving?"

"Just for the weekend." Lily sat down at the table near the crate. "For the opening of the Rockefeller."

"Okay, then." Avi got up and reached for an empty basket from the pottery rack. "You can take fruit with you."

"Too much to carry on the bus," Jamal said.

"You're taking a bus to Jerusalem?" Avi asked.

Jamal unfolded his arms. "How else?"

"Pretty blonde ladies aren't safe riding by themselves through Hebron," Avi said. "These are bad times. They shoot at buses." Avi sat down next to her. "I have the lorry here. I'll drive you to Qiryat Gat to find a taxi."

"Too expensive," Lily said.

"A shared taxi. A *sherut*. Costs the same as a bus." He waited while she thought about it. "There's a *hamsin*." He picked up a grapefruit and began to peel it. "You want to sit in a smelly bus with broken springs?" He offered her a section of the grapefruit, and said she could leave now instead of tomorrow morning.

"I have work to do," Lily said. "Clean up my notes, draw plans and sections."

"You can do that in Jerusalem."

Jamal leaned forward. "Go with him." He spoke with the same hushed voice that he had used in the kitchen.

Lily hesitated, looking from one to the other. Then she picked up the dusty field notebook from the table, told Avi to wait, and went back to her tent.

When she returned, Jamal, still frowning in the kitchen doorway, was eating a grapefruit section by section, as though it were an orange.

Avi left the crate on the table. "*Shalom, shalom*," he said, and carried Lily's bag to the lorry parked behind the dining tent.

They rode along a dirt road lined with orange groves. Avi asked Lily about Eastbourne. He asked why Kate and Eastbourne were not at tea; he asked who Eastbourne's friends were; he asked where Eastbourne went in Jerusalem.

"Why do you want to know?"

"There's going to be a war. Hitler is mobilizing on the Czech border. Archaeologists sometimes dig for more than antiquities."

He talked about Lawrence of Arabia and his archaeological survey of the Negev in 1914, just before the war; of Palmer, who did a survey of the Sinai in the last century and made friends with the Bedouin when the British were building the Suez canal. "Palmer was killed as a spy," Avi said, "by his Bedouin friends."

"How do you know all this?"

Avi shrugged and lifted his hands from the wheel in a questioning gesture. "Common knowledge. Even the director of the American School works for the intelligence agency. That's why he's doing the Trans-Jordan survey."

Lanes of eucalyptus from Australia, planted for shade and windbreaks in the orange groves, lined the route. The Fertile Crescent, Lily thought. Where agriculture was invented. Where the oranges came from China, the peaches from Persia, and the prickly pears growing on the side of the road came from Arizona.

"Are you a native of Palestine?" she asked.

"I was born here. I'm a sabra. But I'm no bloody native."

"I didn't mean it that way."

"I hate the British. Wherever they go, they make trouble."

"They're only trying to keep peace."

"Before the British came, Arabs and Jews were friends. They're our cousins, you know. We fought together against the Turks in the war."

"Cousins?"

Avi laughed. "The children of Ishmael, Abraham's other son."

Dust blew into the lorry. Lily covered her hair with a scarf and closed the window.

"The Brits took up the white man's burden," Avi said. "They pit one side against another and then say. 'These people are incapable of ruling.' Divide and conquer. That's their policy."

"The partition plan . . ."

"Is a bunch of bull. Partition won't work. It's doomed to failure."

"Don't be so cynical. Something has to work."

"Who wouldn't be cynical?" He downshifted and carefully drove around a pothole in the dirt road. "There's a saying in the Talmud: If I am not for myself, who shall be?"

"Sounds like an excuse to be selfish."

"It's political. Written when the Romans controlled Palestine. Things are not much different now. The rest of the text goes: And who am I?" The motor whined as they started up a small hill. "Everything is in the Talmud. There's another maxim: The fish say there is too much land. It all depends on your point of view, doesn't it?"

"And what do Arabs say?"

"With my brother against my cousin. With my cousin against the world."

They drove through foothills covered with stone terraces planted with figs and grapes, the slopes criss-crossed by goat paths.

"It's nice of you to drive me," Lily said.

"An excuse to be with you." Avi blushed. "Besides, it's not safe now. Not since the Grand Mufti began to conspire with Hitler to get the British out of Palestine."

The lorry groaned up a steep incline. "Things are worse since the general strike started two years ago. Violence escalated. Brits lost control of the mandate, can't keep the peace. The Hebron Massacre in '29 was bad enough. I was just a little kid, but I remember it." He shook his head and stared straight ahead. He stepped on the gas, and the motor stammered and stalled. "But this time . . . Jews are always the victims, never the victors. I'm getting sick of it."

He downshifted and let out the clutch. "There's just so much you can take. There's not a Jew in Palestine who hasn't had a friend or relative killed by the Mufti's men."

"I was in Jerusalem two weeks ago during the riots," Lily said.

"Then you know." He looked over at her. "We're beginning to organize to fight back."

"Stockade and tower settlements like the new kibbutzim?"

"What good is a water tower with a searchlight and a barbed wire fence without arms? I'm thinking of joining the *Irgun*."

"*Irgun?*"

"Organized about a year ago. Now the Mufti's mob won't kill us and get away with it."

"Doesn't the Jewish Defense Force stop the attacks?"

"The *Haggana*? They hem and haw, and use 'admirable restraint' according to the British. The *Irgun* retaliates with reprisals." Avi pushed his foot down on the accelerator until the lorry retched and sputtered. "In this part of the world," he said, "no one forgives, no one forgets."

His words hung in the air.

"You know what I think?" he said after a while. "I think the Mufti is angry because Abdullah is Emir of Trans-Jordan instead of him. Now he gets revenge with these bloody raids on settlements and bombs in markets. Riots in Jerusalem and Hebron."

They rode in silence until the truck hit a rock in the road and they bounced in their seats, landing with a jolt on the springs and bounding up again, their heads almost hitting the roof of the cab. Both of them laughed.

"Sometimes I dream that we are married and have three children," Avi said.

"How old are you, Avi?"

"Nineteen."

"I'm six years older than you. When you're thirty, I'll be almost forty."

"Thirty-six to be exact. Anyway, I won't reach thirty."

"Don't be so dramatic."

They drove between distant hills on one side, the sea on the other, through orange groves and melon patches, along the dusty road to Qiryat Gat. Orange groves fluttered in Lily's side-vision and she closed her eyes, thinking of the day a few weeks after her tenth birthday and the long drive to the cemetery with the heavy scent of orange blossoms in the April air. She had sat numb in a limousine following a hearse, listening to her mother sob behind a drapery of black veils. She clutched the blue vial that her father had given her on her birthday. He had held it out to her after she blew out the candles on her cake, turning it so that the dark cobalt reflected the light from the chandelier like a jewel. "This is for you," he had said. "A gift from the past." It was the last thing he gave her. Two weeks later, she had opened the door under the stairs.

And now, to have found another amphoriskos. She knew from the moment that she saw the deep blue shimmer in the dust. She knew as she brushed away the dirt and saw it emerge a few centimeters at a time. She knew when she finally freed it with a careful stroke of the dental pick. Her father had sent it.

The amphoriskos. It was registered in the site catalogue all right, but she didn't remember writing it up in her field notes. She had fastened a slip of paper with its description and mea-

surements to the notebook with a paper clip. I'll fix it in Jerusalem, she thought, and pulled the bag up from the floor.

"Oh damn," she said.

"What?" Avi said.

"I forgot my field notebook. Left it in the tent."

"You want to go back?"

"It's okay. I'll take care of it Monday."

"You work too hard anyway. You deserve a few days rest."

"You work hard, too."

"But I don't have to sleep in a tent. On a cot."

"Neither do I. In Jerusalem at the American School I have a
real bed. And a bathtub."

* * *

"I'm not sure we can find a *sherut*," Avi said. "It's a matter of
luck. You might need a bus after all."

"You and Jamal…"

"Jamal is in love with you."

"Don't be silly. He's a cook."

"And I'm a tractor driver."

"That's different. You're an American."

"Only my passport. I told you, I was born here, on a kibbutz
in Palestine. Don't be so class conscious. You've been working
with the Brits too long."

"Defending your cousin?"

Avi smiled and nodded. "With my cousin against the world,"
he said.

A taxi chugged along in front of them. It pulled to the side of
the road to let them pass.

Avi skidded the lorry around it and stopped. "A *sherut*. You're
in luck."

"The way you drive, I would have been safer on a bus through Hebron," Lily said.

Avi got out of the lorry. "Come on," he said to Lily and called out to the driver of the *sherut*. "*Yerushalayim*? You going to Jerusalem?"

Lily reached for her bag and followed.

The driver didn't answer and turned away.

"Beni?" Avi leaned his arm on the window frame of the cab. "That you, Beni?"

Beni motioned his head in the direction of the back seat. A pretty, pregnant girl, who seemed broader than she was tall, sat between two men in khaki shorts and white shirts open at the collar. The girl began to giggle. Beni spoke to Avi in Hebrew, his voice hardly audible. Lily could make out only a few words.

"You know what's happening," Beni said. "I'm taking Ora . . ."

The man behind the driver's seat interrupted Beni. "We're taking her to the doctor." He spoke in English. "It's an emergency."

Avi leaned further into the taxi to speak to him. "Rafi, this is Lily. I told you about her."

Rafi looked toward Lily, pushed back a strand of dark hair that had fallen onto his forehead, then glared at Avi. "You know better than that. There's no room."

Lily noticed Rafi's foot resting on a folded jump seat. "There's plenty of room," she said. "It's a seven-passenger car." None of this made sense. "And I don't have any communicable diseases."

"For God's sake, Rafi," Avi said, exasperated.

Ora put one hand over her mouth, the other on her stomach, and tittered again.

"It'll be all right, Rafi," Avi said. "I can't leave Lily here in the middle of the road." Rafi scowled at him. "For me, Rafi."

Beni, the driver, pointed to the seat next to him. "She can sit here. In front."

Rafi frowned, shrugged, and pushed back his hair again. "Get in," he said to Lily.

"The best seat," Avi said, leading her around to the other side of the car. "Right next to the driver," and he opened the door for her.

He put her bag in the trunk, slammed the lid and stood in the road waving as they drove away. "Have a safe journey. I'll visit you," he called after them.

FIVE

LILY SAT IN THE FRONT seat of the *sherut*, the wind blowing against her face as the driver gripped the steering wheel, his hands slippery with sweat. From time to time, she glanced at the back seat in the rear-view mirror. The pregnant girl laughed about her ill-fitting dress, about the size and shape of her stomach. They talked about going to Patt's on the Street of the Prophets for special pastries, about yesterday's ambush on the road near Tulkarm, about the bombs in Haifa market.

The man on the left was called Gadi. Rafi, the good-looking one, the one who spoke English, leaned forward to tell the driver, "Don't go so fast. The police will stop us." He had green eyes.

Beni shook his head and clicked his tongue against his teeth to show he disagreed. "Any slower and we'll be an easy target."

They rode in silence for a time, Gadi reading a newspaper; Ora, eyes closed, leaning back in the seat. Lily stole a glance in the rear-view mirror and saw Rafi staring at her. She watched him, watched the flashes of sunlight filtering through passing trees play on his face, his eyes greener in the bright light, his hair dark and shining.

He winked into the mirror. She turned away, embarrassed, and looked out the window. Haughty camels, loaded with sheepskins, trekked across the horizon from a village beyond a hill.

"It's as peaceful as a poster for Travels through the Holy Land," Lily said.

"An illusion. Children used to hike through this countryside by themselves with water and sandwiches in their rucksacks." Rafi said. "They can't anymore. Too dangerous."

They drove around a truck groaning up the hill and stacked with water bottles.

"How long have you known Avi?" Rafi asked the mirror after a while.

"I'm digging at a site near his kibbutz, that's all."

"He talks about you a lot."

Beni swerved to avoid a bundle in the road, and Lily heard the faint ring of metal on metal.

"What was in the road?" asked Gadi, looking up from the paper.

"Just garbage," Beni answered. "Melon rinds, probably. Want to go back to look?"

Ora laughed unexpectedly. "It could have been a bomb."

They bounced over a pothole and this time it was clear that the metallic clang came from inside Ora's dress. Lily turned around to look at the girl's stomach. Bulging and knobby, it shifted with each bump in the road.

They drove past rocky hills scarred with goat tracks, the taxi droning, still climbing toward Jerusalem. A turbaned Arab on a mule jolted along the edge of a distant path.

Beni careened around the next crack in the road in an elaborate slalom, throwing the occupants of the back seat together against the window, first to one side, then the other. Lily glanced in the rear view mirror again and saw the distinctive outline of a gun jutting from the bulge around Ora's middle.

Rafi patted it back in place. "Pull yourself together." She giggled once again. "And for God's sake, stop that laughing."

"I cannot help it. Always, I laugh when I'm nervous."

Lily turned around to watch Ora adjust the bundle around her waist. "That's all I need," Lily said. "To be arrested for smuggling arms."

No one answered from the back seat.

"Either you're hiding weapons under your dress or you're pregnant with a strangely shaped robot."

"You insisted on going with us," Rafi told her.

"Not to get arrested."

They passed a truck loaded with crates of purple grapes spilling through the slats, exuding the smell of ripe fruit.

Melons grew on tangled vines in the fields. An Arab woman in an embroidered dress sat under a green silk parasol next to a pile of ripe melons for sale. Lily glanced in the mirror again. Rafi was still watching her.

"It reminds me of a story," Rafi said. "Jacob and his son were traveling from Minsk to Pinsk. . . ."

"In Palestine, everything reminds someone of a story," Lily said. "And they all take place on that crowded road from Minsk to Pinsk."

"Jacob didn't have enough money for two tickets," Rafi continued, as though she hadn't spoken. "So he told his son to hide in a sack under the seat when the conductor came to take the fares.

"When he asked Jacob what was in the sack under the seat, Jacob told him, 'Just some glass that my poor sick mother is sending to my daughter's wedding.' The conductor had heard it all before, and he kicked the lumpy sack. The sack jumped and Jacob's son said . . ."

Rafi paused here for emphasis. They drove over another bump and another clank came from Ora.

"Tinkle. Tinkle." Rafi said and leaned back, holding out his hands, palms up like an offering.

"It doesn't make it any better," Lily said. "Last month they sentenced a Druze woman to ten years in Acre prison for smuggling arms."

"Maybe next time you should ask if anyone is breaking the law before you get into a taxi." Rafi rolled down the window next to him and closed his eyes as the wind ruffled his hair back onto his forehead. "Anyway, they don't arrest pretty blonde American ladies."

"Or pregnant women, I suppose." Lily wound up the window next to her against the gusts of wind that blew dust into the taxi. "I could always tell the police that you forced me into the car at gun point."

They were coming into the hill country now. They passed terraces planted with grapevines and olive trees, passed Arab men at bus stops who were squatting on the side of the road, smoking.

"I knew it." Rafi leaned forward.

"We thought you were a friend of Avi's so you'd be all right. Now I'm not so sure."

"I'm fine. But I don't know about you."

He sat back again with a grunt.

They drove through villages where boys rode alongside them on rusted bicycles and men in white *kefiyas* sat at small tables drinking coffee and playing shesh-besh. Women with white veils covering their heads and spilling down their backs, the hems of their black embroidered dresses scraping the rutted mud, struggled with bundles of vegetables.

And 400 yards up the road, two British constables were flagging down cars.

Beni slowed the taxi, maneuvering it onto the shoulder. "Roadblock ahead." He gestured toward the army lorry and the striped black-and-yellow barriers that blocked the highway.

"Don't stop here," Rafi told him. "It looks suspicious."

A taxi with Arab farmers had pulled up to the checkpoint. The police gestured for them to leave the car, and they stood on the side of the road, one holding a chicken by its legs. The bird cackled and fluttered while a constable searched the trunk and under the seat.

Ora laughed again. "If they make me leave the car, I give birth right here on the side of the road."

Beni drove up behind the Arab taxi and stopped. The *sherut* idled noisily, swaying from side to side while Ora gripped her stomach.

"Don't worry," Lily said. "They'll let us through. They always wave me through roadblocks."

"Why?" Rafi asked. "You have a special pass?"

"I wondered myself. Last week on the Ashkelon road near Negba, when they waved me through, I pulled up and asked." She looked pointedly at Rafi. "They told me they don't stop blondes."

"Can you make it work again? "

"As long as Ora doesn't clang."

They waited, motor idling, and watched the *fellahin* pile back into their taxi, the chicken flapping and losing feathers in a struggle to escape.

"How do you know you can trust me?" Lily asked.

"I don't. I trust Avi."

The taxi in front of them pulled away and Beni drove slowly up to the roadblock and brought the car to a careful stop.

Lily rolled down the window and smiled at the soldier. "What seems to be the trouble, officer?"

"Just checking for weapons. You have any guns?"

"Why? Do we need them?" she asked, still smiling.

He laughed. "I hope not, luv. I'd hate to have anything happen to someone who looks like you."

"We're archaeologists. On our way to Jerusalem for the reception at the new museum tomorrow." Lily heard mumbling in the back seat. In the rear view mirror she saw Ora clutching her stomach and holding a handkerchief over her mouth. Rafi had one arm over her shoulders, the other tight across her belly. "You all right, dear?" he asked Ora.

The constable leaned into the car, his hand on the window, peering into the back of the taxi.

"We're graduate students from the University of Chicago," Rafi told the policeman. He nodded toward Ora. "This is my wife. I'm taking her to the doctor in Jerusalem. Hope we make it in time."

The soldier hesitated. Lily laid her hand on his arm. "Are you married, Constable?" she said. "Pregnant women are so touchy. The least little thing upsets them."

He looked at her and smiled. "My sister in Colchester has five children. Whenever she gets in a family way, I give her a wide berth. No pun intended."

"Colchester," Lily said. "A lovely town, full of history, with Roman walls and castles. Where Queen Boadicea led the revolt of the Britons against Roman rule."

The constable nodded. "When I was a lad, I would find bits and pieces of Roman pottery in the lanes after a rain and dream I was a Roman soldier. I've always been partial to archaeology."

Lily glanced at the back seat again. Rafi and Ora were still clutched in an embrace. Lined up behind the *sherut*, she saw a lorry piled with bundles of hay, and beyond that, an old Arab in a white *kefiya* sitting in a cart filled with melons. Behind him were two taxis and a bus.

"Heavens," said Lily. "There's a queue behind us. We're holding up traffic. I'd better let you get back to your duties."

"Oh—yes." The constable stepped back from the sherut. "Yes, of course. Nice to meet you. Have a safe trip." And he waved them through.

Ora waited until the checkpoint was out of sight before she began laughing. "Sorry," she said. Her shoulders shook; her stomach rattled and banged. "*Kol hakavod*. Well done, Lily."

"She had no choice," Rafi said.

Ora laughed again. "The constable will tell all his mates tonight about his friend the archaeologist."

"And he'll remember us," said Rafi.

After a while, Rafi said to the mirror, "Come to Patt's sometime and try the special pastries."

* * *

Lily left the *sherut* on Jaffa Road in Jerusalem. She passed shops burned in the riots, their floors blanketed with blackened remains of counter tops and fallen beams. The acrid stench of stale fire from the charred debris filled her with unexpected panic. In two thousand years, Eastbourne had said, only a layer of charcoal, wall-stubs, foundations, sandwiched between other strata, would remain.

She ran across the street in the face of the traffic near the corner of the Old City, toward the White Sisters and Notre Dame.

She cut through a courtyard where a nun struggled with freshly washed sheets that billowed in the wind. A gust lifted the wings of her coif and whipped the sheets, with their fresh smell of soap and sunshine, around Lily's head.

Laughing, the nun untangled her. "*Bonjour*," she said, still laughing.

"*Bonjour*," Lily answered.

"*Va bien?* You are all right?"

They both laughed, together. "*Va bien. Merci,*" Lily said.

Still smiling, she crossed the field where villagers in white *kefiyas* and long cloaks, *abayas* they called them, came into town from Nebi Samwil and Beit Safafa, Beit Hanina and Deir Yasin, with vegetables to sell, with watermelons and figs, and oranges from Jericho. A Bedouin woman held out a bundle of spices, of thyme and capers. Blue and green tattoos, the colors of paradise, decorated the rims of her eyes and mouth and guarded the entrance to her soul. Women from Lifta in dark embroidered dresses squatted on the street next to baskets of beans, of okra, with piles of apricots—holding them up for display, calling to passersby.

Lily hated walking through this section. No matter how she behaved, no matter what she wore, it was like running a gauntlet. Men would step in the way to brush against her; women gestured and shouted at her with guttural cries that sounded like curses.

Lily threaded her way between rickety wooden buses with peeling paint and shattered windows; scribes sat with old typewriters perched on card tables, writing letters and completing forms for clients. Vendors with goatskins of water and shiny bottles harnessed to their backs pushed through the throng, the bottles filled with colored syrup and sticky with flies. The street was slippery with discarded and half-rotted fruits and vegetables, crowded with people milling and pushing, and heavy with the smell of sheep.

She broke through the crowd onto the quiet street where sheep grazed in the field near the high walls of the École Biblique, and rounded the corner. She crossed the road to the gate of the American School, lifted the latch, scurried up the walk and climbed the steps into the calm of the entry hall next to the library.

* * *

Lily heard the bell for dinner and started down the stairs, bathed and rested. A tall man with straight shoulders, a tanned face, and a prominent jaw stood at the bottom of the steps. His hand clutched the newel; he looked up as if he were waiting for someone. Lily recognized him as the man in the Panama hat whom she had seen the day of the riots in front of the King David.

"It's you," she said, and continued down the stairs. "Secretary's gone for the day."

"I came here especially to speak with you, Miss Sampson."

"You know my name?"

"May I see you a moment?"

"What's wrong?"

"I'm Henderson. Colonel Keith Henderson. From the consulate."

"What happened?"

"Can we go outside?" he asked. "Not the garden. Too many people."

Lily led the way down the steps to the tennis court. Only Sir William and Lady Fendley were in the garden. Lily looked back over her shoulder to see if Henderson followed. He took long, loping steps, his hands in his trouser pockets.

"You been keeping up with the news?" he asked.

Where was this leading? "I've been on the tel for the last six weeks. When I come to town I sleep and bathe and see old friends."

"There's going to be a war," he said. "Hitler is mobilizing to enter Czechoslovakia. Over the Sudetenland."

That was the second time that day that someone talked about war. Avi had said the same thing in the lorry. "What does that have to do with me?"

"You heard about the bomb at Jaffa Gate last month. It killed four people. Thirty-eight more and one hundred and fifty wounded in the riots that followed. You were here then, in Jerusalem. I saw you." He watched her, waiting for her to speak. "Last week, forty-five people were killed by a Jewish bomb in the *souk* at Haifa." His voice was taut. "You know the situation in Jerusalem. The British are proposing partition." He paused. "Arabs and Jews are both against it."

"I'm not interested in politics," Lily said. "As a scholar, I can't take sides."

"The Grand Mufti—al-Husseini—is allied with Hitler."

"I have to go to dinner," she said, starting back toward the garden.

"Would you like to have your own site?" He asked so quietly that she wasn't sure she heard him.

She turned around and looked at him. "I couldn't get a permit." Her voice was almost a whisper. "And the funding..."

Something was wrong with this conversation. She didn't know him. She had no idea why he was talking to her, and now he was making some kind of incomprehensible offer.

"You have a good reputation as an archaeologist."

"What is this all about?" she asked.

"With the right recommendations, the Smithsonian would look favorably on a grant proposal from you."

Lily felt a momentary thrill of excitement and danger.

"Archaeologists can go anywhere," said Henderson. "I thought you might like to do a little archaeological survey before you select a site."

There was something vaguely disturbing and unethical about this, and she shook her head.

"You have nothing to fear," Henderson reassured her. Almost as an afterthought, he added, "They never hurt women." He waited again for her reaction.

Who are "they"?

"Think about it," he said. "I'll call you in a few days."

SIX

LILY PIROUETTED IN FRONT of the mirror at the top of the stairs, composing a smile, turning this way and that, watching the fringe of her shawl slither. Her eyes reflected the blue silk, bright against her tan; her hair shone pale and sun-streaked.

Sir William came out of his room on the arm of his wife. "You shouldn't preen like that. It's bad for your character." His eyes were bright and amused and he was laughing, anticipating attention and admiration at the museum reception. Lady Fendley smiled and brushed a stray hair from his forehead.

"We called a taxi," he said. "Care to join us?"

Lady Fendley hesitated and glanced at Sir William. Her smile stiffened. "She's not ready."

As welcome as an ant at a picnic. The curtains at the window next to the mirror wafted clear summer scents from the garden toward Lily. "Too beautiful a day to be inside a musty taxi," Lily said. "I'd rather walk."

"Remember, my dear," said Lady Fendley, "you take your life in your hands near Herod's Gate." Now she seemed offended. What's wrong with her today? "You have a habit of roaming the streets during riots."

Only one riot. "I'll be all right."

"Everyone has guns these days. Someone took a shot at Eastbourne's car a few weeks ago near Solomon's Pools." Lady Fendley brushed a speck from Sir William's collar. "No one is safe in this Godforsaken country."

Not even Englishmen with public school educations, Lily thought.

*　*　*

Lily wore high heels for the first time in months. They pinched her toes. She limped along to the museum, feeling broken bits of sidewalk and pebbles through the thin soles. And next winter, she thought, after the rain begins, it will all be knee-deep in mud.

The new museum sat grandly on raw ground, planted across from the northwest corner of the Old City, just past Herod's Gate. Smooth blocks of creamy gold Jerusalem stone glared in the sun. Ladies in broad summer hats and flowered dresses, men in dark jackets and white trousers crowded the steps before the high open doors of an octagonal tower. Bastardized Moorish like the YMCA, Lily thought, the British vision of East meets West.

Inside, a cacophony of shrill voices echoed in the stone halls. A dense press of people talked in groups, men nodding, smiling, women waving gloved hands, all looking around, waiting to be noticed. Lily pushed her way through the crowd, searching for a familiar face—Eastbourne, Sir William, Lady Fendley. She saw the entire staff of the excavations at Hazor, the senior staff from Jericho and Samaria, even the new High Commissioner from Government House.

It was too crowded to see anything in the cases. In the exhibit hall, men in striped school ties ate canapés in front of stone carvings from Hisham's Palace in Jericho. People lounged against vitrines stacked with ancient jugs and jars.

"Hello, hello," Lily said to no one in particular.

"My God, it's a sea of pots," she heard a woman's voice call out, "and every one of them has a name." The woman wore a hat with an ostrich feather shaped like a question mark that trembled with each word.

"Have you seen Eastbourne?" Lily asked someone who looked familiar. Before she could get a reply, she was driven back toward an exhibit case by a new surge of people.

Rickety in her high-heeled shoes, she stumbled against a physical anthropologist from the hospital. "So sorry," she said.

The press of the crowd was suffocating. Lily forced her way toward the open air of the courtyard, repeating "Beg your pardon, excuse me," in a rhythmic murmur.

Outside, a fountain, dancing and dappling, caught the rosy evening sun. Guests jammed into the shade of a loggia, leaned against stele carved with ancient inscriptions, elaborate sarcophagi and empty stone ossuaries with peaked tops and rosette decorations. In the first century, the ossuaries had held the bones of the dead.

She found a gin and tonic at the bar, already poured and waiting for someone. No ice; they never have ice.

Sir William held court for a brace of admirers in the comparative quiet of the loggia, nodding graciously and offering his cycle of recollections. Lady Fendley stood a little behind, smiling as she watched his animated face. Words came in and out of his head all day long, Lily thought. Some stayed, some slithered away like water. And if they stayed, he repeated them over and over for the comfort of their sound.

"The germ of the idea came from my friend Francis Galton," Sir William was telling a young man, who listened dutifully and nodded deferentially. "Darwin's cousin, you know. He did a study on family resemblances. I just transferred the idea to pottery."

"There you are, my dear." Lady Fendley said to Lily, and continued to scan the crowd. "Arrived safely, I see. I don't see Kate. Isn't she coming?"

"Stayed in camp again. She's anti-social."

"Just shy," Lady Fendley said.

What was wrong with Kate, hiding behind her square shape and face like a cartoon in *Punch*? Someday, when he's in the right frame of mind, I'll ask Sir William about her. He knows about everyone.

"Pity," Lady Fendley said. "It would be to her advantage to show here."

"She never goes anywhere. Except some mysterious place in Ashkelon. Sometimes she stays the night."

"Probably because of the curfew," Lady Fendley said.

"She goes there every day. Eastbourne here yet?"

"Haven't seen him."

Sir William was telling an admirer in a mustard-colored jacket, "I landed in Alexandria during the uprising of '82."

"Must have been an exciting time," said Mustard Jacket. He had a Cambridge accent.

"Much like what's happening here. In those days, the Sultan of Turkey paid the rebels. Today it's Hitler. We put a stop to it then. Arrested the leader, put him on trial."

"Those were the glory days of the empire," Mustard Jacket said. He looked off into the distance, and his eyes misted over.

"We had to protect Suez. Lifeline of the empire."

Across the courtyard, leaning against a column, the woman with the feathered hat was talking to a short, balding man, her feather wavering like punctuation.

"Is that Margaret Sotheby?" Lily asked.

"That?" Lady Fendley followed her gaze.

"The one with the feather."

"Oh that. Yes. Elliot Blessington's wife. She's a novelist."

"I think I met her once," Lily said.

"Writes about one murder after another. I think she's de-ranged." Lady Fendley leaned forward and lowered her voice. "Her first husband was a philanderer." She came closer to Lily, almost whispering. "She's terribly extravagant. Last year, she spent a hundred pounds for a desk she kept in the tent at Eliot's excavation. Writes in the dig house while he excavates." Lady Fendley leaned closer still. "Won't let Eliot out of her sight. Older than he is, you know," she said into Lily's ear.

"I never heard about the desk. Who's she talking to?"

"Haven't the slightest. I never saw him before. Looks American."

"She's coming this way," Lily said.

Lady Fendley straightened up, but continued in a low voice. "They just finished at a site in Turkey. On their way to Mesopotamia, I think. We'll ask."

Margaret Sotheby approached and nodded at Lady Fendley. "Cordelia." The feather danced. Dame Margaret took both of Lily's hands in hers. "Lily darling," she said. "It's been ages since I saw you."

We hardly know each other. Why the effusive greeting?

Dame Margaret dipped her feather. She exuded a pleasant scent of vanilla. "You're working with Geoff Eastbourne now at Tel al-Kharub," she said while she continued looking around the room. "I don't see him here today."

"I haven't—"

"You didn't you drive up with him?" Dame Margaret held onto Lily's hand while her eyes searched the crowd. The short man she had been talking to earlier signaled her from the other side of the loggia. "Will you excuse me?" Dame Margaret said and left, her feather fluttering in the wind. The short man followed her.

"What was that about?" Lily asked, watching them disappear into a side room.

Lady Fendley glared after Dame Margaret. "Rudeness. That's what it was about."

A British major pushed past, almost knocking against a stone column. He made a circuit of the courtyard, glanced around the loggia, tapped his hand on a Roman sarcophagus, and went back into the building.

The hum of conversation from inside the museum stopped. Lily heard the cadence of a garbled announcement. A sound like a collective sigh reached the courtyard. Then silence.

The major returned, followed by the pale, distraught director of the British School. The director took a position in front of the fountain, cleared his throat, tapped on a glass with a spoon, and turned to speak to the major, who nodded.

"Ladies and gentlemen, if I may have your attention . . ." His voice broke. Perspiration stood on his upper lip and ran along his temples. He whispered to the major again. This time the major shook his head and shrugged.

"I have the unfortunate duty to announce that Geoffrey Eastbourne . . ." He reached into his pocket for a handkerchief and wiped his face. "Geoffrey Eastbourne was killed this morning on the Beit Jibrin track near Hebron."

He wiped his face again. The handkerchief fell to the stone pavement of the courtyard. For a moment, Lily wasn't sure what she heard. She felt the blood drain from her cheeks. The courtyard hushed. People stood in clusters, shaking their heads, murmuring in low voices.

All around her, she heard snatches of conversation ". . . died in the line of duty . . . a terrible waste . . . a brilliant archaeologist . . ."

Recollections of the moment when she found her father in the dark closet under the stairs surged through her again—the specter of desolation, the loneliness that came with news of sudden death.

She watched the water play in the courtyard fountain, burbling and flashing in the dusk, and stared at the sarcophagus next to her. A plate with a half-eaten canapé was balanced on the rim.

She remembered Eastbourne pacing along the shadowy stub of an ancient wall; swaggering along a balk, his eyes squinting at the faint outline of stratigraphy emerging on the side of the square; kneeling down on one knee, tracing the outline of the wall on the site map.

Sir William's voice broke into her reverie. "What happened?"

"It's Eastbourne," Lady Fendley said, reaching for his hand. "I'll tell you about it later. We must leave now."

Lily stopped the major before he left. "How did it happen?" she asked. "A traffic accident? Did he skid? Was he speeding? Was he hit by another car?"

"No accident," the major said. "He was shot." He walked away.

People began to leave. Dame Margaret emerged from the side room and looked at the thinning crowd and grave faces.

"What happened?" she asked. Lily told her about Eastbourne.

Only her feather trembled. "I'm not a bit surprised," she said. Lily had no idea why. Dame Margaret leaned forward as if to explain. "We have to talk. Stop at the American Colony on your way home. I'll buy you a chocolate gateau."

She moved into the scattering crowd, her face expressionless, her feather erect.

SEVEN

LILY PUSHED HER WAY through the crowded street across from the Old City wall, thinking of Eastbourne's death. Killed in a flicker on a dusty road in a strange land. He had missed the Great War with its poets and heroic good-byes, its nightmares and festering trenches. Now he died on a desert track, a meaningless death in a nameless by-lane.

Across from Herod's Gate, she turned up Salah-edh-Din Street. An accident? A case of mistaken identity? An angry workman? It made no sense. "The Arabs are my friends," Eastbourne had always said. "There's no danger here for me."

Jamal had warned her. Jamal knew something was going to happen.

Distracted, Lily passed the American School, passed the Tombs of the Kings. She stepped around the bends and cracks in the narrow sidewalks, her feet aching, her toes pinching.

Dame Margaret knew something. I'll find out when I talk to her, Lily thought. She turned into the narrow lane that led into the entrance of the American Colony Hotel, passed the whitewashed walls of the anteroom decorated with tiles, passed the lobby, the air permeated with deep-scented tuberoses in

vases of Hebron glass, brilliant as jewels on the glistening copper tables.

In the courtyard the polite murmur of voices and quiet sounds
of china and silverware moving gently on linen tablecloths were
punctuated by the peaceful splash of the fountain in the center.

Dame Margaret waited at a table in the corner, beyond two
tall palms that wavered above the flagstone pavement, beyond
the blooming roses, near the bright masses of red and orange
and purple bougainvillea tumbling against the stone walls. Dame
Margaret had already shed her hat.

Lily took the chair across from her. "You wanted to see me?"

Dame Margaret didn't look up. She rearranged the spoon
and fork in front of her. Lily expected her to express some sort
of half-hearted condolence, to say something like, "Sorry about
Eastbourne."

Instead, Dame Margaret asked, "Why were you working
with Geoffrey?"

Is that what she wanted to know?

"He was willing to put me on the staff."

"Why not Megiddo? That's a Chicago dig."

Lily was startled. She knows more about me than I thought,
knows I'm from the University of Chicago. "They don't mix
the sexes on American excavations, say it's bad for morale."

"Nonsense. Sex has nothing to do with gender. Wooley and
Lawrence always dug together, and the British Empire survived."

"The Turkish Empire didn't," Lily said. So the stories about
them were true?

An enormous brass key lay on the table in front of Dame
Margaret. She moved it aside. "You're thinking of Ned
Lawrence's friend, that little Saudi sheik? It had nothing to do
with archaeology."

"He became king of Iraq."

"Political obligation, that's all. Ned had to make promises."

"Balfour made promises too," Lily said.

Dame Margaret shrugged. "All's fair in love and war. Without promises, Turks would still control the area. I ordered tea for you."

"Thank you."

"You could have worked with Hetty Goldman at Tarsus." Dame Margaret straightened her fork again, ran her finger along the handle of the spoon. "Kathleen Kenyon and John Crowfoot worked together at Samaria without any trouble. We've come a long way since the twenties. You have Fendley to thank for that. As long as students put up with his field conditions, he took them on. Cordelia ran the camp and mothered them all, men and women alike."

"I have to thank him for more than that. He's responsible for my being on Eastbourne's staff. I came to Palestine on my own, used my fellowship money. When they turned me away at Megiddo, Sir William found me moping in the library at the American School and called Eastbourne."

We should be talking about Eastbourne, Lily thought, should be lamenting his untimely death. "Eastbourne's murder is a terrible shock to me," Lily said.

They sat in silence, Dame Margaret glancing from table to table around the courtyard. Lily waited.

"What did you mean when you said you weren't surprised?" Lily finally said.

"At what?"

"That Eastbourne was killed," Lily said.

"Nothing. Nothing at all. He may have made enemies. The workmen or other archaeologists may have resented him. He was not a pleasant man."

"Unpleasant enough to be killed?"

"He was secretive and bad tempered."

"He had good points too, you know," Lily said, surprised that she felt forced to defend him.

"*De mortuus nil nisi bonum*? Speak only good of the dead? No, my dear. Quite the contrary. The dead are beyond hurting. It's the living who deserve kindness."

Dame Margaret picked up the key and put it down again in front of her. "I have that room over there." She pointed to double doors heavy with paint that led from the courtyard. "They tell me it was Lawrence's room. When he died, he was working on a survey of Crusader castles."

Most of the castles were in the north—on either side of the Palestine border, like Monfort in the upper Galilee and Nimrod in the Golan. Some were along the coast, Caesarea, Atlit; or in the Judean hills, like the ones at Latrun and Ramle.

"You're smiling," Dame Margaret said. "What's so funny?"

"I was picturing Lawrence, getting into that role. Lumbering around the countryside in costume, clattering in medieval armor, mapping a castle keep."

"Ned was an unhappy man," Dame Margaret said. "Maybe a little insane. But he was no buffoon." She paused and fingered the key again. "He worked with Eliot and me at Ur." She looked away at the fountain, watching the water splay and whisper as if it held some secret, and then looked back to Lily. "How did Eastbourne get on with Kate?"

"All right, I suppose." Lily said. "Well, I'm not sure."

Dame Margaret shook out her napkin and laid it in her lap. "Tea is here." She moved the brass key to the side and sat silently while the waiter arranged plates and cups. He poured with an elaborate show of arcs and dips. She waited until he left before she spoke again. "When did you last see her?"

"Kate? Yesterday, when we came in from the field for lunch. I left the tel early. Why do you ask?"

"No reason. There was a time when they had a problem, that's all. I know her well. We worked with her once. You didn't see him leave or know who drove up with him?"

"No. I took off too early for that."

"You'll be going back after the funeral? Will you continue digging?"

"It all depends on Beacon Pharmaceutical. They sponsored the dig."

"By the way, is anything missing from the excavation?"

The question seemed offhand, almost an afterthought. So this is what she's after, Lily thought. "Not that I know of. Why do you ask?"

"No reason. With the situation in Palestine now, the British police are helpless. You might need the protection of your own consulate."

"You think things will get worse?"

"Who knows? For the past two years, with this awful general strike, there's been nothing but violence—a thousand people killed in the last two months alone." Dame Margaret seemed more impassioned than Lily expected. "The whole thing is orchestrated by the Grand Mufti, you know. Inspired by the Nazi forte—to magnify small fears and disagreements. They tease at wounds until they fester, nurture hatred until it erupts."

"Divide and conquer?" asked Lily.

Dame Margaret took a sip of her tea and put the cup down carefully. "The British are the bastion of civilization in the Near East."

"I didn't mean it that way."

Dame Margaret narrowed her eyes. "You were in Jerusalem with him that day." Another casual statement that seemed to come out of nowhere.

"What day was that?"

"July tenth."

"The day of the riot? We were working on pottery at the YMCA."

Dame Margaret paused, wiped the spoon with her napkin, and put it down again. "Both of you disappeared that day from the YMCA."

What is she trying to say? Is she accusing me of something?

"See anyone else?" Dame Margaret asked.

"Just . . ." Lily hesitated. What was Dame Margaret after?

"Just what?"

"Just a tourist," Lily said. "Sir William thinks the whole thing, the riots, the general strike, is a plot to sabotage Suez and destroy the empire."

"He may not be far off. Where do you think the poor *fellah* gets guns and ammunition? We know the Mufti gets his money from Hitler." She picked up the brass key and held it in her hand, idly polishing it with the napkin. "You know Henderson, the new American military attaché?"

"I met him yesterday."

"He's just arrived." Dame Margaret seemed surprised. "His predecessor was killed in an accident near the Kastel on the road up to Jerusalem."

"I know that curve. It's dangerous. The road is narrow there and slippery when it's wet."

"Wasn't raining when he skidded off the road."

"Henderson's a nice-looking man," Lily said.

Dame Margaret shrugged. "There's no accounting for tastes." She put the key on the table next to her spoon and picked it up again. "I'm concerned for your safety, my dear. What will you do now?"

"I don't know. I thought I might do a survey. Iron Age fortresses, maybe. And then write up some proposals for my own excavations."

Still holding the key, Dame Margaret stood up. "Will you excuse me? I'm very tired."

She headed toward Lawrence's room. Lily was dismissed.

* * *

The murder made the front page of the *Palestine Post* the next morning, right under the headline "Eleven Separate Incidents within Seventy-Two Hours." Lily read it at breakfast.

BRITISH ARCHAEOLOGIST MURDERED NEAR HEBRON

Geoffrey Gorton Eastbourne, distinguished British archaeologist and director of the Beacon Research Foundation excavations at Tel al-Kharub, was killed Saturday morning on the Beit Jibrin track northwest of Hebron. Eastbourne was shot in the back and sustained a crushing blow to his head.

Eyewitnesses, including his driver and a member of the excavation staff who witnessed the shooting, say that armed bandits stopped their car two kilometers from the main highway and ordered Eastbourne out of the car. The driver was told to continue on to Hebron. Two shots were heard as they drove away.

The car was intercepted as Eastbourne was on his way to the opening of the new Palestine Archaeological Museum.

According to a spokesman from the British Archaeological School, "Eastbourne demonstrated his usual rash courage and conscientious attention to his professional responsibilities" by insisting that work on the tel be completed before leaving camp. The director of the British School said that Eastbourne had no known enemies but had often been warned against traveling unarmed in the present political climate.

The body was brought to Jerusalem by ambulance late Saturday. Funeral services are scheduled for 2:30 p.m. today at the Protestant Cemetery on Mt. Zion.

* * *

When Lily finished breakfast, she brought the newspaper inside to the telephone table in the alcove next to the Common Room and put it on top of the stack of old papers. She remembered the morning of the riots, when Eastbourne had folded the paper and put it in his pocket, and searched through the stack for July 10, wondering what he had been hiding, and where he had gone that day.

She scanned the headlines from twenty days ago. Air raids in Canton; Spanish insurgents thirty miles from Valencia; Haifa curfew in force after yesterday's bomb; Nazis demand self-determination for Sudeten Germans; arrival of the Italian steamship *Marco Polo* in Haifa port; record New York-Paris flight by Howard Hughes; Aspro tablets cure hay fever, nervous exhaustion, neuralgia, colds, malaria, asthma, sleeplessness.

Nothing there.

She remembered Sir William's joke about a lonely heart's notice in the personal columns. Flats for rent; English-speaking secretary wanted; shipment from the Marco Polo to arrive at the King David this morning; new dresses at Rosenthal's Clothing Emporium.

Nothing there.

Lady Fendley came into the Common Room and Lily handed her the morning paper. "The funeral is at 2:30."

"It's so sad," said Lady Fendley, sighing. "Geoffrey was a fine young man, really. He did it all on his own, you know.

With scholarships and hard work. His father was just a clerk in a haberdashery."

"You really liked him."

Lady Fendley nodded. "It wasn't just that. He had responsibilities that would have distracted another man who wasn't that dedicated. People laughed at him for being stingy. But the truth is, he was just squeaking by financially. He was sympathetic and helpful to all his workmen, seeing to their health and comfort. And he was good with children." Lady Fendley looked down at the paper and then at Lily. "Village children adored him."

"*De mortuus nil nisi bonum?*" asked Lily.

"Of course."

EIGHT

THE HIGH COMMISSIONER himself delivered the eulogy. Lily, drowsy from the sun, listened to his voice drifting in and out with the breeze that floated through the tall cypress and gently shifted their branches back and forth.

Snatches of his words reached her. "Brutally shot down in mid-career . . . outstanding discoveries . . . a scientist and a leader of men . . . inestimable loss."

The whole British community was there—the Anglican Bishop who read the service; the Chief Justice; Dominicans from the École Biblique, dressed in their light linen summer robes; the Attorney General; the Special Commissioner; members of the British School; bearded scholars from the Hebrew University. They crowded around the open grave and coffin draped with the Union Jack. Perspiration beaded on upper lips and ran down temples.

Jamal was there, watching from the verge of the path. Kate, buttoned into an ill-fitting black dress, her face puffed and blotched with tears, lingered on the edge of the crowd. A child sat near her in the shade of a tree.

Sir William stood in front, erect and resolute, looking toward the tawny desert hills and the Dead Sea, the water clear

and blue as the sky and rimmed with white patches of salt crys-
tals floating like miniature icebergs. Lady Fendley held his arm.
Dame Margaret stood next to them, wearing the hat with the
astonished feather.

"Gave his life for this land . . ." the High Commissioner was
saying. Bees and butterflies hovered among wreaths that separated the funeral from tombstones that grew like broken teeth
out of the dry weeds. Fresh graves, decked with faded flowers,
were scattered here and there under soft and irregular ground.

Dame Margaret approached Lily. The breeze straightened
her feather into a point, trembling a moment at apogee and
then subsiding.

Lily heard whispers behind her, ". . . that's not what I heard.
I heard he was killed by some dissatisfied workmen."

Before Lily could turn around to see who was talking, Dame
Margaret reached her. The pleasant scent of vanilla mingled
with the pungent odor of cypress and the fragrance from lavender growing on the side of the hill.

"We have to talk," Dame Margaret said. "Not tomorrow.
Tomorrow's Tuesday. Let's make it Wednesday, for lunch. At
the American Colony." What is it this time, Lily wondered?
Dame Margaret left without saying goodbye, her feather rising
again, the smell of vanilla wafting in her wake.

Sir William tossed the first shovel of dirt into the grave after
the coffin was lowered. He turned away to take his wife's arm
and they walked down the path to a waiting taxi before Lily
could reach them. Kate had vanished before the group dispersed.
Only Jamal remained.

Lily left the cemetery. Weeds brushed against her sandals,
releasing the pungent aroma of wormwood. She scrambled past
the Church of the Dormition at the crest of the hill, past its
turrets and conical dome. Jamal followed her down the hill to
Zion Gate.

They went through the great double doors, heavy with iron hinges. Jamal strolled by Lily's side, silent and watchful, through the crowded lanes—past donkeys and camels that blocked the way; Jewish men with fur hats and black, belted suits; women with head scarves and shapeless, long-sleeved dresses.

Jamal stayed with her as she maneuvered through the swarming bazaar of the Khan ez Zeit, through the slippery streets, past butcher shops redolent with flyspecked legs of lamb. The ruddy-faced woman behind her, wheezing garlic, had her ample belly caught in the small of Lily's back. A man wearing a *kefiya* and a long, loose *abaya* jostled her. For a moment, the crush was so dense that Lily could barely breath.

Jamal was still with her.

Through the stifling throng snaked priests in long black robes and thin-lipped Protestant missionaries in dark suits leading their pale wives in baggy print dresses with dainty lace collars. Jamal glanced at Lily with his hooded eyes and smiled.

Somewhere near the Via Dolorosa, he disappeared.

* * *

Lily arrived at the American school hot and tired. She went to the kitchen and reached into the icebox for the water pitcher. The telephone rang. It was Henderson.

"Can you meet me at Samir's Patisserie inside Damascus Gate in half an hour? Something urgent we must talk about."

"Make it forty-five minutes."

"Forty-five minutes then."

She washed her face and took the glass of water outside into the garden, pressing its cool surface against her cheek and temples. She sat in the quiet of the garden with her feet up, her eyes closed, under the shade of the cedar tree until the lift of the late afternoon breeze revived her. Then she went back to the Old City.

She elbowed her way through Damascus Gate, avoiding beggars with swollen legs lying on the pavement in the shadow of the gate; beggars with pitiful faces and outreached hands; beggars sitting cross-legged on the ground, praying, their copper begging bowls silent reminders; beggars with accusing eyes who babbled and reeked of old urine. Assailed by a swarm of the destitute—by urchins and greedy children snatching at her—she reached into her pocket for a mil, a penny, a dime, anything to ease the guilt, to counteract the curses of their eyes. There but for the grace of God . . .

"Don't give them anything." It was Henderson who came up behind her. "Only encourages them."

He led her to Samir's Patisserie at the corner. "European Pastries," the sign said. "We deliver tarts to your home for your pleasure." The window was banked with sticky cakes and pastries mounded in geometric patterns, like three-dimensional optical illusions. A boy stood near the cakes with a whisk, beating back the flies drawn by the redolence of clarified butter and sugar syrup.

The proprietor smiled, with a sweeping bow. "*Ahlan wa sahlan.*" He waved them to a table. "Welcome in peace."

"*Fiq,*" Henderson answered. "*Minfadlak*, please, just some coffee." He sat down at the table and pointed to the seat across from him.

He waited until she was seated. "Have you thought about the survey of Iron Age fortresses?"

"It depends on whether we continue digging at Tel al-Kharub."

"Without Eastbourne?"

"Kate knows what she's doing."

"You think Beacon Pharmaceutical would sponsor an excavation headed by a woman?"

"The Brits don't mind. Excavations have woman directors, trained on the playing fields of England. Women play field hockey there."

A fly danced along the ceiling, swooped down toward the top of Henderson's head in wide arcs and then back up again, flitting across the room.

"You've heard of the Tegart lines?" he asked.

"I'm not sure."

"Double electrified fences. The Brits are installing them along the northern border," he said. "Two sets of barbed wire, about three meters high, ten meters apart. And roles of barbed wire between."

"To prevent infiltration from Syria and Lebanon by the Mufti's men?"

He nodded. "Personnel, arms, ammo. Tegart wants to build fortified command posts. The best locations were worked out in antiquity. We're looking for defensible hillsides with a good overlook."

"Maybe they weren't the best locations," Lily said. "Assyrians and Babylonians invaded and conquered anyway."

"Depends on the terrain and back-up."

"Locations of Iron Age fortresses were based on the use of fire signals from hilltop to hilltop," Lily said. "Now there are radios."

"The principle's the same."

She leaned closer. "You believe the new forts will keep out the Mufti's men?"

"I don't know. He's daring, resourceful."

"He hid in the Haram-al-Sharif and sneaked away in the night to Beirut disguised as a woman," Lily said. "You call that daring?"

"I call that resourceful." The fly buzzed above his head in narrowing circles. "I met him once."

"What was he like?"

"Disarming personality—a gentle man, smiling, soft-spoken. Light eyes. Pleasant."

"He kills people."

"To defend his home. The Jews are trying to drive Arabs from their own country, murdering their sons, burning their houses. Probably plotting to destroy the Dome of the Rock," he hit the table for emphasis, "as we speak."

"He kills Arabs too."

"Only traitors. Like a surgeon cutting away diseased tissue." Lily moved back in her chair. "He sounds like Hitler."

"Exactly." The fly lit on the rim of his cup and he brushed it away. "Hitler is giving Germans back their pride. Like the Mufti is doing for Arabs."

"I suppose you met Hitler and found him charming too."

Henderson lifted his cup, and spooned some sugar and water into the saucer. He held the cup in his hand, waiting for the fly to light, then slammed the cup into the saucer, turning it around and around.

"You have to understand Hitler," he said. "He was wounded in the Great War. Trapped in a trench for two weeks with a dead comrade who'd been blown to bits. He was shell-shocked—blind for two months. Recovered his sight, but not his naiveté. He swore vengeance."

"That's no excuse," Lily said.

Henderson lifted the cup, put a paper napkin on the saucer over the splayed fly, and took a sip of coffee. "Something similar happened to me. Horrible. Buried with the dead. Hemmed in for a week. I'll never forget the stench, the bloated stomach, the eyes open to the rain."

"Yes, but you didn't . . ." Her voice trailed off. "Hitler behaves like a madman," Lily said. "Especially toward the Jews."

Henderson shrugged and took another sip of coffee. "He blames them for the war and the defeat. I don't trust them either. Most of them are Communists. They control the press and banking."

"Communist bankers?"

He grasped the coffee cup in his fist. "Between Marx and Rothschild, they control the world."

"You forgot Freud and Jesus."

He tried to smile. "Them too." The knuckles of his hand tightened around the coffee cup.

"Confucius and Buddha probably had Jewish mothers."

He nodded. "I wouldn't be surprised."

"And Mohammed and Chief Sequoia."

"Chief Sequoia?"

"A member of the Lost Ten Tribes. Where were you brought up?"

"Cincinnati."

"It sounds like a whole different world. Keep talking," Lily said. "It's time to put the other foot in your mouth."

Henderson leaned forward. He was looking at her carefully now, ignoring a second fly that danced around his head, his deep-set turquoise eyes glinting. "You are a very attractive woman. The gold of your hair and the blue of your eyes . . ."

"Is a blend of the western skies?"

"Yes. Something like that."

Lily moved her chair back. "I'm the sweetheart of Sigma Chi."

He leaned his arms on the table. Lily stared at the napkin in his saucer, puckered and discolored. "I have to be going." She started to get up.

"By the way." He reached for her arm. "Something is missing from your excavation. You registered it in the catalogue."

Another offhand statement, this time from Henderson.

"What is it?" she asked.

"Nothing much. Just a little blue glass vial."

Her amphoriskos! "What do you mean 'missing'?"

"Not at the site or in the stuff Eastbourne was bringing to the museum," he said.

"How do you know about it?"

He didn't answer. His nostrils flared for a split second and he narrowed his eyes. "I'm not at liberty to say." He glared at her through icy slits. "Let's just say it's a matter of great interest to the State Department."

"What's this about?"

"It's hush-hush." He stood up. "You're too upset to talk now. You just came from Eastbourne's funeral." He tossed two piasters on the table. "We'll talk about this another time. How long will you be in Jerusalem? When do you go back to the excavation?"

"I'm not sure."

"There's a reception at the Austrian consulate tomorrow evening. I have to be there. What say I pick you up tomorrow at six and we have dinner at the King David before the reception. We can talk then."

"Talk about what?"

"The blue glass vial, of course."

NINE

THE NEXT MORNING LILY slept late. She dressed quickly, reached for her saddle shoes, considered disguising the scuffs under a coat of fresh polish, and then thought better of it.

She carried her breakfast into the garden. Avi sat at the table under the pine tree, his legs up on the chair next to him, his face hidden behind the front page of the *Palestine Post*.

"*Boker tov*," he said. "Good morning."

Lily read off the headlines. "Bomb Outside Hotel in Tel Aviv Wounds 21; Air Raids in Barcelona; Henlein Bloc Victorious in Czech Poll. Not very good as mornings go."

"We're alive." He looked over the edge of the paper. "I was waiting for you. Thought you might like company after the funeral yesterday."

"You came to Jerusalem to console me?"

"I had errands." He closed the paper and looked around the garden, at the roses dropping their petals on the flagstones, stretched his arms and took a deep, satisfied breath. "A beautiful day. Flowers are blooming. The sky is blue. Finish your breakfast and we'll go for a walk."

He went back to the paper. "I see they arrested someone and let him go."

"For Eastbourne's murder?"

"Police dogs tracked a scent from the murder scene to a house in Kharass."

He took his legs off the chair and sat up. "'The dog followed a trail for 22 kilometers to Kharass where it went straight to the house of the accused,'" he read aloud, "'stopped at the door and went to the wall of the courtyard, jumped against it and barked. A German Luger loaded with four rounds was found hidden behind a stone in a hole in the wall. The firearm was handed to Sir Charles Tegart, who assisted in the investigation.'"

"They let the man go?"

"He said he was looking after a sick cow when Eastbourne was shot. He claims he never locks the courtyard and anyone could have hidden the gun."

"What was Tegart doing there?"

Avi shrugged. "Eastbourne was an important man."

"How much does a Luger cost?" Lily asked.

"I don't know. Fifty pounds, maybe."

"Where would a poor *fellah* get the money? It would take years to earn that much."

Avi shrugged. "From the Waqf, maybe?"

Lily shook her head. "That's a religious fund. For widows and orphans, maintaining holy places."

"It's a form of religion. The Mufti feels he has a sacred duty to kill anyone who doesn't agree with him. That's what religion is all about."

"Don't be so cynical."

Avi put down the paper and began to chant. "Who killed Geoff Eastbourne? I, said the sparrow, with my little bow and arrow."

"It was a Luger."

"Sorry. Make that: I said the Hun, with my little German gun."

"You're pleased with yourself today."

"Ever walk along the ramparts on top of the city wall?" Avi asked.

"Spying on secrets hidden in the old stones and crooked alleys?" she said. "Let's go."

They spent the morning in the tangle of streets—Feather Lane, Watermelon Alley, Dancing Dervish, Needle's Eye—crowded with camels and donkeys, sheep and goats. They made their way through water vendors and men sitting on the stone pavement with olivewood camels for sale. They listened to nasal love songs of Umm Kousum blaring from shops.

They ran along the catwalk on the top of the city wall, looked down at traffic on Suleiman Street, at tourists studying maps. They peered into courtyards with wash hanging on the line, at spires of churches, at children playing in schoolyards, at the arches of the Church of the Holy Sepulcher.

"I feel like a peeping Tom," Lily said, and stopped to watch tired buses on Suleiman Street gasp up the hill between carts drawn by donkeys or spavined horses.

Avi stood on the parapet facing the Old City. He spread out his arms and declaimed, "If I forget thee, O Jerusalem, may my right hand forget her cunning, let my tongue cleave to the roof of my mouth, if I remember thee not; if I set not Jerusalem above my chief joy."

"And is Jerusalem your chief joy?" Lily asked.

Avi dropped his arms. "I don't know. Sometimes I wonder how many lives must be lost for this pile of stones. Then I remember all the stories of Jerusalem. This is where my forebears wrote the Bible. Over there," he pointed to the Dome of the Rock, "King David bought the threshing floor of Araunah the Jebusite."

He gestured at the narrow lanes of the Old City. "This is where David danced when he brought the ark from Kiryat Yearim. And over there," he pointed toward the cemetery on the Mount of Olives, "are the tombs of my ancestors."

He turned to Lily. "Did you know that if you're not buried in Jerusalem, you must tunnel your way back on your hands and knees? Just think, Eastbourne is already here."

He gazed across the hills. "At the end of days, the Messiah will sacrifice a red heifer and a miraculous bridge will lead from the Mount of Olives to the Temple Mount. Souls of the dead will walk across it for divine judgment." He gestured toward a wadi where small rubbish fires burned. "All the dead will rise from the Valley of Hinnom, right over there." Avi swept his arms from hill to hill like a conductor at a concert. "Franciscans will rise from the Olivet, Eastbourne from Mount Zion. The dead from everywhere will come to Jerusalem."

"There's not enough room."

"It is written." He dropped his arms. "That's the tragedy of Jerusalem. There's always room for the dead." His voice dropped to a hoarse whisper and his tone flattened. "There are no more red heifers. The species is extinct. The Messiah can never come."

The sounds of a quarrel seemed to erupt in the street outside the Old City. Lily looked down at vintage taxis parked in front of Damascus Gate. A flock of sheep blocked traffic. The shepherd leisurely guided them down the center of the street, ignoring the man shouting and shaking his fist from the running board of a Pierce Arrow marooned in the sea of sheep.

"Don't argue with the past," Avi called down in a mournful voice to the red-faced man. "You can't win."

"I had enough of the Old City," Lily said. "Let's go into town. I'll buy you an ice cream."

"Had enough of my sentimental hogwash?" He gave her a nervous smile. "Better yet, let's go to Patt's, and you'll buy me lunch."

They descended from the city wall at Jaffa Gate and started down Bethlehem Road toward the Sultan's pool.

"The Old City looks different," Lily said. "Last year it was full of men in red tarbooshes. It looked like a Shriner's convention. Now they all wear *kefiyas*, like *fellahin* from the villages."

"Statement of political solidarity," Avi said. "Even Arab judges wear *kefiyas* nowadays. Everybody wears costumes." He stopped and looked at her dress and down at her shoes. "I know you're an American because of your funny shoes."

Lily was sorry that she hadn't covered the scuffed toes with shoe polish.

"You know I'm a kibbutznik because I wear sandals and shorts and a *kova tembel*." He pointed to the white hat perched on the top of his head. "My idiot hat."

He grinned and started uphill toward Mamilla Street.

A bearded man from one of the yeshivas, dressed in black from his homburg to his shoes, strutted past them on the narrow sidewalk. Fringes of a prayer garment peeked from beneath his open frock coat. Side curls hung along his curly beard down to his lapels and danced with each step.

The man covered his eyes with his hand in an elaborate gesture and turned his face away.

Avi chuckled. "You see, everywhere silent messages shout at you. He was flirting, letting you know you make him think carnal thoughts."

They had reached Julian's Way and were near the King David Hotel.

A taxi, its motor idling noisily, waited at the corner of Mamilla. Two Arabs sat in the front seat.

A man dressed in a striped vest over baggy pants, his head encased in a bright turban, strolled down the street toward the King David Hotel. He carried a brown paper package tied with string.

"Another costume," Avi said as the man approached. Avi squinted at him. "Isn't that the workman from your site?"

"Abu Musa?"

Abu Musa looked up at the sound of his name and ducked into a shop near the entrance of the hotel.

Avi watched him scurry out of sight. "He looks like an illustration from a David Robert's print."

"Costumes again. He's Samaritan," Lily said. "I wonder what he's doing here." The shop had a gold-lettered sign, Judah Arnon, Antiquities. "I know Judah, the owner of the shop." Lily approached the display window adorned with Roman lamps and coins and peered inside. "Sometimes he works with archaeologists. Dug with us one season at Kharub."

Ancient bowls and jars stood beneath tiny spotlights on lacquered stands. Abu Musa, holding an Iron Age decanter, gestured and argued with a man who stood behind a glass case laden with jewelry.

"That's Judah," Lily said. "Behind the counter. The decanter looks like one from Tel al-Kharub."

Abu Musa waved his free hand insistently while Judah shook his head.

With a final nod of dismissal, Judah turned away from Abu Musa. The Samaritan wrapped the decanter in newspaper, put it back into the brown paper sack and retied the string. He came out of the shop with the package under his arm.

This time, he grinned at Lily. "I go to Ramallah. Wrong bus." He slid his tongue around the gaps in his brown teeth. "Ask in shop to find bus."

The taxi on the corner of Mamilla and Julian's Way pulled away from the curb and started toward them.

"Bus terminal is on Jaffa Road," Avi pointed up the street toward town. "That way."

Abu Musa's glance followed Avi's finger. "You sure that the way?" He flashed his stained teeth in a friendly leer.

Behind Abu Musa, Lily saw the driver of the approaching taxi lean back in the seat while the passenger reached down and brought up a rifle.

The man with the rifle swung it across the steering wheel to aim in the direction of the shop.

Judah looked through the window, waved his hands in warning, opened the door and grabbed Lily's arm. "Inside. Quick."

Abu Musa, alerted, ducked into the hotel entrance.

"Down!" Avi shouted.

An explosion erupted from the cab with a fiery flash. A loud pinging sound reverberated somewhere near the shop window and something flew past Lily.

Lily brushed her hand against her cheek. "What was that?"

The taxi sped away and Lily saw Abu Musa run down the alley that led to Herod's family tomb.

"Rifle shot," Judah said. "Hit the building."

"Don't be silly," Lily said and felt her knees buckle.

"There." Avi pointed to a spot near the door. "Took a chunk out of the stone."

Judah grabbed Lily's arm and propelled her inside. "Worry about that later."

He pulled at the straps that closed the metal shutters. They clattered down. He settled Lily into a chair in the back of the darkened shop. "You all right?" He held out a glass of tea in a silver holder. "Why would someone try to shoot you."

"I don't know." Her hand was shaking as she reached for the tea.

"First Eastbourne. Then you." Avi's high-pitched voice and rapid speech echoed his alarm. "Something to do with Tel al-Kharub?"

"I don't understand." Lily took a sip of the tea. "There's nothing there. No reason I can think of." She dropped a cube of sugar into the glass and stirred the tea. "You were at the site, Judah. Can you think of anything?"

Judah held out his hands and shrugged.

Avi said and leaned forward. "Think. There must be a reason."

Lily took a deep breath, sipped from the glass, shook her head. A marble clock on the shelf behind the counter ticked with a steady rhythm. She stirred the tea again. "What did Abu Musa want?"

"Tried to sell me an Iron Age decanter. Said he found it when he was plowing fields near his village."

"You didn't buy it."

"It wasn't from Samaria. Rim and neck were wrong. More a Judean type. Still . . . You think it's a fake?"

"Or stolen."

"From Kharub?"

"Maybe. I couldn't swear to it."

The clock whirred as if it took in a breath. Soft chimes carefully struck twelve o'clock. Lily finished the tea and handed the glass to Judah.

Avi glanced at the clock. "We have to leave."

Judah set the glass on the counter. "You sure it's safe?"

"I'll be all right," Lily said and stood up.

"I have an appointment. At Patt's," Avi said. "We'll be fine."

* * *

They headed for the New City through narrow alleys redolent with garbage, where armies of cats stalked and perched on the lids of cans, ready to pounce on their prey. Iridescent pigeons pecked at melon seeds and detritus scattered around the edge of oily puddles the same color as the birds.

"Wild life in the city," Avi said. "Years ago the British brought cats here to control the rats. And now look." He skirted a discarded melon rind. "I could never live in a city."

They continued up the hill toward Zion Circus, passing machine shops, skirting grimy pools of grease, passing a Hebrew sign painted on the wall between two doors.

"Holy place. Forbidden to urinate here," Avi read. "You see, even that is forbidden." He smiled at the sign and the faint dark rivulets trickling along the wall below it.

"You know what happened back in the twenties?" he asked. "The Brits built a public toilet near Zion Circus. They were miffed when the Arab mayor refused to commit public urination for the opening ceremony. Told him they do it in France. He said he didn't have to go, he went before he left his house."

"Ever seen a photo in the *Illustrated London Times* of the Lord Mayor of London in full regalia," Lily asked, "using a public latrine in Picadilly Circus?"

"No."

"Neither have I," Lily said, and was surprised that she had almost forgotten the rifle pointed in her direction and the stone chip from the building that had flown past her cheek.

At the sidewalk outside of Patt's, Avi pulled a canvas chair away from one of the small wooden tables. "We can sit out here and watch the world go by. Sooner or later, everyone comes to the Street of the Prophets." He gestured up and down the empty street. "It's like Times Square."

The only other person on the street was a woman who hurried out of the little grocery at the corner, weighted down with full shopping bags balanced from each hand.

A waiter stepped outside, wiping his hands on a towel.

"Cheese sandwich?" Avi asked Lily.

She nodded.

"Two. And orange juice twice," he said to the waiter. He turned to Lily. "You don't want the coffee. It will dissolve your teeth."

The waiter continued wiping his hands on the towel. "The shipment of *rimmonim* you brought this morning from the kibbutz?" he said to Avi. "Some of them were rotten."

Avi pushed away from the table. "The pomegranates? Maybe the whole crop is spoiled. I better go see."

He entered the shop and disappeared through a door in the back of the bakery. Lily waited for a while in the shade of the locust trees, watching occasional passersby. An old man wearing threadbare, faded clothes shuffled along on the other side of the street, hugging buildings, tilting his face to the sun as though he were blind. A ButiGaz truck stacked with cylinders of butane for kitchen stoves rumbled by.

Lily fidgeted in her seat and wondered what was keeping Avi. A boy carrying a soccer ball ran down the street. A pale young woman in a long-sleeved dress pushed a child in a carriage.

Finally, Lily left the table and opened the door of the café to the yeasty aroma of bread and pastries fresh from the ovens, the bitter smell of boiled coffee, the clatter of dishes on small marble tables where people leaned toward each other and murmured in quiet voices. She walked past them to the back of the room where Avi had gone through the door. She turned the knob.

The door was locked.

TEN

LILY KNOCKED. SHE HEARD movement behind the door and knocked again.

Avi's voice, strained and apprehensive called out "Who is it?" He opened the door a crack and looked through the narrow opening still secured by a chain bolt. "Oh, it's you." He hesitated. "Sorry I left. Emergency."

"A shipment of over-ripe pomegranates?" Lily looked past him into the back room, unfurnished except for a sink and towel roller in the corner.

What was so secret about a shipment of pomegranates from a kibbutz? Pomegranates—*rimmonim*. There's another meaning, Lily remembered.

Hand grenades.

Ora stood in the middle of the room, in the same baggy maternity dress, this time loose around the waist.

"Ora gave birth to an unhealthy brace of hand grenades, didn't she?" Lily said.

Avi flushed. "Who told you that?"

Ora twittered.

"You did," Lily said. "Just a little while ago. The waiter said something about a shipment of pomegranates, *rimmonim*—hand grenades in Hebrew. That's what you and Ora brought to Patt's this morning."

Ora giggled, sending the ripples of loose fabric from the dress surging around her middle like the tide.

Rafi, his hands white with flour, emerged into view, coming up from below. He stopped on the stairs.

"Are there flour bins in the basement?" Lily waited for a confirming titter from Ora. "Is that where you hide them?"

Rafi moved to the sink to wipe his hands. "Get her out of here," he said in a low voice.

"She's all right, Rafi. You told me . . ."

"I'll take care of it." Rafi reached for the towel and looked Lily over speculatively. "We'll go for a walk." He started for the door.

Lily heard the lock click behind them as they went back through the café and into the street.

They strolled under the trees, not looking at each other, brushing leaves out of the gutter with their shoes.

"Where are we going?" Lily asked.

"I don't know." He walked slowly, looking down at his feet, his hands in his pockets. "I'm just a tourist here."

"Sure you are."

They turned the corner at Rothschild Hospital and continued on toward Ethiopia Street.

"What are you really doing here?" Lily asked.

"Not much to tell. My name is Ralph Landon. I'm an orthopedic surgeon from Chicago, here for a few months to demonstrate new trauma procedures at Strauss Hospital."

"I'll bet."

"A tourist. Here for a couple of months."

Lily watched him as they sauntered up Ethiopia Street in the quiet of the siesta. "You want the grand tour," she asked, "or the intimate one of back streets that tourists never see?"

"Intimate is always better."

She smiled. He took his hands out of his pockets and smiled back.

"Over there," she waved toward a building on the other side of the road, "is the former home of the American School. Before they built the one in East Jerusalem."

"That where you live? The American School?"

"Where do you live?"

"I rent a bed-sitting room with board and laundry in Katamon, for eight pounds a month."

"You're overpaying. You can get a whole apartment for five pounds a month."

Lily pointed to a house next door to the black-domed Ethiopian Church. A guard in a white uniform stood at the door. "Haile Selassie, the Lion of Judah, Emperor of Abbysinia, descendant of Solomon and the Queen of Sheba, lives right there, in the Abbysinian Palace."

"In parts of Chicago," he said, "the South Side, some people think he's the new Messiah. A new religion, Ras Tafarians. We used to get called to the South Side sometimes to fix up knife wounds when I was a resident at Michael Reese. That's when I found out."

"You really are a doctor, aren't you?"

"I told you."

"You said Ora was your wife."

"I don't always tell the truth."

"You honestly work at Strauss Hospital?"

Rafi nodded and kept walking, slower, his hands in his pockets, brushing his shoe along a pile of leaves on the curb, scattering them into the roadway.

"I like the quiet this time of day," Lily said.

They strolled along the street, the only sounds their own footsteps, the crickets, and leaves stirring in the afternoon breeze.

"But that's not the real reason you're here, to teach trauma techniques," Lily said. "You're smuggling arms."

"Where'd you get that idea?"

Lily shook her head. "I caught you white-handed. Why the alias?"

"Don't know what you're talking about."

"I'd have to take lessons in stupidity to miss what you're doing."

"I don't have an alias. Just simpler to use a Hebrew name. Raphael."

"You said you don't always tell the truth."

"And you believed me?" He stopped walking and faced her. "I'm getting hungry. How about you? There's a new café on Chancellor Road, across from the hospital."

They turned left on Chancellor Road, their footsteps echoing in the silence. In front of the cafe, they sat at a table under an umbrella and waited in the eerie hush of the siesta.

A car was pulled up on the sidewalk in front of an arched doorway; bits of torn gray paper scudded among the leaves on the pavement and eddied in the wind.

A beggar sat cross-legged next to the steps of the Health Center across the road, his eyes closed, an open book across his lap, an engraved copper begging bowl next to his knee.

Rafi went into the café, emerging after a few minutes with two bottles of orange soda. "We have to make do with this. *'Geschlossen zwichen Zwie und Vier fur Schlafstunde.'* Closed between two and four for the siesta."

Lily took a sip of the soda. "What are you doing here really?" she asked.

"I told you. Demonstrating techniques for treating traumas at the hospital."

"Just working at a hospital? Every fourth man in Jerusalem is a doctor," she told him. "Taxi drivers and hod carriers are doctors. They don't need one more doctor in Jerusalem. You're here to smuggle arms."

"What makes you think that?"

"The *sherut* for one thing. And today at Patt's."

"I don't know what you mean."

"Why would a doctor take chances like that?"

Rafi shifted in his chair. He looked down at the table and took a sip from the soda bottle. "That reminds me of a story," he said. "Moishe and Chaim . . ."

"Were on the road from Minsk to Pinsk?"

Rafi shook his head. "No. This time they were on the high seas in a leaky boat. In a storm. The boat was pitching and tossing, pitching and tossing." Rafi rocked back and forth like the tide, his hands and forearms rising and falling. "Moishe cried, 'Help! Help! The ship is sinking! The ship is sinking!' And Chaim answered, 'So why are you worried? Is it your ship?'"

Lily sat quietly for a moment, not smiling, her arms crossed over her chest.

"You were supposed to laugh," Rafi said.

"Why were they in a leaky boat?"

"It was the only one they had."

She leaned forward and touched his arm. "You have to be careful. Penalties are getting more severe. They sentence people to death for smuggling arms now."

"I am careful. Besides, they always seem to commute the sentence."

He took another swallow of soda, tapped his foot and looked toward the beggar asleep at the steps of the Health Center. "What would you like to do now? We could go tea dancing at Café Europa. Or to the Edison and watch a movie. Walter Huston is enlarging the British Empire in *Rhodes of Africa* this week. We can spit shells from sunflower seeds onto the floor the whole afternoon. Or we could go to a salon—a genuine salon—at an artist's house."

"I have to meet someone for dinner at six o'clock."

"The salon it is," he said and tilted the soda bottle to finish it. "We'll drop in and leave after an hour, like important people."

"I've never been to a salon. What do people do?"

"Sit around in a circle and take turns talking about themselves."

"Does anyone reveal a guilty secret?"

He shook his head. "They come to flex their egos. They say, 'I won this prize; I invented that; I wrote that.' It's edifying."

"Sounds boring."

"It is. High society in Jerusalem. For visiting dignitaries like us." He stood up. "Leave the bottle on the table."

"Where is the salon?"

"A little way from here. Kalman House. He's an opthamologist. Runs an eye clinic out of his house. She's an artist and has her studio there. They hold open house every Thursday afternoon."

"How do you know them?"

"From the hospital." Rafi looked at his watch. "If we walk slowly, we won't arrive too early."

They strolled in the direction of Zion Circus. In a small alley with steps that led down a steep incline, the sensuous smell of roasting nuts drifted toward them from a shop built into the stairway.

"Someday I'll buy you a bag of pistachios," Rafi said.

"I'd rather have rubies."

Dissonant sounds of muezzins' calls for prayer wafted toward them from loudspeakers on a multitude of minarets near the Old City.

"It's three-thirty," Lily said. "Siesta's over."

"That's how you tell time?"

"Muslims are called to prayer five times a day—when they wake up just before first light, in mid-morning, at noon before the mid-day meal, at the end of the siesta, at sun-down, and before they go to sleep. Like a factory whistle. Tells you the time, even though you don't work in the mill."

People appeared in the streets; shopkeepers unlocked their doors. Ancient cars gasped along the road; motorbikes squealed between sputtering trucks and careened around horse-drawn wagons.

A man in a black felt fedora brushed against Lily, knocking his briefcase against her leg as he hurried past.

From somewhere near the Old City, hoarse shouts drifted toward them, faint and indistinguishable at first, then growing in intensity, punctuated with cries and shrieks. Lily stopped and grabbed Rafi's hand. Not another riot, another bomb, another lifeless face like Dr. Stern's. Rafi pressed her hand for a moment, then put his arm around her waist.

Around them, traffic slowed, people stood silent with harried faces animated by fear. Lily waited, anticipating horror, waited for the sound of gunfire, the jolt of an explosion, the howl of sirens through the streets.

ELEVEN

THE HAIRDRESSER, READY to open his shop, left the shutters half-closed; the greengrocer, carrying a box of apricots, halted on the sidewalk. Traffic on the road barely moved. A man on a motor bike lingered at the corner, one foot on the ground, the bike canted against his leg, his head tilted toward the Old City. All waited, listening in mute fellowship for echoes from the Old City.

The man in the black fedora knelt on the sidewalk, opened his briefcase and took out a gun that glinted blue-black in the sun. He thrust it into his belt, catching it in the fringes of a prayer-vest that dangled beneath his shirt. A tall man behind him peered over the rim of his sunglasses and backed away. A woman glanced at the gun, smiled at her friend and raised an eyebrow.

Noises from the Old City abated. Fear dissipated; shoulders that had been hunched relaxed. People still waited until the street filled with familiar sounds—mothers calling to children, taxis honking, buses coughing their way through the streets—and then turned away from each other. They walked around the man in the fedora, their eyes straight ahead.

Rafi let out a long breath. "Well, that certainly got my adrenals flowing."

Lily noticed that her fingers were still shaking. "The man in the fedora . . ."

"He wasn't Hagganah," Rafi said.

"How do you know?"

Rafi put his hands in his pockets. "What were you going to say about the man in the fedora?"

"He could be arrested for carrying arms," Lily said after a while.

Rafi kept walking, kicking at imaginary pebbles with the toes of his shoes. "Not if he's a supernumerary." He didn't look up.

"Supernumeraries carry spears. At the opera."

"British police recruit locals, Arabs and Jews, as reserves." He took his hands out of his pockets. "Call them supernumeraries."

"What kind of gun was it?"

"A Luger."

"The Brits issue German weapons?"

"Probably his own."

"Are they expensive?" Lily asked.

"Forty, fifty dollars." Rafi reached for her arm. "You want one?"

"Where would a *fellah* get the money?"

"A *fellah*? What makes you ask that?"

"It said in the paper that the police tracked Eastbourne's attackers to an Arab village and found a Luger hidden in a wall."

"Maybe he stole it?" Rafi shrugged. "Got it from the Mufti?"

"I think it's odd, that's all. They didn't arrest the man, or question him, just let him go when he said he didn't put it there. . . ." Her voice trailed off.

They strolled in silence, Rafi's fingers still lightly on her elbow. She could feel the warmth from his body, and was surprised at how comfortable she was with it.

After awhile, he pointed down the road to a house where green shutters stood open on the upstairs balconies and white curtains fluttered softly in the afternoon breeze. "Kalman's is over there, the big house with the awnings, near the corner."

Rafi rang the bell. The sound echoed inside the house, and penetrated through the tall arched windows. Footsteps clattered on a stone floor.

A small, bald man with glasses and a gray mustache opened the door. "*Baruch haba*. Come in. Come in." He swept his arm in a welcoming gesture. "What was the commotion in the Old City?"

"Who knows," Rafi said.

The man shook his head. "It's getting so bad, I can't even count sheep to go to sleep. In the middle of counting, someone shoots them."

Rafi's hand still rested on Lily's elbow as they entered the hallway. The man looked from Lily to Rafi and winked. "This is the first time you brought a friend."

Rafi winked back. "Lily Sampson," Rafi nodded at Lily. "Albert Kalman."

Kalman led them into a room with whitewashed walls and a high domed ceiling. Four blue settees were arranged around a polished brass table exactly in the center of a Persian rug. Bookcases ran the full height of two walls, the books punctuated with blown glass pitchers and vases—blue, deep red, green. Lily stopped in front of a wall hung with framed woodcuts and drawings of street scenes in Jerusalem, old Turkish houses, bearded Hassidim in the religious quarter of Mea Shearim, women shopping for vegetables among the stalls at Machneh Yehudah.

A woman came into the room, her sandals slapping on the marble floor, her loose skirt swaying with each step. "You like them?" she asked of the drawings. Her thick gray hair was pulled into a coil at the back of her neck, her cheekbones shone in the light, and her eyebrows, heavy and dark, underscored the intensity of her large brown eyes.

"Very nice," Lily said. "They look like a Jerusalem version of Kathe Kollwitz."

"Really? They look like Anna Kalmans to me."

Albert Kalman came up to them, smiling. "Here you are, Anna. You met Rafi's friend Lily?"

"Anna? I didn't mean . . ."

"Of course you didn't. Actually, I'm flattered," the artist said, and tilted her head to look at Lily. "It's time Rafi brought someone here." She took Lily's arm. "Come out to the garden. You need a bit of sunshine." She called over her shoulder to Albert, "Two more spritzers," and turned back to Lily. "Our holy water. Wine from the Galilee and soda water from Jerusalem."

Steps led down to a garden shaded by Aleppo pines, filled with the sweet scent of Victorian Box and blooming roses. A dark man stood on the edge of the terrace, looking out over the garden.

"This is Rafi's friend Lily," Anna said. She turned to Lily. "Yaacov is in Jerusalem to learn trauma techniques from Rafi. He's a doctor at Hanita."

"Hanita?"

"The new Hagganah settlement near the Lebanese border," he said. "Built the watchtower and stockade last March."

"I read about those settlements in the *Palestine Post*," Lily said. "They're built like Iron Age forts, inside a double wall of wood filled with rubble."

"Exactly. We have to protect ourselves. Armed bands from across the border are killing Jewish farmers, attacking buses and trucks on the highway."

"And they had a time building it," Anna said.

Yaacov beamed at her. "It was quite a day. Got there before dawn. We thought we'd finish before nightfall, present the Brits and Arab villagers with a *fait accompli*. But..." he shrugged.

"What happened?"

"We had to leave the vehicles behind. Hill was too steep; there was no road. We hacked out a trail to carry equipment and supplies up the hill by hand. And the wind! Couldn't even put up tents. It took longer than we planned—hadn't finished by dark. They attacked at midnight."

"You lived to tell the tale," Anna said.

"Drove them off, thanks to Orde Wingate."

"The British army captain?"

Yaacov smiled. "He trained us. Carries a Bible with him. He says he's working for the victory of God and the Jews."

"You see, God works in mysterious ways." Albert Kalman said. "He gave us Rafi and Orde Wingate. And Yaacov, still a student who learns from everyone. He learns from Rafi, who learned to treat wounds in Chicago, the Sodom and Gomorrah of America where gangsters roam the streets."

"And what did you learn from Orde Wingate?" Lily asked.

"I learned how to move in the darkness, how to whisper orders, how to shoot, how to hide, how to anticipate an attack," Yaacov said. "In the Hagganah, I swore by candlelight, with a Bible and a revolver on the table before me. When I was a boy, growing up in Peqi'in, I never dreamt that all but one family would flee from our village."

"Peqi'in?"

"Mountain village in the Galilee. A Jewish community since the days of the Temple," Yaacov said. "Everyone else is just a newcomer."

Anna sat in one of the garden chairs and pulled another closer, gesturing for Lily to sit. "So you've come to visit Rafi while he works in Jerusalem?" She leaned toward Lily with a conspiratorial smile. "Tell me all about it."

"Actually," Lily said, "we met in a *sherut*."

"And since then you've become friends?"

Albert came toward them carrying a tray, with Rafi close behind. Rafi brought a small tiled table from the other side of the terrace, then carried two more chairs to where Anna and Lily sat.

"You're a tourist, then?" Yaacov asked.

Lily took a sip of her drink before she answered. "I'm an archaeologist."

"Ah, the archaeologists," Albert said. "They flit here in the spring like flocks of migratory birds. They peck at the ground all summer long and fly away in the fall. Only three industries in Jerusalem. Hospitals, British, and archaeology."

"I work at Tel al-Kharub."

Anna passed a plate of orange slices. "Unpleasant, that unfortunate incident with the director. My condolences. Things are completely out of hand." Anna shook her head.

Lily placed her glass back on the table. "What do the Arabs want?"

"Arabs?" Yaacov answered immediately. "To stop Jewish immigration, prohibit sale of land to the Jews."

Albert reached for an orange slice. "In the end, the British may have to give in. They have to put a stop to this brouhaha before the war with Germany. And then, who knows?"

"And the Jews?" Lily asked. "What do they want?"

Albert's sigh was deep and thoughtful. "Just a little corner of the world where we can live ordinary lives in peace."

"Why are the British so interested in Palestine?" Lily asked. "It isn't exactly the land of milk and petroleum."

"The gateway to Suez," Albert said.

"It's the poor farmer I feel sorry for," Yaacov said. "The *fellah*. He's caught in the middle. If he obeys the law, he's a target for the Mufti's men. If he doesn't, the British throw him in jail."

"Not to mention armed brigands who infiltrate from Syria and Lebanon to steal crops and animals," Anna added.

Yaacov nodded. "The *fellah* can't sell his land for fear of reprisals."

"It's not all bad," Albert said. "The Arab strike of the last two years is the best thing to happen to the *Yishuv*. First they closed the port at Jaffa, so we built one in Tel Aviv. Then they closed their shops. Been a stimulus for our economic development."

"Maybe if it hurts their pocketbooks enough they'll mutiny," Anna said. "The Mufti's men murder any Arab who has commercial dealings with Jews. Nobody stops them."

Albert leaned over his wife, shaking his head. "It won't help. German and Italian propaganda fan the flames."

Lily picked up her glass and held it in her hand.

"More spritzer?" Anna asked.

"Not really. It's making me a little sleepy. I haven't had lunch."

"Oh, dear," Anna said, and picked up a bowl from the tray to move it closer to Lily. "Here. Have a peanut."

Albert looked at his watch. "Time for the BBC. Maybe today we'll be able to hear some news."

He led the way inside. A glistening mahogany cabinet with dials for a short wave receiver stood in the corner. Albert squatted in front of the radio, twisting knobs until they heard a faint crackling. "This is BBC calling with news of the world. Today in China, the Japanese bombed . . ." The voice faded in and out.

"Where did they say?" Anna asked. "Nanking? Peking?"

Kalman put a finger to his lips. He sat in the chair next to the radio, listening, frowning in concentration, his eyes focused on the tip of his sandal.

". . . On the streets of Barcelona . . ." the voice said before it faded again. "In Czechoslovakia . . . Konrad Henlein . . . the Sudetendeutsche Party . . . eight-point program. . . ."

Intermittent high-pitched screeches and the dead noise of static drowned out the words. They all leaned forward, watching the loudspeaker like lip readers.

"Ah. The Italian air war," Albert said. "They're strafing the broadcast frequencies."

Anna looked at her watch. "Try the BBC Arabic broadcast. They increased the signal."

Kalman turned the dial until they heard a few words in Arabic. This time Morse code signals and the voice of a soprano singing *Un Bel Di* cut off the sound.

"I've always enjoyed Puccini," Anna said, and glanced at the wall clock.

Albert turned off the radio. "Hopeless." He stood up and began to pace, his hands behind his back. "The only thing that's certain is that to the victor belong the ruins."

"Not that the British are all that impartial," Anna said. "Lloyd George says that Hitler is the greatest German of the century."

"He's a bastard," Rafi said. "All Nazis are bastards."

"Thank God all bastards are not Nazis." Albert sat down and looked toward Lily. "We must be more careful of our language in the presence of the young lady." He inclined his head in her direction. "Did we insult you?"

Lily shook her head. "Not me. Just bastards."

"So tell me," Albert said to Lily. "Will you remain in Jerusalem?"

"I go back to the University of Chicago when the digging season is over to work on my dissertation."

"Just as well. No room at the Hebrew University. Since the *Anschluss*, the university is full, gymnasiums are overflowing, and every hospital is overstocked with physicians. Soon doctors will pay hospitals to practice instead of vice versa," Albert said. "Every one is an exile. Strangers here, strangers there, strangers everywhere, filled with longing for the past, the familiar smells of their childhood."

"The influx of immigrants from Europe is crowding every-one out," Anna said. "That's what makes the Arabs angry."

"Arabs are no better," Yaacov said. "They immigrate here from neighboring countries at the Mufti's instigation. Most of the immigrants of the last fifty years have been Arabs. Last century there were about 25,000 Jews in Jerusalem and only 14,000 Arabs. Now the proportions are reversed."

Anna looked at the wall clock again. "It's almost five o'clock, and almost no one is here. I'm beginning to worry. Something must have happened in the Old City," she said to her husband.

"Wait another fifteen minutes," he told her. "If no one comes, then you can begin to worry."

Chimes from the wall clock interrupted their conversation. Anna looked at her watch, threaded her fingers together and looked at her watch again.

"It's getting late," Lily said. "I have to go."

"Stay a little longer," Dr. Kalman said. "We hardly got to know you."

"Besides," added his wife, "we don't know what's happening in the streets."

"I have an appointment," Lily said. "At the King David for dinner. I still have to change."

"Rafi won't mind if you're a little late," Anna told her. "Will you, Rafi?"

"She's not going with me."

Lily was already in the hall when the doorbell rang. Anna opened the door to a short round woman with reddish hair and sharp features and a small dark man. Both began speaking at once in an excited mix of German, English and Hebrew.

"The *ganze* city is a *balagan*, everything is topsy-turvy," the woman said. "We saw it. The whole thing. From Jaffa road."

"Sorry we're late. We were held up at check points."

Anna leaned forward to kiss the air behind the woman's ear. "*Ma kara*, Tsipi? What happened?"

"*Alles* is *beseder*. It's all right," Tsipi said. "This time the police were ready."

"It started at Al Aqsa mosque," the man said. "The Arabs were whipped up by a sermon after someone passed around fake photos of Jews attacking the Dome of the Rock."

"Poured out of the mosque like madmen," Tsipi said. "We saw them at Damascus gate, shouting and waving their fists, running up the hill."

"Police surrounded them before they got to New Gate," the man broke in.

"The police blocked the roads into the New City and the gates of the Old City." She stopped to catch her breath. "The crowd threw stones and bottles and the police charged with batons."

"Anybody hurt?" Rafi asked.

The woman turned to her companion. "*Welche Nummer, Pauli? Ulai*," she began in Hebrew, "Maybe?" she switched back to German. "*Sechs? Sieben?*"

"Six Arabs, five policemen," Pauli said. "Light injuries, nothing serious."

"This time," Anna said.

Albert shook his head. "The Mufti hangs over Jerusalem like the angel of death."

They stood at the crowded doorway, Tsipi's hand on Pauli's arm.

Lily looked at her watch. "I have to leave. Thank you both for a lovely afternoon."

Albert walked down the steps with them. "Don't take the bus," he said. "Walk. Between snipers and ambushes and gelignite bombs, buses are too dangerous." He took Lily's hand. "It was good to meet you. Come back soon."

"*Shalom*," Rafi said.

"*Shalom, shalom ve ein shalom*," Albert said. "'Peace, peace, there is no peace.' They said that in the ancient days in Jerusalem. Little has changed." He pointed to metal disks hammered into the asphalt to mark the crosswalk. "You see how bad things are," he said and smiled at them. "They have to nail down the streets so that no one will steal them."

TWELVE

IT WAS A QUARTER TO six by the time Lily returned to the American School. Hardly enough time to dress for a gala evening at the King David. A note from Lady Fendley, tacked on the message board under the stairs, said that Kate had called and wanted Lily to come down to Tel al-Kharub to help close the camp. I'll call her in the morning, Lily thought, and ran up to her room to wash and put on the blue dress and high-heeled shoes she had worn at the museum reception. On the way to the mirror at the end of the hall, she glanced out the back window and saw Henderson waiting in the garden.

"Be right down," she called to him, ran the comb through her hair, tossed the fringed scarf over her shoulders and hurried down the stairs.

* * *

"Wrong side," Henderson said when Lily opened the door of the sleek green car. "Right-hand drive."

"What kind of car is it?" Lily asked, looking over the polished chrome trim and leather seats.

"Jaguar. Like it?"

"Nothing is in the right place."

"Depends on your point of view."

Henderson turned the key and the car purred to life. The powerful motor vibrated gently. "Motor mounts need adjustment," he said.

The Old City gleamed in the evening sun as they turned down St. Paul's Road.

"Beautiful, isn't it?" Lily said.

Henderson eyed the array of gauges that decorated the burled wood dashboard. "Not a bad car," he said, "but expensive to keep up."

They turned down Julian's Way, toward the King David Hotel.

The domed bell tower of the YMCA stood against the soft glow of the evening sky, serene with its graceful proportions, its tiles and vaulted arches. The morning of the riots still quivered in Lily's memory—the face of Dr. Stern, lax and pale in death on the sidewalk—her first glimpse of Henderson, buffeted by the mob in front of the King David.

Henderson drove past the grand entrance of the hotel, where the doorman, in a turban and galabia, unloaded cars and taxis under the porte-cochere. He turned onto the side road on Abu Sikhra Street. They pulled up in front of the ancient tomb with the rolling stone where Herod had buried his murdered relatives.

"We'll park here," Henderson said. "I may have to leave early."

Inside the rotating glass doors of the entrance, tall Sudanese waiters wearing white pantaloons and red tarbooshes glided along the marble floors of the majestic lobby.

"Looks like the British Colonial Office conquered the Ancient Near East too," Henderson said, eyeing the ornate lobby with its Assyrian décor, the dining room's ancient Phoenician theme. "They think they own the world."

They waited for a table in a lounge that was ornamented with Hittite motifs. A *thé dansant* trio played the *Tango de la Rose*. Lily watched couples twirl, stiff-backed, on the tiny dance floor.

"What would you like to drink?" Henderson asked signalling a waiter. "Two Scotch and Coca-Colas." He ordered without waiting for her answer, pulled out a chair at a small table and sat down.

"Is that what they drink in Cincinnati?" Lily asked.

"What?"

"Cincinnati. Your hometown."

"Oh, yes. Of course."

Lily picked a pretzel from the dish on the table.

"About the blue glass vial," Henderson said.

"Amphoriskos."

"Yes. Of course. Amphoriskos. You have any idea where it is?"

"It was on a shelf in the pottery shed when I left the camp. The day before the museum opening."

"You haven't seen it since?"

Lily shook her head. "What makes you think it's missing?"

"Tell me something about it," Henderson said.

"Dates to about 800 BC, made of sand-core glass. More opaque than the blown or molded variety."

"How's that?"

"Before glass-blowing was invented, a core of sand used as a mold was coated with viscous glass, and the sand was removed when it cooled."

"What's it look like?"

"Dark, opaque blue. Small, about three inches high and one and a half inches around. Pear-shaped, with a long neck and handles from the shoulder to the neck. It was wound with yellow glass threads combed into an ornamental pattern."

The waiter appeared behind Henderson, arched the tray downward with a flourish and poured their drinks.

Lily took a sip. "Interesting taste."

"Never had Coca-Cola before? It's the great American drink."

Of course I've had Coca-Cola. Not with scotch. Lily tried it again. She rolled the sticky sweetness on her tongue. There was an aftertaste of peat. "It tastes like cotton candy made of mildew," she said.

"The glass vial—amphoriskos," Henderson said. "Is it worth a great deal of money?"

"You mean, would someone steal it? I suppose a collector might pay as much as a thousand dollars for it in a New York gallery." Lily picked up another pretzel and broke it in two. "I don't know what people pay for these things. I don't approve of the antiquities trade. Artifacts mean more in an archaeological context than in a vitrine in a New York apartment."

A pageboy, his uniform jacket buttoned up to his neck, a little cap slanted on his forehead, came toward them. "Mr. Henderson, sir. There's someone to see you at the concierge desk."

Henderson said, "Excuse me a moment," and left the table.

Lily could see him, nodding and gesturing, intent in conversation with someone who remained out of her line of vision. She watched couples on the dance floor, pomaded and bejeweled. She picked up another pretzel and tried the drink again. She decided she didn't like it.

The music was smooth and soothing. "Let's Face the Music and Dance." She took another sip of the drink. It was still too sweet.

After a few minutes, Henderson returned and asked for the bill.

"What is it?" Lily asked.

"They were looking for someone named Karl."

"What did they want?"

"How should I know?"

"Well, maybe . . ."

"There must be two hundred Karls in Jerusalem. I'm not one of them. Finish your drink. We have to stop by the Polish consulate."

* * *

At the consulate, Henderson deposited Lily next to a buffet piled with plates of herring and sausage, little fish balls on toothpicks, platters of bread and mounds of butter. A large bowl of shaved ice embedded with small silver cups of vodka stood in the center of the table. Henderson disappeared into a side room.

A tall gray-haired man with a trim goatee unexpectedly grasped Lily's hand and bent over, kissing the air above her fingers.

"Charming," he said. "Now you try our Polish vodka. Better than the Russian." He plucked a silver cup out of the mound of ice as if it were a grape and handed it to her, skewered a piece of herring on a toothpick and pressed it to her mouth.

Lily had swallowed three cups of iced vodka, two little sausages, and a piece of herring by the time Henderson returned and told her that they had to stop at another reception, this time at the Austrian consulate.

"Don't worry," he said. "Their buffet is good. Champagne, pastries, and of course," and now he smiled, "*schlagsahne.*"

"*Schlagsahne?*"

"Whipped cream. A Viennese specialty."

* * *

They rode south on Julian's Way, past the railroad station and into the German Colony, with its Bavarian houses and window boxes bright with geraniums. They parked in front of a large house.

"Here we are," Henderson said.

Lily was startled to see a Nazi flag flapping on the flagpole over the doorway. When she hesitated before getting out of the car, Henderson said, "Austria is part of Greater Germany now. Since the *Anschluss*."

A red carpet, anchored with polished brass rods, covered the marble steps in the entry. In the whitewashed foyer, a large black eagle hung against the wall.

In the inside rooms, Arab waiters in starched white jackets stood behind tables lavishly laid with pastries and wine. Small groups of people—some men in uniforms encrusted with medals, others in tailcoats and high wing collars, and ladies in long dresses—leaned toward each other, talking earnestly. The lilt of a Strauss waltz emanated from an adjacent room. Here and there, the sound of laughter punctuated the quiet murmur of conversation.

Lily noticed an Arab in a dark suit near a table in the corner. He stood apart, and his dark eyes moved from one group to another.

It was Jamal.

Henderson followed her gaze. "You know him?"

"Who?"

"The Arab. You know him?"

"I didn't notice," Lily said. "What Arab?"

Henderson watched her for a moment. "I'll be back soon. Someone I have to see." He disappeared into another room.

THIRTEEN

LILY MOVED TO THE TABLE. "A glass of wine, please," she said to Jamal. "Didn't expect to see you here."

Jamal asked a waiter for two glasses of wine and handed one to Lily.

"You don't work here?" she asked.

"I'm working right now. Attending physician at the reception."

"Physician?"

"Graduated the American School in Beirut," Jamal told her. "That's where I met Eastbourne."

"You worked at Kharub as a cook."

He took a sip of wine. "To earn extra money. Hospitals don't pay enough to live on. There are more doctors in Jerusalem than patients."

"I didn't know Arabs drank wine."

"I'm not a Moslem."

"There's a lot I don't know about you. I didn't know you were a doctor."

Jamal reached for a plate and contemplated the pastries on the table, looking over eclairs, cream puffs shaped like diminutive swans, little tarts, mocha and chocolate tortes. "I'm on staff at the Austrian Hospice," he said. He heaped pastries on the plate and handed it to Lily. "They do wonderful sweets here. Try a cream puff and some *Sacher torte*. Viennese specialty."

Lily put down the wineglass. "You were on the Beit Jibrin road with Eastbourne when he was killed, weren't you?" she asked. She tasted the *Sacher torte*.

"They reported it all in the newspaper," Jamal told her. "Gunmen ordered him out of the car and told us to drive on. Then we heard the shots. Nothing I could do."

"You didn't go back to see if you could help?" The *Sacher torte* was delicious.

"Driver wouldn't turn around."

Lily took another forkful of torte, luxuriating in the rich chocolate, rubbing her tongue against the roof of her mouth. After a while, she said, "Did Eastbourne have the amphoriskos with him when he was shot?"

"The one you found in the tomb? He might have done. Could have been bringing it up to the museum."

She tried the cream puff. "Henderson told me it's missing."

Jamal glanced toward the door to the other room. "Henderson? That his name? The man you came with?"

"You know him?"

"Henderson? No."

"It wasn't found in the car or on Eastbourne's body." Lily took another bite of *Sacher torte*.

"Might have dropped on the road," Jamal said.

"Could you take me there? To the exact spot?"

Jamal shrugged. "Police have been all over the area."

"I want to look for glass shards."

"Is it so important?"

Lily nodded. "When can we go?"

"I have to arrange for someone to cover for me at the hospital."

* * *

Henderson came back into the room, shaking his head and holding out his hands in apology.

"Have to go," Jamal said. "See you."

Henderson looked after him. "You do know him."

Why was he so interested? "We just met."

"There's champagne in the other room," Henderson said. "And an orchestra playing waltzes. Come on. I'll teach you the Viennese waltz."

He took Lily's arm and led her through the door. Dancing couples careened in patterned circles, around and around the floor in time to a Strauss waltz—*Blue Danube? Voices of Spring?*—circling the ballroom in wide arcs.

"A toast," he said, handing her a champagne flute and clicking his glass against hers.

"To what?"

Henderson flourished the glass, swirling it in a little circle. "To our friendship. To the blue glass vial. Drink up and we'll dance."

She felt queasy for a moment—but it passed. "I've never danced a Viennese waltz before," she said. When she ducked her head in apology, the room moved—just a small motion—but it passed.

"It's easy," he said, looking down at her with his handsome face. "Just follow me. *One*, two, three, *one*, two, three, *one*, two, three," and they whirled in time to the music, arching and swaying and twirling around the room.

One, two, three. *One*, two, three. *One*, two, three.

He smiled at her, the light from the chandeliers bouncing off his teeth and eyes, the colors of the room twinkling and flashing past his head. Turning and swirling, tilting at the waist—*one*, two, three; *one*, two, three.

Behind him, streaking light and blurring shapes kept moving, kept moving, two three; *one*, two, three. Red tracks flickered behind his ears, his forehead was growing and his eyebrows were getting longer—two, three; *one*, two, three; *one*, two three.

Those horrible cocktails. Two, three; *one*, two, three. Scotch and Coca-Cola.

One, two, three; *one*, two, three.

She was getting dizzier. The Polish reception with herring and sausage and little glasses of iced vodka. "Butter the bread thick, then a bite of herring. It lines the stomach and you can drink all night." They gave her one cold glass and then another. "Specially for the American lady."

One two three. Her head felt as if she had drunk Novocain. *One* two three—one—two—three. Her legs were heavy; her mouth was taut and dry.

It was the sausage. You never know what they put in sausage. One two three, one two three, one two three. And the vintage wine. Who knows one wine from another—red wine, white wine, with a nose, without—two three, one two three. And all that pastry. Whipped cream. On everything. Two three, one two three, one two three.

She saw his interminable smile, reeling and gyrating, with the chandelier twirling carelessly on the top of his head, and the room spinning out of control. One—two—three. One. Two. Three. One two three.

"I'm going to be sick." When she stopped, the walls were still heaving and moving. There was no way out. No doors, no windows, just the tilted floor and pulsating walls, waving toward her and receding, one two three, one two three, in and out, two three.

Jamal grabbed her arm and pulled her outside to the terrace, where the cool air was as sharp as an ax. She groped for the railing and leaned over, facing bushes garnished with thorns and little pink roses with open mouths. She bent over, her jaw slack, her stomach cramping, gagging and retching on the roses—two three, one two three. Go away. Leave me alone, two three. One two three. Hold my head.

Behind her, the ballroom was still spinning, the whipped cream still billowing, and the Viennese were still dancing and laughing in the woods, two three.

One two three, *one* two three.

FOURTEEN

AT BREAKFAST, SIR WILLIAM nattered on. "I met him," he was saying to Lily, "Konrad Henlein and his brother Karl."

Her eggs were swimming in grease; her toast was cold and wilted. The sun was too bright; she had a headache; she was sick to her stomach. And now, he was babbling about the Sudetenland crisis. And Konrad Henlein.

"It's the same as my pottery styles," he droned. "Just small changes—in rim shape, curvature of the shoulder—"

Lily tried another sip of coffee

Sir William prattled on. "Galton worked with family resemblances. I knew Sir Francis. Darwin's cousin, you know."

Lily tried the toast.

"… Just small changes," he was saying, "just a line of the lip, the tip of the nose. Police use it for composite portraits."

Lady Fendley said, "Finish your breakfast, William darling, before it gets cold," and tucked a napkin under his chin.

"Please. Don't interrupt, my dear," Sir William told his wife. "This is important."

He turned back to Lily. "Where was I?" He paused a moment, pressing his hand against his forehead.

Would he never stop, Lily thought? I have to call the police about the amphoriskos. When does Kate want me to come down?

"I remember," Sir William raised his index finger heavenward. "I was telling you about Konrad Henlein and your young man."

"I have a touch of stomach flu," Lily said. "I have to make a telephone call," and left the table.

At the phone under the hall stairs, she tried Kate's number, letting it ring until the operator came back on the line and said there was no answer.

"Connect me with the police post in Jerusalem, please," Lily said. "I don't know the number." When a voice finally answered, she said, "I would like to speak to the officer in charge of Eastbourne's murder investigation."

"Is this an emergency?"

"No," Lily said. "I worked with Eastbourne, and I wanted . . ."

"Sorry," the voice said. "We have no new information."

"I have something—"

"We are making every effort to find his killers, madam."

"But I want—"

"Thank you for your interest, madam. As soon as we finish investigations, information will be released to the public. Goodbye, madam." The line went dead.

Nothing was going right this morning. She felt dizzy, and her head hurt to the tip of her nose.

Must be a migraine, she thought. Or a sinus attack.

The only thing to do, Lily decided, was relax in the shade and close her eyes until it was all over. She went out to the garden.

Avi was waiting near the fountain. He said, "I hear you were out dancing last night," and he raised his arms to hold an imaginary partner and began to waltz over the flagstones.

"Five foot nine; eyes that shine; and he comes from Palestine . . ." he sang, pirouetting around the fountain and turning past the table.

"Oh shut up."

"A bit testy this morning? Don't look to me for sympathy."

He danced around the edge of the terrace, twirling around the roses, almost losing his balance. "You could have spent the evening with me at the Orion, cheering for Jeanette Macdonald as she sang through the San Francisco quake, reformed Clark Gable and defeated the forces of evil, all in less than two hours. You could have done that.

"Instead," he said, still circling, "you chose to carouse with the descendants of the Knights Templar and the minions of Mad Adolf from Berchtesgaden."

"They were Austrians."

"So is Adolph." Avi stopped dancing and dropped his arms. "Some of my best friends are Austrians," he said, "but they don't behave like that."

"The amphoriskos is missing," Lily said.

"Yes?"

"Eastbourne had it with him. He was taking it to the Rockefeller."

"Yes?"

"Henderson told me."

"Is that his name?"

"I tried to tell the police just now on the phone. Something's wrong there."

"If you ask me, Henderson's what's wrong there."

"I didn't ask you. The police wouldn't listen. They hung up on me."

"Not to worry," Avi said. "I'll speak to Auntie Major. She'll get you in touch with the police."

"Auntie Major?"

"Her real name is Greta Landau. She's having an affair with a British major. She says he'll do anything for her. He brings her gifts. Things in short supply, like lipstick and perfume."

"What does she give him?"

"Oranges?" Avi shrugged. "She says he's her fiancé."

"Are you going back to the kibbutz today?"

"I could."

"I have to go down to Kharub. Kate's going to close the camp."

"When do you want to go?"

"Not 'til the afternoon. I'm having lunch with Dame Margaret."

"Don't look so unhappy. Dame Margaret's not so bad. She writes about bloodless murders, she wears funny hats, and she smells like a cookie."

Lily was staring at the table. "Things are worse than I thought," she said. "I see little black spots before my eyes. And they're moving."

"Those are ants," Avi told her.

Lily pressed her fingers against the bridge of her nose. "I don't feel well."

"Serves you right, *habibi*."

Lily said, "I'm going to take a nap," and lay back on a lounge chair with her eyes closed.

She heard Avi tiptoe away and return. He brought a soft, lightweight covering that smelled of mothballs, draped it over her, then tiptoed away again.

Lily fell asleep and dreamed she was whirling in a storm-tossed dinghy, getting seasick as the boat eddied round and round. And the ship was sinking.

When she awakened, it was almost one o'clock. Her insides were churning, her head was aching, and she felt worse than before.

* * *

Dame Margaret waited at a table in the American Colony, crowned with a hat that looked like a miniature garden. If Lily felt better, she might have smiled.

"You look dreadful," Dame Margaret said.

"I feel dreadful."

"Eat something. They do a nice omelet here."

"Nothing fried," Lily said and made a face.

"Some steak tartar?"

Lily pictured the meat, buzzing with flies, hanging in the bazaar of the Old City. "I'm a vegetarian."

Dame Margaret called the waiter. "Bring her a tomato juice with a raw egg."

Lily groaned. "Oh, God."

"As bad as all that? What did they serve at the King David? Or was it the Austrian Consulate?"

"Everybody knows where I went last night?"

"You got a bit tiddley. And with a tall, good-looking man." Dame Margaret's tulips shook in admonition until they rattled. "You left with one man and came home with another. There are no secrets in a small town. Rumors are the only entertainment."

"I don't remember going home."

Dame Margaret leaned forward. The whiff of vanilla stung Lily's eyes and stirred her stomach.

"You think Henderson is good-looking?" Lily asked. "You didn't before."

"I still don't." Dame Margaret sat back in her chair and her tulips swayed in the breeze. "I've been meaning to ask you. Is anything missing from the site inventory?"

"An amphoriskos. You think it has anything to do with Eastbourne's murder?"

Dame Margaret shook her garden. "Who knows? Anything else missing?"

"I don't know. I'm going back to Kharub this afternoon to help pack up."

"They're closing the camp?"

Lily nodded. Her brain tossed around inside and ricocheted against her skull. She was sorry she moved her head.

"Too bad," Dame Margaret said. "Kate is competent. She should have a chance."

The waiter brought the tomato juice and put it in front of Lily. She looked at it with distaste.

"Drink up," Dame Margaret said. "You'll feel better."

Lily took a sip. "Oh, God," she said, "excuse me," and ran from the table.

* * *

They reached Kharub in the late afternoon. Avi swung the lorry onto the rutted field where the excavation's wagon was parked. "How do you feel?" he asked.

"Better, thanks," she answered with a dramatic whine. "But far from well." She placed the back of hand against her forehead and sank back in the seat. "The doctor says I never will be strong."

"Poor *habibi*. That'll teach you."

The camp was deserted. Kate's car was nowhere in sight, and some of the tents had already been taken down.

Avi parked next to the wagon. "Where's Kate?"

"I think she has a house in Ashkelon. Maybe she's there."

"You want to wait here? Go to Kate's? Drive over to the kibbutz?"

"I'm not sure where Kate lives. Anyway, I have work to do," Lily said. "And I want to look for the amphoriskos. In the wagon, maybe. Or the shelf in the pottery shed."

"I'll help." Avi opened the camp wagon, felt under the seats and looked in the glove compartment. "What does it look like?"

"A dark blue vial, decorated with wiggly yellow lines."

He pulled out the back seat. "It isn't here."

"It's in a box, a small cardboard box, maybe three and a half inches long."

"When did you last see it?"

"In the pottery shed. I labeled the box and covered the shelf with a tarp. That was before I left for Jerusalem. Let's look there."

The tarp was gone. Avi looked at cardboard cartons neatly ranged on the shelves. "What are all these numbers?" he asked.

"Kh is the site name, Kharub; 38 is the year; 3 would be the area of the site; T 104 would be the number of the tomb; g, for glass; 3321 is the catalogue number."

"You put these numbers on everything you find?"

Lily nodded. "I put a tag on an artifact and enter it in my field notes. The registrar adds it to the field catalogue and also makes out a card for the other registry over there." She pointed to a speckled file box on the shelf.

"Like double entry bookkeeping."

"Triple entry," she said. "I haven't written it up in my field notes yet." She felt ashamed of her carelessness. "If the amphoriskos is lost, it's my fault."

"Naughty, naughty," Avi said and flipped open the field catalogue on the table.

Lily looked over his shoulder to check the registration number of the amphoriskos. "It's in the registry, but not on the shelf."

"You want to look in all these boxes?"

She shook her head. "Maybe later. First I have to finish my field notes."

"I'll look in the boxes while you work on that."

"It can't hurt." She turned toward her tent to get her field notes. "Don't mix anything up. Watch how you repack the artifacts. Handle them carefully. I'll be right back."

The notebook was still on her cot, lying on top of the sleeping bag. She slapped the dust off the loose-leaf binder and brought it back to the pottery shed.

Avi waved a small box at her. "I found it. I found it."

"Where?"

"It fell behind this pile of cartons." He shook the box.

"Careful with that."

He placed the box on the table and lifted the lid. "It's heavier than I thought it would be."

Inside was a rectangular stainless steel object. Lily placed the notebook on the table and took it from the box.

"It's a cigarette lighter," she said and turned it over in her hand.

The back was inscribed with the word MINOX inside a lozenge with the letters VEF breaking the line at the top. Underneath, it said Riga, and at the bottom the legend "Made in Latvia."

"Latvia? Where did Eastbourne get a cigarette lighter made in Latvia? And what's it doing in this box?"

"It's a camera," Avi said.

"It's too small to be a camera."

"Rafi has one, uses it to copy documents." He reached for the camera. "Let me show you."

He let Lily's notebook fall open and pulled at both ends of the camera. It opened with a click. There was a tiny eyepiece that seemed to be a viewfinder and a lens. He held the camera over the page with the viewfinder to his eye and clicked it shut.

"That's how it works," he said and put it back into the box.

Lily looked over at the open notebook. "Something's wrong," she said and sat down. "These aren't my field notes."

Lily turned page after page filled with Eastbourne's cramped handwriting. She picked up the book and shook it. A map and plans fell out of the back pocket.

FIFTEEN

"It belongs to Eastbourne. Some kind of journal." Lily flipped the pages of the notebook. "He left it for me. Why?"

Avi reached over her shoulder and pointed to an entry. "*July 10. KH at the King David, 9:30 a.m.* I thought so. He met someone."

"That morning in Jerusalem—the day of the riots. I couldn't find him all day. Maybe he kept the appointment."

"A scandal." Avi licked his lips and rubbed his hands together. "KH. You think it was Kate Hale?"

"It's not a joke," Lily said. "Anyway, it could be anyone."

"Who then? Kareem Husseini? Some bimbo with a name like Karla Habibi? Or your own Keith Henderson?"

Lily thumbed through the binder. "He's not my Keith Henderson."

"No. That one belongs to the world." Avi sat down next to her, moved the notebook toward him and turned the pages one by one.

"Don't do that," Lily said. "It makes me feel guilty. Like we've opened someone else's mail."

"If he left it for you, you owe it to him to read it." Avi read an entry and turned another page. He tapped the journal. "Here's the amphoriskos," he said. "*July 30*—the day he was murdered."

"Let me see."

He ran his finger along the page. "Right here. *Pack amphoriskos.*" He read the next entry. "*July 31. KH at King David, 9:30 a.m.* What did I tell you? Another tryst."

Avi began to hum. "Who killed Geoff Eastbourne? I, said his lover, and I did it undercover."

"Stop it," Lily said and took the journal away from him.

They were interrupted by the noise of Kate's Austin. It sounded like a sewing machine that needed oiling as it struggled up the road toward the camp. The dull blue paint of the Austin was streaked and dappled from the sea air.

Lily closed the notebook and slipped it into her bag.

Kate set the brake with an audible ratchet. The motor churned while she squeaked the car open. She got out and pushed against the door with both hands to close it. She had lost weight. There was a fragility about her that Lily hadn't noticed before.

Kate's face was more blotched than ever, her eyes swollen from crying. "I've been trying to reach you," she told Lily. "Beacon Pharmaceutical wants to close the camp."

"I'm sorry," Lily said.

Kate took a ring binder from the shelf near the kitchen door and handed it to Lily. "You forgot your field notebook." It seemed like an accusation.

Lily flushed. "I've been looking for it everywhere."

With a heavyhearted sigh, Kate sat down at the table. "We have to finish the site report." She looked toward the boxes on the shelves behind Lily. "You can do the section on the cemetery. That is, if you want to."

"I meant to work on my field notes last weekend in Jerusalem. But . . ." Lily wondered whether Kate was listening.

It didn't seem to matter. Kate's arms drooped at her sides, her dress hung loosely from her shoulders and had a stain in front, and her face looked like a wound. Her eyes were filling with tears. She doesn't understand what I'm saying, Lily thought.

Lily kept talking, trying to diffuse the dejection that radiated from Kate with an incessant patter. Lily told Kate that the amphoriskos was missing, told Kate about her frustration when she tried to get in touch with the police. Kate listened with a dazed, uncomprehending look.

"I'm awfully sorry," Lily said. "Awfully sorry."

Kate reached for the handkerchief balled up in her sleeve. "Geoffrey was taking the amphoriskos up to Jerusalem for the opening of the Rockefeller. Ask the museum registrar."

She heard what I said after all, Lily realized.

Kate wiped her nose. "All the tomb finds have to be photographed for the site report." She continued to sniffle and looked down at her hands, twisting the corners of the handkerchief into a damp point. "Why don't you pack up the cemetery stuff, work on it in Jerusalem?"

Kate shouldn't be alone, Lily thought, and reached out to touch her arm. "You look tired. You need help here."

"No, no. I have to keep busy. It's the only way." Kate looked at her watch. "I have to get back now."

She rose slowly, faltered to the car, started the motor, and clattered down the road toward Ashkelon.

"Four o'clock." Lily watched Kate drive away. "She always leaves around this time."

Avi stood up. "Let's follow her." The car turned the corner toward the Ashkelon Road. "Find out where she goes."

"Probably goes home. Every day at four o'clock. You think it has anything to do with the entries in the journal? KH."

Avi started toward the lorry.

"Wait a few minutes," Lily said. "So she doesn't know we're following."

They took the Ashkelon road, past orange groves and stands of eucalyptus. The asphalt was white with the sun, and tiny mirages glimmered and disappeared as they bounced over the dips and gullies. The trees thinned out near the dune area, and they could make out Kate's car, shimmering in the heat, about a quarter of a mile ahead. The road went past half-buried brick walls from Byzantine houses punctuated with the bright flowers of wild oleander; past stubs of ancient columns, festooned with tangled branches and thickets of bramble. As they approached the sea, drifts of sand scarred with tracks from bus tires coated the roadway. Spikes of wormwood and dune grass anchored small sand hillocks on the abandoned sidewalks. Here and there, gray, leafless branches of white broom jutted from the cracked macadam.

A lone grocery, its door bracketed with stacks of soda bottles and a small refrigerator, was on the left. A row of small stone houses with flat roofs stood facing the sea. Past the houses, an incongruous Bauhaus structure with a faded sign that said Club Casino overlooked the beach. A single date palm with a leeward bend, hunched and distorted by the wind, grew near the corner of the building.

Kate's car was parked next to a tumble of bougainvillea at the side of the last house. A bright blue door was half-hidden by swags of jasmine that drooped from a matted trellis.

Lily got out of the lorry and started toward the house. "Mind if I go in?"

"Go ahead. I'll walk on the beach."

Lily rang the bell and heard a rush of footsteps. A sandy-haired boy, about six years old—the boy Lily had seen at Eastbourne's funeral—pulled open the door. He had the same imperturbable blue eyes as Eastbourne.

"Geoff. Don't open the door without knowing who's there," a guttural voice called from behind him, and a plump Arab woman in a striped Gaza dress came puffing up to the door after him. "I can help you?"

"I came to see Kate Hale," Lily said.

Kate appeared behind them. "It's all right, Faridah. She's a friend." Kate put her hand on the boy's shoulder. "This is my son, Geoff." Kate smoothed the child's hair and kissed his forehead. "Now you know." She stared at Lily, as if waiting for a comment.

The boy reached to shake Lily's proffered hand. "How do you do?"

"We're having tea." Kate's fingers continued to stroke little Geoff's hair. "Care to join us?"

"Just came to see if you're all right. I can't stay." Lily gestured toward the lorry. "Someone's waiting."

Kate led her into a light-filled room. Deep red Bukharian rugs were scattered over the floor, the marble tiles beneath so loose that they rasped and echoed with a hollow sound as they wavered beneath Lily's feet.

A table in front of a window overlooking the sea was set for tea and covered with a starched, embroidered tablecloth.

Geoff smiled up at Lily. "We have strawberry jam today," he said. "Would you like some?"

"You and Faridah have your tea," Kate told him. "Miss Sampson and I have to talk."

She gestured toward two small armchairs in the corner that stood on either side of a table inlaid with mother of pearl. A glass door behind it led to an atrium with a dusty table and chairs and forsaken bracts of bougainvillea that swirled in the corners like broken paper lanterns. A cluttered desk nearby was surrounded by a typewriter table and bookshelves made of planks and glass bricks. Piles of books were stacked on the desk and spilled haphazardly over a heavy plush chair.

Kate sat down, looked at her hands, limp in her lap, and ran her fingers along the folds of her skirt. "Were you surprised when you met Geoff?" she asked Lily.

"It wasn't what I expected."

"He'll be going back home this fall. To public school."

"You and Eastbourne never married?"

"We couldn't. We were both graduate students. It would have been the end of our careers." Kate looked over at Geoff and smiled. "Lady Fendley took care of everything. She's been a brick. Geoff adores her. He's called her Auntie Cordelia ever since he could talk."

This was a new aspect of Lady Fendley, Lily thought. The doting aunt. "She arranged the public school too?"

Kate nodded. "She told them little Geoff was her dead sister's child. Things are pretty tight financially. But Geoffrey came up with the money. He always does."

"Is that why you went up to Jerusalem to meet Eastbourne?"

Kate shook her head. "I never met him in Jerusalem. Just here. In private. Besides, I wouldn't leave Geoff for a whole day."

"Then who did he meet?"

"I don't think he met anyone. He may have done consulting work for some collectors. We needed the money."

Kate sighed. A picture of Eastbourne and a bowl of apples were on the table next to her. Her nose was still red from crying. She picked up the photograph and cradled it, stroking it with her finger, tracing Eastbourne's forehead and cheek. A tear formed on the rim of her eye and ran down along side her nose, trembling on the edge of her nostril before it dropped to her blouse.

She put the picture back on the table and lifted an apple from the bowl. "He brought these from Lebanon," she said. "They don't grow here. Not enough frost." She ran her finger along the surface of the apple, around a dark spot on its skin. "He was like the apples, you know. A beautiful blossom in its youth and shining in its maturity, with a few surface flaws here and there. But the taste is crisp and sweet. And at the core are seeds for a thousand orchards."

This was the first true moment of mourning that Lily had witnessed through all the speeches and eulogies of the past week. "You really miss him," she said.

"Of course I do. Who wouldn't?" Kate put the apple on top of the table next to the picture. "There was trouble at the site toward the end, you know."

"Oh?"

"Things were turning up missing. Small things. Geoffrey's extra pair of linen breeches, some frying pans from the kitchen, a black juglet, a horse-and-rider figurine." Kate pressed her hands to her face as if they could staunch the tears. "At first he thought it was the Bedouin. It turned out to be Abu Musa. Geoffrey told him to clear out."

"When was that?"

"That last morning."

"You think he stole the amphoriskos?"

"He could have done."

"And waited at the Beit Jibrin track?"

"He was angry enough." Kate's shoulders shook. She took a deep breath and looked out the window toward Avi's lorry. "You can drive the station wagon up to Jerusalem," she said after a while. "I don't need it here. I don't want to see it day after day." She shuddered. "Let me fetch the keys."

She disappeared into the bowels of the house. "You have to bring back the wagon eventually," she said when she came back into the room. "It belongs to Beacon's Pharmaceutical. We have to return it after the camp is closed."

Outside, Avi was waiting in the lorry. "Well?" he said.

"Well what? I have the keys to the station wagon," Lily said. "I can use it until we close camp. I'll bring some of the material up to Jerusalem, work on it there."

"You know what I mean."

"Eastbourne didn't meet Kate in Jerusalem. I'm afraid it was that bimbo with a name like Karla Habibi."

"Bimbo is right. With a name like that, she'd go out with anyone."

On the way back, Lily told him about little Geoff and Lady Fendley, and about Eastbourne's accusations against Abu Musa.

She mused about it until they reached the camp.

"I'll help you load the boxes," Avi said on the way to the pottery shed.

"I must talk to the police." Lily picked up a box to carry to the station wagon. "About Abu Musa."

Avi reached for a carton and stacked it against the back seat of the station wagon. "I'll get hold of Auntie Major," he told her. "She'll arrange it."

* * *

Lily maneuvered the station wagon along the track to Qiryat Gat, distracted by a whirlwind of thoughts about what Kate had said, about Abu Musa, about the amphoriskos. July tenth, July tenth, echoed with the hum of the tires bumping over the ruts in the road. If not Kate, then who did Eastbourne meet that morning?

On the road, she passed the place where Avi had stopped the *sherut* with Rafi in the back seat. Lily smiled and wondered where he was, what he was doing at that moment.

At the American School, she parked the wagon near the tennis courts and brought the boxes into the back hall, one by one. She hoisted one of the boxes, balancing it against her hip, and unlocked the library door, ready to carry the box down to the pottery laboratory in the basement.

A man stood at Lily's carrel, pawing through books and notes scattered over the desk and onto the floor. Lily recognized him as Eliot Blessington, Dame Margaret's husband. He looked startled when Lily opened the door.

He grabbed for a book.

"Ah, here it is," he said and held it up for her to see. "I was looking for the site report from Tel Beit Mirsim. It was checked out to you. I need to borrow it."

"I don't have the site report from Beit Mirsim at my desk."

He made an elaborate show of reading a title on the spine of the book. "Sorry. My mistake." He put down the volume, left the chaos on her desk and started for the door.

"I hope you're feeling better," he called over his shoulder. "Margaret still wants to talk to you. She'll ring you tomorrow." He closed the door behind him.

"You left a mess," Lily said and heard the front door slam. "I know ancient curses for people like you."

While she rearranged the books in the carrel and picked the papers off the floor, the rhythmic repetition, July tenth, July tenth, continued in her head. The day of the riots. Something happened that day, Lily thought, something that involved Eastbourne.

She went out into the hall to look for the pile of old newspapers. They were still there, on the shelf on the bottom of the telephone table. She hunted through the stack for the newspaper. When she found it, she folded it up, just the way Eastbourne had done, and put it in her pocket.

SIXTEEN

RAFI WAS WAITING in the foyer when Lily came down the stairs the next morning. She felt her face flush.

"Had breakfast yet?" he asked. "We can go into town. My treat."

"We could eat here." The idea of making breakfast for him appealed to her. "Save you money."

"Can't." He shook his head. "I'm on call. I told them I'd be at that little place near the hospital."

"I'm not sure I have time," Lily said. "I'm waiting for Avi to call. I have to get hold of the police. Abu Musa may have killed Eastbourne to steal an amphoriskos—a blue glass vial—from Kharub."

"Who's Abu Musa?"

"One of the workmen at the site."

"Was the amphoriskos valuable?"

"Eastbourne was taking it to Jerusalem for the museum opening."

"Maybe you should let it alone." Rafi's hands were in his pockets. "Let the police handle it. It's a British matter. Eastbourne was a British subject."

"I can't do that. I have to find the amphoriskos. Besides, the police aren't handling it."

"They may have their reasons."

"As far as I can see, it's because they lost control of the Mandate," Lily said. "The terrorists have taken over."

"All the more reason. The same people that went after Eastbourne might go after you."

"They already have. Someone took a pot shot at me a few days ago."

He took his hands out of his pockets and reached out to her.

"They missed," she said.

"Those are famous last words. Maybe the amphoriskos is still at the site. You looked through everything?"

"Its not there. But I found a camera in the box where it was supposed to be."

"A camera?"

When he touched her arm, she noticed his fingers were red and sore. "What happened to your hands?"

"It's nothing." He shoved them back in his pocket. "It's just a rash. I got it in the darkroom."

"You don't use gloves and tongs?"

"I use a special developer for fine grain film. The fumes are pretty strong and there may have been a pinhole in the gloves."

"You need that developer for the film you use in that little camera you have?"

His eyes widened in surprise. "What little camera?"

"The one you use to copy journal articles."

"Who told you I used a camera to copy journal articles?" His voice was edgy.

"Avi told me."

"Avi?" He kept his hands in his pockets.

"Yes. He said you had a little camera like Eastbourne's."

"Eastbourne had a little camera to copy articles?"

"I told you. We found it in the box that was supposed to have the amphoriskos."

"Any film in it? I might be able to develop it in the lab."

"I don't know. I didn't open it."

"I suppose you should go to the police." He looked past her at the wall and seemed to be thinking. "But they won't talk to you without an appointment."

"How can I get one?"

"I'll see what I can do," Rafi said. "I'll get back to you." He turned and hurried out the door.

*   *   *

Lily had almost finished breakfast when the telephone rang. It was Rafi.

"Avi said you wanted Auntie Major to arrange an appointment with her officer," he said.

"Yes?" Lily was surprised at the glow of excitement she felt at the sound of his voice.

"We made one for ten o'clock, Monday morning," he told her. "Auntie Major will meet us at Patt's at 9:30 and take us to the police post in the Russian compound."

"Can't it be sooner?"

"I wish it were. But today's Friday—Moslem Sabbath. The Brits close offices for everybody's holidays—Moslem, Christian, Jewish, Chinese New Year. And any day that has an 'r' in it."

"I want to talk to the police as soon as possible."

"I'd like to see you before then." There was silence at the other end. When Rafi spoke again, his voice was muffled. "You sure the amphoriskos was stolen? Maybe it's in the Rockefeller."

Lily could hear Rafi chewing. "What are you eating?"

"Breakfast. How did you know it was missing in the first place?"

"Someone told me."

"Who?"

"I'm not free to say."

"Oh, come on."

This time, Lily heard Rafi sip and swallow. "Coffee?"

"Juice."

Another moment of silence, and Rafi said, "You rilly thimk Abby Musim milled—?" He swallowed, and repeated it. "Abu Musa killed Eastbourne for a glass vial?" Another pause, another bite. "You mink Abumus dukit?"

"You got crumbs in my ear," Lily said.

"Mo do bell."

"*Bon appetit*," Lily said and hung up.

She sat next to the telephone for a while. Better check the museum first, she thought, before I go to the police. She picked up the receiver again and jiggled the hook to get the operator.

Lily finally got the registrar of the Rockefeller on the line and asked if the amphoriskos was in the museum. "Eastbourne was bringing it up to the museum for the opening," Lily told her.

"We don't have it on exhibit in any cases on the floor."

"It would have come in too late for that. Maybe the police brought it. During the murder investigation."

"Murder?"

"Eastbourne was killed on the way to the opening."

"I know that."

"Do you have the amphoriskos?"

Lily heard the rustle of papers. "I have to check the accession record," the registrar said.

"It's not the sort of thing you could forget."

"You have no idea. It's a madhouse here. We weren't ready by the opening. Haven't caught up since. Nothing in the cases is labeled. We're behind in our records."

"Will you look it up?" Lily asked.

"I'm awfully busy. It may be misplaced. Other things are missing too. It'll turn up."

"It's important." Lily said.

"I'll get back to you."

So much for that, Lily thought. She tried the American consulate next and asked for Henderson. He had gone to Haifa for the weekend, the clerk said, and wouldn't be back until Monday.

She went into the library, sat down at her desk and took Eastbourne's journal off the shelf above her carrel. If Eastbourne had left the journal where he knew she would find it, there must be a message for her in it, something that he wanted her to know.

Lily opened it to July 9, the day before the riots. "KH arrives," it said. The same KH that Eastbourne was scheduled to meet in Jerusalem the next day?

The telephone rang again, just as she started up the stairs to get the July tenth newspaper. The museum registrar, Lily thought, and hurried to answer it.

This time, it was Dame Margaret. "We never did get to talk," Dame Margaret said. "How about lunch tomorrow? One o'clock at the American Colony," and rang off before Lily could answer.

Command performance, Lily thought, another session of casually worded questions. Maybe Dame Margaret knows something about the amphoriskos.

Back in the library, Lily spread the newspaper on the empty desk next to her carrel. She looked at the personal column again, at ads for secretaries and furnished flats. What had she overlooked? What had Eastbourne hidden from her? What really brought him to the YMCA at Julian's Way that morning?

The sentence jumped out at her. How could she have missed it? *The shipment from Marco Polo will arrive at King David this morning.* Marco Polo? A code name?

Something nagged at her memory. She almost had it, when the telephone rang again. Maybe the museum registrar this time, Lily thought.

It was Henderson.

"You got my message?" Lily asked.

"What message?"

"They told me you were in Haifa."

"No, I'm right here in Jerusalem, getting my car fixed. In this damned country, nobody knows what they're doing."

"I wanted to talk to you. About Abu Musa."

"Who?"

"One of the laborers at Kharub. I think he stole the amphoriskos. And killed Eastbourne."

"Do you, now? Meet me here at the garage and tell me all about it. Nissin's, next to the radio station on Queen Melisande Street."

Lily hesitated. "I'll be there in twenty minutes," Lily said. Henderson may know who Marco Polo is.

Lily went back to the library to stash the journal and newspaper upstairs in her room before she left. As she folded the newspaper, a line from the shipping news caught her eye.

The Italian steamship Marco Polo arrived in Haifa port yesterday afternoon. KH had arrived in Haifa on the *Marco Polo* and met Eastbourne at the King David the next day.

She put the paper and journal under her arm and started up the stairs. Lily remembered that morning, remembered looking from the balcony toward the King David just as the riots began, and remembered Henderson in his Panama hat, buffeted by the crowd.

She shoved Eastbourne's journal into the top drawer of her desk, stashed the newspaper on top, and locked her door.

Henderson was the shipment on the *Marco Polo*.

SEVENTEEN

HENDERSON WAITED IN FRONT of the garage, standing near a clutter of engine parts between cars that were pulled up onto the narrow sidewalk.

"Let's get out of here," he said as soon as she came into sight. He glowered at the gutted cars with their engines disgorged on the ground. "They look like torn intestines. And they smell of axle grease and old oil."

He started up a steep alley in the direction of Zion Circus. "Who is this Abu Musa?"

"A laborer at Kharub."

"One of the Bedouin?"

"A Samaritan."

Henderson shrugged. "Anyway, an Arab."

"They claim to be the lost ten tribes. Some scholars say they are the descendants of the Macedonian soldiers Alexander settled in the ancient city of Samaria-Sebast."

Henderson stopped and turned toward her. "Can you find him, get hold of the vial?"

Abu Musa should be easy to trace, she thought. Only about two hundred Samaritans are left, some in a little village near

Nablus at the foot of Mount Gerizim, some still in Sebastiye. She regretted telling Henderson about him. "Abu Musa disappeared after he left Kharub," Lily answered.

Henderson began walking again. "I hate this place," he said. "They can't do anything right here. They'll probably wreck my car."

"Why did you take it there?"

"It's the whole damned city. The whole damned country. Can't do anything right."

He was moving faster now, and Lily had to hurry to keep up with him. "Why don't you wait until you get home to fix it?" She was almost out of breath.

"Bring it back to Cleveland?" he asked.

"Cincinnati," Lily said.

"Right," Henderson said, increasing his pace, forcing Lily to trot after him. "No choice. If the motor mounts give way, I could turn a corner, the car would go one way, the engine another."

He strode into the narrow lanes that led through Nachlat Sheva. "For all I know, they'll bollix the job." He stopped and looked around him. "Where the hell are we?"

They were in the alley smelling of urine that she and Avi had walked through on Tuesday, where pigeons strutted through puddles of oily residue, where cats prowled for their dinner, where the sign said, "Holy place. Forbidden to urinate here."

Henderson stepped on the cobbles carefully as if he were wading in excrement. "Cats and pigeons, pigeons and cats," he said. "The whole damned city is nothing but pigeons and cats. And fleas."

"It's a beautiful city," Lily said, "with unexpected charm. For instance, that sign on the wall behind you—"

"I don't give a damn what the sign says."

A cat rubbed against Henderson's leg and he kicked it away with the toe of his shoe. It slinked toward him—its back poised for pouncing, its tail straight up—and scratched at his trouser leg.

"The sign says—" Lily began.

Henderson and the cat glared at each other. The cat bristled and hissed, its sharp teeth bared.

"I hate it here," Henderson said.

"It says 'Holy place—'"

He reached down and picked up the cat by the tail. The cat squalled and spit, struggling at the end of Henderson's arm.

Henderson mumbled, "Look at that. Look at that," gesturing with his free arm up and down the alley while he swung the cat by the tail.

Its head hit the wall with a hollow thump, leaving a trickle of blood behind.

"Filthy, dirty scum of the earth." He whirled the cat against the stones again, once, twice, as if he were handling a tennis racket.

"Oh my God," Lily said.

He smashed it against the wall again and dropped it on the ground.

Henderson leaned against the wall, next to the sign. His hand shook; he gasped with spent emotion.

"Holy place—" Lily repeated automatically. The narrow alley began to tilt and waver. Cobbles shivered beneath her feet. Walls quivered and closed in on her. Not enough room to swing a cat. Isn't that what they said?

Lily's skin went cold. She backed away from the trickles of blood; away from the cat, one eye smashed and closed, its neck awry, its teeth still bared; away from Henderson, leaning against the bloodstained wall.

She ran through the alley toward Jaffa Road, hardly seeing where she was going, doors and stone walls of houses blurring as she hurried past.

EIGHTEEN

LILY FLED THE DARK ALLEY, the smell of kerosene and dank stones. She ran toward Zion Circus, where she knew the sun was shining, where crowds of orderly people carried shopping bags and waited at crosswalks for the lights to change.

"Lily," a voice called after her, and she kept running.

"Lily," it repeated, and she felt a hand on her shoulder, slowing her flight. Ready to cry out, she turned around.

It was Rafi.

"What happened?" He put both hands on her shoulders. "You're pale as a ghost."

"The cat," Lily said, panting and pointing toward the alley.

"Sure it's not a tiger?"

She was still pointing. "No, no. It's him. He—" She still pictured the cat, discarded on the ground. She shuddered.

"Someone is chasing you with a cat?"

Lily shook her head, still out of breath.

His hands kneaded her shoulders and he spoke in a low, measured tone. "Take a deep breath."

He smelled of soap and bay rum. His fingers, warm and pacifying, rubbed the muscles of her neck and spread across her back, moving gently against the tension. She leaned into him, resting her head against his shoulder.

"That's better," he said and steered her toward Ben Yehuda Street, his arm around her waist, and sat her at a table in the shade of an umbrella in front of Café Atara.

Rafi put his hand on her arm. "Brandy," he said to the waiter and turned back to Lily.

"Before lunch?" she asked.

He stroked her arm, like a mother calming a baby. "You look like you're in shock."

The waiter put a bottle of the local brandy and a shot glass on the table. Drops of water glistened on the exterior and ran down the outer surface. Rafi filled the glass to the brim. Lily sniffed, held her nose, leaned down and sipped. "It tastes awful." She pulled back her lips in distaste.

"Brandy always burns on the way down."

Lily sat back in the chair. "It's dissolving my teeth."

"You want to tell me what happened?" Rafi's hand was still on her arm.

"Not really." She reached for the brandy glass, lifted it, and put it down again. "I'm awfully thirsty. Don't they have water here?"

Rafi signaled the waiter for a bottle of Vichy. She drained one glass, then another. She stopped once for breath, gasping, then drank again.

"What were you running from?" he asked after a while.

She turned the bottle around and around, leaving a track on the table. "He killed a cat. Casually, while he was talking." She reached for a napkin and wiped at the wet circle. "Back there." She nodded her head in the direction of the alley. "He grabbed it by the tail and slammed its head against the wall."

"You saw the man?"

"No expression on his face. And his eyes," Lily shuddered. "His eyes were blank. As if he were dazed. He just kept swinging the cat."

"Dangerous man. Keep your distance if you see him again." Rafi leaned toward her. "Take another sip of brandy." He glanced at the glass she was clutching. "Your hand is still trembling."

"You're trying to get me drunk."

"I could ply you with a cheese sandwich instead."

"Orange juice."

He called the waiter and watched her pour the rest of the water from the bottle, watched her reach for her sunglasses. "You shouldn't wear dark glasses," he said. "Your eyes are too beautiful to hide."

Lily felt her face flush. "The sun is too bright."

Rafi eyed her pensively. "Better?"

She nodded, put down the glass and smiled back.

He turned her palm up and traced her heart line. "It says here," he said, "that love has a deep meaning for you. Are you in love?"

She shook her head; her skin tightened as he ran his finger along her palm.

His hand was still on her arm when the waiter brought lunch. "Are you and Avi close friends?" Rafi asked.

"He visits the tel sometimes."

"He likes you, you know."

"He's a nice boy."

"Boy?"

"He brings me oranges. Sometimes he drives me if I need a ride."

"That's all? Does that leave a clear field for me?"

Lily felt a tick of satisfaction and looked away. Couples around her sat at the tables in front of Café Atara, murmured in soft voices, bent toward each other, their eyes locked. Rafi was still brushing his fingers along her arm. Without thinking, she placed her hand on top of his.

Rafi picked up the sandwich with his free hand. "What were you telling me about this morning?" he asked and bit into the roll.

"You always talk with your mouth full? *Bon appetit.*"

He swallowed. "That reminds me of a story."

"About a storm at sea in a leaky boat?"

"This time, Sammy Goldberg was traveling to Europe for the first time, first class on the *Queen Mary.* The first night, he went to dinner all spiffed up in his tuxedo and found out he shared a table with an elegant Frenchman. Just as Sammy sat down, the Frenchman bowed and said, 'Bon appetit.' So Sammy bowed back and said, 'Goldberg.'"

"Very funny," Lily said.

"Wait. I'm not finished. The next night and the night after, it was the same thing. The Frenchman would say, 'Bon appetit' and Sammy would answer, 'Goldberg.' Then Sammy found out what *bon appetit* meant, that it wasn't the Frenchman's name. So on the fourth night, Sammy came to dinner early. This time he was ready. When the Frenchman arrived, Sammy bowed with a flourish and said, 'Bon appetit.' So the Frenchman answered, 'Goldberg.'"

"That's it?" Lily said.

"That's it." Rafi took another bite of the sandwich.

"*Bon appetit,*" Lily said again.

"Goldberg." Rafi reached for a napkin. "You said something about Abu Musa this morning? The Samaritan who worked at the tel? And a blue glass vial."

"I went to Kharub yesterday. Kate told me that Abu Musa was fired for stealing."

"That's why you think Abu Musa killed Eastbourne for a blue glass vial?"

"For revenge."

"Anything's possible."

"Abu Musa comes from a little village near Nablus—Sebastiye," Lily said. "I have to go up there to talk to him."

"Don't go alone. If he killed Eastbourne, he might do the same to you."

* * *

Lily went as far as the hospital with Rafi. He paused at the steps, bent to kiss her lightly on the cheek, cupped her chin in his hand and kissed her again, this time on her lips.

People smiled at her as she floated home along the Street of the Prophets. Summer breezes bent leaves to shade her all the way to the American School. The sky was a brighter blue today. Even Sinbad's dogs sniffed gently at the fence when she passed. And a pleasant whiff of vanilla that reminded her of Dame Margaret lingered at her carrel in the library.

* * *

She sat in her room, reluctant to begin working. Too much had happened today to spend time with dusty potsherds and pour over drawings of tombs and the placement of skeletons. She reached for Eastbourne's journal instead, then turned on the radio, moving the dial back and forth until she found an English program with a studio orchestra that played gentle music.

Plans and sections of rectangular buildings were in a pocket in the back of the notebook. They were not Iron Age forts, nor Roman *castella*. Plans of modern buildings. What had Kate said—

something about Eastbourne doing consulting in Jerusalem for extra cash? Consulting? About what? Lily felt a chill of misgiving.

She unfolded the largest sheet in the pocket. It was a topographic map of Northern Palestine—the scale, 1 to 100,000. Sites were marked along the northern and eastern borders. He's been doing some kind of survey, she thought, maybe the one that Henderson had proposed.

She spread the map on the table and traced what she knew of ancient roads and trade routes, trying to make sense of the settlement pattern. The ancient Kingdom of Israel? The Roman period? Crusader castles? Nothing fit except the present. These were the borders of the Mandate.

* * *

A tone sounded three times on the radio to announce the hour, paused, repeated, and then a bland voice announced, "This is the news from the Palestine Broadcasting Service."

The British voice intoned, "In local news, two more bombs were exploded in Tel Aviv. The wounded were taken to Government Hospital. The Jaffa-Tel Aviv death toll for the last two days is now five.

"Emergency Regulations curfews have been imposed between the hours of 7 p.m. and 5 a.m. in the municipalities of Haifa, Jerusalem, Tel Aviv-Jaffa border, and Nablus; the villages of Jenin, Taiyiba, and Umm al Fahm; and all roads and tracks between municipalities, settlements and villages.

"Shots were fired at a bus between Affuleh and Mesha settlement. The attackers fled before police arrived at the scene. Shots were fired from ambush at a taxi traveling along the Haifa-Nazareth road. Troops quickly arrived at the scene and engaged an armed band, inflicting one casualty and capturing three of the bandits.

"German rifles were found in a taxi near Rehovoth. The Arab driver and his passengers were arrested.

"Security in the south is deteriorating. . . ." Lily turned off the radio.

* * *

Lily didn't notice the peal of the telephone until the third or fourth ring. Breathless, she ran into the hall to answer it.

It was Rafi. Lily smiled at the sound of his voice and ran her fingers up and down the telephone as he spoke.

"You're in luck, little tiger," he said. "We have an excuse to go to Abu Musa's village. I have a Samaritan patient who invited me to a wedding there on Tuesday."

"We can drive up. I have the station wagon from Kharub."

"Good. I knew there was a reason that I asked you to go with me."

* * *

That night, Lily couldn't sleep. She stroked her arm where Rafi had touched it, smiled and stretched under the covers.

She listened to the sounds of Salah-edh-Din Street—an occasional car, the angry dogs tethered in the yard of Samir's Taxi, the clop of donkeys and the strain of cartwheels rolling up the hill toward the American Colony.

She lay awake for hours, hearing the incessant tick of the clock on the bedside table, the dogs barking and growling at shadows in the dark night, footfalls echoing in the empty street outside her window, the clatter of an empty can scudding along the sidewalk as the steps faded.

Eastbourne's murder, the maps and plans in his journal, Kate's tear-ridden face, blood-haunted visions, rumbled through her head. When she closed her eyes, she saw the bloodied cat, its neck askew, lying on the cobbles. Sometimes it looked like Mrs. Klein, with her toothless stare, crumpled on the asphalt in front of the YMCA the day of the riots.

Toward dawn, after the muezzin called the first prayer of the day, Lily fell asleep and dreamed of Eastbourne lying bullet-ridden and bloody in a trench at Tel al-Kharub. In her dream, Kate was keening as his body turned to sand, while Lily brushed away the particles with a camelhair brush and a dental pick. The skeleton of a cat with a crushed skull and a broken tail lay next to him, its sharp teeth, like fangs, buried in Eastbourne's bony hand.

*   *   *

At lunch, Lily's eyes were gritty from lack of sleep; her neck ached with fatigue. Nothing that Dame Margaret said made sense.

Lily rested her chin on her hand and closed her eyes. "I couldn't sleep at all last night."

Dame Margaret leaned forward, exuding her usual scent of vanilla. She was saying something about the Grand Mufti-Nazi connection.

"By the way," Lily said. "You haven't heard any rumors about the missing amphoriskos, have you?"

Dame Margaret ignored her question. "The danger is real."

"We can't locate it. There's a possibility that one of the workmen stole it."

"You're not listening to me."

"Sorry. I'm tired," Lily told her. "I haven't slept well lately. First the riots, then Eastbourne's murder. And now this missing amphoriskos. I don't know what's going on, or why it's all happening."

"But you do know. You even know who KH is, and what Eastbourne was doing in Jerusalem."

Dame Margaret had been at Lily's desk after all and had looked in the journal.

Lily shook her head. "I haven't the slightest."

The big yellow rose balanced on the brim of Dame Margaret's hat began to quiver. "The Arabs have a saying—He who knows not and knows not he knows not is a fool. Shun him." Lily felt dizzy. Dame Margaret went on relentlessly. "He who knows not and knows he knows not is a child. Teach him. He who knows and knows he knows—"

"Is too darn nosy?" Take that, Dame Margaret.

"There's your problem right there." Her rose waggled like a reprimand. "The rest of it goes—He who knows and knows not he knows is asleep. Waken him."

"I'm too tired to waken. Too tired to think about it."

"Not too tired," Dame Margaret said. "Too frightened."

"Frightened?"

"You escape into the past. You probe old archives of disaster layer upon layer, but your ruins are memorials for bloodless deaths. That's why you're an archaeologist."

"You disapprove of archaeologists?"

"Of course not. I adore them. When you marry an archaeologist, the older you get, the more he loves you." Dame Margaret smiled at her. Lily had heard the quip before.

"I really should go home and lie down," Lily said.

"You refuse to face facts. Americans are so naive. Why don't you look at things head on? This is no time for optimism."

Lily formed her lips to answer but said nothing.

"There's going to be a war. All over Europe, people know. What's happening here and in Spain and China is only the prologue." Dame Margaret's rose was trembling now. "Before it's over, the world will be bleak and changed forever."

"You're afraid."

Dame Margaret reached across the table. "Of course I am. The Great War was just the beginning. The horrors are yet to come."

Lily blinked at her.

"You can't keep your eyes open," Dame Margaret said. "Go home and take a nap."

NINETEEN

LILY SPENT THE MORNING in the basement of the library, taking artifacts out of boxes one by one, tomb by tomb, marking notes on the brown paper she had spread over the long laboratory tables. She had propped open the basement door and the sun shone in from the garden. Site reports were stacked on a small desk next to the accountant's ledger she used as a register.

She reached for a Cypriote juglet with bands of black painted on the shoulder just as Lady Fendley clattered down the stairs in her sensible shoes.

"Someone to see you." Lady Fendley raised her eyebrows and jiggled her head coquettishly. "A young man."

Henderson? "What does he look like?" Lily put down the juglet.

"Like someone very nice."

Rafi?

"You're blushing to your earlobes," said Lady Fendley.

"Tell him to come down."

Rafi had already started down the stairs. "Had an hour to spare. Thought I'd visit. You busy?"

"Working on the pottery from Kharub."

"I'll help." He reached for a small black burnished juglet. "What's this?"

"A perfume juglet. Put it back. I'm working on the artifacts from tomb 104, the one that had the amphoriskos."

He reached into a box labeled tomb 104, grasped two handles with his forefingers and lifted out a large pot. "What's this?"

"Don't pick it up by the handles. It's a store jar."

"Why three handles? And what's this, where the fourth handle should be?" He canted the jar against his hip and pointed.

"Be careful. It's called a pillar handle. It's hollow, a resting-place for a little dipper juglet, like this." She picked up a small-necked, round-bottom juglet to show him. "The jar was used for oil. They dipped it out with the juglet." She made a scoop-ing motion with the juglet in her hand and replaced it on the table. "After it was emptied, they placed it on the pillar handle and the drippings went back into the jar."

"Pretty clever." He balanced the store jar with both hands and brought it to the table. As he carried it, a faint sound, like metal rolling seemed to come from the bottom of the jar. "Something's in here," Rafi said, and turned the jar upside down.

"Don't—"

A tiny aluminum cylinder bounced on the table and rolled onto the floor. Rafi placed the jar on the table and picked up the cylinder.

"What's that?" Lily said.

Rafi turned it over in his hand. "A film cassette."

Lily glanced at it. "It's too small."

"Eight millimeter. A new kind of film, fine grain with high resolving power, used in that camera. . . ." He stopped and looked over at Lily. "You say that this is the tomb the amphoriskos came from?"

"Yes."

He twirled the cassette between his fingers. "It's used in a miniature camera with a special macro-lens for copying documents. Like the one you found, no bigger than a cigarette lighter. Snap it open and shut and the copy's made."

"It's used to copy texts, manuscripts, record shots of small inscriptions, coins?"

Rafi nodded.

"Maybe there's a shot of the amphoriskos. Look inside, see if there's film."

He unscrewed the lid of the cassette and looked inside. "Not this time. Film's gone."

"Usually Eastbourne used a professional photographer. They use mechanical boxes with special lights and platforms," Lily said.

"Cameras like this are easier to conceal." Rafi edged toward her field notebook and flipped a page. "What's this?"

"My field notebook. Gives the exact find spot of every artifact. A three dimensional record. All very scientific."

"Will it cure the common cold?" He continued to turn the pages of the notebook.

"You're losing my place." A gust, carrying the scent of lemon blossoms, blew in through the open door and ruffled another page.

Lily looked out into the garden. "Let's go for a walk." Rosebushes along the gravel path bent and smiled in the breeze and offered their buds to the sun. "It's time for a break."

* * *

They strolled along the Street of the Prophets, back toward the hospital, hand in hand, their gaits matching. He asked her about Eastbourne's murder, about the amphoriskos, about Abu Musa, about Kate and little Geoffrey. "I still don't think you should interfere with what the police are doing," Rafi said. "Just let the police take care of it."

"But they're not taking care of it."

"Don't get tangled up in this. It could be more complicated than you think."

"I can't help it. Curiosity, for one thing."

"And another?"

"An instinct for self-preservation, maybe. I owe it to Eastbourne. And myself, I suppose. I promised Kate I'd find out what happened. Anyway, I have to find the amphoriskos."

"That's too many reasons. One would be more convincing. Give it up. I worry about you," he said. "I think I'm in love."

Lily glanced at him, flushed with pleasure and squeezed his hand. The wind had blown the cowlick onto his forehead, and she resisted the urge to push it back. "Is it anyone I know?"

"What a self-satisfied smirk," he said. "I'm not sure you know her. She does strange things. Sticks her nose into affairs that don't concern her. Most of the time, she lives in an imaginary world of long ago, like a child."

Lily slowed her pace. "Are you in love with who she is or who you want her to be?"

"I'm not sure of that either." Rafi let go of her hand.

"The amphoriskos is my responsibility."

"Don't talk about responsibility. There are people who are sick, people who are hungry, and children who can't go to school because they have no shoes, while you play in the dirt and look for old glass bottles."

Lily lagged behind him now and stopped walking. "You want me to go door to door, collecting pennies for the poor?"

"Better than escaping into the past." He turned around to face her. "You're as oblivious as a snowflake. With your brains, it's a waste."

"You think everyone has to cure the sick?"

"It would be a start." He pushed back his hair. "I care what happens to you. I don't want you running into harm's way for no reason."

"And if there is a reason?"

Rafi looked down the street toward the hospital.

"What about you?" Lily said. "You put yourself in harm's way."

"That's different."

"Because it's you, not me?"

"I have to get back to the hospital." He put his hands in his pockets, stepped off the narrow sidewalk and strode up the street.

She caught up with him. "I must talk to the police, give them information that might help the investigation."

"That's not what worries me." His face was turned away from her. "It's the trip to Sebastiye."

"I excavated the amphoriskos. I must find it. It's part of my report, my responsibility."

Why couldn't she tell him it was about her father?

He walked faster now, not looking at her. "Do what you think is best."

They trudged in silence, Lily on the sidewalk, Rafi in the street, looking at the ground instead of each other.

Lily thought about the appointment with the British police the next day. "Why do you call her Auntie Major?" she asked.

"It's all she talks about. My friend the major this, and my friend the major that."

"Is she really your aunt?"

"My father's sister." He stopped, looked at Lily without speaking and smiled. "Bet you were a terror when you were a child," he said after a while.

"Matter of fact I was. I always won whenever we had orange wars in the groves, girls against boys. We lobbed oranges at each other instead of snowballs."

"Orange groves?"

"In Pasadena, where I was raised. My father was Orville, my mother Mathilde. She was a proper Pasadena matron—marcelled hair, pearls. So when I came home with scruffy knees and orange peels in my hair, she would be outraged."

"Your father was Orville Sampson?"

Memories of her father eddied through her head. "He died when I was young."

"I'm sorry." He took his hands out of his pockets for a moment to gesture. "Orville Sampson. I've heard the name. Famous for something, wasn't he?"

"He—" Lily felt tightness in her chest. "He was a friend of Harding."

"President Harding?"

"Yes." Lily's answer was scarcely audible.

"I remember now." He eyed her speculatively. "He was involved in that oil scandal."

"He was a friend of Harding."

"I heard what you said." He scanned her face intently. "He killed himself when the scandal became public, didn't he? I was just a teenager at the time, but I remember my parents talking about it, something in the paper. . . ." His tone was hushed. "I'm so sorry."

"No need to be sorry. He was a wonderful man."

"I only meant—"

"I know what you meant. I loved him very much. I still love him."

"Of course you do." Rafi began walking again, scuffing fallen leaves aside with the toes of his sandals.

Lily strolled alongside him. "My father collected antiquities," she said. "He gave me an amphoriskos like the one from Kharub."

"You still have it?"

"We lost everything in the Crash." She looked down at the sidewalk, stepping carefully to avoid cracks in the pavement. "We seemed to manage at first. Then we ran out of money. My mother hung wash on the line at night after dark, so that no one could see that we didn't have servants. We lost the house, lived in a hotel on Green Street. My mother sold everything she could get her hands on to keep us going."

"She sold the amphoriskos?"

"Yes."

They stopped in front of the hospital. The beggar with the copper bowl was across the street, a book open in his lap.

"He never said goodbye," Lily said.

"Your father?"

Lily nodded.

"That's why you have to find the amphoriskos?"

She nodded again.

"You get to keep it? Finders keepers?"

"No. It belongs to the Department of Antiquities. We make a division at the end of the season, and Eastbourne gets to—got to—take some of the things back to London for analysis."

They stood next to the steps leading up to the hospital facing each other.

"I have to go," Rafi said finally. "Tomorrow morning at Patt's."

"For breakfast."

"At eight o'clock." He gave her a light peck on the cheek. His hands were still in his pockets.

All the way home, the conversation bothered her. Why doesn't he want me to go to Sebastiye? Why does he want me to stop looking for the amphoriskos? Or find out who killed Eastbourne, for that matter?

"He's being unreasonable," she said out loud, and a man passing by turned to look at her.

* * *

Back home, Lily went directly to the library. Eliot was at Lily's desk again. When she entered, he made an elaborate show of reading book titles.

"Tel Beit Mirsim?" Lily asked.

Eliot was red-faced. "Beth Shan."

"I don't have it."

"So I see."

"Try the library shelves. The site report section." She pointed toward the stacks. "DS 110."

"Yes. Of course. I didn't think of that." He backed away from her desk. "We probably have it at the British School. I'll just pop around the corner." He started for the door. "Sorry to bother you," he called back over his shoulder and slammed the door behind him.

* * *

In the morning, Lily reached Patt's by five minutes before eight.

Rafi was already waiting. His seat faced the door.

This morning, the coffee was almost drinkable. Often it was thick, the texture of sludge.

Bots they called it—mud. They ate in companionable silence. The rolls were crisp and warm enough for the fresh butter to melt into them.

He had just put down his cup and looked up. "There she is." He stood up and indicated a woman dressed in flounces and furbelows who sailed in their direction. "Auntie Major."

She carried a ruffled parasol, wore white cotton gloves and an enormous hat covered with blowzy pink roses. She descended on Rafi, arms extended as if to smother him with an embrace and a kiss.

He stepped back. "May I present Lily Sampson. Lily, this is my aunt, Mrs. Landau." He looked at his watch. "I have to leave now. I'm due at the hospital."

"Our appointment with my friend Major Fogarty is in half an hour," Auntie Major said. She looked like the drawing room of an English cottage at the end of a Sunday afternoon, slightly rumpled and padded with chintz. "My friend the major has an office in the Russian compound." Her dress was tight as a sausage casing.

She reached for Lily's hand, as if Lily were a child. "My friend the major will be waiting for us." She hustled Lily down the street, leading with her parasol. "I told him about your little problem."

"What problem?"

"You know. The threat on your life."

"What threat?"

"The one from the Nazi agent, of course. That day in front of the King David. My friend the major was quite concerned."

"What Nazi agent? Why did you tell him a thing like that?"

"You wanted to get in to see my friend the major, didn't you? Besides, that's what Rafi told me."

Burbling and cooing, she towed Lily down St. Paul's Road and up the steps to the Russian compound toward the elaborate white, onion-domed Cathedral. She said that she was pleased about Lily and Rafi; that her friend the major came from an important family in Sussex; that Rafi needed someone, and it was about time. She said her friend the major understood the Middle East well. She said Lily would adore her friend the major.

Lily nodded and grunted from time to time to indicate that she was listening as Auntie Major prattled on until they reached the block of government offices in the Russian compound.

"The law courts are in the Sergei Building." Auntie Major waved in the direction of a wide, two-storied building with a row of arched windows along its façade. "That's where my friend the major has his office."

Auntie Major smoothed the lines of her dress and cinched her belt before she knocked with the handle of her parasol. A man in a colonel's uniform opened the door part way.

"Dear Colonel Darnell. How nice to see you again." Auntie Major gave him a lustrous, expectant smile, accompanied by a lissome tilt of the head.

"I'm sorry, Mrs. Landau. This meeting is confidential." He looked past her and motioned for Lily to enter. "Please wait outside," he said to Auntie Major.

She leaned on her parasol and smiled again. "You don't understand. Major Fogarty expects . . ." she began.

"I'm sure you don't mind," the colonel said to Auntie Major. He led Lily into the office and closed the door. "Miss Sampson? You were Eastbourne's assistant?"

"I worked with him at Tel al-Kharub."

He pointed to a chair and sat down next to her.

A man with a trimmed British moustache was seated behind the desk. "Major Fogarty?" Lily asked.

He nodded. "Mrs. Landau said you wanted to see me?"

"I wanted to talk to you about Eastbourne."

Fogarty reached for a pipe and tobacco pouch on his desk. "What about Eastbourne?"

"He wasn't killed by bandits."

The major continued to fill his pipe, tamping down the tobacco and running his fingers along the bowl. "What makes you say that?"

"Eastbourne was bringing an amphoriskos from the site to the Rockefeller for the opening of the museum the day he was murdered. It's disappeared."

"And you think Eastbourne was killed for the amphoriskos?"

Lily nodded. "I think a laborer who worked at Tel al-Kharub stole it. A Samaritan named Abu Musa."

Darnell rose and started toward the door. "Young lady, there must be a thousand Samaritans. And they are all named Abu Musa."

"I plan to go to their village near Nablus," Lily said. "Ask around, see if I can find him."

The colonel moved closer to the door and tapped his hand against his thigh. "You do that, young lady," he said, reaching for the knob.

"And then there's Henderson," Lily said.

Darnell dropped his hand from the knob and started back toward the chair. "The American attaché? What about Henderson?"

"He was in Jerusalem the day of the riots. I saw him in front of the King David. I think Eastbourne went to meet him."

The colonel and Fogarty exchanged glances.

"Henderson?" asked Darnell. The major began to light his pipe.

"There was no mistaking him. He stood out—at least six inches taller than the mob around him. Sandy-haired, lantern jaw."

Fogarty drew on his pipe in great draughts, filling the room with smoke.

"Thank you for the information," the colonel said.

The sticky-sweet smell of tobacco smoke filled the room. Both men stood as a signal for Lily to leave.

The colonel walked with her to the door. "It's almost no use trying to find the killers." He opened the door and kept his hand on the knob. "Sad to say, the Mandate has many more pressing concerns."

Auntie Major waited in the hall, brimming with curiosity and indignation. "What was that about?"

"They just don't care," Lily said. "Too busy to be concerned with the murder of a British national?" She glared at Auntie Major. "Is that likely?"

"There's no reason why they made me wait out here," Auntie Major said.

"If I want to know what happened to Eastbourne, I'll have to find out for myself."

"After all," Auntie Major said, as they began to work together. "Major Fogarty is my friend."

"And why should I care who killed Eastbourne, anyway? It's not my job. I just feel sorry for Kate, that's all."

Auntie Major adjusted her dress again, pulling it down around her waist. "I can't let it bother me." She paused, took a deep breath and smiled at Lily. "Tell me about you and Rafi." The dress began to ride up again.

Lily stopped walking and faced Auntie Major. "The amphoriskos. That's my responsibility. Not who murdered Eastbourne."

Auntie Major narrowed her eyes and looked at Lily. "Young lady, you make no sense at all."

They had walked as far as the Palace Hotel on the corner of Mamilla. Auntie Major said, "Rafi tells me that you're going to Nablus with him tomorrow."

"We both have errands there."

Auntie Major seemed in the mood to gossip. "You two make a handsome couple."

"And furthermore," Lily said, "I don't just play in the dirt. Archaeology is important, too." She lifted her chin and gazed at the box tree on the corner. "No one can understand the future until they have viewed the past." That sounds like a quote from a textbook, she thought, and grimaced.

"I'm not at all sure I approve of the way you're behaving," Auntie Major said. "I live near here in Rehavia." She waved her arm in the direction of King George Street. "Why don't you come home with me and have a nice cup of real English tea?"

I can't stand another minute with this woman, Lily thought. She looked at her watch and shook her head. "Some other time. I have an appointment."

Lily left Auntie Major at the corner of King George and headed toward Ben Yehuda Street. "I enjoyed our little talk," Auntie Major said. "Shalom. TaTa. Give my regards to Rafi."

Maybe Rafi is at a morning break in Café Atara, Lily thought. I have to talk with him anyway about the curfew tomorrow. I may as well stop for a sandwich and coffee.

Lily passed a perfumery. I should buy a lipstick, she thought, and went inside. She came out of the shop into the bright sunshine a few minutes later, carrying a small packet containing lipstick and face powder.

Maybe Rafi is at that café near the hospital on Chancellor Road. Maybe he isn't eating lunch at all. She passed a beauty salon near the corner of Ben Yehuda and King George, then turned back. "I should get my hair done for the wedding tomorrow," she decided, and went inside.

For a moment the sharp odors of shampoo and lotion, of ammonia and acetone, stung her eyes. A bank of women doggedly perspired under hairdryers that looked like helmets from Buck Roger's world of the twenty-fifth century.

A young woman in a starched pink dress sat at a counter, with bottles of lotions and pots of cream displayed on the wall behind her. "May I help you?" she asked.

Lily sneezed. "I would like a shampoo and a set." She looked down at her hands. Her nails were uneven, her cuticles ragged.

"And a manicure." She held her arm out in front of her and spread her fingers. "Yes. A manicure."

The woman behind the counter picked up a white pen with a plume. "Would you like a facial today? We have a special on Mondays—facial, shampoo and set for only fifty mils." She waited, her pen poised above a yellow pad. "Your skin will be smooth and glowing."

Lily ran her finger along her chin and across her cheek to her temple. "Yes. Of course. That too."

* * *

Lily arrived late at dinner. Sausages of hair framed her face. She was pleased with the glamorous image she had seen in the beauty salon mirror until Sir William looked at her when she sat down and said, "Good God! What happened to you? You're made up like a corpse."

He launched another endless lecture, all the while dripping food on his jacket. He mumbled about pottery classification, the Czech Nazi Henlein, Galton's family resemblances. Lady Fendley interrupted now and then to wipe his chin or smooth his hair.

Lily, exhausted from her afternoon at the beauty parlor, the heat of the dryer, the face patting and chemical odors, listened to Sir William drone until the sound of his voice made her dizzy. She imagined Sir William, lecturing with a pointer in front of a huge clay pot, a caricature of a Toby mug shaped like the face of Henderson. His exaggerated jaw and deep-set eyes moved and shifted while the pot shouted orders in an incomprehensible staccato. She pictured them crammed inside an army tank that crawled, snakelike, along a hillside, while the fluid features of Henderson and the pot changed bit by bit, taking on the face of an anonymous gymnast she had seen in a film about the Olympics, then Henlein.

"Pay attention," Sir William said. "This is important."

"Of course it is," Lily answered.

Sir William mumbled on and on.

When she left them, Sir William and Lady Fendley were drinking coffee in the common room. Tired and irritated, Lily fetched Eastbourne's journal from her room and brought it downstairs to the library.

She sat in the large leather wingback chair at the far end of the room and opened Eastbourne's journal to the back pocket.

When she put the journal away earlier, she had folded the map carefully into the back pocket, beneath the plans and sections of buildings. It was now on top.

She propped her legs on the ottoman in front of the chair and spread the map over them.

She had seen the contour map somewhere before—without the checkmarks and zigzag lines Eastbourne had drawn on it. She remembered Kitchener's map, prepared for the Palestine Exploration Society in the 1880s. He had gone as far as the border between present-day Palestine and French-controlled Syria. "Kitchener of Khartoum," she said aloud, rolling out the last word like a parody of the voice of a stuffy British colonel.

She took Condor and Kitchener's British Ordinance map off the shelf. That was it. There were the same contour lines defining the hilltops in Eastbourne's photostatted copy. But Eastbourne had drawn a scroll along the boundaries with Lebanon and Syria, marked checks on the hilltops and joined them with jagged lines that looked like connect-the-dots from a children's playbook. Lily noticed that the marked hills were near the border and within sight of each other. But why? And what were the herringbone lines between them?

She put away the Condor and Kitchener, sat in the chair, spread the map on the ottoman and puzzled over it. She opened the journal to July 10 and turned the pages. There must be something she missed. She curled her legs under her and turned the pages. *July 15. One and a half kilometers north of Montfort.* She looked at the map again. There it was, marked with a check, a hill north of Monfort. Was he doing a survey of Crusader castles? The Ladder of Tyre on the coast north of Nahariya was marked, but Caesarea wasn't. Neither was Atlit. Latrun—the Crusaders *Le Toron des Chevaliers* built to defend the road to Jerusalem—had a small square.

What was Eastbourne looking for? And why had he entrusted the journal to her keeping? Someone wanted to know what was in the maps.

If whoever it is wants maps, I'll give them maps, Lily thought.

She found a piece of scrap paper and copied the coordinates of Eastbourne's symbols along the Lebanese border and the crusader forts, making it look like a list of telephone numbers. She found a copy of Crowfoot's *Early Churches in Palestine* on the library shelf, carefully erased Eastbourne's marks from the map and replaced them with checkmarks at sites of Byzantine churches in the Jordan Valley on both sides of the border between Palestine and Transjordan—at Beth Shan, and Madeba, at Jericho and Nebo.

She practiced forging Eastbourne's cramped handwriting, made a list of the sites she had marked and put it between the pages of the journal.

And then she leaned back in the large leather chair and contemplated the newly marked map.

Pretty good. She rested her head against the wing of the chair and idly turned the pages of the journal. Another meeting with KH on July 20th.

The doorbell rang and rang again. Lily put the journal and map under the chair cushion.

Rafi stood on the porch, holding out a rose, wearing an abashed smile. "Just finished at the hospital. I wanted to see you." In the entry hall, he handed her the rose. "About the curfew. We'll have to leave early tomorrow."

"I know."

"No. That's not the reason I came."

She bent her head to sniff at the rose and felt her hair brush against his sleeve.

"I wasn't very nice to you yesterday," he said.

He fingered the rose petals and ran his hand along her arm. "I didn't mean to criticize you."

She moved closer to him, and he stroked her hair. "You smell like a hospital," she said. He laid her head against his shoulder.

"I never want to argue with you." His hand ran along her back. "I was looking for an excuse to see you." He held her close. Her hands caressed his shoulders and she reached under his collar to feel the curve of his neck.

"It's all right," she said. She lifted her face when he bent down toward her, nearer, nearer, until she felt his breath on her, and she closed her eyes.

When they kissed, the skin along her spine prickled and the room began to waver. She leaned against him. Breathless and light-headed, she clung to him while he held her. She stroked the back of his neck, his shoulder.

They moved to the bench in the hall, sat down and clung to each other. They heard Sir William open his bedroom door upstairs and shuffle toward the bathroom.

"Tomorrow," Rafi said. He kissed the top of her head gently, put the rose in her lap, went out into the hallway and closed the door softly behind him.

Still trembling, Lily retrieved Eastbourne's journal from under the seat cushion and brought it upstairs.

This time, she put the notebook under the mattress near the foot of her bed. She found a piaster and a roll of adhesive tape, used a coin to open the back of the radio, taped her list of Eastbourne's coordinates onto the inside of the radio back, and screwed it in place.

"Tomorrow," she repeated as she fell asleep.

TWENTY

Lily pointed to the top of a hill. "That must be Sebastiye." It was two hours since they left Jerusalem. She looked up at the houses built against tumbles of fallen stones, scattered among ruins of ancient buildings and shattered columns. "Looks like the photos from the site report."

Rafi turned onto the bumpy track that led up the hill. Dust eddied around them. The station wagon sputtered, then died.

"We'll never get up there," Rafi said. He scrambled out of the car and propped open the hood. "The carburetor needs cleaning, the fuel pump is clogged, and everything makes noise but the horn."

"There's a little butterfly thing you have to wiggle," Lily said.

He held up his hands and waggled his fingers. They were streaked with grease. "I can't go to a wedding like this."

"There's a towel under the seat," Lily said.

With his hands still in the air like a surgeon who had just scrubbed, he tried to open the car door with his elbow.

Lily reached under the seat and pitched the towel to him through the open window.

"What's the rattle and bang in the back of the car?" he asked.

"Digging equipment. Picks, shovels, brushes. A folding ladder. And a dining canopy."

"In case you find a site somewhere and need to dig an emergency hole in the ground?"

"Exactly."

"Try the choke." He put the towel on the fender and reached under the hood again. "This car reminds me of a story."

"About the *Queen Mary*?"

"About a Texan who was visiting a kibbutz." He wiped his hands. "Turn on the ignition."

The engine whined; the wagon shook from side to side. "There it goes." He slammed the hood shut. "Anyway, this Texan said to the kibbutznik, 'Mighty nice little farm you have here, but my spread in Texas is so big that it takes a day and a half to drive around it.'" Rafi got back into the car and shifted carefully into low gear. "And the kibbutznik said, 'I used to have a car like that.'"

The wagon heaved, lurched and chugged up the hill.

Lily pointed out the remains of a crumbling structure where weeds grew from stubs of stone walls. "That's the palace of Omri the king of the Israelites. The town's built over ruins of their royal city, Samaria. Harvard dug here before the war, then the British in the twenties."

Five or six men in vivid striped cloaks and baggy pants tied at the ankles smoked hookahs, leaning against an ancient foundation in the shade of the wall of a house built of scavenged ashlars. "Over there, where the men are sitting, is the Temple of Augustus, built for him by Herod."

Two of the men sat in chairs; the others squatted on the ground. They spoke in low voices, arms sweeping the horizon, their bright turbans swaying with each nod of their heads. One of them called out to a man who came through the courtyard.

After a bawdy laugh, he, too, sat down and grasped one of the pipes.

"Wedding must be over there," Lily said.

Rafi parked in the shade of a carob tree. "Not under this tree," Lily said. "Carob sheds this time of year."

Rafi backed up the station wagon and it rattled into the shade of a building. "That must be the groom's house. My patient said you can't miss it. He said men and women celebrate separately."

"I'll find the women. Keep your ears open for any talk about Abu Musa."

Rafi reached for the door handle. "Meet me here at three o'clock. We have to leave early so we can make it back to Jerusalem before curfew."

He turned off the ignition, set the brake and listened to the car gasp and knock. "Cheap gas. Idles too fast, too." He got out and went around to Lily's side. "They call this the Red Day of the wedding. The fourth day. I've no idea why."

A large stone bathhouse, the rooftop studded with rounded domes inlaid with thick bubbles of green Hebron glass, stood beyond the pillars of an ancient ruin. Women came and went from there, crowding around the door. Lily strolled up to the bathhouse and looked inside.

Lit by a ghostly green light from the skylights, women, all talking at once, clustered around tables and peered into baskets overflowing with striped cloth, dishes and bowls, kitchen gadgets, and copper pots. Jewelry clinked as the women moved. Rhythmic music, throaty singing, clapping of hands, and an eerie, throbbing, cry flowed from another room.

A soft voice sounded in her ear. "Welcome, welcome. I speak English." Lily turned to see a matron wearing a long white cotton dress woven with green, red, and yellow stripes and tied with a broad sash.

"You look at my dress." The woman stroked her red-and-yellow satin chest panel. "Here we do not embroider. We have special cloth. Very good. Very expensive." She wore a bonnet decorated with antique coins and covered by a white gauze veil that fell down her back; on her arms, silver bracelets; around her neck, gold and silver chains and glass beads strung with magic eyes and the hand of Fatimah.

"Come. Come. We go to the wedding." She grabbed Lily by the hand and made a path to the door.

"My name is Yohevet, like the mother of Musa in the Holy Book." She gestured toward the baskets. "Wedding gifts from the groom's family." She thumped her chest, and the beads jiggled and tinkled.

The heat of the room, the crowd, the noise were oppressive.

Yohevet indicated a woman fingering a dress with a nod of her head. "That one is saying, 'Not good enough.' She lies. I buy the cloth myself in Medjel. I watch them weave and dye. The best silk and cotton."

She gestured toward another, holding up jewelry to the light. "She say the wedding will put him in debt for the next ten years. Is true. It cost more than five years of oil from all the olive grove." She shook her head and sighed. "Come. We eat."

The town gossip. She'll know about Abu Musa, Lily thought.

Yohevet led Lily into an open courtyard lined with tables—tables piled with fruit; with pastries of savory chopped meats; with saffron-colored cakes, sticky with honey. Smoke from braziers of charred meat hovered in the air. Lily tried to snake her hand between two women in the throng around the table to reach a pastry.

Yohevet jammed one into Lily's hand. "You like? Is special. I make myself. With minced meat and sumac." She pounded her chest again, then stuffed another tidbit into Lily's other hand.

Lily bit into one and savored the crisp texture of the flaky pastry, the pungent taste of sumac. A woman leaving the table knocked against Lily's elbow as she lifted her hand for a second bite. The delicacy fell to the floor.

Yohevet said, "Come. See the bride." And she beat her way back through the crowd, dragging Lily behind her through the stifling crush.

In the next room, a fourteen-year-old sat on a carved chair like a queen on a throne, with cushions and rugs and quilts piled around her. The girl wore bright patterned pants with a long sash wound around her waist. A coat, striped red, black and yellow, draped gracefully over her head like a veil, fell around her neck and down her back. Necklaces and earrings trembled among braids that peeked out from under the coat.

"Her new husband's coat," Yohevet said. "Now he protects her."

"She's just a child," Lily said.

"No, no. I examine myself. She is woman."

Mothers led little girls by the hand to the bride. They touched her dress with awe, bowed before her, and brought their fingers to their foreheads in deference.

At the far end of the hall, a woman beat a tambour and another sat next to her on a low stool, playing an instrument that resembled a guitar. "An oud," Yohevet said.

A high pitched trill vibrated from women on the bride's side of the room, reverberating back and forth in the crowded space from one side to the other.

"To keep away evil eye," Yohevet said.

Bangles jangling, jewelry clinking, they clapped their hands in rhythm to the music. The groom's family began to sing in a minor key, melodies that seemed to echo unrequited longing.

"*Dodi li,*" they sang and clapped their hands.

"A love song of King Solomon from our Holy Book," Yohevet said.

They danced to the sensuous rhythm of the tambour, to sentimental laments plucked from the melodic oud. Their silver hair ornaments dangled from false braids and swung with the cadence of the music.

The overpowering smell of jasmine water and attar of roses, the smoke from lamps that lit the room, mesmerized Lily. She began to sway with the rhythmic throb of the tambour and the nasal whine of the singers.

"*Dodi li,*" they sang. They were answered with trills and songs from the bride's side of the room.

The music swirled around Lily; the dancers twisted and gyrated. The shrill warbling of ululation rang in her ears.

"*Dodi li,*" Lily sang, "*v'li dodi,*" and clapped her hands. *I am my beloved and my beloved is mine.* Lily's feet moved in time to the music, her shoulders and hips whirled and pivoted. *He feedeth among the lilies.*

The women passed copper dishes from hand to hand, dipping their fingers, wetting their palms, rubbing amber liquid into their hair.

"This is the night of the henna," Yohevet said. "Tonight, we make everyone beautiful, but most of all the bride."

Lily looked down at her own hands, with the bright red polish of yesterday's manicure, and at the women seated cross-legged on the floor, with their red palms and auburn-streaked hair, giggling like little girls as they groomed each other. Different countries, different customs, she thought, and sat on the floor next to Yohevet while the copper pot passed toward her slowly from one woman to another.

What did the woman say? Yohevet is the mother of Musa? "You are the mother of Musa?" Lily said to Yohevet while they waited.

She clicked her tongue against her teeth. "Yohevet."

"You know Abu Musa?"

The woman shrieked. The clapping and trilling stopped and the sound of singing trailed away. Yohevet held the henna dish in the air without moving, her face blank and cold. "Who?" Yohevet spilled henna on Lily's skirt and glared at her.

"Abu Musa. You know him?"

The bathhouse became silent. The women formed a circle around Lily, as if to cut her off from the rest of the room. One by one, they lifted their left hands, their palms red with henna.

"*Hamsa b'aynik,*" one of them said. Five times in your eyes— the curse to avert the evil eye.

A woman pushed her way through the crowd and stood before Lily, her arms across her chest, her nostrils working in anger, her dark eyes burning into Lily's face, a guttural tirade spilling from her, swelling the veins in her neck.

"She say you may not say that name at her daughter's wedding. An evil man. A wicked man. We celebrate for joy, and do not call on the name of a devil." The mother of the bride tossed her head with contempt. "She say you are not welcome here. You will leave this wedding. You will leave this house."

They cleared a path for Lily and she walked slowly to the door, her wet skirt flapping against her knees.

She stood in the shade of the carob and looked back toward the bathhouse. The ground beneath her feet was thick with litter from the tree: fallen leaves, acrid-smelling red blossoms, and rotted pods that were moldy from the dew. After a while, she heard a tentative ululation, and then an answering trill. The singer's voice began to intone a love song. By the third verse, Lily heard the rhythmic click of cymbals and the beat of the tambour drum.

She looked down at the stain on her skirt, leaned back against the tree and waited for Rafi.

TWENTY-ONE

RAFI SWERVED AROUND sun-hardened grooves left by wheels of donkey carts.

Lily pointed to the mountains shimmering in the distance. "That's Mount Gerizim, the holy Samaritan Mountain. The other is Mount Ebel."

The equipment in the back of the station wagon clattered with each rut in the dirt track. Dust billowed behind them.

"So," Rafi said. "You're *persona non grata* in Sebastiya. You and Abu Musa."

"It's nothing to laugh at." They hit a furrow and Lily bounced in the seat.

"About Abu Musa," Rafi said. "I think he tried to seduce the bride. And raped a girl in Ramallah."

"Are you sure?"

"My Arabic isn't all that good. But that's what I think they said. The girl in Ramallah—her brothers killed her."

"For being raped?"

Rafi nodded and gunned the engine. They hit another bump, and Lily held onto the strap over the window.

"Drive carefully. It isn't safe here." She stared at the road in front of them, at the gray stone houses of Nablus that floated on the top of the hill visible between the shifting outlines of the mountains. "The newspaper says police are searching the whole area."

"Patrolling the terror triangle." Rafi said. "Nablus. Tulkarm. Jenin." He dodged another pothole, tilting the car and slanting Lily toward him. She stroked his arm and he grinned at her, reaching for her hand. "Rough roads have compensations."

"You suppose Abu Musa really did that? Raped a girl?" she asked.

"Who knows? I'll find out from my patient."

"He won't tell you."

"I'll be more subtle than you were back there at the wedding. Dissimulation is the key."

"You'll lie?"

"I told you once, I don't always tell the truth." When turned toward her, the car veered. Lily slid against him again.

"I'll miss this when we reach the paved road in Nablus," he said.

"Watch the road," she told him.

They jolted along the rutted track and Lily careened against Rafi, swayed toward the door, and slammed back in the seat. He concentrated on the jagged surface, meandering over the track to avoid dips and troughs, until the car rattled over another gash in the dirt.

They were halfway to Nablus, almost as far as Deir Sharaf, when Lily saw the row of massive stones obstructing the road. "Looks like an ambush!"

Large boulders on either side shut off access to the shoulder. Footprints and telltale gouges—scratched across the road by rocks lugged into place to block their passage—slashed the ground.

Rafi slowed. "You're right."

He stopped the car and threw it into reverse. The station wagon bucked, groaned and stalled.

"Oh, God." Lily said.

"Don't give out now," Rafi muttered to the steering wheel. He patted the knob on top of the gearshift. "You know how to turn over. You've done it before." He let out the clutch slowly. "Get us out of this, and I'll buy you a new horn."

The wagon lurched, gasped, heaved and backed along the track, gathering speed. Rafi stroked the dashboard.

"Good girl," he said as he grasped the gearshift again, and turned the car around.

He turned to Lily "We have to go through Tulkarm."

Lily shook her head. "Tulkarm's too dangerous."

"And this isn't? Bandits hiding behind a roadblock?"

"We don't know what we're getting into there. Nobody's following us. Maybe no one was there."

"They're there, all right. Waiting for the next damn fool to get out of his car to clear the road."

"We don't have anything of value. They can see that."

"Doesn't matter." The steering wheel shimmied in his hand. "They'd kill anyone for two piasters."

The folded hills on either side of them were green with orchards. They drove through rolling countryside where villages dotted the hilltops and stark, gray-white rocks stood like sentinels in fields scarred by goat paths. Stone walls of terraces hugged the steep slopes like steps of a great Olympian stairway.

They hit another bump. Lily bounced. Her head almost hit the roof of the car. "Let's hope we'll make it as far as Tulkarm."

A boy in a striped vest, a turban wound around his head, tended a flock of sheep that moved slowly along the track in a cloud of dust. The boy drove the herd with a long stick while two mangy dogs ran around the animals, snapping at their heels when they strayed.

Rafi careened around them, through a dry ditch at the side of the road, the dogs snarling at the wagon, leaping at the fenders and doors. The boy watched with dark, impassive eyes.

They sped and bumped along the corrugated road, the dogs barking in their wake, until the flock was out of sight.

They were almost as far as Tulkarm when the station wagon sputtered, wallowed and shuddered to a stop.

Rafi sighed and looked at Lily. "Your car has palsy." He got out and kicked the fender. "Bad car."

He sat on the running board, shaking his head. "This car is nothing but a *tarrantah*."

"*Tarrantah?*"

"Means jalopy. The word came into Hebrew from the French by way of Russia."

"How—?"

"When Napoleon invaded Russia, the camp followers came along with the army. Russians would ask the women how old they were, and they would say '*trente ans,*' thirty years. So in Russian it came to mean anything old and worn out."

After a while, he stood, went to the front of the car and pulled open the hood.

"The engine is full of grit. We're stuck."

"What are we going to do?"

"I need something to clean it out. Maybe I can prime it."

Lily went to the back of the wagon to open the tailgate. "There's water in the cooler and gasoline in the jerry can. Will that help?"

"Maybe. Maybe. Give me the gasoline. And that rag we had before."

"Towel."

Lily waited near the verge of the track, feeling the wind change as the afternoon breeze came off the sea. "Hurry up. It's almost four o'clock."

"Not to worry." Rafi's voice resonated under the hood. "We'll make it in time." He lifted his head and wiped his hands. "I almost have it."

Lily paced the side of the road, glancing back at Rafi. He ran his tongue along his upper lip. His forehead wrinkled in concentration. She wandered past a weedless patch of fresh dirt, sunken lower than the surface of the surrounding soil, and felt a draft of cool air blow against her ankles.

"I think this may work," Rafi said, ready to close the hood.

Lily knelt on the ground, passing her hand over the surface of the depression. The cool air was still there, coming from somewhere underground. She stood up, went to the back of the wagon, took out a pickaxe, a shovel, and a roll of string wound around four surveyor's pins and dropped them next to the patch of dirt.

She put her hand close to the ground, felt for the direction of the draft again, used the pointed edge of a mason's trowel to sketch a rectangle around the patch and jammed the surveyor's pins into the corners of the square she had outlined, stretching the string from pin to pin.

"What in hell are you doing?"

Lily reached for the shovel and began clearing away loose dirt. "There's something here."

"What are you talking about?"

"Something's buried here." She knelt down and scraped with the side of the trowel in quick, steady strokes. "The soil is loose. Freshly dug in the last few weeks."

"Leave it alone. It could be a dead body. Or a sick animal."

"It's not here long." She brushed aside a cigarette butt, brown and desiccated from the sun, then picked it up again, rolling it between her fingers. The paper crackled, and the tobacco spilled out. "My guess is two weeks."

She picked up the shovel and began digging. "If it were a dead animal, there would be a smell. Somebody hid something here. In a cave."

"What do you mean, a cave?"

"I can feel cool air coming from a hole under the ground." She stretched out her hand and passed it over the surface. "See for yourself."

Rafi knelt down and spread out his fingers. He looked baffled, wiped his hand and tried again. "What do you expect to find?"

"Pirate treasure, of course. Grab a pick and shovel. Make yourself useful."

He stood up. "We don't have time for this. We won't get back to Jerusalem before the curfew. We can come back tomorrow."

"That'll be too late. We've already left tracks. They'll know whatever it is has been spotted. Dig."

Rafi lifted a shovel out of the back of the wagon and moved some soil halfheartedly. "I think you're crazy."

"Try to stay inside the square marked with the string. And keep the side walls straight."

"Why?"

"Otherwise, it'll collapse. The whole thing will fall in on us."

"Helpful hints from the professional ditch-digger."

Lily worked quickly, filling the shovel and tossing the dirt outside of the square in a rhythmic motion.

Rafi stepped back. "Be careful. You're getting dirt on both of us."

"Shut up and dig."

*　*　*

With both of them digging in the loose soil, it went fast. By the time the long shadows of late afternoon etched the ground and cool breezes came off the ocean, the hole was almost chest-deep.

"Not much further now." Lily leaned down and held out her hand. "You feel the draft?"

Rafi reached toward the bottom of the square. "It's coming from over there."

"Get a whisk broom. And the little ladder."

He tossed the brush he had retrieved from the station wagon into the square, jumped in after it, and propped the ladder against the sidewall. She felt for the draft again, scraping with the trowel, then swept the surface with the whiskbroom.

"There it is," Lily said. "You see the top of the cave?" Lily traced along an edge of stone at the side of the square with her hand. She brushed again and stepped back. "Wooden boxes. Big ones. Crates more than three feet long."

Rafi jumped into the hole and wiped at a box. "Something's printed here. Stenciled on the side." He stepped back and cleared away more dirt. "Holy Moley."

"What?"

"12 *Shutzen*. 98 *Mauser*."

"What's that?"

"German rifles. Probably hidden by the Mufti's men. Precisely what the patrols are hunting for."

Rafi climbed out of the square and went back to the station wagon. He emptied tools and supplies from back of the wagon and dumped them on the ground. "Help me with this."

"What are you doing?"

"Clearing a space for the rifles."

"Who's crazy now?"

"We'll cover them with the tarp from the dining canopy. With the tools on top, no one will know they're there."

"I'll know. What if we're stopped?"

"We can't just leave them."

"It's almost six o'clock," Lily said. "We can't get back to Jerusalem before the curfew."

"We're not going to Jerusalem. We're going to Netanya."

"What's in Netanya?"

"A basement."

Rafi jumped back into the square and cleaned off a crate. He tugged at it, pulling first one side, then the other. "This must weigh a ton."

"You can't do that. It's too heavy."

"If I can get some leverage, I can get it out of the hole." He knelt down and pulled the long wooden box onto his shoulder. When he tried to stand, the weight shifted and slid toward the ground. He grunted and reached down to steady it.

The veins in his neck stood out. "Help me with this, can you?" His voice was strained.

Summoning all the strength she could, Lily pushed at the side of the crate to balance it on Rafi's shoulder.

"Why am I doing this?" she said. "You'll get us both in trouble."

Rafi went up the ladder one rung at a time. "Oh, God. This'll break my back."

He carried the load to the station wagon, dropped it behind the back seat with a clang and leaned against the tailgate, grunting and struggling for breath.

"My, you're strong," Lily said, laughing.

"Oh, stuff it." He tugged at the crate and wedged it into the space behind the seat. "We can't fit more than one box in here. We have to come back tomorrow with a truck."

"What do you mean, 'we'? This is the second time you got me mixed up in something like this. Third strike, you're out."

A cloud of dust approached from one of the hilltop villages, and as it came nearer, Lily made out a mule-driven cart, driving toward them along the sinuous path that led back and forth along the hill from the village to the road.

"Hurry up. Someone's coming," Lily said.

Rafi jumped back into the hole and picked up the whisk-broom again. "A desperado in a donkey cart?"

"He could be one of the Mufti's men. For God's sake, what are you doing?"

"Looking for ammo." He kept brushing. "Here it is." He tugged at a carton. "500 *Einsteckmagazin*; 8 mm."

"Hurry," Lily said.

The cart swerved back and forth along the path to the road as it lumbered down the hill toward them.

"We'll make it before he gets here." Rafi jammed the ammo into a space in the back of the car beside the crate of rifles and covered both with the tarp of the dining canopy, then piled the digging equipment on top and slammed the tailgate shut.

"There. No one can tell." He climbed back into the car. "Let's go."

The mule cart was less than fifteen feet above them. They could see the angry scowl of the *fellah* as he pulled the mule around another turn in the path. Rafi turned on the ignition, carefully let out the choke. The motor rocked. The car bucked and trembled and staggered forward. The mule brayed in fear. It backed against the cart, tumbling cart and driver onto the terrace.

"I told you we'd make it." Rafi patted the trembling steering wheel affectionately. "We'll be in Netanya by six thirty."

"The curfew is at six. We'll be stopped."

"We'll burn that bridge if we get to it."

Lily could see the *fellah* in the rear view mirror, running down the road after them.

"Where are we going in Netanya?"

"Leora's house. Leora and Gadi."

"Who are they?"

"You met Gadi. In the taxi to Jerusalem. When you were on your way to the opening of the Rockefeller."

"That time the guns were Lugers."

"You did this yourself. You're the one who found the cache."

"You're not going to get me embroiled in this."

"You're already involved."

"Why are you doing it?"

"Let's just say I am my brother's keeper."

"That's no excuse. You'll get us both in trouble."

He turned to face her. "We can fight the Nazis here, now, or later on the streets of Chicago. Which do you prefer?"

"People who feel that way go to Spain and join the International Brigade. Just send some tinfoil and scrap metal to the Loyalists."

He shifted gears and swerved around a rut in the road. "When I was a child, my mother kept a little tin box in the house for pennies to buy land from the Turks in Palestine. One evening— I was only about eight or nine—Louis Brandeis came to Chicago to give a speech. He had just been appointed to the Supreme Court. He came to dinner at our house."

Rafi paused. His eyes clouded as he evoked the memory. "My aunt, Avi's mother, came down from Milwaukee with her friend and they talked all evening, about his struggle to get working women the minimum wage, about the Balfour Declaration. I didn't understand what they talked about. I fell asleep at the table and someone carried me to bed."

"But you remembered it all."

Rafi nodded. "I'll never forget that night, everything about it. Crumbs and poppy-seeds scattered on the plates; seltzer bottles; cut-glass goblets; reflections from the chandelier, like little rainbows on the white tablecloth; a bowl of green gage plums that made my mouth pucker."

"What happened?"

"As soon as the war ended, my aunt came here. The British had just taken over. My aunt and uncle joined a kibbutz. They had tough times. She was pregnant with Avi. They had nothing, lived in a mud hut while they built the kibbutz with their own hands, the children's house first."

"And her friend from Milwaukee?"

"Golda? She followed a few years later. Got involved in politics, in this committee and that. The right to be hired as a fruit picker, minimum wage, all the things that she and Brandeis talked about that night. I never met a woman with such determination and energy. She's like a steam-roller."

"And now you smuggle arms on your summer vacation. What are you going to do with the rifles?"

"Leora and Gadi have a root cellar."

"They live in a kibbutz?"

"They have an orange grove. On a bluff overlooking the sea. With a little truck garden."

"And you'll hide the guns in the cellar."

"A root cellar in the chicken house."

"Chicken soup with a vengeance."

"Why not? Chicken soup is the universal panacea." Rafi turned to her and smiled and they hit another bump.

"Watch the road," she said.

*　*　*

An armored car blocked the road ahead of them. A soldier in a red beret leaned against it, waiting.

"Oh damn," Lily said. "A British patrol."

As they came closer, the soldier moved to the center of the road and signaled for them to stop.

"See if your blond hair can get us through this one," Rafi said.

TWENTY-TWO

LILY SMOOTHED HER DRESS, wiped her face and rolled the window down as they pulled up to the barrier.

"Officer," she said, as breathlessly as she could, "I'm so glad we found you." She smiled, took a breath, and went on sounding agitated, her tone pitched high and tremulous. "Three men. Back there," she waved vaguely in the direction of the road. "They buried some boxes." She held out her arms like a fisherman describing the one that got away. "Big boxes. In a cave, near Tulkarm."

The soldier looked first at Lily, then at Rafi, and glanced at the equipment in the back of the wagon.

Rafi leaned forward. "Boxes maybe three feet long. They looked heavy."

Lily noticed Rafi's soil-smeared shirt and her own dirt covered arms. "We're doing an archaeological survey. For the Department of Antiquities. We put in test trenches near Atara. No luck." Her voice rose half an octave and she spoke more rapidly. "We were coming home. That's when we discovered them."

"Madam," the Englishman said.

"They ran back to the village when they saw us."

"Madam," he said again.

Lily pointed to the road behind her and kept talking. "Near Nur-e-Shems, or Danibeh." Her voice shook and increased in tempo. "We thought it was a funeral. But it wasn't."

"Please, madam," the soldier said, "calm down."

"I'm all right." She ran her fingers through her hair and looked at her hands. "My. I'm covered with dust." She turned to Rafi. "What did the writing on the side of the boxes say?"

"Mausers. They were burying Mausers. It looked like an arms cache."

"You saw this?" the soldier said.

Rafi nodded. "If we hurry, we can get back there before they get away."

"How many men were there?"

"Three or four," Rafi said. "At least a dozen boxes. As long as rifles."

"Can you show me where this is?"

"I'll take my wife home and meet you back here." Rafi said. "There may be trouble. No place for a lady."

"Right. We'll need reinforcements," the Englishman said. "Meet me at the police post in Netanya. We'll take an armored car and a couple of supernumeraries. Can you handle firearms?"

"We have to get back there before they move the stuff again."

"Right."

"I'll hurry," Rafi said. "They may get away." And he started the wagon and drove in the direction of Netanya.

"Your wife?" Lily said when they were back on the road.

"Why not? We make a good team."

"Is this a proposal?"

"It could be."

"You're married to Ora. The girl with the giggle."

"Only on Tuesdays and Thursdays."

The road was smoother now, and they sped along the macadam. "I'll drop you off at Leora and Gadi's. Tell them to put the Mausers and ammo with the rest of the weapons in the root cellar. Under the onions and potatoes."

"Where do they get the other weapons?"

"From friends. Gadi has a shop in Netanya. A linen shop. He goes to Belgium twice a year to buy tablecloths and lace."

"He must have a good business."

"He goes mostly to see friends. They give him gifts."

"Chocolates?"

"Chocolate gives him hives. So they send other things. Special delivery."

"To the beach? At night?"

Rafi nodded.

"What about Ora?" Lily asked. "Does she go along?"

"She lives in Hedera."

Lily had been there once. It was another small, isolated beach town, north of Netanya. "She has a linen shop too?"

"A gift shop. Delft. Bohemian glass."

"And her friends send her gifts from Holland and Czechoslovakia?"

"Not for much longer. She'll close the shop after Hitler takes over Bohemia."

"Then it will be the Mufti's turn to shop for cut glass."

"Exactly."

"You won't be able to go back tomorrow and get the rest of the guns after all," Lily said.

Rafi reached for her hand. "If we get back to Tulkarm in time, the Mufti's men won't be able to use them, either."

The road leading into Netanya was smooth and paved; close to town, the air lifted and wafted toward them with the soft tang of the sea. They passed the police post, stark and rigid as a prison, at the edge of town and drove down the main street of the little resort.

Couples strolled along a promenade or rode in horse-drawn carriages that clop-clopped gently along a broad avenue. Roses blossomed in the center divider and bright flowers bloomed on either side of the street—beneath the trees, in front of the shops, along the walks of *pensiones* with broad porches where people sat drinking tea.

Rafi pulled the car off the road into an orange grove and bumped along in tall weeds toward a white stucco house on a bluff. Faded green paint flaked from the window frames and a wooden door. Two bicycles rested against the side of the building.

He went toward the house and Lily followed. A woman in a flowered cotton dress answered Rafi's knock. Her face, her arms, her neck were covered with freckles. A single, long, ginger-colored braid reached halfway down her back.

"Gadi here?" Rafi said.

"In the orange grove."

"Tell him to empty the station wagon and park it out of sight, in the back. I have to get to the police post as quickly as possible. I'll borrow a bicycle. Lily will fill you in on the details."

He started down the road and turned back again. "I forgot," he said, got off the bicycle, leaned over and kissed Lily on the forehead. "I'll be back soon."

"You're Lily?" Leora said after he rode away.

"And you're Leora."

"Rafi talks about you all the time."

Lily felt herself blushing. "Good things, I hope."

Leora smiled and looked out at the grove toward the station wagon. "What's going on?"

Lily told her about the cave filled with German guns, about the boxes with rifles and ammo in the back of the station wagon, about the encounter with the British patrol. "Rafi said to hide the rifles in the root cellar. The Brits don't know we have these. Rafi is leading a police patrol back to Tulkarm to recover the cache, maybe catch the gang with the guns."

Leora listened carefully, nodding and smiling.

"I like you," Leora told Lily when she came back from speaking with Gadi. "You'll be good for Rafi."

Everyone's a matchmaker, Lily thought.

Leora stepped back and examined Lily. "You look a mess," she said. "Wait here."

She returned with a bucket, a towel and two bars of soap. "This one's for your clothes." She held out a chunk of white soap. "And this one," she brought the wrapped bar up her nose and savored the aroma, "is for you." A whiff of jasmine wafted from the soap.

A dark red silk robe smelling faintly of lavender and mothballs was draped over her arm. "You can wear this while your clothes dry."

"It's beautiful," Lily ran her fingers along the smooth surface of the robe. The silk was as smooth as cream. "Are you sure?"

"Gadi brought it back from Europe. It's the wrong color for me. Makes me look like a spotted hen." She handed Lily the bucket. "The shower is down that hall, on the right."

*   *   *

Lily stood in the hot shower, soaped the dirty clothes as she peeled them off, scrubbing one piece at a time, dropping it in the bucket filling with water and stomping on it until she thought it was clean.

She unwrapped the bar of perfumed soap that Leora had given her and rubbed it back and forth against the sponge, releasing the sweet scent of jasmine. She squeezed the sponge. Bubbles spurted out, glistening on her arms and breast and clinging to her skin with milky softness. She slicked it gently against her shoulder, humming to herself, remembering Rafi's fingers reaching out to stroke the curve of her neck.

*　*　*

In the kitchen, Leora was cutting cucumbers.

"Can I help?" Lily asked.

"All done. We'll have supper after Rafi gets back." She tilted her head and looked at Lily. "That looks good on you."

Lily lifted the bucket of wet clothes. "Where can I hang these?"

"The wash line is just past the rose garden, near the stairs to the beach."

Lily went through the house to the garden and felt the faint evening breeze caress her skin. It carried the scent of roses and the sea. Off to the left in the orange grove, Gadi was washing the station wagon. He paused to look at her walking among the roses, waved and turned back to the car.

Lily hung the clothes on the line at the far end of the garden. Beyond the road, the sky over the hills was already darkening. She walked around the rose beds, bending down to breathe in their perfume or to stroke velvet petals of a long bud.

She found steps that led down to an isolated cove, hidden from the garden, where dune grass bent and wavered in the evening breeze and the golden sun, low on the horizon, dappled the sea.

In the cove, she walked barefoot along the beach, the silk of the robe caressing her like a second skin. Wet sand crunched under her steps, and she dug into it when the surf lapped against her feet, squeezing the slurry of sand and water between her toes.

She paused at tide pools to watch the edge of the sea roil among the rocks; watch dentalium and cowrie tumble, water-washed in the foam; watch sand crabs wink at the rim of tiny breakers and sea anemones waver and undulate in the current.

She waited impatiently for Rafi to come back, to hear what happened at Tulkarm, listening for the tenderness of his voice.

She watched the sea inch up the beach, the cool water licking at her toes, advancing and receding, each time a little higher on the strand. She stood at the edge of the water, until she became a creature of the tide, feeling it billow back and forth, moving against the arch of her foot, caressing her ankles. She felt the sea retreat, pulling grains of sand back to the surf from under the soles of her feet.

She glanced back at the bluff. Rafi appeared at the top of the stairs. He came down the steps toward the beach, and she went to meet him, to ask what happened. "Did they . . ."

He stroked the side of her cheek, and she leaned into the fold of his arm.

"It went without a hitch," he said.

She felt his hands trace her neck, felt the silken robe slip from her shoulders, felt it fall from her arms onto the ground, felt his hand along her back, felt the texture of his chest and shoulders, the curve of his neck. He kissed her cheek, her chin, her eyelids, the curve of her neck, and she felt the flow of skin against skin, smooth as water rippling in the wind. She leaned into the taste of him, the smell of him, while the sea pounded in her ears, and they clung together on the beach, bathed in the golden sunset, while the night overtook the sky.

TWENTY-THREE

LILY WATCHED RAFI'S HANDS at supper, imagining them stroking her shoulders, reaching along the curve of her back. "We got there just as they were moving the guns." She watched his lips as he talked about the police expedition to Tulkarm. "Police arrested four men. They'll be sentenced to hang. Tomorrow the military command will bulldoze their houses. That's standard punishment for terrorists."

He has a beautiful mouth, his lips flexible and strong—and the line of his jaw—

"They'll be released," she heard Gadi say. "There's always some excuse to free those brigands—not enough evidence, they were burying a dead donkey—anything will do."

She watched Rafi butter a roll. "They claimed that they were digging up the arms to turn them in to the British authorities. A *fellah* told the police that I took a box of rifles, that I was the one who had buried the guns." He paused. "Please pass the cheese."

Lily's fingers lingered on his forearm when she handed him the plate. "The one who chased us?"

Rafi nodded.

"You think the Brits will bulldoze the Strauss Hospital?"

"Of course," Rafi said. "And the American School. They're onto us."

"Oh stuff it," Lily said.

Gadi speared a slice of tomato with his fork and waved it in the air. "You're in the clear. No one in the English-speaking community smuggles arms. Everyone knows that."

"And a good thing too," Lily said.

* * *

In the morning, Rafi took the station wagon to a garage in town. Lily and Leora had brought their coffee out to the bluff, where Lily sat on a bench overlooking the sea, her skirt spread around her, a smile on her face.

Children's voices, high pitched and laughing, drifted up from the cove. Lily's newly washed clothes were crisp and bright and smelled of sunshine and fresh air. She felt the sun brighten her cheeks, felt its warmth on the soft down of her arms, and she tilted her head back, throwing out her arms to embrace it all. Dawn had washed the world and the morning danced under a cloudless sky.

* * *

Lily and Rafi arrived at Chancellors Road in Jerusalem in late afternoon, in time for his shift at the hospital. She drove to the American School through the narrow lanes behind Mea Shearim. Bearded men in black suits pressed against buildings waiting for Lily to pass. Tired housewives lumbered along the pavement.

Boys with long side-locks and milky-white skin, miniature adults in black cloaks, somberly kicked a soccer ball. The ball hit the station wagon with a thump. The boys stopped the game, waiting silently for the station wagon to pass as it bumped over the cobbles. The side-curls gave the boys a look of sadness, like basset hounds.

A woman blocked the way. Lily sounded the horn. The woman, a black scarf tied over her shaven head, her shoulders drooping from sacks of groceries, turned around, glared at Lily and continued trudging down the middle of the road.

Lily parked the wagon in the back of the garden and ran up the steps to the portico. Lady Fendley sat at the desk in the office and called to Lily as soon as the door opened. "You were gone a long time for just a wedding." It sounded like an accusation. "There are all sorts of messages for you."

"The car broke down."

"You should have called." Lady Fendley put down the pen and drew in a breath. "In these times!" She shook her head and wagged her finger—as Lily's mother had done when Lily had come home late—then ticked off messages one by one. "Kate wants you to bring the wagon back down to Kharub." She turned down her index finger. "Someone named Jamal said he has to-morrow off and can go with you to Beit Jibrin. You going there? It's morbid." She was up to her ring finger. "And your friend Avi called. Something about an amphoriskos."

"I'm sorry. Next time I'll call." Lily started up the stairs. "What about the amphoriskos?"

"And Eliot came by," Lady Fendley called after Lily. "He was looking for the site report from Tell Abu Hawam. It wasn't at your desk. He said you took it upstairs. I had to get the extra key so that he could look on your desk."

"In my room?"

"You shouldn't take books upstairs unless you leave a note on the shelf," Lady Fendley said.

"But I—Never mind," Lily said and hurried up the stairs to unlock her door.

The desk was in order, but her closet door stood open. The coverlet lay smoothly over the foot of the bed. Lily reached under the mattress where she had hidden the journal and pulled it out.

The drawings of plans and sections fell, loose, onto the floor. Lily remembered folding them carefully into the pocket at the back of the journal before she slid it under the mattress. The list of sites she had forged in Eastbourne's handwriting was gone.

She unscrewed the back panel of the radio. The coordinates she had copied were still there.

Lily put the maps back in the folder and spread the plans on the desk. This time she focused on the sheet with drawings of small, round semi-subterranean structures with slotted, high windows and thick walls; plans of larger, square edifices with even thicker walls, casemates and turrets, similar in plan to ancient fortresses; and cross-sections of wide concrete culverts. A detailed illustration of a turret included plans for a revolving steel cupola, that could disappear and be raised or lowered by a lever and counterweight.

Lady Fendley's voice called from the corridor. "Are you in there, Lily?" She knocked. "Telephone for you. Your friend Avi."

Lily folded the map and plans, put them in the pocket of the journal, placed it in the desk drawer and headed for the phone in the upstairs hall.

Avi's voice was almost drowned out by the rattle of dishes and the sound of running water in the background. "I'm in the kitchen," he shouted, "and can't hear very well. You have to yell." He told her he had heard that someone brought a blue glass amphoriskos to an antiquities dealer in Tel Aviv.

"I have to bring the wagon back to Kharub tomorrow," Lily said.

"I could meet you at the tel tomorrow afternoon, say four-thirty. We could drive up to Jerusalem together, go to Tel Aviv the next morning early."

"Great. See you tomorrow," Lily said. She put the telephone back on the table, then picked it up again. "Thanks," she shouted into the mouthpiece and hung up.

She went back to her room to find Jamal's number at the Austrian Hospice, and left a message for him to meet her at Damascus gate the next morning at nine a.m.

*   *   *

Jamal was waiting for Lily in the morning. He ran across the road from Damascus Gate in the face of traffic, and climbed into the seat next to her in the station wagon.

The road south to Bethlehem curved along the crest of the ridge. They drove through the German Colony with its staid Bavarian villas trimmed with green shutters and pots of red geraniums. They passed the stone houses of Bakaa with their flat roofs and wide, vaulted porches; passed row on row of long stucco buildings at Allenby Barracks.

Jamal slumped in his seat, chewing on the cuticle of his thumbnail, his eyes large and staring at the dash.

"What's wrong?" Lily asked.

"I don't like this. I don't feel comfortable going back there. Maybe we should turn around and drive back to Jerusalem."

The road crossed through the Judean Hills, covered with stone terraces, green with olive trees and grapevines. An ancient cinder-cone from a long dead volcano stood out against the golden hills of the Judean desert that cradled the blue mist of the Dead Sea.

"I told Kate I would bring the station wagon down today," Lily said.

"How will you get back?"

"Avi will drive me."

"Avi again," he said, and examined his thumb, running a finger along the edge of his nail.

"Avi's a nice boy."

Ahead of them, Lily saw the church steeples and spires of Bethlehem. Just before they reached the kibbutz of Ramat Rahel, they came to a pillbox. Narrow slots below the conical roof squinted at them like eyes in an angry mask. It looks like the circular structures in the drawings in Eastbourne's journal, Lily realized with a jolt. Why would Eastbourne have plans of modern military installations?

Why not? Yigael Sukenik, son of the chair of the Department of Archaeology at Hebrew University, was researching warfare in Biblical times and doing a survey of ancient Judean fortresses. "If we ever have an ancient war," Sir William had once said of him, "Yigael will make a perfect general."

Lily waved her hand in the direction of a kibbutz. A stone wall enclosed a water tower, some barracks-like buildings, and weed-covered knolls. "That's Ramat Rahel," Lily said. "Those mounds are probably the remains of a Judean fortress from over twenty-seven hundred years ago."

"Canaanites were here before that."

"Canaanites?"

"My ancestors."

"I thought you were a Philistine."

"Both. Canaanite and Philistine. This is the home of my ancestors. That's why it's called Palestine. Others come and go, like guests. Brits, Turks, Romans, Jews. But we were always here. And we will be here forever."

"So you agree with the Mufti?"

Jamal clicked his tongue against his teeth and gave a quick

shake of the head to indicate 'no.' "I understand him," Jamal said. "I don't agree with him. I don't like violence."

"You back his opponent, Khalidi?"

He clicked his tongue again in a gesture of denial. "Palestinians have a hundred factions, each with a different point of view. It's all a matter of perspective."

"That's what Avi says."

"Avi again." He went back to biting the edge of his finger.

Lily had already passed Rachel's Tomb near the entrance to Bethlehem and Shepherd's Field with its terraced olive groves. She drove through the narrow streets of Bethlehem.

"It seems to me," Lily said, "that the Mufti has caused economic disaster for Palestinian Arabs. His men kill anyone who won't go along with his dictates—farmers who sell land, merchants who don't join the strike."

"He says if we don't act together, we'll lose the land."

"You agree?"

Jamal sat rigidly in his seat, absorbed in private thoughts. He stared straight ahead, toward the Bethlehem market. Franciscan monks in brown habits carried baskets filled with fruit. Lily glanced at Jamal. His cheeks were suffused with an angry glow, the wings of his nostrils dilated.

A fly came in through the open window next to Jamal, buzzed around his head, and flew out the back window.

"Haven't you ever wondered what a fly sees with all those lenses in its compound eye?" Jamal asked. "Humans have two eyes, and see in three dimensions. The fly sees a hundred pictures. What does he see that you and I can never grasp? Can he understand more than we do?"

Greek Orthodox priests with black robes and rigid hats like crowns draped with cloth passed in front of them.

"Where are the tourists?" Lily asked.

"Who?" He looked around, at coffeehouses where old Arab men played shesh-besh and smoked; at laden donkeys struggling along the cobbles. "Too early in the day."

They drove through the empty expanse of Manger Square. Souvenir shops surrounded the Church of the Nativity, with its low entrance door. Proprietors of the shops sat in arched doorways on low stools, arms crossed across their chests, smoking hookahs, sipping coffee, waiting for customers to buy their mother of pearl rosaries and olivewood camels. They called out, "Welcome, welcome," to Lily as the station wagon crawled along.

"I always get lost here," Lily said.

"Keep going," Jamal told her. "Hebron is straight ahead."

He was silent as they drove on. Hill villages with stone houses and flat roofs surrounded by rough fieldstone walls looked down on the road. On either side of them fields were green with vines and fig trees; men and boys winnowed wheat with pitchforks; women sifted flour in flat baskets, donkeys pulled large rolling stones to crush olives.

Every man under his vine and fig tree, Lily thought.

"I don't like the Mufti," Jamal said after a while. "Violence in the name of patriotism is still violence. I think he's despotic, maybe a little corrupt. He took money from the Waqf—the widows and orphans fund—to buy arms."

"Why do people put up with him?"

"You know the Bible?" Jamal asked.

"I use it sometimes in my research. For historical references."

"You know the part in Deuteronomy where Moses promises that in Canaan, Israelites will have cities that they didn't build, cisterns they didn't dig, vineyards and orchards that they didn't plant?"

"I don't recall exactly."

"Take my word for it. It's there. That's what Palestinians fear the most. To be exiles in their own land, laborers in their own groves."

"But Jews don't steal the land. They buy it."

"That's why the Mufti doesn't let people sell."

They passed the burned-out houses of the Jewish settlements north of Hebron. Jamal turned in his seat to look back at them. "The Mufti's men killed my uncle. There's blood between us."

"Your uncle sold land?"

"Near 'En Kerem."

"To Jewish settlers?"

"It was his to sell."

The road went through Hebron, where Abraham built his altar and buried his family. "According to legend," Jamal said, "the stones of the Cave of Machpelah, Haram al-Khalil, were laid by djinns under orders from Solomon. You believe it?"

"I believe they were laid by Herod, with the help of taxes and enforced labor."

"Like your friend Avi says, it's all a matter of perspective." Jamal looked down at his hands and picked at his fingers. "I remember a Bedouin workman at the tel who had tuberculosis. I tried to get him to the hospital. He insisted that his cough came from an evil djinn, commanded by one of his enemies. I tried to explain about bacillus in his lungs. He said I was naïve and gullible."

"Oh?"

"He asked if I believed the story that at the North Pole, the sun didn't set in the middle of summer and didn't rise in the middle of winter."

"Yes?"

"He said I was foolish to believe it. Because people who live at the North Pole couldn't celebrate Ramadan, and Allah would never permit it."

"Does your Bedouin observe Ramadan even in summer in the desert?"

Jamal nodded. "Even on the hottest days of July, he doesn't eat or drink water from dawn to dusk for the entire month. But he smokes cigarettes."

"Isn't that allowed?"

"The Arabic word for smoking is the same as that for drinking. When he smokes, he hides in his tent, so Allah cannot see him."

Lily grinned. "Surely Allah has more eyes than a fly. Even a fly has a hundred eyes. You said so yourself."

They continued down the road, past the souk.

"Keep going, keep going," Jamal said.

They drove past glass factories with open-air furnaces and glass blowers forming bowls and vases and lamps in jewel-like colors, past shops festooned with glass bracelets and beads.

"Turn to the right there, after that house." Jamal pointed to a stone building just ahead. "The road's paved with gravel for a while and then turns into a dirt track."

The track narrowed after about a hundred yards. Lily drove slowly over the rutted road, her hands tight on the steering wheel.

Jamal fidgeted in his seat. After about twenty minutes he said, "We're coming up on it soon." A little later, he pointed toward a pair of boulders on the side of the track. "They were hiding behind those rocks. Three of them. We came up from the other side. We were attacked just beyond there."

Lily turned off the engine and got out of the car. Multiple tire tracks and footprints scarred the ground. The stench of a dead animal hung in the air. She shuddered.

Jamal walked past the boulders. "They jumped out from behind that rock and told us to halt. They leveled their rifles at him and shot him point blank."

"The newspaper report said that he was shot with a revolver."

He shook his head. "They used rifles. Two were armed. I don't know about the third—he hung back. I told that to the police." Jamal looked at his watch. "I don't have much time."

Lily examined the ground, trying to imagine Eastbourne facing his murderers. Was he frightened? Was he defiant? "Exactly where did you stop?"

He walked a few paces in the direction of Beit Jibrin. "Right about here. They ordered Eastbourne out of the car and told me to drive on to Hebron. I heard the shots as I drove away. There's a terrible odor here."

"Did you see them shoot him?"

"I looked back. He was stumbling along the track, and then they shot him again."

Lily felt a sudden surge of anger toward Jamal. "Why didn't you go back?"

"I was only one person and they had guns." He shifted uncomfortably, looked at his watch again. "I'm on call tonight."

Lily searched the ground carefully. It showed evidence of heavy traffic—footprints that overlay one another, wheel marks from carts and lorry tires. At a point about five yards further on, there was a jumble of marks from sandals, boots, and at least three different pairs of shoes near a dark stain on the ground. Eastbourne's blood, Lily thought. One set of footprints near the stain meandered unsteadily. Eastbourne's steps.

Lily wandered over the ground, expanding her inspection of the area, searching for signs of the amphoriskos. As she neared the boulder, the smell became overwhelming. "There's a dead animal here."

"I have to leave. It's just garbage. Someone probably picnicked here."

Lily walked back toward the rock. The smell was stronger now. The freshly dug, uneven surface of the ground was pocked with small rodent holes and animal tracks. Lily bent down to look at a small bone lying loose on the ground. The odor, un-pleasant and almost overwhelming, triggered an atavistic fear and revulsion. She picked up the bone. The sinews were almost dry and still attached. The bone was still fresh, scarred with small parallel scratches where rats had gnawed it.

Jamal held a handkerchief to his face. "It's a chicken bone."

But it wasn't and Jamal knew it, Lily thought.

"Left over from a picnic," he said.

"This is human bone." He knows that. "A metatarsal. Some-one was buried here. Recently. We have to report it."

Jamal looked at his watch again. "There's a police post about five minutes further on at Beit Jibrin. I don't have time to go with you." He walked back to the car for his bag. "You go ahead. I'll find a ride." He started walking up the track toward Hebron.

"But you—"

"I'll get someone in the village to take me to Hebron so I can catch a bus. Don't worry. I speak the language."

Lily hesitated.

Jamal waved "You'll be all right. It's not far."

Only five minutes, she thought. Closer than Hebron.

She got in the car and started toward Beit Jibrin.

TWENTY-FOUR

THE RANK SMELL OF DEATH stayed in her nostrils as Lily shifted the car into first gear. She felt the tires grab the dusty surface of the track. Distracted, she drove automatically, bumping over furrows and troughs.

Her mind churned with questions about the burial behind the rock. What connection did it have to Eastbourne's murder? Why was Jamal so anxious to get away?

The ruins of the Crusader Church of St. Anne on the hill above Beit Jibrin loomed in front of her. With Beit Jibrin so close, why did Jamal drive to Hebron the day Eastbourne was killed? Hebron was more than twenty minutes away.

Bandits. Were they really bandits? Lily wondered if Jamal could have saved Eastbourne if he had tried, could have skirted back? Eastbourne still may have been alive when he left. Maybe not. Two shots, Jamal had said.

* * *

The police post turned out to be a small concrete building. A Union Jack flapped from a pole in front. Inside, a constable sat at a desk, a cup of tea next to his elbow.

"Can I help you, miss?" He looked up at Lily from the book he was reading and smiled as if they were old friends. "Why, it's the lady archaeologist."

Lily peered at his sandy hair and ruddy face, trying to recall if she had seen him before.

"Remember me?" he asked.

It was no use. All ruddy-faced Englishmen look alike. "Of course I do," Lily said.

"At the road block? The day you drove up to Jerusalem for the opening of the Rockefeller?"

"Oh." The day she met Rafi. "Of course. The man from Colchester. Interested in Roman ruins."

He spread the book, spine up, on the desk and gave her an encouraging smile. "What can I do for you today, luv?"

"I found a dead body."

"Oh?"

"On the Beit Jibrin track. Buried behind a rock, near where Eastbourne was killed."

"You're quite sure, now?"

Lily nodded. "In a shallow grave."

"If it is buried, like you say, how do you know—?"

"Animals burrowed into it and brought bone up to the surface. Human bone."

"What makes you think it's human?"

"I know, that's all."

"I see. Archaeologists know those things." He took a sip from the cup. "And now you want to dig it up?"

"It's not an archaeological site. Not a regular grave either. Too shallow, too recent."

"You suspect foul play?"

Lily nodded again.

"And you want us to investigate?"

"Yes."

"We have our hands full as it is without going out to look for trouble." He sat down at the desk and reached for the book. "Digging up every corpse in Palestine."

He seems to have time today, Lily thought. She twisted her head to read the book title. "What are you reading?"

"Just a novel. A detective novel by Margaret Sotheby."

Lily read the title out loud. "*The Body from Baghdad*. Dame Margaret is a friend of mine, you know."

"Of course she is, luv. And now you think you found a body. Like the archaeologist in the book."

"It's not like that at all. The body was hidden behind a rock, covered with dirt."

He closed the book this time and pushed back the chair. "All right. It's a dull morning. Suppose you take me there, luv."

Lily thought of the smell, the rat-gnawed metatarsal, and the dark stain left by Eastbourne's blood on the dusty track. "I can't go back to that place."

"Isn't that what archaeologists do? Dig up dead bodies?"

"I don't deal with the wet dead."

"Wet dead?"

"Fresh cadavers. I only work on skeletons at least five hundred years old—clean and dry. Just skeletons."

"Same thing, luv. A body is a body."

"No, it's not. A skeleton is data. But a dead body is—"

"Carrion?"

"Exactly. I have an appointment at Tel al-Kharub."

"That's where you dig?"

"I did. We're closing down the excavation."

"You worked with Eastbourne?"

"Yes."

He stood up again. This time, the amused smile was gone. "My sympathies, ma'am." He looked at Lily speculatively.

"Were you one of the investigating police?" she asked.

"I handled the team of bloodhounds. We tracked a scent as far as Kharass. Turned out to be a false trail." He looked away for a moment. "Where did you say this body is?"

"Near where Eastbourne was killed. You can't miss it. Just follow your nose, officer."

"Meriman's the name. Sergeant Meriman." He sat down at the desk, opened a drawer and brought out a pad and pen. "I have to write out a report, ma'am. Name?"

"Lily Sampson."

"Address?"

"American School in Jerusalem. 26 Salah-edh-Din Street."

"You have a telephone?"

"One three one."

"Location of the disturbance?" he said, looking up. "Beit Jibrin track, behind a rock." His pen scratched along the page. He scanned his watch. "Eleven-thirty." He stopped writing and read the paper over. "That's all for now."

"I can go now, officer?"

He smiled at Lily. "You'll still have to come back. If we find anything, you'll be a witness. Have to make a statement."

Lily moved toward the door. "This afternoon. In about an hour and a half." She hurried to the door and waved at him over her shoulder. "See you later."

* * *

Where the camp had been, the hill was bare, the earth scarred with tire tracks, postholes from vanished tents, and old foot-prints. Nothing grew on the hard-packed ground, not even weeds. The corrugated tin walls of the dig house kitchen remained. That too was being dismantled, the roof already gone.

Kate stood next to a hired lorry, directing Bedouin workmen who were stacking boxes on the flat bed of the truck. "Cartons with blue labels go on that side," she said, gesturing to the right. "Orange labels on this." Her voice was authoritative.

Nothing about Kate was the same. Even her posture had changed, the apologetic droop of her shoulders gone. She seemed taller. I never realized how much she shrank in Eastbourne's shadow, Lily thought.

Kate paused when Lily drove up. "You brought the wagon." She smiled at Lily. "I'll miss working here." She looked around as if she still saw the absent camp, the dining tent and the pottery shed.

"It looks denuded," Lily said. "Like a man with too close a haircut."

"So sad." Kate gestured with a nod of her head toward the ghostly corrugated walls. "Park over there, behind what's left of the dig house."

Kate signaled to a workman. "Be careful with that. Don't stack the cartons more than two deep." She turned back to Lily. "We'll be finished packing tomorrow. Help me check the inventory of boxes. The registry is on the front bench of the lorry, passenger side."

Kate picked up a clipboard from the top of a stack of boxes and climbed into the truck bed. "How will you get back to Jerusalem?" she asked Lily.

"Avi will meet me here this afternoon. About four."

"We'll be done long before that." Kate pointed to the area next to the dig house. "I put aside two more boxes of material from the tombs for you. Over there, next to the dig house. When you finish your dissertation, ship the whole lot to me at the Institute of Archaeology, University of London."

In a little more than an hour, they finished the inventory of boxes stacked in the truck. There was a rhythm and satisfying comfort in the mindless busy work, Kate calling out numbers of artifacts from labels on the side of the cartons, Lily checking them off in the registry.

"That's it for today," Kate said and slapped her hands together in a gesture of finality. "*Helas. Basta*. Beacon Pharmaceutical will be here in the morning for the lorry and the wagon." She climbed down from the truck bed. "You'll come to the house for tea?"

"I have to go back to the police post at Beit Jibrin," Lily said.

Kate leaned forward. Her hand clutched Lily's arm. "They found the killers?"

"It's not about Eastbourne. I found a body."

"What kind of body?"

"I don't know. They're recovering it now. I have to go back to give a statement."

"Better drive the wagon to Beit Jibrin. No other way to get there. Bring it back and leave the keys under the seat."

"Will all this be safe—the cars, the material in the boxes? It won't be stolen?"

"Thieves aren't interested in sherds and scraps. Most of the whole pots were shipped to the Rockefeller. I gave the foreman of the Bedouin a few pounds to guard all this." She indicated the camp, the tel, the boxes with a sweep of her arm. "It's all safe, such as it is," she said. "They'll keep an eye out for Abu Musa." She paused. "Some things are gone. Like the amphoriskos. You found it yet?"

Lily shook her head and clicked her tongue against the roof of her mouth like an Arab. "I heard a rumor that someone sold it to an antiquities dealer in Tel Aviv. I'll check it out tomorrow."

Kate reached for Lily's hand. "This is goodbye for now, then. Little Geoff and I are going up to the British School Thursday evening and sailing for England Friday morning."

"You're leaving?"

"I have packing to do in Ashkelon. Put a note on the lorry telling Avi to wait in case you're not back by four."

"I'll be here long before that."

"You never know with the police." Kate still held Lily's hand.

"Will you be all right," Lily asked, "when you're back in England?"

"I'll get on. I took a flat in Bloomsbury, on Gower Street. Beacon Pharmaceutical gave me a stipend to work up the material for the site report." Now she clasped Lily's hand between both of hers. "And Sir William arranged for the Egyptian Exploration Society to hire me on. At the University of London, for a course of lectures on the Archaeology of Palestine, and as Keeper of Antiquities for the Fendley Collection."

"And little Geoff?"

"He goes to public school. Geoffrey received a consulting fee of five thousand pounds from somewhere, the week before he died. Used it to set up a trust fund for little Geoff's education. His patrimony." She pumped Lily's hand up and down. "It was good working with you. See you next summer in London to work on the site report."

Kate strode to her battered Austin. Lily stayed on the desolate hill, watching Kate's car until it was out of sight.

*   *   *

"I'm sorry, ma'am," Meriman said, "but you'll have to view the body. It's required by law. We need to know if you recognize whoever it was. Being an archaeologist, maybe you can help."

The stench permeated the police post. Meriman took two handkerchiefs and a small bottle of lavender water from the desk drawer, sprinkled some of the lavender on one of the cloths and handed the other to Lily with the bottle. "You might need this." He hesitated. "Sorry, ma'am," he said again. "It's the law."

He led her down the corridor. When he opened the door, she staggered back, assailed by the overwhelming stench that filled the room.

A body with an embroidered white dress lay on a table. "Oh my," Lily said and backed toward the corridor.

Maggots billowed around the neck, over what had been the cheeks, and festooned the dress, undulating and fluttering on the red embroidery. The dress seemed to shimmy as if it were alive.

"Oh my," Lily repeated, closed her eyes and turned her head.

"So sorry, ma'am."

Lily gagged and leaned against Meriman. "It's a wedding dress. From Ramallah."

"How do you know that?"

"Red embroidery on white linen and silk. The design—rosettes—is from Ramallah. Each village has its own pattern."

"A wedding dress? We thought it could be a man. But it's hard to tell. The body is in bad condition. In this climate, with the bugs and rodents..." His voice trailed off. "I hate to ask you this, ma'am. Could you go closer? See if you recognize the deceased?"

She took a deep breath. The effluvium of decay overwhelmed her with primal fear, invading her senses, forcing her back against her will.

"I'll try." She shook a few drops of lavender water on the handkerchief, covered her nose and mouth, and stepped forward, controlling the urge to run from the building.

It was impossible to tell what the body had been in life. The cheeks were gone. Maggots swarmed and jostled in the eye sockets and over the brows, a pulsating mask that flowed like pointelles in an Impressionist painting come to life.

But the mouth, set into a gelatinous rictus, had Abu Musa's unctuous smile. There was no mistaking it—the brown teeth, broken left incisor, missing lower incisors, and gaps where the right canine and first left premolar should be. Alive with maggots crawling and squirming and tumbling over one another, it was Abu Musa's face.

Lily retched. She felt the bile rise in her throat and stumbled outside.

Sergeant Meriman followed. "You all right, miss?"

"I know him," Lily said. "He was one of the workmen at Tel al-Kharub. Abu Musa."

Meriman looked surprised. "Abu Musa?"

"You know the name?"

"Why should I?" He took Lily's arm. "You need a drink. We both need a drink. Come back to my office."

* * *

Meriman took another sip from the teacup on his desk. His breath had a whiskey smell. "Something to calm the nerves," he said, and reached into the desk for a bottle of Dewars and a glass. He poured two fingers of Scotch and handed it to her.

"Drink it down. It will do you good."

Lily's hand shook as she brought the glass to her lips.

"You're too upset to drive right now," Meriman said. "I know a little pub, on the seashore near Ashkelon. Why don't we go there? It will give you time to relax. Come along." He took her arm and led her outside. "Ever been in a Q car?" He gestured toward a vehicle parked at the side of the police post.

"It looks like an ordinary panel truck."

"That's the idea. We use them on patrol." He knocked against the side panel with his knuckles and produced a heavy thud. "You're safe in here. Armor-plated sides. Terrorists think it's a commercial van. When they attack, we meet them with rifle fire."

* * *

They pulled up to a small building with a gas station on one side and a lunchroom on the other.

"Charlie has fish and chips. And cold beer," Meriman said.

The door was open. Beyond the scattering of small linoleum-covered tables and straight-backed chairs, a small, dark man sat behind a counter, a newspaper spread out before him. It was difficult to think of the place as a pub.

"Hello, Charlie. No customers today?" Meriman called to him. The man folded the paper. "Any good news?"

"Hello, constable. There's never good news in this bloody country."

"Charlie here is from Bombay," Meriman said to Lily.

"Madras," Charlie said.

Meriman shrugged. "Same country."

"Not really."

"Give us two of your nice cold American beers."

"I only have Stella beer today."

Meriman pulled out a chair and sat at one of the tables. "Stella, then. It'll have to do."

The waiter brought two bottles and two chilled Pilsener glasses beaded with cold water from the icebox.

Meriman tilted the Pilsener glass and poured the beer slowly. "Have a beer?" he said to Lily.

"I don't drink."

"Religious reasons?"

Lily decided that was as good an excuse as any. She composed her face into the smug mask and resigned air of the truly holy. "Yes," she said.

"You want a tea?" Charlie said.

Lily nodded.

"Nothing like a cool beer on a warm day." Meriman savored the beer and sighed contentedly. "My mates drink it warm, but I like it American style, kept in an icebox." He took another long draft. "No offense," he said.

"We can't stay too long," Lily said. "I have to be back in Jerusalem before the curfew."

"Not to worry. Curfew's called off. We found what we were looking for. Cache of arms near Tulkarm."

"Imagine that," Lily said.

Meriman held the bottle in his hand, and studied the label— a drawing of two camels in front of the pyramids. "Stella Beer," he said. "Egyptian. My father told me about this beer. He was stationed in Cairo during the war." Meriman poured the second bottle into the glass.

"Two more beers, Charlie," he said. Charlie had already opened them and was carrying the bottles to the table on a tray.

"My father told a tale about this beer. It tastes awful, you know. He said he sent a sample to a local chemist to find out what was in it. The report came back that his horse had kidney stones." He chuckled and sighed.

By now, he was drinking straight out of the bottle.

"Who do you think killed Abu Musa?" Lily asked.

"Haven't the slightest. The whole bloody place is full of armed brigands. It's like your American Wild West. And I'm supposed to keep order." He lifted the bottle with a broad gesture that encompassed the bar and the world outside. "In this whole bloody place." He shrugged and a few drops of beer spilled on his sleeve. "It can't be done."

He took another pull at the beer. "Not going to waste time on it. He's only another bloody wog. They have all sorts of vendettas. He could have looked cross-eyed at somebody's sister, for all I know."

"But whoever killed him stole the amphoriskos."

"The what?"

"A blue glass vial. It's missing from the excavation. We think Abu Musa stole it."

"In this bloody country they'll kill for a shilling, much less a piece of old glass."

Meriman finished the beer and put the bottle down. "Don't you worry your pretty head about it," he said. "Have another beer." He signaled the waiter.

Meriman's face was flaccid, his eyes drooping and unfocused. There were four empty bottles in front of him now. He arranged them in a square, two on a side.

"Two more beers, Charlie." Meriman looked across the table at Lily. "It's warm today, isn't it?"

He sighed again. "Things are seldom what they seem. At first, I was happy to be posted here. I thought it would be more romantic, more exotic. East of Suez, and all that. The Holy Land. But it's not, you know. Englishmen sell out their own country here for five thousand pounds."

"How is that?"

He paused dramatically, sipped from the bottle and put it down again. "Can't tell you that, luv."

What was it Kate had said? Eastbourne got a consulting fee, five thousand pounds. Was it Eastbourne? "You're right. It is warm today," Lily said to Meriman. "Certainly makes you thirsty. Two more beers, Charlie."

"You sure?" Charlie asked.

Lily reassured hum with a smile. "Please."

The drawings in the pocket of the journal, Lily thought. A line of forts—and along the border, the Tegart lines.

"It was Tegart's idea, wasn't it?" Lily said. "Forts to control the gun running and terrorist activities. Keep the avenues open between Jerusalem and the Suez Canal in case of war." She took in her breath. "Eastbourne was supposed to scout out the locations."

Meriman leaned forward confidentially, tipping a little beer on the table and blinked. "How-d'ya find out?"

"Same way you did," Lily told him.

"The Arab who came to the police post with a story about Eastbourne meeting Nazis in Jerusalem?"

So that was it. The Mufti is working with the Nazis, Jamal had said. There's blood between us. Don't ride with Eastbourne to Jerusalem, Jamal had said.

"Jamal," Lily told Meriman.

"Don't know his name. The cook, he said he was."

And Jamal, not Eastbourne, had left the notebook in her tent.

Meriman grunted, shook his head and lifted the bottle again. "Your friend Eastbourne sold the whole thing, kit and caboodle, to the Nazis." He put down the bottle with a bang. "Had to scrap the entire idea. We started some forts, like the one at Latrun. Had to turn them into police posts."

"That's why Eastbourne had to be killed, isn't it?" Lily said.

Meriman's head rocked unsteadily up and down in agreement.

"The newspaper report said that you tracked a scent to Kharass and found a revolver hidden in a wall," Lily said.

"Lily, is it?" He lowered his vice to a conspiratorial whisper. "Eastbourne wasn't killed by a revolver, Lily. He was shot with an Enfield rifle."

"A British weapon?"

"My job was to lay a false trail and take the bloodhounds in the wrong direction so the newspapers could report that he was shot by armed bandits from one of the villages." A tear lingered in the corner of his eye and ran down the side of his nose.

Oh God, a maudlin drunk, Lily thought. "You know who shot him?"

He fingered the bottle and nodded. "A Jewish supernumerary. One of those religious types, the kind with the black fedoras. We set it up so that three men dressed like *fellahin* would waylay the station wagon. We knew the route Eastbourne would take. Hired a workman from the tel to identify him, make sure we got the right man. The rest was easy."

He leaned back in the chair and closed his eyes. "The supernumeraries told me that the workman went through Eastbourne's pockets afterward, stole money from his wallet."

"Abu Musa?"

"Don't know, luv. Never met him."

So Abu Musa took the amphoriskos. But what did Henderson and Dame Margaret want with it?

Meriman placed three more bottles on top of the four that already sat in front of him. Slowly and carefully, with his tongue sticking out of the side of his mouth, he tried to balance one more on top of those. "I'll make a pyramid of pyramids," he said and began to chuckle. "See?" He held the bottle out to Lily. "Pyramids on the labels." He knocked his elbow against his pyramid and it tumbled, spilling beer across the table.

Lily looked at her watch. It was almost four. "I have to get back."

He didn't hear her. He was already asleep, face down on the table.

"I'll help you pour him into the lorry," Charlie said. "This isn't the first time."

Lily searched Meriman's pocket for the keys. "Passenger side," she told Charlie.

She started the truck and headed for Beit Jibrin. All the way back, Meriman slumped beside her, his eyes closed, his head lolling, his mouth hanging open. After a while, he began to snore.

She parked the Q car in front of the police post, started to get out but sounded the horn instead. Even from here, she thought, she could smell Abu Musa.

An Arab supernumerary opened the door of the police post and walked toward her, smiling. "He's at it again. He drinks as a Sphinx."

"He what?"

"Isn't that the expression?"

"Drunk as a skunk."

The supernumerary shrugged. "He does this all the time. Passes out in the lorry. Sometimes he doesn't make it home."

Lily handed him the keys. "You can take care of him?"

He nodded and grinned at her. "I always do."

She got into the station wagon, started the motor and drove back to Kharub.

TWENTY-FIVE

ALL THE WAY BACK TO KHARUB, the vision of Abu Musa's eyeless grimace haunted her. Lily coaxed the station wagon up the bald hill to the site. For the last time, she thought.

Avi's lorry was parked squarely in the empty field. He sat on the running board by the open door, leaning back against the seat.

The dining shed was dismantled, its corrugated tin sides stacked neatly next to the rented truck. Lily parked the wagon on the other side of the truck.

Avi stood up. "What happened?" He gestured toward the bed of his lorry. "I put your boxes in the back. Let's go. We have to be in Jerusalem before curfew."

Lily climbed into the passenger seat. "Curfew's over. Meriman told me."

"Who's Meriman?"

Lily told Avi about finding Abu Musa's body, about going to the police station to identify it. "I asked about the amphoriskos. No sign of it."

"You smell like a brewery," Avi said. "Spent a lot of time with Meriman, didn't you?"

"We went to a pub in Ashkelon. Not much of a pub. He got drunk, I had to drive him back."

Avi let out the throttle. The motor turned over. "I heard that Abu Musa raped a girl in Ramallah the day before her wedding. Her brothers killed her."

"That explains the wedding dress Abu Musa was wearing when they found him."

"Did they do anything else to him before he died?"

"Like—?" The stench, the rat-gnawed cheeks and arms were bad enough. "I don't know. The body was too far gone to tell."

Avi backed the lorry and turned it around. "You remember the day after Eastbourne's funeral, when someone shot at us in front of the King David?" They bumped over the field toward the road. "They may not have been after you. It was probably Abu Musa."

"How do you know all these things?"

"This is a small country. If I didn't mind everybody else's business, I wouldn't be doing my civic duty."

"You were right about something else."

"Oh?"

"Eastbourne was a spy."

"And that's why he was killed?"

Lily nodded. "He . . ." She hesitated. Speak only good of the dead. The rest of it, the maps in the journal, the five thousand pounds that Meriman spoke about, could wait for another time.

Avi shifted gears and the lorry groaned up the hill. "You think Eastbourne sold the amphoriskos? He was strapped for money."

"I think he sold more than the amphoriskos," Lily said.

*   *   *

In the morning when Lily brought her breakfast into the garden, Avi was already waiting.

"It's getting late," he said. "It'll be hot and sticky in Tel Aviv today."

The lorry careened down Jaffa road, past the warren of nineteenth century stone houses of Nahalat Sheva.

"Take it easy," Lily said.

"Sorry."

The streets smelled of dampness and kerosene.

"Something bothering you?" she asked.

"No. Yes."

The shops at Ben Yehuda Street and King George were still shuttered.

He shrugged "Maybe I just got up on the wrong side of the bed."

"Where do you stay in Jerusalem?" Lily asked.

"With Auntie Major. She told me all about you and Rafi in Netanya."

"Your Auntie Major has the brains of a tiddley-wink. I hope it's not hereditary."

"Why? You planning to have my child?"

"Not yours."

"Rafi's?"

"Avi . . ." she began and then thought better of making an excuse.

The street narrowed. They bumped along the cobbles. Avi drummed on the steering wheel, the lorry crawling behind donkey carts and porters who bent under the weight of chests and boxes that clogged the road.

"What did you call Auntie Major before she met Fogarty?"

"The *Mezuzah*."

"The little prayer scroll rolled inside a container that they nail on door jambs?"

Avi nodded. "'You shall write them on the doorposts of your house and upon your gates.' Religious people kiss them when they go into a house."

"*Mezuzah*? Because she was religious?"

"No. Because everybody kissed her."

They slowed when they passed Machane Yehuda, the Jewish market where hawkers cried out prices of fruits and vegetables. Fat women in dark dresses, heads covered with scarves, lumbered through stalls shaded by burlap. Their arms were filled with sacks that brimmed with flapping chickens and the green tops of carrots.

Avi gestured in the direction of a hospital surrounded by a wall that enclosed a cow pasture. "That's Shaare Zedek," he said. "The cows give fresh milk for patients. Old Dr. Wallach rules the place with an iron hand. He came from Germany in 1890. This was wilderness then. That's why the wall. Protection from bandits.

"Down in the basement, there's a room full of automobile batteries that provided electricity until Wallach got a generator. The Turks surrendered to the British right there on the balcony. Because of Schwester Zelma. You heard about her?"

Lily shook her head.

"Head nurse at the hospital. Came here maybe thirty years ago. When the Brits took Jerusalem, General Allenby arrived on foot, like a pilgrim. Schwester Zelma met him on the road with a cup of tea. When I am mortally wounded in the service of the *yishuv*, bring me to Schwester Zelma."

"You joined the *Irgun*?"

"Not yet. And if I did, I couldn't tell you."

They left the city, driving rapidly downhill, through hairpin turns. The houses of Deir Yassin clustered on top of the hill above the road. Terraced orchards lined the hillsides. At each curve, Lily held onto the door and stomped on the floorboard of the lorry, reaching for a brake that wasn't there.

They drove around the Kastel. She looked at the sheer drop to the valley below and stamped her foot against the floorboard again.

"Dangerous curve. People go off the road here," Avi said, turning toward her. "Especially when it's raining."

"Don't look at me," Lily said. "Watch the road."

They drove in silence for a while, through Bab al-Wad. Calcareous and rocky earth was dotted with Aleppo pine seedlings.

"Reforestation," Avi said. Pine trees three or four feet tall were planted in pockets of dark brown soil. "The great forest of Jerusalem. I don't know if anything will take. The hills are so eroded even the ribs of the earth are showing."

They passed the ruins of a watchtower. A single wall stood like a sentinel above a tumble of rocks on the bare hill. On the left was a small stone house where a weatherbeaten sign announcing food and lodging flapped above the door.

"You shouldn't travel alone on these roads," Avi said. "It isn't safe."

"I don't."

"That's right. You went with Meriman to Ashkelon, with Jamal to Beit Jibrin, with Rafi to Netanya. A regular *mezuzah*."

"It's really none of your business."

"And to the German Colony with Henderson. I forgot that one."

"That's in Jerusalem."

"It was a foreign country," Avi said.

Lily bristled, remembering the Nazi flag that hung from the balcony of the Austrian consulate. She crossed her arms and looked out the window at the rock-strewn hills.

"I'm sorry," Avi said after a while. "Don't mind me. I had a terrible dream last night. I can't shake it."

"What?"

"I was in terrible pain. At a funeral. Everyone was crying. It didn't make sense. I don't know what it means."

"Whose funeral?"

"I don't know. But it left me with this awful feeling. Like something bad is about to happen."

"Like what?"

"I don't know. Just that it's bad."

Lily waited for him to say more. "You want to go back?"

"No. It's just so strong." He shook himself. "Probably just coming down with a cold." He squinted at the road through the bug-spattered windshield and kept driving.

"That's Latrun over there," he said and pointed toward the ruins of a Crusader church and tower on a hill above an Arab village. "Next to Imwas. The Brits built a police post there."

Latrun had been marked on the map. "I know," Lily said.

*　*　*

The minarets of the Great Mosque of Jaffa stood out against the sea on their left. The lorry inched north toward Tel Aviv along the crowded street, wedged between carts and vans, cars and wagons. Everything stopped for a flock of sheep meandering down the middle of the road, goaded by an old shepherd with a long stick that had a strip of cloth tied to the end.

"The clock tower says two o'clock," Lily said. "We weren't on the road that long."

"Ignore it. It's always two o'clock at the Jaffa souk."

"How much farther?"

"Not much. Tel Aviv is a suburb of Jaffa." Avi sighed. "Twenty years ago, this was only sand dunes. Some Jews from Jaffa built little houses with gardens. And now look."

The lorry crawled through bustling streets, past hovels and new apartments, and through the Carmel Market, swarming with push-carts, live chickens, and throngs of jostling housewives picking through stands packed with pots and pans, vegetables and shoes.

"The amphoriskos is on one of these pushcarts?"

"The shop we want is in a fancy neighborhood, a new hotel on the beach. Not much further." He maneuvered the lorry around large vans blocking the street, parked near the entrances of warehouses. "None of this was here four years ago. Since the Mufti called the general strike and the Arabs closed Jaffa Port, shipping has gone through Tel Aviv."

They turned onto Hayarkon Street near the port. Avi parked in an empty lot. They walked along the sand-covered sidewalk toward hotels that faced the beach. Near the harbor, construction workers in the shade of buildings ate lunch and napped.

"We've arrived during siesta," Lily said. "The shop will be closed."

"Not here."

People came and went from hotels. Some were dressed for town. Some, in broad-brimmed hats and sunglasses, wore bathing suits and had towels slung around their necks. Along the sand, bathers in bright woolen suits shouted and splashed, weaving among umbrellas, lounging in beach chairs. Girls and boys linked arms and strolled along the dunes; children filled buckets with sand; mothers, their skins tanned or angry red from the sun, pushed squalling babies in wicker prams.

Avi led Lily to a hotel with an imposing curved entrance. The ground floor was studded with shops and travel agencies.

"In here. Inside the hotel."

They went through the revolving door, out of the humidity and heat, into an air-conditioned lobby. "Oh my," Lily said. "How grand."

"The shop is along the corridor next to the newsstand." He looked down at his shorts and sandals. "We don't look rich enough for a place like this. They'll probably ask us to leave."

From the outside, the shop looked like an elegant room in the house of a private collector, with deep leather chairs, a Persian carpet. Mahogany breakfronts with softly lit shelves lined the walls. A buzzer sounded when they opened the door. The muted strains of a Bach concerto lingered over the dark, polished wood of the cabinets.

A tall man with a goatee came out from the back of the shop. He eyed Avi and Lily and pursed his lips. "The newsstand is next door."

"We're looking for an amphoriskos," Lily said.

"You're a collector?"

"Of course."

"I have something that would interest you." He opened a drawer and brought out a small velvet box. "An intaglio that belonged to a queen." He opened the box and held a small gold ring with a carved stone up to the light. "Aphrodite." He looked Lily up and down. "A portrait of you," he said and bowed.

"I collect glass."

"Ah." He reached for an iridescent long-necked vial from one of the shelves. "From the tomb of a prince." He held the vial carefully between two fingers and turned it so that it shimmered silver, blue, and green, with a myriad of colors. "Beautiful, yes? It once held the tears of the prince's beloved. She wept into it at his funeral."

"Too common," Lily said. "I'm looking for something special. In sand-core glass."

"Those are rare and expensive. It would cost at least two hundred pounds."

"You have one?"

"An Arab brought one in a few weeks ago. He pretended that it came from an excavation. It was a fake." He inclined his head with modest pride. "I can tell at a glance."

"What excavation? Where was he from?"

"Told me some bizarre story he concocted. I didn't pay much attention. They're all the same."

"Did he have anything else?"

"He had a decanter with him."

"A decanter?"

"You're interested? You want to see it?"

"Please."

He disappeared into the back of the shop and emerged a few minutes later. He held out a Judean-type decanter from the eighth century BCE, like one she found in a tomb at Tel al-Kharub.

"And the amphoriskos?"

The man eyed her quizzically and hesitated. "I told you it was a fake. I didn't buy it."

"You expect the Arab to come back?"

"Not likely. I never saw him before."

"Too bad." Lily turned to go.

The man bowed and clasped her hand. "The intaglio would look beautiful on your finger." He held her wrist and bowed again, kissing the air above her hand. "*Küss die Hand, Gnädige Frau.*"

She pulled her arm away. "We have to go."

"If I find such an amphoriskos, I shall call," he said. "Just give me your address. . . ."

"I'm at the hotel. Leaving this afternoon." She reached for the door of the shop and opened it. The buzzer sounded.

Out in the street again, Lily squinted in the bright sun. "I think Abu Musa was here. That decanter looks like the one he tried to sell to Judah at the King David. I think it's from Tel al-Kharub."

"You want to go back into the shop? Maybe he can tell us more."

Lily shook her head. "We came here for nothing. That man's a charlatan."

"It's all right. We're on holiday." Avi linked his arm in hers. "We'll go *spatziering*. It's what everyone does in Tel Aviv."

"I suppose," Lily said. "When in Rome, do like the Rumanians."

They strolled up Allenby Street toward Mograby Square.

"Tel Aviv has all the modern conveniences," Avi said with a wave of his arm toward the confusion of traffic, the cacophony of horns and angry drivers stalled behind a farmer churning down the middle of the road in a tractor. "Cinemas, pedestrians who cross the street in the face of traffic, modern shops with fashionable clothing."

A man in black slacks and a straw hat hurried past. He carried a briefcase. The corner of the case knocked against Avi's leg. Avi glared after the man, bent down and rubbed his shin. "It even has men who think they're too important to be polite, who carry briefcases that hold nothing but their lunch."

"How do you know they carry lunch? How do you know they don't carry bombs?"

"Tel Aviv already had a bomb this month."

"Bombs are rationed? Only one to a city?"

Avi bent down and rubbed his leg again. "I wish that were so."

"Could be poison," Lily said. "Your leg feel numb?"

"Poison?"

"I read in the paper that sometimes a needle in the corner of a briefcase . . . Oh, forget it. Why would anyone want to kill you?"

"That day outside the King David, when someone took a shot at us?"

"They were after Abu Musa," Lily said.

"Now I'm not so sure." He took a few limping steps. "If anything happens to me, would you miss me?"

"Very much," Lily said. "You joined the *Irgun*, didn't you?"

"Would you remember me forever?"

"Forever," Lily said.

"And light a candle for me every year?"

"Every year."

He rubbed his leg again and looked up at Lily, his eyes clouded with an unknown grief. He straightened up, took her arm and started laughing. "I was kidding. Really." He smiled. "We're on holiday."

"Where are we?"

"Allenby Street, the Rue de la Paix of the Middle East. We'll sit and watch the riffraff pass our table at a sidewalk café."

Behind him, a dark green car darted around vehicles and started a new wave of impatient shouts and curses. The driver seemed to be a young Arab; the passenger looked exactly like Henderson.

"Was that Jamal?" Lily said.

"Where?"

"In the green car."

Avi squinted at the car, already halfway to the next corner. "What would Jamal be doing in a Jaguar? In Tel Aviv, no less."

"Maybe I was wrong." But it was Henderson. Lily was certain. Who else drove a Jaguar in Palestine?

They sauntered arm in arm, keeping to the curb and out of the way of the tables scattered in their path. Avi stopped now and then to inspect a café, looking for some nuance that Lily couldn't decipher. To her, one café looked much like another. Small white tables and chairs spilled out onto the sidewalk, and umbrellas advertised Cinzano.

"Here we are," Avi said after inspecting at least half a dozen. "This year's fashionable café. Everyone comes here."

"Everyone?" Lily asked.

"Even Einstein. He was here the other day."

"He's in Princeton."

"Max Einstein. The waiter." He pulled out a chair for her.

Men in open-collared shirts read newspapers, women nodded their heads under floppy hats. People at the tables smiled, talked, leaned back in their chairs, watched passersby, brandished cigarettes in the air. Men leaned back in their chairs to stare at Avi and scan Lily from head to toe.

"They're famous for their dobish torte. You want coffee? I'll be back in a minute," Avi said.

"You want me to go in with you?"

Avi smiled at her, bowed and pulled out a chair for her. "Please, madam. Pretend we're on a date. Wait here. I'll bring it out to you."

Lily watched the man and woman at the next table, who leaned toward each other, talking softly, the woman in a dress with a broad belt and a halter top, her white gloves next to her on the table. The man placed his hand over hers and squeezed her fingers. The woman hunched her bare shoulders, said something to him in a low voice, and smiled. They glanced at Lily. She looked away, embarrassed, at the street heavy with traffic then at Avi inside the cafe.

He was standing at the bakery counter, pointing to pastries in the case.

Lily noticed a dark-haired man inside the shop, paying for pastries. He seemed to jostle Avi and then ran out the door. He darted in and out of the tables on the sidewalk, dropped his bag of pastries near Lily's table, and rushed off down the street.

Lily called after him. He didn't turn around. She called again, picked up the bag of pastries, and started to run after him.

He had reached the corner when a sudden clap of noise enveloped her with a rush of air, pressed against her head, reverberated against her chest.

Then silence.

A numbness in her ears.

She looked back at the café. Glass erupted toward the tables, the frame of the window shivered, wood splintered, plaster burst and ricocheted. The café ceiling sagged and fell, dangling wires, collapsing like a tired sigh.

Again and again. Wave after wave of heat and silence throbbed against her. Glass from the window marked with red splotches. Hot blasts of wind. Bits of cake exploding from the bakery.

Avi? Where was Avi?

Sights and sounds pulsating with fire, with darkness, with noise too loud to be heard.

"My gloves," said the woman at the next table. Aimless. Helpless. Turning around and around. The man clutched her chair and blinked.

I must find Avi.

"All those cakes," a woman with a piece of glass wedged in her back was saying in a plaintive, flat voice. "All those cakes. Cakes are everywhere." Her dress had large white buttons with big red spots.

"I must find Avi," Lily told her.

Flames erupted in the shop, flowed like water along the floor, up the walls. Pieces of lath hung by loose nails and ruptured into an inferno. Chairs burst into tinder. Avi's foot stuck out from beneath a fallen table. It twitched and kicked. Lily moved forward. Fire licked his sandal, caught at the leather. The shop flooded with flame and smoke.

"In the courtyard," Lily said to the woman next to her, "the woman was clutching her child. I found a severed arm at Tel al-Kharub. Kate did. And broken pots under a pile of mud-brick."

"You saw that?" the woman with the bloody back said, and fell against her.

Lily propped her on the table. "I must get Avi. I must." She moved toward the shop. Heat from the fire, the terrible smell of burning, beat against her in waves. She peered through fallen beams and buckled walls. "I must get Avi."

A heavy arm grabbed her and pulled her back.

"I must get Avi."

"You must get out of here."

It was Henderson.

TWENTY-SIX

∿

LILY STARED IN FRONT OF HER at the glossy polished wood of the dashboard, at a bug flattened against the windshield, at an incomprehensible range of dials and knobs in front of Henderson. They had already rushed past the clock tower of the Jaffa souk.

Nothing was right. Henderson drove from where the passenger seat should be, his face an implacable mask.

"I'm on the driver's side." Lily said.

Henderson kept his eyes on the road. "Jaguar. Right-wheel drive."

"Where are you taking me?"

"Jerusalem."

Why am I in this car? How did I get here?

Stay calm.

"We have to go back." She tried to sound as reasonable as possible. "We have to get Avi."

"He's dead." Henderson's tone was cold and brusque.

"You don't seem to understand." She spoke slowly, as if to a child. "He went inside to buy a cake. He'll look for me when he comes out."

"He's not coming out." He smiled at that.

"You're not frightening me," she told him. "You've been in my nightmares before."

This time he didn't smile. His jaw began to work. "You're awake."

"Oh, God," she said and pressed her palms against her face, felt the hollow below her check bones, the curve of her brow. She held her hands over her eyes to combat waves of nausea, to block out the sight of Avi caught under the debris of the café, the witless stare of the woman with the bloody back, the smell of burnt cloth and hair, of gelegnite, and the cloying odor of scorched sugar.

The road climbed through olive groves. She lurched with the motion of the car as it swiveled around hairpin turns.

Try to sound casual. Just make conversation.

"I saw you driving down Allenby Road," Lily said.

"Feeling better?" Henderson asked.

She ran her fingers along the burled wood of the dash and the shining chrome.

"Don't do that," he said.

"What are all these dials?"

He pointed to the one nearest her. "Throttle." His hand moved to the knob below it "Choke."

He stepped on the gas. The needles on the dials wavered as the car lunged forward. "Motor mount's still loose." He grunted. "Damn. Someday I'll turn a corner and the motor will go in the opposite direction."

"You were with Jamal." She said, still conversational.

"The Arab who took you home from the German colony?" The side of his face twitched. "Your friend Jamal," Henderson paused, "had an accident."

"Where is he? What happened?"

Henderson glanced at her through narrowed eyes. "Terrible accident." He spoke slowly, as if he savored each word. "He fell into a pit. Impaled on a stake in the bottom of a pit." His voice was oily and resonant.

"How—?"

"Carelessness. It could happen to anyone." He looked over at Lily again and his right hand reached inside his jacket. "Could happen to you."

"I don't understand. He said he had to work at the hospital in Jerusalem."

"Never got there."

"He's dead?" Lily's fingers grew cold. She felt the blood drain from her face. "What were you doing in Tel Aviv?"

"Why were *you* in Tel Aviv?"

"Looking for the amphoriskos."

He slowed the car and withdrew his hand from his jacket. "Find it?"

She shook her head.

He dropped his hand into his lap. He slowed as they drove through Ramleh and concentrated on the road clogged with children ducking between bicycles and donkeys, women trudging under heavy loads from the market, men smoking and talking.

The dead donkey that she and Avi had seen this morning still lay in the ditch, its stomach distended, its odor a leitmotif that carried in the wind with the buzz and murmur of the street sounds. Henderson was steering with both hands now. "Stinking country."

He wiped his forehead with his right hand, patted the bulge on his jacket. The car wavered. The powerful motor whined as they left the town and began to climb.

Lily thought of the first time she had seen Henderson, the day of the riots in front of the King David. KH. Keith Henderson.

Was that his real name? And was he from Cincinnati?

Lily had been in Cincinnati as a child. Her father had taken her on a tour of Harriet Beecher Stowe house. Anyone from Cincinnati would know the house.

"You remember Eliza?" Lily said. "She jumped from one clump of ice to another, as though they were stepping stones. Does the river freeze in winter?"

"What are you talking about? What river?"

"The one in Cincinnati. I forget the name."

He glanced at her, then looked back at the road. "Ohio."

At least he knows the name of the river.

"Who's Eliza?" he asked.

"You know. Uncle Tom."

"You have relatives in Cincinnati?"

"Everyone knows Uncle Tom," Lily said.

"Never met him."

He's not an American. Who is he?

They had passed Latrun. They approached Bab al-Wad and the pathetic clump of saplings struggling to grow in the rocky soil. Avi had called it the forest of Jerusalem.

Lily stared at Henderson, watching his impassive face. His hands held the steering wheel lightly, and he drove as though nothing had happened. He had killed Jamal. And Avi. He didn't even know Avi, and he killed him.

Angry tears burned in her eyes. Henderson's the one who rouses them to frenzy, the one who pays them to kill.

And the amphoriskos. Why did he want it?

"They're looking for a man named Karl," Henderson had said that night at the King David.

She scanned his jutting jaw, his burning eyes, and in her mind she heard Sir William's reedy voice droning, "I met Konrad Henlein. He has a brother Karl." Sir William, spilling his soup on the table, repeating, "Your young man . . . family resemblances, like pottery types . . . a nose here, an angle of the jaw there."

Karl. Of course, Karl, that must be his name.

"Karl," she said out loud, and he turned.

"What did you say?"

That was a mistake. "You remind me of someone named Karl."

"I told you. I don't know anyone named Karl."

"I meant Karl Marx." He glared at her. His face was stony.

"The man with the lamp shop on Jaffa Road," she added quickly. "I left my desk lamp to be fixed."

She flinched in the acid wash of his eyes. The muscles around his powerful jaw churned.

He kills for a living. He'll kill me too. As easily as he'd kill a fly, as easily as he'd kill a cat.

His eyes slashed at her. He put his hand in his jacket pocket again.

The car swerved around the curve. "You should have believed me," he said, his jaw still working. "Too bad. I liked you."

The road was narrow here. Barely wide enough for two cars. The car wound around the edge of the precipice. Lily looked down at plowed fields and terraces far below. "Beautiful view," he said. "We'll step out so you can appreciate it."

Henderson had one hand on the wheel. His eyes shifted from Lily to the road and back again.

The car swayed toward the sheer drop of the cliff edge. Henderson yanked the wheel back sharply.

A thump sounded from under the hood. The car veered.

Henderson turned toward the sound. "Shit."

Almost by instinct, Lily hoisted herself up, with one knee on the seat, and pulled out the throttle. She grasped the steering wheel. She shoved it hard to the right, heard a jarring noise, felt the jolt of impact. The car hurtled into the wall of the cliff.

The dashboard crumpled and showered her with broken glass. A numbing pain shot through her leg. Henderson's head jerked back and forth through the windshield.

He slumped in the seat, his face bloody with cuts.

She tried to move. Pain throbbed in her leg, wedged between the crumpled remains of the seat and the crushed dashboard.

"Oh, God."

She closed her eyes and still saw Henderson's bloody face imprinted on the exploding café, the fallen beams and twisted rods, the flare of the fire, the woman with glass in her back, Avi's twitching foot.

Lily heard the sound of a car coming around the curve toward her.

She began to sob uncontrollably.

TWENTY-SEVEN

A CREAM-COLORED BENTLEY with Eliot at the wheel purred into sight and slowed. Dame Margaret peered through the windshield.

"Hold on," Eliot called out and stopped the car. He hurried toward Lily, his sandals slapping the road.

Lily tried to move again. A sheet of pain ran down her left leg. "I'm pinned."

Eliot pulled at the shattered door of the Jaguar. "Stuck." His face flushed with effort.

He placed one hand on the window, braced a foot against the fender and yanked again until the door rasped open. A hinge clanked on the ground. Eliot tugged once more. The door fell loose, tumbling from his grasp onto the road.

"Try moving now."

Lily strained. Another stab of pain thrust through her. She scraped her bottom teeth against her upper lip and shook her head.

Dame Margaret leaned out the open window of the Bentley. "What about him?"

Eliot glanced at Henderson. "He's not going anywhere."

The wide brim of Dame Margaret's hat flipped back and forth. "We'll take care of him later." She reached up to steady the hat.

Eliot turned back to Lily. He struggled to lift the dashboard, nudging it just enough to relieve the pressure on Lily's thigh. "Try again." Beads of sweat glistened on his forehead.

"I can't." Lily licked her lip and caught a glimpse of her ashen face in the mirror. "I think my leg is broken."

He indicated the dash. "Put your hand under there," he directed and slid Lily along the seat, mumbling, "Carefully. Carefully."

Lily winced.

He lifted her out of the car. Lily cringed with each jarring motion.

"Hold on, girl." His voice rasped with exertion. "We'll make it, girl."

Panting, he hoisted Lily to the Bentley. Dame Margaret stood by the opened door of the back seat, leaning on a stadia rod. "All I could find in the boot. Give me your belt."

Dame Margaret gently raised Lily's foot with both hands, rested the broken leg on the seat, and used Eliot's belt to lash the stadia rod to Lily's leg. "We'll be in hospital in no time," she said and stroked Lily's arm.

"What about Henderson?" Lily asked.

Dame Margaret straightened up. She rubbed the small of her back with both hands and looked back at the Jaguar. "His name is Henlein." Her voice was glacial and deliberate. "He told you he's Henderson?"

Eliot strode to the driver's side of the Jaguar, reached through the window and put a finger on Henderson's wrist.

Not Henderson, Lily reminded herself. Henlein.

"Pulse is faint. But there."

Dame Margaret stood next to him. She tilted Henderson/ Henlein's head back against the seat, pulled at his eyelids, took a handkerchief from her sleeve and dangled the corner in front of his nose. Almost imperceptibly, it wavered with his breath.

"Still alive."

She shrugged. Eliot and Dame Margaret exchanged glances.

A sudden gust of wind lifted the brim of Dame Margaret's hat and carried it off. Eliot and Dame Margaret watched it waft back and forth, dancing in the wind past the rocks at the edge of the cliff, across the ruins of the Kastel, as it sailed into the valley below. They glanced at each other again and nodded.

Dame Margaret tucked the handkerchief back into her sleeve while Eliot scurried to the other side of the Jaguar. Together, one on each side of the car, they pushed it backwards, leaning their weight into it. Slowly, it moved away from the cliff face toward the center of the road.

Lily watched Henderson's head sway with the impact, watched a thin trace of blood seep from his mouth, heard a faint moan.

Eliot and Dame Margaret didn't seem to notice. Both were frowning, intent on shoving the car across the road.

"He's alive," Lily said. Were they deaf? Lily shifted in her seat, felt the stab of pain in her leg and gasped. "What are you doing?"

The car crept toward the embankment. Eliot grunted. "Nothing, really."

And they continued to push the car.

Dame Margaret's face was crimson. "This is a dangerous curve." She halted, panting, and pushed back her hair. The handkerchief fell from her sleeve and fluttered across the road. "Slippery in the rain."

"It isn't raining," Eliot told her.

"But it could be." Dame Margaret pushed against the car again.

"Why are you doing that?" Lily asked, starting to rise. A spasm in her leg threw her back on the seat.

"Cars skid off this cliff all the time." A streak of perspiration stained the back of Eliot's shirt.

"Stop it," Lily said.

Eliot's face reddened with exertion and the Jaguar moved to the edge of the cliff.

Eliot and Dame Margaret gave the car a final thrust and watched it tumble. The clang of metal struck against the rocky slope, dust billowing with blow after blow as it shattered down the hillside, hood over trunk, until it came to rest.

Then silence.

"You killed him," Lily cried. "Just like that. You killed him."

"I certainly hope so." Dame Margaret wiped her hands against her dress. "Poetic justice. The attaché before Henderson went off the road at the Kastel." She pointed down the valley. "Right here."

"It won't do any good." Eliot went back to where the car door lay on the asphalt. "Henlein will be replaced."

"What have you done?" Lily shouted. "Are you mad?"

"We gained time." Eliot moved back to the door of the Jaguar lying on the road. "It will be days before he's missed. Maybe a week."

Dame Margaret nodded in agreement. "Then they have to train his replacement."

"Delayed them for two weeks, a month at the outside." Eliot's voice was hoarse with his struggle to hoist the remnant of the car with both of his hands. He bent under its weight. As he carried it to the edge of the cliff, the hinge clattered onto the road.

"Wind and weather permitting," he said between breaths, "we only saved twenty, maybe thirty lives."

He heaved the door over the precipice, retrieved the hinge, and still panting, tossed it into the canyon. Dame Margaret watched it clang to rest.

"*Inshalla*. God willing," she said. She picked up the other door hinge, threw it after the door, and wiped her hands against each other with a cheerful slap.

Dame Margaret returned to the Bentley with a satisfied smirk on her face, then turned to Lily with a puzzled look. "What were you doing in the car with that man?"

"The fire," Lily said, "the explosion—he pulled me away."

"You were in the café that was bombed."

Lily nodded and closed her eyes. "And Avi."

"We know. We've been following you since you left Jaffa," Eliot said.

"I didn't see you."

"Take heart," Dame Margaret said to Lily. "We'll have you at hospital in the blink of a sheep's eye."

They started up the incline toward Jerusalem and drove over the tire tracks that ran across the road into the cliff wall. "Won't the police notice the skid marks?" Lily asked. "They go in the wrong direction."

Eliot turned slightly. "Not for days. Besides, there's no connection to us. We've all been in the southern Shephelah at Zakariya today. We surveyed the archaeological site, measured the walls, checked the fortress. That's how you broke your leg. Didn't you? You fell off the tower. Didn't you?"

"But—"

"It's an important site. Probably ancient Azakah. Next year we may excavate there. Won't we?"

"I—"

"You're on the senior staff. You remember, don't you?"

"I suppose," Lily said.

"Next time," Dame Margaret wagged her finger at Lily, "be more careful."

Eliot slowed as they went around the next curve. "She's doing all right, considering," he said to Dame Margaret.

"Considering what?"

*   *   *

Each nick and bulge in the road, each jolt, sent a shock of pain up Lily's leg.

"Only a little farther," Eliot said. "We're coming into Jerusalem."

Rafi will take care of it, Lily repeated to herself, closed her eyes and licked her lips again. "I want to go to Strauss Hospital. On Chancellor Road."

"Strauss it is."

Lily tried to smile through cracked lips.

Dame Margaret tilted her head out the window, wiping at her forehead with the back of her hand. "Hot today." Her hair blew across her face and she pushed it back, narrowing her eyes against the wind.

They slowed for a barrier that blocked Jaffa Road just past the entrance to the city. "Now what?"

Eliot braked. "Another bomb?" he asked the policeman who directed traffic to the right and left with broad sweeps of his arm.

"This time a bus. On Jaffa road." The policeman gestured to the right. "Have to detour."

"Left," Lily said.

Only a little way to go.

The blare of an ambulance horn keened behind them. Eliot pulled to the side of the road. The ambulance bellowed again and continued along the Street of the Prophets in the direction of Rothschild Hospital, rocking the Bentley as it passed. Clouds of dust swirled in its wake, obscuring the red Star of David painted on its side.

Another red-starred ambulance whined behind it and turned onto Ethiopia Street.

They followed it to the emergency entrance of Strauss Hospital.

"We need some help here," Eliot called to the orderlies who were lifting a stretcher onto a gurney.

A nurse in starched white emerged from the hospital, pushing an empty wheelchair. She peered into the back of the Bentley. "Another victim? Broken leg?"

Eliot helped transfer Lily into the chair and smoothed her skirt over her knees. "They'll fix you in a jiffy," he said. "You'll be all right now," and returned to the Bentley.

* * *

The hospital smelled of antiseptic and sour flesh.

"I want to see Doctor Landon," Lily told the nurse over the moans and sobs and voices on the edge of hysteria that permeated the crowded waiting room.

The nurse didn't answer, continued to push the chair with one hand, and raised the other above her head. "Anglit. English." She pointed down to Lily with a flick of the wrist.

Another nurse, this one in a blue uniform, snaked through the bevy of wheelchairs, gurneys, and benches toward Lily. "It's a *balagan* here today. A madhouse."

"I want to see Dr. Landon."

"All in good time." The blue one adjusted the wooden leg rest of the wheelchair and carefully lifted Lily's leg. "You weren't the only one on the bus."

"I wasn't—" Lily took in her breath and wet her lip again. Where's Rafi?

"First we put you in the queue for Xray," the blue nurse said, parked the chair next to a table, and disappeared behind some swinging doors.

Lily looked around, at a man who held a bloodstained arm in an improvised sling, at a woman who pressed a gory piece of gauze to her eye, at a child sobbing against the shoulder of a stolid woman who stared straight ahead.

They could all be dying. I only have a broken leg.

Someone slammed against her chair and a spike of pain ran up her leg. Surprisingly, the wheelchair moved. Her leg throbbed; her head eddied with nausea.

Where was Rafi? Please, Rafi.

Lily reached for the table to pull the chair out of traffic. She closed her eyes while the murmur of voices washed over her, individual inflections lost in a whirlpool of sound. Her head jerked forward. Startled, she opened her eyes again to watch for Rafi from her roost at the side of the table.

An orderly pushed a cart through double doors at the opposite end of the room. Lily caught a glimpse of Rafi at the end of a long, sloping corridor.

Tentatively, Lily pushed away from the table. She reached backward, clutching at the large wheels of the chair, and rolled herself, inch by inch, across the room toward the double doors.

The room wavered in front of her. Perspiration ran down her spine.

The doors opened again. She saw Rafi, intent on Xrays that hung in front of light-boxes lining the hallway.

She pushed herself past the doors and into the corridor.

A pink lady carrying a tray brushed past Lily, bouncing against the chair. It caromed against the wall. From the opposite direction, an attendant grasping a stainless steel pitcher rushed toward them, while Lily struggled to shove away from the wall.

The attendant and pink lady collided. The tray and the pitcher clattered to the floor.

Lily's wheelchair slid away from the wall.

"Cleanup," the attendant called.

A girl with a bucket and mop appeared from a side room. The attendant pointed to a widening puddle of tea that swept down the hall. The girl dabbed at it and tossed the soapy contents of the bucket onto the terrazzo floor before she mopped.

The wheelchair gathered speed. Lily skidded through the slippery layer of soapsuds, careening toward Rafi.

"Look out," someone shouted.

The sharp pain of impact was sudden and unexpected. Rafi, reaching toward the chair, was knocked off balance.

A flash of blue flared out of his pocket and crashed to the stone floor. Lily looked down at the shatter of broken glass.

It was the amphoriskos, splintered into a hundred tiny shards, lying next to Rafi's foot.

A tiny roll of film spun away from it, rotating down the corridor.

Lily licked her lip again. Then she passed out.

TWENTY-EIGHT

LILY HEARD MURMURING around her, and muffled voices that seemed to come from another room. Her mother sat among weeds on the rotted steps of a shuttered house. Dead leaves swirled around her. Lily's mother looked up, her face shattered with grief, her eyes uncomprehending and swollen. "It's all gone, you know. All gone." Crimson rivulets seeped through the fingers of her mother's clenched hand. "You see. Gone."

"What are you holding?" Lily asked, and gently opened her mother's clenched fist to find blue splinters of shattered glass smudged with blood.

"We must go to the hospital now," Lily told her.

"You came at last," her mother said to a private ghost behind a broken window. "At last."

* * *

"Coming around at last," Rafi's voice was saying.

Lily's leg, encased in a massive cast, throbbed. She lay under a burden of sheets, heavy and crisp with starch.

She opened her eyes to see Rafi leaning over her, his face so close that she felt his breath on her cheek.

"Go away." She closed her eyes again.

"Are you in pain?"

Silence engulfed her and ticked around the room, covering the table beside her, the dresser, the chair next to the bed.

"I don't want to see you," she said after a while. "I don't want to see anyone."

When she opened her eyes, Rafi still leaned over her. She felt a flush of anger and turned her head away. A pepper tree nodded and bowed in the window.

"Avi's dead." The words caught in her throat.

"I know." Rafi took in his breath. Something about his voice made her look at him. The rims of his eyes were moist and tinged with red.

Behind him, a candle sputtered in a glass on the corner of the dresser. Rafi followed her glance. "I lit it for Avi. Hope you don't mind."

"I promised him," Lily said.

"Why was he in Tel Aviv?" Rafi asked.

"We went to find the amphoriskos." Lily fingered the sheets. "The amphoriskos," she repeated. "Don't you understand what you've done?" She felt a void, deep as a chasm, in her core. "I trusted you. I believed you."

"You can still trust me."

"I trusted Eastbourne too."

"And now you don't? What do you know about him?"

"You lied to me. You had the amphoriskos all along."

"I found it in the house in Sebastiye," Rafi said. "During the wedding. Abu Musa must have stolen it when Eastbourne was killed."

"You know about Eastbourne? For all I know, you killed Abu Musa too," she said, and for a moment, the horror of the thought stuck in her head. An angry tear spilled down her cheek.

"I'm sorry. I'm awfully sorry about the amphoriskos. But we needed it."

"We?"

"Eastbourne hid the film inside the amphoriskos. That's why he was bringing it to Jerusalem."

"Why didn't you give it to me when you found it?"

"It was evidence. I couldn't get out the film. The inside of the vial was rough. Sand core glass, you said. The neck was narrow and the film stuck. I needed a long-nosed tweezers from the lab to get it out."

"You carried it around in your pocket."

"I came in to develop the film in the hospital darkroom. Have to use a water bath to control the temperature because of the sensitivity of the film. There was no time. The bomb on the bus, one trauma after another."

He reached toward her, his hand poised to stroke her cheek.

"Get away from me." She turned away and looked out the window. "What did you expect to find in the film? And who is 'we'?"

"I've been working with Henderson. He's here. He's waiting for the film."

A stab of fear numbed her. "Here?" The bough of the pepper tree shook as if to warn her. "He's alive?"

"Of course he's alive."

She tried to get out of the bed. The movement jarred her leg and the pain shot through her body.

Rafi adjusted the covers. "You look uncomfortable. Too warm? In pain?" He held out a glass of water and two pills that glistened in his hand.

"What's in the pills?"

"Just something to take away the pain."

She looked toward the other bed in the room. It was empty. The pills were a nauseous green. "I don't need them."

"I'll leave them here." He put the pills and water on the nightstand. "In case."

The only thing to do is bluff it out. "It was foolish of me to be so clumsy." She tried to smile.

"Something's fishy." Rafi sat down on the chair next to the bed.

"What do you mean, fishy?"

"For one thing, I don't think you broke your leg falling off a tower."

"What makes you say that?"

"Your femur has a spiral fracture, not a transverse fracture."

"What's the difference?"

"If you broke it in a fall, you'd most likely have a transverse fracture—straight across—unless you got yourself tangled. But you don't. Your leg twisted. I've seen breaks like that from automobile accidents."

He knew. Henderson told him. *They're both in this together and I have to get out of here.*

She tried to sit up, to swing her leg over the edge of the bed. The sudden clap of pain made her gasp.

"Sit back. I'll get what you need."

I must get help. The call button for the nurse was pinned to the pillow. Lily reached for it and fell back panting.

"You *are* in pain." Rafi picked up the water and pills again.

"No, no." She pulled up the covers, as if she could hide under them. "I have to go to the bathroom."

"Let me help you."

"It's all right. I'll wait."

"You weren't at an archaeological site," he said. "You were in Tel Aviv with Avi."

"How do you know?"

"You just told me."

A light knock sounded at the door. *Henderson?*

A small bald man in a summer suit stood at the door. He held three roses wrapped in green wax paper. "I'd like to speak to you." He waggled the flowers and came into the room. "If you're up to it."

Who is this man? "What do you want?"

Two of them. Somehow, I have to get out of here.

"I tried to contact you earlier," the stranger said to Lily. "When you phoned me at the consulate, I was in Haifa. I expected you to call back."

"Haifa?"

"Clearing customs. I had just arrived a few days earlier. Wasn't settled in at the consulate yet. And I wasn't sure how to reach you."

"I called you at the consulate?"

"This is Henderson," Rafi said. The man bowed again. "Colonel Keith Henderson. He's attaché at the American consulate."

Lily felt a surge of relief, and then a jab of anger. "Your name really is Henderson?" How can I be sure? "You don't—"

"I had a lot to organize when I arrived. But I knew you were in good hands with Dr. Landon. He said he'd watch out for you."

"He told you that?"

"I understand that we're responsible for breakage of an artifact accidentally removed from your archaeological site. We'd be glad to reimburse the excavation."

"The amphoriskos. Dr. Landon told me you needed it. I don't understand why."

"Nothing to be concerned about. Had to do with some maps. The originals had been damaged—altered."

Rafi glanced in Lily's direction.

"Photocopies of the maps were inside the vial," Henderson said.

"She's exhausted," Rafi told him. "Can you come back later?"

The little man looked from Lily to Rafi and back again. "I'll let you get some rest now. We can talk more tomorrow." He put the flowers on the nightstand and left.

Next to the bed, Rafi picked up the bouquet. "I'll get these in water." He started out the door.

"Rafi?"

He turned back to her.

"I think I'll take those pills now."

He handed her the glass. "They'll make you a little sleepy."

She swallowed the pills, and he leaned down to kiss her forehead. She turned away to the window again. Red peppercorns dangled in the lacy leaves like drops of blood. The pepper tree shook and curtsied back and forth, back and forth in the wind. She watched the delicate pattern of the branches dip and bow, back and forth, back and forth, until her eyes grew heavy.

*   *   *

Her father held the blue glass vial delicately between thumb and forefinger. "This little bottle," he was saying, "is a talisman. It guards your life."

She reached for it, and he held it away from her, up to the light. "It diverts danger, takes the blows itself and shatters. Then the danger is past."

"Is that what happened, father?" She held out her hand to him, and he disappeared.

*   *   *

She opened her eyes to see Sir William and Lady Fendley seated next to her bed, watching her.

"You've had a bit of a bother," Lady Fendley said. "Didn't mean to disturb you."

"This last month—" Lily said.

Sir William took her hand. "I know. It's like when I first came to Alexandria, long, long ago," he said. "Nationalism is as bad as religion. I used to think they were a good thing, God and country and all that. Now I don't know."

A nurse bustled into the room, carrying a vase of flowers. "Visiting hours are over." She put the vase on the dresser. Rafi waited in the doorway. "Doctor wants to examine you."

Sir William turned to go. He leaned on his wife's arm, saw Rafi near the door, and turned back to Lily. "Don't let him bully you. Don't let him tell you that archaeology is just an excuse for self-indulgent adventure, the world's most expensive team sport. We are in the business of inventing memories. A necessity in the modern world. We are as necessary as water." Sir William waved at Lily, wiggling the fingers of his free hand. "Ta ta," he said.

Lily turned her face to the window.

"You still angry with me?" Rafi asked.

"Of course.

He came closer to the bed. "You don't understand."

"Oh, but I do," Lily told him. "It reminds me of a story."

"Please . . ."

"You want to hear the story?"

"Not really."

"A scorpion and a duck were on the banks of the Jordan."

"I know the story," Rafi said. "I know what you're going to say. But the whole thing is more complicated than you think."

"The scorpion said to the duck, 'I need to get to the other side of the river. Will you carry me on your back?'"

"I had to get hold of the plans before Henlein," Rafi said.

"And the duck answered, 'Certainly not. If you get on my back, you'll sting me. That's the nature of scorpions.'"

"It wasn't what you think," Rafi told her. "You told me you wanted to find Abu Musa."

"So the scorpion said," Lily continued, "'I can't swim. If I sting you, you'll sink and I'll drown.'" Lily pushed the button to raise the back of the bed and ignored the twinge in her leg it caused. She was enjoying this. No wonder Rafi had a story for everything. "When they reached the middle of the river, the scorpion stung the duck. As they were sinking, the dying duck said to the scorpion, 'But you gave me your word.' And the drowning scorpion said—"

Rafi finished it for her. "'How could you believe me? This is the Middle East.'" He reached out a hand to adjust her coverlet. "Did I ever say I was telling you the truth? I've always been honest about lying. It's a matter of principle."

"That's the nature of scorpions."

Rafi flashed her a tentative smile and spread his fingers. "You're pretty sneaky yourself, you know." He reached into his pocket and took out a piece of paper. "The note you left in the journal."

"You're the one who took the note? Who looked at the maps?"

"You're the one who changed them."

He leaned over her and brought his lips close to her forehead. "By the way," he murmured, "where are the coordinates of the original map?"

"Go away."

"I can't go away," Rafi said. "Too much has happened between us."

Were they were all linked together—conquerors and madmen, the Hitlers and el Husseinis and Henleins, who gorged on hatred and moved people around like chess pieces? The Eastbournes and Hendersons and Dame Margarets, who played at intrigue like fractious children, convinced that they were making history? Even Rafi? Weariness overwhelmed her.

"I can't forgive you for the amphoriskos. You lied to me. You had it with you in Netanya."

"It isn't me you can't forgive. You can't forgive yourself."

"Forgive myself? You took the amphoriskos. It fell from your pocket."

"It's more than that. You told me you never said goodbye to your father. You think you could have stopped him if he told you?"

"Maybe.

"That's a terrible burden for a ten-year-old."

"I thought the amphoriskos was his message to me, to tell me goodbye." All she could remember was the last sight of her father, when the door opened to the closet under the stairs.

"And the amphoriskos broke. Maybe that was the message. To break with the past."

Restless, she fingered the sheets and drew her hand across her forehead. "Maybe . . ." she said, but her voice choked.

Why hadn't she remembered the laughter and smiles and limitless love of her father, the marzipan automobile hidden under her napkin, sitting on his shoulder to watch the Rose Parade?

Tears clouded her eyes and started down her cheek.

Rafi brushed them aside.

She turned her face away. He sat on the edge of the bed, and she turned back to him.

"You must hate me," he said.

Her eyes began to sting. "Not really."

If I start to cry now, I'll never stop. She felt warm tears on the back of her hand, the fold of the sheets. She felt a heaving in her throat and sobbed without end as she leaned against Rafi's shoulder.

"It's time to say goodbye now," he said.

Tears kept coming. She hid her face in the curve of his neck, and he kissed her neck, her cheek, her lips.

"Time to say goodbye," she echoed.

TWENTY-NINE

Ꙩ

RAFI CALLED EVERY MORNING after Lily came home from the hospital.

Each time he called, Lily felt a wash of excitement and leaned into his voice. And each time, after she hung up, misgivings eddied through her. She would walk back to her room, the words "he lied, he lied," thrumming in her head, still angry at his deception, fearful that someday, he too, would be gone. As her father had done, leaving nothing behind but empty rooms.

"I'll have ten days to woo you on the way home," Rafi had said that morning. "Taxi will be there at two," he reminded her. "Be ready or we'll miss the boat."

Lily closed the trunk filled with field notes, pottery and artifacts from the tombs at Kharub. Her leg still bothered her when she was tired. That too will pass, Rafi had told her.

She had just finished packing when Rafi came upstairs with the porter. He looked at the trunks and suitcases stacked on the floor.

"All this?" he asked. "It won't fit in your cabin, much less the taxi. I have a few bags, too."

"Only the Gladstone bag goes in the cabin. The trunks go in the hold."

The porter, heavy and sad-eyed, wore a shirt that was too small and gaped between the buttons, exposing smudged portions of a sweat-dampened undershirt.

Rafi helped lift one of the trunks. "What do you have in here? Lead pellets?"

The porter bent forward with a grunt while Rafi helped secure the load on his back with a tumpline.

"Books. Papers. Artifacts. The weight of history."

The porter staggered into the hall, and Lily heard the trunk clatter between the wall and the banister all the way down the stairs.

"You go ahead and say your good-byes," Rafi said. "I'll stow the baggage in the taxi."

Lily went into the garden. Dame Margaret was there, ensconced behind an open *Palestine Post*. Only the feather of her hat could be seen, wagging in the wind.

The headline covered half a page. *PEACE IN OUR TIME.* Lily sat down across from the newspaper. *CRISIS AVERTED.*

"Good morning," said Dame Margaret. "There's going to be a war." She was still hidden behind the paper. "I came to say goodbye."

"Now that it's over," Lily said, "I wanted to tell you that I'm glad we became friends."

"It isn't over. It's hardly begun. Austria and Czechoslovakia are just the beginning. Poland may be next. Hitler's already talking about violation of Germans' rights there." Dame Margaret lowered the paper.

Arrays of sparrow hawks, one formation after another, soared overhead, sailing on the wind, dipping and gliding across the sky like vast *corps de ballets*.

Lily watched them. "Where are they going?"

Dame Margaret looked up. "Somewhere in Africa." She folded the paper and put it on the table. "We leave tomorrow for Mesopotamia," she said. "Just for the digging season. Until the rain sets in."

"What will you do if war breaks out?"

"It won't. Britain isn't ready for war yet. It will be at least a year. First we have to get all our ducks in a row. There'll be more concessions. The Mandate will have to accede to Arab demands to stop Jewish immigration."

"Why?"

"The Chinese sages say that every battle is won before a war begins. Victory is based on deception, my dear. The winners are those who can turn harmony into chaos, certainty into confusion."

An involuntary shudder surged through Lily. "That's horrible."

"More horrible than we ever imagined, thanks to the miracle of modern science." Dame Margaret shook her feather. "Before it's over, we'll all be collaborators, steeped in silence and guilt."

Dame Margaret folded her hands and hesitated before she spoke again. "Good luck to you and your young man. I'm sorry about Eastbourne."

"You mean about his defection?"

"I'm sorry that he was killed," said Dame Margaret, smiling. "Always remember that it was the work of unknown bandits. He was warned so often about traveling on the Jerusalem-Hebron road."

"And Henderson?"

"You mean Henlein?"

Lily nodded.

"He seems to have left the country. No one has seen him for over six weeks."

Dame Margaret's feather still wavered in the breeze as Lily went into the Common room to say goodbye to Sir William.

The old man, seated in the big black chair, looked smaller and more frail than ever. He glanced up at her. "You're going home to write your dissertation?"

"Yes."

"About the graves at Tel al-Kharub?"

Lily nodded. "Perhaps you should go back to England. It's no longer safe here."

"There's nowhere else to hide," said Sir William. "I shan't see you again, you know."

Lily bent down to kiss him. She brushed against his dry cheek and touched his crackled skin.

"After this, archaeology will never be the same to you. When I was young, I wandered the streets of Alexandria through snapping fires and thought only of Caesar and the sack of the city, delighted at the chance to witness the recreation of a great event. Then I saw their eyes, and their fear."

"You understand then," Lily said. "I can't escape into the bloodless deaths of the past any longer." Just layers of charcoal and burnt beams, charred bones and shattered jars.

"It's not just data." The woman cowering in a gutted courtyard at Tel al-Kharub; the dead with wounded arms and smashed heads, shoveled into an ancient trench like sticks of broken wood. Now they had names—names like Avi and Eastbourne, like Dr. Stern, and even Abu Musa.

Will I be like this someday, lost in a chair, recounting tales of the violent days in Jerusalem?

Tears welled up in her eyes and she left, going through the hall and out the door to the waiting taxi.

Lily hesitated for a private moment of goodbye to Avi, to Jamal, and even the corrupt Abu Musa. Just one more layer in the archaeology of Palestine, Eastbourne had said.

Rafi stood by the car. He had already stowed bags in the trunk and the front passenger seat. Suitcases filled the floor of the cab and occupied the back seat. "I don't know if there's room for us with all this baggage."

I'm bringing home more than baggage, Lily thought, and leaving more than keepsakes behind. "That's all right," Lily said. "We'll sit on top."

She climbed in, mounting the running board and the suitcases as if they were stairs. "We'll manage," she said. "I'm Lily Sampson, girl archaeologist," and she reached out her hand to help Rafi into the cab.

ACKNOWLEDGMENTS

My thanks go to Linda McFadden, Cathy DeMayo and Sally Scalzo, who read draft after draft with keen insight and endurance; to Don Sheppard, Terri Eselun, and Toy King, who nursed the book through the first rough draft, and cured it of the purple passive; to Barbara Collins Rosenberg, who gave me sage counsel and encouragement; to Buffalo Boots Tiemann, for advice on the development of the Minox and its uses in the years just prior to the outbreak of WWII.

The ostraka mentioned in Chapter 3 are modified versions of those found at Lachish in Israel that refer to the invasions of the Assyrian army under King Sennacherib (Torczuner, L.I., et. al., *The Lachish Letters*, Oxford, 1938).

Most of all, I would like to thank Anita and Jordan Miller and the staff at Academy Chicago Publishers for their work on the book and their patience and support.

Aileen G. Baron
August, 2002

GLOSSARY

kefiya .... head scarf
fellahin .... farmers
finjan .... coffee pot
sherut .... jitney cab
hamsin .... desert wind
souk .... market
fiq .... a greeting
kova tembel .... "an idiot's hat"
habibi .... darling
mezuzah .... a religious amulet

Human beings at this point have already begun a fundamental psychic transformation: they feel amour-propre. Self-love transforms itself into amour-propre the moment we become aware of another human being as another will independent from and aware of our own. Our previously independent existence is now comparative. We become relative beings, aware of the possibility of superiority and inferiority, and determined to assign ourselves first place. Contentious passions—hate, anger, shame, envy—develop, because we not only seek superiority, but vainly insist that our superiority be acknowledged by others. Our awareness of others and of our relations with them transforms us into moral beings, beings who want not only to have goods, but to "be" good, to be "someone": amour-propre is the "true source of honor" and of all "our virtues and our vices." With this most comprehensive and explosive source of all the passions, we are "truly born to life" and become human, or at least what we recognize as human.[19]

Amour-propre can assume more and less healthy forms: its character is entirely determined by our sense of strength or weakness relative to our needs and relative to others. Amour-propre can foster a proud demand for independence and great generosity. Since it insists upon the position of superiority, however, it can do so only under certain conditions. When amour-propre is not carefully controlled, it becomes incessantly occupied with the slightest fancied slight, and gives us a powerful but necessarily impotent desire to make others, and even the world itself, do our bidding. At its worst, it transforms us into a weathervane blown by the winds of other people's fancies.

Yet it is not the development of amour-propre that according to Rousseau now confines human beings "everywhere in chains."[20] What then is the core of his many repeated denunciations of modern society as nothing but systematic subjection? All the "contradictions of the social system," the heart of Rousseau's diagnosis of our ills, arise from the disjunction between the mere appearance of the extension of our freedom to do as we will, and the actual servitude to the wills of others that results from our efforts to benefit from their aid.[21] The watershed of human misery, in his account of our development, is the invention of division of labor. The more inventiveness and inventions increase, the more we become habituated to new comforts and commodities, and the more we soften our bodies and spirit, multiplying our dependencies upon others all the while. The more a complex economy based on division of labor develops, the more we are compelled to serve others in order to serve ourselves.[22]

Society excites our desires and expands our vision of the possible by holding out an imaginary tool or weapon through which immense power seems to be within reach: the possibility of influence, authority, or even mastery over others. Once we have developed imagination and foresight, the limits of our imagined well-being extend far beyond our own powers to procure it. Civilized human beings are thus entangled in the contradiction that arises between their imaginations and their true power to satisfy the desires imagination suggests to them: we become dwarves with the appetites and hopes of a giant. Civilized society is enslavement because it inescapably places us in a situation in which the independence that is the deepest goal of self-love cannot be obtained. Independence can now only be pursued through the very means that cause it to recede ever further: dependence upon, and so submission to, the wills of others. A civilized being always says "I want," and must always do what others want.[23]

Society created in accordance with modern principles would, in Rousseau's view, bring to a head the corrupting contradictions at work within developed society. Modern society increasingly loosens bonds of sentiment or affection that are the basis for mutual esteem and good-will, and turns human beings into vain, grasping competitors. Thus, modern society would tend not only to destroy gradually its own political health, but the moral and psychic health of the human beings living within it. The fundamental task for a political thinker, then, is how to create a basis for real concord between individuals, lacking which society remains a covert state of war. Health or corruption, happiness or misery, depends upon our capacity properly to mold the relations to which we are subject within society, for society and its effects upon us are now inevitable. Opinions and passions must be transformed, identities must be shaped, in order to recapture some measure of the "sweetness of independent intercourse" enjoyed by the members of tribal societies.[24]

The political solution to the civilized war among individual wills is to reduce the opposition between them. Each individual must act only as she would wish everyone else to act; each individual must be made to place this "general will" as an inflexible law over his inclinations. Each must thereby be willing in the name of equal subjection to the laws to make the personal sacrifices required of good parents, citizens, and neighbors. Subjection to laws that come from all and apply to all is the necessary condition of freedom from subjection to any particular groups or individuals. Within society the "impulse of appetite alone is slavery," because by it we must submit to others; the cultivation of "virtue," which demands that we conquer our appetites in the name of moral freedom, returns us to self-mastery within society. Submission to the general will is therefore the condition of freedom within society.[25] Nonetheless, the fundamental political problem always remains: the private will always seeks to prefer itself, at the expense of others. The full force of education and political institutions must therefore be brought to bear to transform each citizen's amour-propre so that it leads us to identify with others, rather than to contend with them. Each naturally recalcitrant being who is a "perfect and solitary whole" must be shaped into a part of a larger whole to which he or she is so passionately attached that pride, joy, and life itself seem impossible without it.[26]

As Rousseau makes clear, however, the conditions required for such a society to arise are not only very rare, but likely impossible within modern times. The necessary political conditions—among which are a small, homogeneous population, a simple, preferably agrarian economy, rigid sumptuary laws, and censorship—are not compatible with the large, cosmopolitan, commercial, and liberal society envisioned by Enlightenment thinkers and in which we live. Two of the works contained in this volume, the fragmentary *Death of Lucretia* and *The Levite of Ephraïm* show what is involved in the origin of the sort of political community Rousseau admires. Both place special emphasis on the demands the establishment of such communities can place on women in particular.[27]

Those who live in a large modern society in which each pursues his own comfort and prosperity, will generally not be moved by, nor would it be sensible for them to respond to, appeals to Spartan, Roman, or Old Testament virtue. A palliative, however, remains both necessary and possible. While the political institutions and laws of a modern society may be governed by liberal or Enlightenment principles, the morals of its denizens and the smaller societies they form between them might be transformed in ways that could protect them from the larger society's most corrupting influences. Even in the society governed by the general will, the legislator's principal task is to shape the morals and character of the citizens: legislation is only fully effective when the citizens' customary ideas or beliefs about what is to be praised and blamed, what is honorable and dishonorable, accord with the law's demand that they respect and obey the general will.[28] Rousseau himself can be understood to engage in a similar task of shaping the morals and popular tastes of bourgeois society, but he does so against the grain, rather than in accord with what he fears will be its dominant ethos. His best-known efforts in this regard are his highly influential philosophical novels *Emile; or, On Education* and *Julie; or, the New Heloise*. By capturing his readers with extraordinarily rich and charming tales of exemplary men and women, who embody compelling visions of a new form of bourgeois family life centered around romantic love, Rousseau attempts to nourish their hearts, by inspiring in them sentiments that could counteract the narrow and vain selfishness fostered by modern life.[29]

We can now begin to understand the fundamental role that love, the family, and therefore the character of women play in Rousseau's thought. If morals can be so shaped, and amour-propre is the keystone of morals, the critical moments during which it is first, and most powerfully, felt shape the course and character of our passions and therefore of our relations to others. Whether we can be good for ourselves and others, whether we can be proudly independent as well as generous and humane—or will be vain, coldhearted, and scheming—depends on the character of our amour-propre. According to Rousseau, there are two basic turning points in human life, moments when we necessarily experience dependence on others. The first moment is that of infancy. In Rousseau's view, the first impressions we receive of others when we are most helpless and vulnerable profoundly shape our potential for both self-sufficiency and benevolence. Even if we have passed this hurdle and developed benign sentiments toward others, amour-propre inevitably arises during the second and more decisive moment, the "tempestuous revolution" of puberty. Sexual desire subjects us to others, whatever we may do; for to desire others is to want them to desire us in turn, and therefore compels us to make ourselves desirable. If one seeks the love and esteem of another, one must perforce make of oneself what that other wishes. With sexual desire, then, the opinion of others raises its throne in our hearts.[30]

Any attempt to guide amour-propre in one direction rather than another will therefore greatly depend upon the character of those who first love us and care for us, and then upon the character of those whose love we seek. We are formed and transformed, then, most of all by our mothers and lovers. "Do you want to know men . . . ? Study women."[31] Women seek to become what men want them to be; men aspire to what women are pleased to find in them. "Men will always be what is pleasing to women; therefore if you want them to become great and virtuous, teach women what greatness of soul and virtue are."[32] The character of family and sexual relations, then, are central to Rousseau's project.

Left to its natural course, however, sexuality does not reliably point in the direction of lasting romantic love, strong family ties, or any particular kind of masculine or feminine character. By nature, in Rousseau's account, sexual desire is originally a simple physical urge that presses on us infrequently and is easily satisfied. Human desire in general is extremely plastic or malleable: it is not attached to any particular object, and operates under the direction of pleasure. The particular objects we pursue to satisfy our strivings become desirable or not depending on whether we found them pleasant when we first tasted and tried them. What we find pleasant or painful, desirable or undesirable, what we deem attractive in others and in ourselves, therefore, is profoundly shaped by our early, accidental, experiences. Sexual desire, then, is given more specific direction by habit, by experience, and so by what we come to imagine. Imagination and amour-propre in particular play a far greater role in fixing the objects of sexual desire, and in greatly intensifying it, than we realize.[33]

In *Narcissus*, contained in this volume, Rousseau playfully dramatizes a vain young man who falls in love, not merely with an image formed by his personal experiences, but literally with an image of himself. The play explores the question of whether the vanity characteristic of the most sophisticated humans is capable of being cured by love, and even whether such people are capable of loving anything but themselves. In the lyric scene, *Pygmalion*, Rousseau shows the poetic or artistic character of love in its most extreme or most pure form: a man creates an image more beautiful than nature or even the gods and then longs for it to become real. Both *Pygmalion* and the "Letters to Sara" show that even the most intelligent and clear-sighted people fall prey to what they know to be illusions.[34] In short, human beings easily divorce sexuality from its purely natural "end" of procreation; the content and character of desire is filled in by human reasoning and imagination.

Sexual desire is potentially sociable because, unlike our other physical needs, it characteristically involves the participation of others. Understood in a strictly natural or physical sense, however, sexual desire is satisfied as easily and indiscriminately as hunger; in order to satisfy this desire, understood in a strictly natural or physical sense, male and female animals need only couple briefly and go their separate ways. By nature, then, sexual desire is a temporary need that does not fundamentally alter our independence. Hence, in Rousseau's view, the human family as we tend to think of it is no more natural than lifelong marriage. Natural inclination alone, without the intrusion of human opinion or institution, points only toward a family composed of mother and child. Rousseau describes the natural if temporary attachment between the female human animal and her offspring as arising at first from the mother's own need to nurse, and then from habit. Paternal attachment, however, lacking even this basic natural connection, depends far more upon habit and opinions than does maternal attachment. The two-parent family may quickly develop once males come to feel the sweetness of being loved by beings whom they can conceive as part of themselves; but for Rousseau, parenthood, and especially fatherhood, is far more contingent than we imagine or like to think.[35]

If human beings above all seek pleasure and freedom, nothing allows us to assume that either romantic or familial attachment will necessarily arise. In this area as in others, what we take to be nature is "present nature": what seems to be natural sexuality and natural sexual identity is the product of cultured desire; that is, of imagination and circumstance. Yet if sexual desire is amorphous, human invention can transform it and direct it in ways that support our natural health or independence within societies. What is physical in the "most free and the sweetest of all acts" must be turned into a genuinely moral phenomenon.[36] In Rousseau's account, the key to this transformation is that, on the most basic physical level, sex for women involves, or can involve, willingness as well as desire. Beginning from the physical fact that, for intercourse to take place, women need not feel desire, but need only not resist male desire (while the inverse is not true), Rousseau seeks to construct a form of moral love that relies on men's uncertainties in relation to women's wills. Learning to respect someone else's will in this way is a crucial beginning of moral life. Concern for the development of moral authority and respect in sexual relations, rather than a traditional view derived from patriarchal society, would therefore seem to be the source of Rousseau's attention to such things as female modesty and male pride.

On the basis of Rousseau's analysis of the unnaturalness of civilized relations, it might be tempting to recover a more natural sexual life based on the temporary pleasure that the physical act affords.[37] Certainly the romantic heroine and hero of his novel *Julie*, Julie and Saint Preux, understand their love as a natural revolt against the conventionality of the aristocratic ideas of family held by Julie's father.[38] Despite his reputation as the naïve advocate of natural goodness, however, in Rousseau's view a realistic understanding of sexual relations makes a "return to nature" for civilized human beings on this front as undesirable and even impossible as it is on any other. As Saint Preux's letter about Paris[39] shows, sophisticated promiscuity and contempt for matrimony lead to a life that is anything but natural in the primary sense. As Rousseau says in a different but related context, such a life is "a new state of Nature different from the one with which we began, in that the one was the State of Nature in its purity, and this last is the fruit of an excess of corruption."[40] This is necessarily the case because sexual desire is no longer infrequent and easily satisfied, but fueled by imagination and vanity.

Civilized human beings, then, are now inevitably subject to psychological effects from sexual relations, from the often profound miseries and hopes arising from amour-propre. To engage in natural relations is to engage in a meeting of bodies rather than of minds; bodies are readily interchangeable. Rousseau, ever hardheaded, wonders whether temporary associations of mutual gratification make us, in the end, subject to the whims or tastes of others. The more two individuals conceive of themselves as looking for the best sexual deal, the more their pairing risks being little more than corrupt modern society writ small. The unease and pains of such a situation, the flux of temporary bonds built on temporary wants, leads neither to stable society nor lasting happiness.

Bonds must therefore be tightened and made more lasting, and partners made more necessary to one another. If reason's account of nature as it is to be found in the *Second Discourse* does not supply such bonds, human beings within society must be guided by a poetic account of a harmonious and beneficent Nature that does. Rousseau therefore tells a tale of an ordered Nature that fosters love and family by dividing human beings into two natural genders: man and woman, two partial beings whose differences in talents, tastes, and charms complement each other perfectly, so that neither can feel complete without the other. Rousseau appeals to such an ideal while simultaneously revealing his profound awareness of the tensions and limits inherent in what he poetically presents as simply and incontestably natural. When he discusses the "nature" of women, he repeatedly states his view that "[m]oral truth is not what is, but what is good. What is bad . . . must not be admitted, especially when this admission gives it an effect it would not have had without it."[41]

For the creation of mutual, lasting attachment is even more important for women, Rousseau argues, than it is for men: while civilization makes us all dependent, it makes women unequally so. The original equality between men and women, arising from their relatively equal independence and vigor, is compromised not only by the general softening of body and mind within advanced societies, but by the greater frequency of childbearing, and the greater length of time needed to raise little human beings rather than little human animals. Savage women may be able to give birth and then run to catch up with the rest of the tribe. There is now, however, a fundamental inequality between men and women, Rousseau argues, when it comes to sex: the "male is male only at certain moments, the female is female all her life, or at least during her entire youth."[42] The more civilized women become, the more their relations with men make them generally unequally dependent upon them. While men and women are equally pleasure-seeking beings, men can seek pleasure without consequences, while—barring the aid of technology—women cannot. As long as this unequal physical dependence exists, decoupling sexual behavior from its periodic consequence tends to benefit men at women's expense.[43]

In the *Second Discourse*, Rousseau mocks Locke's argument that responsible fatherhood and monogamy are "natural" because that is what women with dependent children need. For, as he says tartly, "moral proofs do not have great force in matters of physics"; nature is not providential.[44] Hence a man can enjoy a "perfect liberty which he then voluntarily alienates." But what forms his will to alienate his liberty? To the degree that biology makes a woman dependent, she is subject to men's opinions: she is "subjected to many laws" that she must learn how to bend to her own advantage.[45] Unless she is wealthy, she must learn how to appeal to a man so that he will willingly alienate his freedom in favor of her needs and those of her children. Rousseau is in this, as in other matters, a realist. If women's sexuality imposes an unequal yoke upon them, lectures and moral declamations against the injustice of this inequality, as well as demands that means be put at women's disposal so as to liberate them from it, no matter how justified, are unlikely to prove all that effective. For Rousseau, no "ought" in the world can effectively be imposed simply by the force of law; nor can it have any effect if people are not moved to act upon it. Paternal care, familial affection, and loyalty do not simply arise by nature; they must be made attractive in order to arise.

Precisely because women are unequally affected by the consequences of sexuality, they are potentially the more political sex. Women have a greater desire and need to shape the opinion of those around them, and must be awakened to their capacity to do so. "Men depend on women because of their desires; women depend on men because of their desires, and because of their needs."[46] In order to offset a natural inequality of need, women must create lasting passion in men; unable to compel aid and attachment, women must attract lovers to want to give these. Physical attraction alone, however, is not durable. Hence the lasting authority of mistresses, as well as that of wives and mothers, rests on virtuous men; that is, men who can be constant, whose devotion will endure. Such devotion, however, is inspired only by the belief that one's beloved is worthy of it. "There is no genuine love without enthusiasm, and no enthusiasm without an object of perfection, either real or chimerical, but always existing in the imagination."[47] Women can govern men indirectly to the degree that men feel they possess beauty of character or strength of soul, so that one must aspire to obtain their consent. But in order to exercise this rule, women must seek to govern themselves in light of men's aspirations, and learn to consent only when men meet them in their turn.

By submitting to public opinion, then, women are also its judges and rulers. Because of this, women play a pivotal political role even where they have no direct share in political rule. Even the sound constitution of a Sparta or a Rome, the cities Rousseau holds up as models of devotion to civic virtue and political freedom, depended on the character of their women. For the austere civic virtue of Spartan and Roman men, in turn, depended greatly on their desire to aspire to the respect and love of mothers, maidens, and wives. Civic virtue depended upon the character of the city's women, the austere morals that governed their relations with men, and the institutions and customs that set men and women apart and made them the public judges of one another's virtues.[48] While Sparta no longer exists, women remain a potent social force. The mutual desire to inspire love creates a web of admiration, honor, and affection that not only draws men and women to one another, but fuels care for excellent and worthy character that benefits society as a whole. This is so much the case for Rousseau that not only can Julie be the governor of Clarens, as Sophie is of Emile, but that Rome can be said to have been governed by her women.[49]

In modern societies, women remain the weft of the social fabric, because they are best equipped to inspire and to maintain devoted family life. "The attraction of domestic life," Rousseau declares, "is the best antidote for bad morals."[50] The little society of the family, if it becomes a central and stable part of our lives, can nurture and strengthen loving attachments that counteract the centrifugal effect of self-regarding individualism. Deep familial love arises between real familiars: it arises from long, intimate habit, and the sweet confidence in the many tender cares its members give one another. It is thus also within the bosom of the family that the human heart can learn to open. For we seek what does us good, but we love what seeks to help us. When we experience the steady intention to care for us, and palpably feel the efforts others expend upon us, we respond with sentiments of gratitude, and come to feel a desire to repay the good we are shown and to be benevolent in our turn. The less we meet with such care during our first experiences, the more our amour-propre tends to become fractious and to concentrate narrowly on ourselves.[51] Our future sentiments toward our fellows, then, are given their direction during our formative years in the home. Thus the romantic novel of "[t]he child-centered family was undeniably born on the pages of *Emile* and *La Nouvelle Héloïse*."[52]

Further, parents who are attached to one another, and to their children, seek a place in which their loved ones will fare well. The "love one has for those near us . . . [is] the principle of the love one owes the State; [it is] . . . through the little fatherland which is the family that the heart attaches itself to the great one; [it is] . . . the good son, the good husband, the good father who make the good citizen."[53] Within modern societies, the family is the foundation of citizenship and of our willingness to do our duty to the laws; sweet and durable family bonds are the cradle of the emotional and moral habits that sustain both personal and civic virtue.

For Rousseau, a home must be a warm, vivid, and constant presence if it is to animate our affections. The family itself must hold a beating heart, and that heart is the nursing mother: "let mothers deign to nurse their children, morals will reform themselves."[54] Rousseau wonders whether the same overflowing bounty, generosity, patience, and sweetness one can experience in the bosom of one's mother can be so readily provided by another. It is also the mother who has a closer natural bond to the children, and is best placed to make the "bother" of children become sweet.[55] Rousseau's romance of the family is, again, based on realism: family is also much work, and an obstruction to many freedoms. Men—and women, too—can all too naturally wish to shift some, or even all, of its burdens onto others.[56] Rousseau's insistence on the central responsibility of the mother, then, as well as the degree to which he paints the two sexes as ruling in different spheres, is an attempt to produce a sexual division of labor within the family that, by making the spouses complementary, will help to produce the need for unity between them.

Poetic artifice is not only at the center of family life; it is also at the heart of what is for Rousseau the most ravishing experience of happiness that most human beings will ever experience. To be swept away by deep romantic love for another is to be moved by the expectation of a complete happiness that is happiness itself. These sentiments that elevate and heat the human heart, however, are the work of the imagination. "If one saw what one loves exactly as it is, there would no longer be love on earth."[57] The fuel for the passion of love is sexual desire. In Rousseau's view, however, it is only when the urge to possess is contained, and we are moved to ruminate over and over again on the desired object that, excited by its tantalizing distance from our grasp and by our own hopes, our imagination turns it into beauty beyond compare, adorned by every sweetness and charm we can lend it. As salt slowly crystallizes on a bare branch, transforming it into a coruscating gem, distance and desire transform our beloved into a resplendent being who transcends our every longing, and yet more.[58]

The imaginary adornment that gives rise to the deepest romantic love does not happen of itself; it is the product of sublimation, that is, of unsatisfied desire. For Rousseau, the character of desire is such that we only long for what we do not have. As such, romantic love is inherently fragile and short-lived, and cannot serve to keep the family together; it even poses a threat to the family. The more our grasp of a good is unsure, the more desirable it seems; the habit of possession saps enjoyment. Hence the "passions languish in boring freedom." Freedom of desire paradoxically makes desire more tepid: the "apparent obstacle that seems to move [the] object farther away" is in fact "what draws it nearer."[59] The differences that Rousseau depicts between the genders are critical here as well, for imagination is brought to life by what is different or new; in everything, habit and familiarity deaden the imagination.

Rousseau makes clear throughout his writings that the visions of family and romantic love he paints are as much questions as they are answers.[60] Nothing makes this clearer than the fate of the ideal couple, Emile and Sophie. Some readers have argued that the sequel to *Emile* shows the failure of Emile's education, although others have read it as an almost comical demonstration of its success.[61] Whatever may be the case for Emile himself, it is clear that the love of this couple who were made for each other seems unable to survive the harsh experience of the world. The uncertain ending of the sequel to *Emile* leaves the reader unsure as to the ultimate fate of Rousseau's lovers, but it is clear that the failure of their marriage launches the ultimate test of Emile's ability to be happy. Moreover, Rousseau makes it clear that this test begins because of a flaw in Sophie's education.[62]

Maternal and paternal devotion are necessary for society. Yet, in Rousseau's view, human sexuality is far more fluid than he depicts it to his wider audience—and, as the example of Rousseau's own unconventional loves would seem to suggest, romantic love and family are in great tension with our natural desire for independence, as well as with one another. While romantic love is "the supreme happiness of life," it is also the source of great instability and terrible pains.[63] Further, to the extent that the unequal dependency, which both subjects women and enables them to play the critical role Rousseau describes, is no longer a necessity as it was when he wrote, it could be argued that he would now explore the possibility of the pursuit of independence for both sexes. Why could not the rule of the general will be established between women and men as equal, independent, and fundamentally similar beings?

Rousseau was certainly capable of taking into consideration the significance of important changes in the conditions in which humans live.

The accidental move from the pure state of nature to nascent society entails a loss of independence, but brings with it the experience of "the sweetest sentiments known to men."[64] When this situation is lost, a successful transition to political life brings with it a moral existence and virtues unknown to the more primitive condition, but only at considerable expense. Even the largely irreversible corruption of political life that Rousseau saw in the large nations of Europe brings with it the possibility of a new sort of family life, with personal satisfactions and domestic morality not found in the healthiest political communities. Every advance comes at a price and, apparently, every failure brings an opportunity. Most of all, Rousseau insists that the fundamental tension between virtue and goodness, or morality and happiness, means that—whatever may be the case for individuals like Emile, Rousseau himself, or reflective women such as Rousseau's correspondent, "Henriette"—a successful social solution to the problems of human life is as impossible as squaring the circle. No reform of social or political life, however radical or successful, would change that fact.

Even if the problem of unequal dependence between women and men, and so the need for gender differentiation that Rousseau recommends in part in order to overcome it, had really disappeared, there remains a fundamental difficulty. Rousseau's account of human relations follows that of Machiavelli: we respect only what we feel we need. Lasting passion is a product of the imagination rather than nature; while nature alone points to similarity, the imagination is fired by difference. Therefore, the "more women will want to resemble [men], the less will women govern them. It is then that men will really be the masters."[65] Moreover, love and mutual dependency must be constructed in order to combat amour-propre's visceral reaction to the imposition of another will on ours. While in a city under the general will, human beings may feel that they are subject to exactly the same general rules, could such an arrangement be made effective within a single home? Family life is governed with a view to all sorts of particulars; therefore one or the other's view must in the end prevail. The relation between two willful beings may in the best case be one of perfect friendship. In Rousseau's view, however, that friendship will be more durable if each friend believes he or she is only a part when apart, and if each believes there is a province of rule particular to him and her. Rousseau presents this division of labor as "natural" because otherwise it would itself be an object of contention.[66] In the end, however, Rousseau's account of relations between the sexes is not only about managing the snarl of human wills, but about clearing a way toward the possibility of happiness.

Select Bibliography

The purpose of this bibliography is to point readers to scholarship in English (or translation) on the works in this volume, rather than to more general works on Rousseau. A number of additional works are cited in the notes to the introduction. A large number of essays on Rousseau have been collected in the four-volume collection *Jean-Jacques Rousseau*, edited by John Scott, Critical Assessments of Leading Philosophers series (New York: Routledge, 2006). This collection is cited as Scott, followed by volume number.

General Works on Women, Love, and Family

Lange, Lynda, ed. *Feminist Interpretations of Jean-Jacques Rousseau*. Re-Reading the Canon Series. University Park, Pa.: The Pennsylvania State University Press, 2002.

Okin, Susan Moller. *Women in Western Political Thought*. Princeton, N.J.: Princeton University Press, 1979.

Schwartz, Joel. *The Sexual Politics of Jean-Jacques Rousseau*. Chicago: University of Chicago Press, 1985.

Trouille, Mary Seidman. *Sexual Politics in the Enlightenment: Women Writers Read Rousseau*. Albany: State University of New York Press, 1997.

Narcissus

O'Neal, John C. "Myth, Language, and Perception in Rousseau's 'Narcisse.'" *Theatre Journal* 37, no. 2 (1985): 192–202.

Queen Whimsical

Murphy, Patricia. "Fantasy and Satire in Rousseau's La Reine Fantasque." *The French Review* 47, no. 4 (1974): 757–766.

Runte, Roseann. "The Paradox of Virtue: Jean-Jacques Rousseau and La Reine fantasque." *Studies in Eighteenth-century Culture* 23 (1994): 47–54.

Letter to d'Alembert

Coleman, Patrick. *Rousseau's Political Imagination: Rule and Representation in the "Lettre à d'Alembert."* Geneva: Droz, 1984.

Jensen, Pamela. "Dangerous Liaisons: The Relation of Love and Liberty in Rousseau." In *Love and Friendship: Rethinking Politics and Affection in Modern Times*, edited by Eduardo A. Velásquez. Lanham, Md.: Lexington Books, 2003.

Wingrove, Elizabeth Rose. *Rousseau's Republican Romance*. Princeton, N.J.: Princeton University Press, 2000.

Emile

Bloom, Allan. *Love and Friendship*. New York: Simon and Schuster, 1993.

Keohane, Nannerl. "'But for Her Sex . . .': The Domestication of Sophie." *Revue de l'Université d'Ottawa* 49, nos. 3–4 (1979): 390–400.

Schaeffer, Denise. "Reconsidering the Role of Sophie in Rousseau's *Emile*." *Polity* 30, no. 4 (1998): 607–626.

Shell, Susan Meld. "*Emile*: Nature and the Education of Sophie." In *The Cambridge Companion to Rousseau*, edited by Patrick Riley. Cambridge: Cambridge University Press, 2001.

Weiss, Penny. *Gendered Community: Rousseau, Sex, and Politics*. New York: New York University Press, 1995.

Julie

Fermon, Nicole. "Domesticating Women, Civilizing Men: Rousseau's Political Program." *Sociological Quarterly* 35, no. 3 (August 1994): 431–442.

Ray, William. "Reading Women: Cultural Authority, Gender, and the Novel. The Case of Rousseau." In Scott, 4:341–362.

Shklar, Judith N. "Rousseau's Images of Authority." In Scott, 4:223–246.

Letters to "Henriette"

Starobinksi, Jean. "The Antidote in the Poison: The Thought of Jean-Jacques Rousseau." In Scott, 1:340–387.

Trouille, Mary. "The Failings of Rousseau's Ideals of Domesticity and Sensibility." *Eighteenth Century Studies* 24, no. 4 (Summer 1991): 451–483.

The Death of Lucretia

Kelly, Christopher. "Taking Readers as They Are: Rousseau's Turn from Discourses to Novels." In Scott, 4:363–380.

Matthes, Melissa M. *The Rape of Lucretia and the Founding of Republics: Readings in Livy, Machiavelli, and Rousseau*. University Park, Pa.: The Pennsylvania State University Press, 2001.

The Levite of Ephraïm

Kavanagh, Thomas. "Rousseau's *The Levite of Ephraïm*: Synthesis Within a Minor Work." In *The Cambridge Companion to Rousseau*, edited by Patrick Riley. Cambridge: Cambridge University Press, 2001.

Kochin, Michael S. "Living with the Bible: Jean-Jacques Rousseau Reads Judges 19–21." *Hebraic Political Studies* 2, no. 3 (2007): 301–325.

Morgenstern, Mira. "Strangeness, Violence, and the Establishment of Nation-hood in Rousseau." *Eighteenth Century Studies* 41, no. 3 (2007): 359–381.

Pygmalion

Weber, Shierry M. "The Aesthetics of Rousseau's Pygmalion." *MLN* 83, no. 6 (1968): 900–918.

Emile and Sophie; or, The Solitaries

Senior, Nancy. "Les solitaires as a Test for Emile and Sophie." *French Review* 49, no. 4 (1976): 528–535.

I

GENDER IDENTITY

CHAPTER ONE

Narcissus,[1] or, The Lover of Himself

Comedy, by J.-J. Rousseau,
Performed by the Actors of the King, December 18, 1752.

CAST

LISIMON.
VALERE, ⎫
LUCINDE,⎭ CHILDREN OF LISIMON.
ANGELIQUE,⎫
LEANDRE, ⎭ BROTHER AND SISTER, LISIMON'S PUPILS.
MARTON, SERVANT.
FRONTIN, VALÉRE'S VALET.

The Scene is in Valére's Apartment.

SCENE I.
LUCINDE, MARTON.

LUCINDE.

I just saw my brother taking a walk in the garden. Let's hurry before he gets back, and put his portrait on his dressing-table.

MARTON.

Here it is, Miss, changed in its attire so as to make him unrecognizable. Although he is the prettiest man in the world, as a woman he shines here with new charms.

LUCINDE.

With his delicacy and with the affectation of his adornment Valére is a sort of woman hidden under the clothes of a man, and this portrait

SOURCE: Jean-Jacques Rousseau, *Letter to D'Alembert and Writings for the Theater. Collected Writings of Rousseau* X, trans. and ed. Allan Bloom, Charles Butterworth, and Christopher Kelly (Hanover, N.H.: University Press of New England, 2004).

cross-dressed this way,[2] seems less to disguise him than to return him to his natural state.

MARTON.

Very well, where's the harm? Since today women try to make themselves closer to men, isn't it fitting for these to meet them halfway, and try to gain in attractiveness as much as the women do in steadfastness? Thanks to fashion, all will put themselves on a level more easily.

LUCINDE.

I cannot get used to such ridiculous fashions. Perhaps our sex will be lucky enough not to please any less even though it becomes more worthy of esteem. But as for men, I feel sorry for their blindness. What do those giddy young fellows mean by usurping all our rights? Do they hope to please women better by endeavoring to resemble them?

MARTON.

As for that, they would be wrong, and women hate each other too much to love someone who resembles them. But let's get back to the portrait. Aren't you afraid that this little raillery will offend the Knight?

LUCINDE.

No, Marton; my brother is naturally good: aside from his flaw he is even reasonable. He will feel that, by making him a silent and teasing reproach with this portrait, I have thought only of curing him of a failing that shocks even that tender Angélique, that lovable pupil of my father whom Valére is marrying today. It is doing her a favor to correct her lover's faults, and you know how much I need the efforts of that dear friend to free myself from her brother Léandre, whom my father wants to make me marry too.

MARTON.

So that young stranger, that Cléonte whom you saw last summer at Passy,[3] still has a strong hold on your heart?

LUCINDE.

I don't deny it at all; I even count on the promise he gave me of turning up again soon, and on the promise that Angélique gave me of inducing her brother to renounce me.

MARTON.

Fine, renounce! Consider that your looks will have more strength to tighten that engagement than Angelique could have to break it.

LUCINDE.

Without arguing over your flattering remarks, I will tell you that since Léandre has never seen me, it will be easy for his sister to warn him, and to make him understand that, as he cannot be happy with a woman whose heart is engaged elsewhere, he cannot do any better than to disengage himself from her with a decent refusal.

MARTON.

A decent refusal! Ah! Miss, to refuse a woman made like you along with forty thousand crowns, this is a decency of which Léandre will never be capable. (*Aside.*) If she knew that Léandre and Cléonte are the same person, such a child would certainly change her epithets.

LUCINDE.

Ah! Marton, I hear some noise; let's hide this portrait quickly. It is doubtless my brother who is coming back, and while amusing ourselves by chattering, we have deprived ourselves of the leisure to execute our plan.

MARTON.

No, it is Angélique.

SCENE II.
ANGELIQUE, LUCINDE, MARTON.

ANGELIQUE.

My dear Lucinde; you know how reluctantly I joined in your plan when you had the adornment of Valére's portrait changed into a woman's attire. Now that I see you ready to execute it, I'm terrified that the displeasure of seeing himself toyed with will set him against us. Let us give up, I beg you, this frivolous teasing. I feel that I cannot find any relish in making fun at the risk of my heart's repose.

LUCINDE.

How timid you are! As long as you are only his mistress, Valére loves you too much to hold against you everything that happens to him because of you. Consider that you have only one day left to give vent to your whims, and that his turn will come only too soon. Moreover, it is a question of curing him of a foible that exposes him to raillery, and that is properly a mistress's work. We can correct a lover's faults. But, alas! A husband's must be endured.

ANGELIQUE.

But after all, in what respect do you find him so ridiculous? As he is lovable, is he so greatly wrong to love himself, and aren't we setting the example for him? He seeks to please. Ah, if that is a fault, what more charming virtue could a man carry into society!

MARTON.

Above all, into the society of women.

ANGELIQUE.

Still, Lucinde, if you take my word for it we will suppress both the portrait and all that air of raillery that might just as well pass for an insult as for a correction.

LUCINDE.

Oh, no! I do not lose the costs of my industry this way. But I am willing to run the risks for success alone, and nothing obliges you to be the accomplice in a business in which it is possible for you to be only the witness.

MARTON.

A fine distinction!

LUCINDE.

I shall be delighted to see the look on Valére's face. However he takes the thing, in any case it will be a rather amusing scene.

MARTON.

I understand. The pretext is to correct Valére: but the true motive is to laugh at his expense. There is women's genius and happiness. They often correct ridiculous people while dreaming of nothing but amusing themselves with them.

ANGELIQUE.

In the end, you intend to do it, but I warn you that you will answer to me for the result.

LUCINDE.
So be it.

ANGELIQUE.
For as long as we have been together, you have done me a hundred turns for which I owe you punishment. If this business causes me the slightest worry with Valére, watch out for yourself.

LUCINDE.
Yes, yes.

ANGELIQUE.
Consider Léandre a little.

LUCINDE.
Ah! My dear Angélique . . .

ANGELIQUE.
Oh, if you estrange your brother from me, I swear to you that you will marry mine. (*Softly.*) Marton, you have promised me secrecy.

MARTON, *softly.*
Fear nothing.

LUCINDE.
Still, I . . .

MARTON.
I hear the Knight's voice. Make your decision as quickly as possible, unless you want to give him a circle of girls while he dresses.

LUCINDE.
We must avoid having him notice us. (*She puts the portrait on his dressing table.*) Now the trap is set.

MARTON.
I want to lie in wait a little for my man so as to see . . .

LUCINDE.
Quiet. Let's flee.

ANGELIQUE.
What ill forebodings I have about all this.

SCENE III.
VALERE, FRONTIN.

VALERE.
Sangaride, this day is a big day for you.[4]

FRONTIN.
Sangaride; that's to say, Angélique. Yes, the wedding day is a big day, and one that even makes the ones that follow it devilishly longer.

VALERE.
What pleasure I shall taste at making Angélique happy!

FRONTIN.
Do you intend to make her a widow?

VALERE.
Malicious joker. . . . You know how much I love her. Tell me; what do you know that could be lacking to her felicity? With much love, a bit of wit, and a face . . . as you see; one can, I think, always consider oneself to be rather certain of pleasing.

FRONTIN.
The thing is indubitable, and you have performed the same experiment on yourself.

VALERE.
What I feel sorry for in all this is I know not how many little persons whom my marriage will cause to pine away with regret, and who will not know what to do with their hearts any more.

FRONTIN.
Oh! but yes they will. Those who loved you, for example, will busy themselves with thoroughly detesting your dear other half. The others . . . But where the devil can those others be found?

VALERE.
The morning is getting on; it is time to get dressed to go to see Angélique. Come now. (*He sits down at his dressing table.*) How do you find me this morning? I don't have any fire at all in my eyes; I have a poor color; it seems to me that I am not at all up to the usual standard.

FRONTIN.

Up to the usual standard! No, you are only up to your usual standard.

VALERE.

The use of rouge is an extremely nasty habit; in the end I shall not be able to do without it and I shall be extremely hard put without it. Where is my patchbox, then? But what do I see there? A portrait . . . Ah! Frontin; the charming object . . . where did you pick up this portrait?

FRONTIN.

Me? I'll be hanged if I know what you are talking about.

VALERE.

What! It wasn't you who put this portrait on my dressing table?

FRONTIN.

No, hope to die.

VALERE.

Who would it be then?

FRONTIN.

By my faith, I don't know anything about it. It can't be anyone but either the devil or you.

VALERE.

Or someone else. Someone paid you to be quiet. . . . Do you know how much Angélique loses by comparison with this object? . . . By my honor this is the prettiest face I have seen in my life. What eyes, Frontin! . . . I believe that they look like mine.

FRONTIN.

That says it all.

VALERE.

I find much of my air in her. . . . She is, by my faith, charming. . . . Ah! If her mind matches all that . . . But her taste answers for me about her mind. The minx is an expert in merit.

FRONTIN.

What the devil! Let's have a look at all these marvels.

VALERE.

Well, well. Do you think you are fooling me with your inane manner? Do you believe I am a novice in intrigues?

FRONTIN (*aside.*)

Am I deceived! It's him . . . it's him himself. How decked out he is! What flowers! What trimmings! Without a doubt it's one of Lucinde's tricks; Marton will have done at least half of it. Let's not disturb their teasing at all. My previous indiscretions have cost me too dearly.

VALERE.

Well then? Might Mr. Frontin recognize the original of this painting?

FRONTIN.

Bah! Do I know it! Several hundred kicks in the ass, and just as many boxes on the ear that I have had the honor of receiving from it in particular have solidified our acquaintance.

VALERE.

A girl, kicks! That's a little lusty.

FRONTIN.

They are little bits of domestic impatience that seize her over nothing.

VALERE.

What? Would you have been in her service?

FRONTIN.

Yes, Sir; and I even have the honor of still being her very humble servant.

VALERE.

It would be rather funny if there were in Paris a pretty woman who was not of my acquaintance! . . . Tell me sincerely. Is the original as lovable as the portrait?

FRONTIN.

How; lovable! Do you know, Sir, that if anyone could approach your perfections, I would find that she alone compares to you.

VALERE, *considering the portrait.*

My heart can't resist. . . . Frontin, tell me the name of this beauty.

FRONTIN, *aside.*

Ah! By my faith, here I am caught without an ace.[5]

VALERE.

What's she called? Speak then.

FRONTIN.

She's called . . . she's called . . . she's called nothing at all. She is an anonymous girl, like so many others.

VALERE.

Into what sad suspicions is this rogue throwing me! Could such charming features be those of a mere wench?

FRONTIN.

Why not? Beauty is pleased to adorn visages that take their pride from it alone.

VALERE.

What, she is . . .

FRONTIN.

A little person, very coquettish, very simpering, very vain without very much reason for being so: in a word, a true female fop.

VALERE.

Look at how these knavish valets talk about the people they have served. Nevertheless, I must get a look. Tell me where does she abide?

FRONTIN.

Good, abide? Does that one ever abide anything?

VALERE.

If you provoke me . . . Where does she lodge, rascal?

FRONTIN.

By my faith, Sir, so as not to lie to you, you know it just as well as I do.

VALERE.
What?

FRONTIN.
I swear to you that I do not know the original of this portrait any better than you do.

VALERE.
You aren't the one who put it there?

FRONTIN.
No, may the plague smother me.

VALERE.
These ideas that you gave me about her . . .

FRONTIN.
Do you see that you are furnishing me with them yourself? Is there anyone in the world as ridiculous as that?

VALERE.
What! I will not be able to discover where this portrait came from? The mystery and the difficulty arouse my eagerness. For, I admit it to you, I am very truly smitten.

FRONTIN, *aside.*
The thing is priceless! Look at him in love with himself.

VALERE.
Nevertheless, Angélique, the charming Angélique . . . In truth, I don't understand anything about my heart, and I want to see this new mistress before settling anything on my marriage.

FRONTIN.
What, Sir! You don't . . . Ah! you are joking.

VALERE.
No, I tell you very seriously that I could not offer my hand to Angélique, as long as the uncertainty of my feelings is an obstacle to our mutual happiness. I cannot marry her today; that's a settled point.

FRONTIN.

Yes, with you. But the Gentleman your father, who has also made his own separate little resolutions, is the man in the world least likely to give way to yours; you know that compliance is not his weak point.

VALERE.

She must be found, whatever the price might be. Let's go, Frontin, let's rush, look everywhere.

FRONTIN.

Let's go, let's rush, let's fly; let's make the inventory and the description of all the pretty girls in Paris. Plague, the good little book we would have there! Rare book, the reading of which would not put one to sleep!

VALERE.

Let's hurry. Come and finish dressing me.

FRONTIN.

Wait, here is the Gentleman your father very opportunely. Let's ask him to be one of the party.

VALERE.

Shut up, torturer. What an unlucky mischance!

SCENE IV.
LISIMON, VALERE, FRONTIN.

LISIMON, *who should always have a brusque tone.*
Well then, my son?

VALERE.

Frontin, a chair for the Gentleman.

LISIMON.

I want to remain standing. I have only two words to say to you.

VALERE.

Sir, I cannot listen to you unless you are seated.

LISIMON.

What the devil! I, I don't want to. You will see that the impertinent fellow will pay compliments even to his father.

VALERE.

Respect . . .

LISIMON.

Oh! Respect consists in obeying me and in not bothering me at all. But, what is this? Still not dressed? On your wedding day? This is a pretty thing! Angélique has not yet received your visit, then?

VALERE.

I was finishing doing my hair, and I was going to get dressed in order to present myself decently before her.

LISIMON.

Is so much apparatus necessary to do up your hair and put on a suit? Zounds, in my youth, we made better use of our time, and without losing three-quarters of the day strutting in front of a mirror. We knew how to forward our business with the beautiful ladies with a more just claim.

VALERE.

Nevertheless, it seems that when one wants to be loved, one cannot take too much trouble to make oneself lovable, and that such neglectful attire might not indicate lovers very occupied with the effort of pleasing.

LISIMON.

Pure stupidity. A little negligence sometimes goes well when one is in love. Women hold us in better account for our eagerness than for the time that we would have lost at our dressing table, and, without affecting so much delicacy in our attire, we had more of it in our heart. But let's leave that aside. I had thought of delaying your marriage until Léandre's arrival so that he might have the pleasure of assisting at it and so that I myself might have that of bringing about your wedding and your sister's on the same day.

VALERE, *softly.*

Frontin, what luck!

FRONTIN.
Yes, a marriage postponed; that's always so much gained on repentance.

LISIMON.
What say you, Valére? It seems that it wouldn't be seemly to marry the sister without waiting for the brother, since he is on his way.

VALERE.
I say, father, that nothing could be better thought out.

LISIMON.
This delay would not cause you any pain, then?

VALERE.
Eagerness to obey you will always overcome all my reluctance.

LISIMON.
Nevertheless, it was out of fear of making you dissatisfied that I hadn't proposed it to you.

VALERE.
Your will is no less the rule for my desires than it is of my actions. (*Softly.*) Frontin, what a fine fellow of a father!

LISIMON.
I am charmed to find you so docile. You will have the merit of it cheaply; for, by a letter that I just received, Léandre informs me that he is arriving today.

VALERE.
Well then, father?

LISIMON.
Well then, son; this way nothing will be disturbed.

VALERE.
What, you would like to get him married as he arrives?

FRONTIN.
Get a man married still in his boots!

LISIMON.

No, not that; besides, as Lucinde and he have never seen each other, they must be left the leisure of getting to know each other. But he will assist at his sister's marriage, and I will not have the harshness of making such a compliant son pine away.

VALERE.

Sir . . .

LISIMON.

Fear nothing; I am too well acquainted with and approve your eagerness too much to play you such a dirty trick.

VALERE.

Father . . .

LISIMON.

Let's leave that aside, I tell you, I can guess everything you could say to me.

VALERE.

But, father . . . I have made . . . some reflections . . .

LISIMON.

Some reflections, you? I was wrong. I would not have guessed that one. Upon what, then, if you please, do your sublime meditations turn?

VALERE.

On the inconveniences of marriage.

FRONTIN.

There is a text for commentary.

LISIMON.

Even a fool can reflect sometimes; but never until after the foolish act. There I recognize my son.

VALERE.

How, after the foolish act? But I have not gotten married yet.

LISIMON.

Learn, mister philosopher, that there is no difference between my will and the act. You could have moralized when I proposed the thing to you, and you were so eager for it yourself. I would have wholeheartedly listened to your reasons. For you know how compliant I am.

FRONTIN.
Oh! Yes, Sir, on that score we are in a position to do justice to you.

LISIMON.
But today when everything is settled, you can speculate at your ease, this will be, if it please you, without prejudice to the wedding.

VALERE.
Constraint redoubles my reluctance. Consider, I beg you, the importance of the business. Please grant me several days . . .

LISIMON.
Farewell, my son; you will be married this evening, or else. . . . you understand me. What a dupe I was of the blackguard's phony deference.

SCENE V.
VALERE, FRONTIN

VALERE.
Heavens! His inflexibility casts me into such trouble!

FRONTIN.
Yes, married or disinherited! To marry a wife or poverty! One would hesitate over less.

VALERE.
I hesitate! No; my choice was still uncertain, my father's stubbornness settled it.

FRONTIN.
In favor of Angélique?

VALERE.
Exactly the opposite.

FRONTIN.
I congratulate you, Sir, for such a heroic resolution. You are going to

die from hunger as a worthy martyr of liberty. But if it were a question of marrying the portrait? Ahem! Would marriage appear so horrible to you any more?

VALERE.

No; but if my father means to force me to it, I believe that I would resist with the same firmness, and I feel that my heart would recall me toward Angélique as soon as someone wanted to estrange me from her.

FRONTIN.

What docility! If you do not inherit the Gentleman your father's goods, at least you will inherit his virtues. (*Looking at the portrait.*) Ah!

VALERE.

What's the matter with you?

FRONTIN.

Since we fell into disfavor, this portrait seems to me to have taken on a famished physiognomy, a certain strung-out appearance.

VALERE.

Your impertinent remarks are costing us too much time. We should already have gone over half of Paris.

He leaves.

FRONTIN.

At the pace you are going, you will soon have gone round the bend.[6] Nevertheless let's wait for the outcome of all this; and, on my side, in order to feign an imaginary search, let's go hide in a tavern.

SCENE VI.
ANGELIQUE, MARTON.

MARTON.

Ah! ah, ah, ah! What a humorous scene! Who would ever have foreseen it? What you have lost, Miss, by not being hidden here with me when he was so completely smitten with his own charms!

ANGELIQUE.

He saw himself with my eyes.

MARTON.

What! You would be weak enough to preserve feelings for a man capable of such a fault?

ANGELIQUE.

He appears very guilty to you, then! Nevertheless, what can one reproach him for but the universal vice of his age? Do not believe, however, that insensitive to the Knight's insult, I will allow him to prefer over me like this the first face that strikes him agreeably. I have too much love not to have delicacy, and from this day forth Valére will sacrifice his follies to me, or I shall sacrifice my love to my reason.

MARTON.

I fear very much that the one will be as difficult as the other.

ANGELIQUE.

Here is Lucinde. My brother is to arrive today. Be very careful that she not suspect him of being her unknown man until it is time for it.

SCENE VII.
LUCINDE, ANGELIQUE, MARTON.

MARTON.

Mademoiselle, I wager that you would never guess what the effect of the portrait has been? You will surely laugh about it.

LUCINDE.

Eh! Marton; let's leave aside the portrait; I have many other things to think about. My dear Angélique, I am disconsolate, I am dying. This is the moment I need all your aid. My father just announced to me Léandre's arrival. He wants me to be ready to receive him today and to give him my hand in a week.

ANGELIQUE.

What do you find so terrible in that?

MARTON.

What, terrible! To want to marry a beautiful eighteen-year-old to a rich and well-formed twenty-two-year-old man! In truth, that is scary, and there isn't any girl of the age of reason who wouldn't be given a fever by the idea of such a marriage.

LUCINDE.

I do not want to hide anything from you; I received a letter from Cléonte at the same time; he will be in Paris right away; he is going to intervene with my father; he begs me to delay my marriage: in sum, he still loves me. Ah! my dear, will you be insensitive to my heart's agitation and to that friendship you have sworn for me . . .

ANGELIQUE.

The dearer that friendship is to me the more I should wish to see its bonds tightened by your marriage with my brother. Nevertheless, Lucinde, your peace of mind is the foremost of my desires, and my wishes are even more in conformity with yours than you think.

LUCINDE.

Deign then to remember your promises. Make Léandre understand very well that my heart cannot be his; that . . .

MARTON.

My God! Let's not swear anything. Men have so many expedients and women such inconstancy, that if Léandre began to get it into his head to please you, I bet that he would completely succeed in it in spite of you.

LUCINDE.

Marton!

MARTON.

I don't give him two days to supplant your unknown man without even leaving you the slightest regret for him.

LUCINDE.

Come now, keep it up. . . . Dear Angélique, I count on your efforts; and in the turmoil that is agitating me, I am hastening to try everything with my father in order to delay, if I can, a marriage that my heart's pre-occupation makes me foresee with fright.

She leaves.

ANGELIQUE.

I ought to stop her. But Lisimon is not a man to give way to his daughter's entreaties, and all her prayers will do nothing but reaffirm this marriage for which she herself wishes even more than she appears to fear it. If I take pleasure in playing on her anxieties for a few moments, it's to make the outcome sweeter for her. What other vengeance could be authorized by friendship?

MARTON.

I am going to follow her; and without betraying our secret keep her, if possible, from committing some folly.

SCENE VIII.

ANGELIQUE.

Madwoman that I am! My mind is occupied in jesting while I have so many things preying on my heart. Alas! Perhaps at this moment Valére is confirming his infidelity. Perhaps informed about everything and ashamed at letting himself be surprised, he is offering his heart to some other object out of spite. For that's the way men are: they never avenge themselves more eagerly than when they are most in the wrong. But here he is, completely preoccupied with his portrait.

SCENE IX.
ANGELIQUE, VALERE.

VALERE, *without seeing Angélique.*

I'm rushing about without knowing where I should look for that charming object. Will love not guide my steps?

ANGELIQUE, *aside.*

Ingrate! It is guiding him only too well.

VALERE.

Thus love always has its pains. I must experience them looking for the beauty that I love, not being able to find her to make her love me.

ANGELIQUE, *aside.*

What impertinence! Alas! How can someone be so conceited and so lovable both at the same time?

VALERE.

I must wait for Frontin; perhaps he will have had more success. In any case, Angélique adores me . . .

ANGELIQUE, *aside.*

Ah, traitor! You know my weak point.

VALERE.

After all, I still feel that I will lose nothing with her: her heart, her charms, she's got everything.

ANGELIQUE, *aside.*

He will do me the honor of accepting me as his fallback.

VALERE.

How whimsical I experience my feelings to be! I am giving up the possession of a charming object to whom, at bottom, my inclination still brings me back. I am exposing myself to my father's disfavor in order to be stubborn over a beauty who is perhaps unworthy of my sighs, perhaps imaginary, based on the sole evidence of a portrait fallen from the clouds and certainly a flattering one. What capriciousness! What folly! But what! Aren't folly and caprice the distinctive traits of a lovable man? (*Looking at the portrait.*) What charms! . . . What features! . . . How enchanting that is! . . . How divine that is! Ah! May Angélique not flatter herself that she can stand up to comparison with so many charms.

ANGELIQUE, *seizing the portrait.*

Assuredly, I do not care to. But let me be permitted to share your admiration. At least acquaintance with the charms of this fortunate rival will soften the shame of my defeat.

VALERE.

Oh heaven!

ANGELIQUE.

What's the matter with you then? You appear completely taken aback. I would never have known that a fop would be so easy to put out of countenance.

VALERE.

Ah! Cruel one, you know all the ascendancy you have over me, and you insult me without my being able to answer.

ANGELIQUE.

That's extremely badly done, in truth; and according to the rules you ought to be paying me insults. Go along, Sir Knight, I have pity for your perplexity. There is your portrait; and I am so little angry over you loving the original, that on this point your feelings are completely in agreement with mine.

VALERE.

What! You know the person . . .[7]

ANGELIQUE.

Not only do I know the person, but I can tell you that that person is the one I hold dearest in the world.

VALERE.

Truly, this is something new, and the language is a little peculiar in the mouth of a rival.

ANGELIQUE.

I don't know about that! But it is sincere. (*Aside.*) If he gets piqued, I win.

VALERE.

She has much merit, then?

ANGELIQUE.

It is up to this person alone to have an infinite amount of it.

VALERE.

No faults at all, doubtless.

ANGELIQUE.

Oh! Many. This is a little bizarre person, capricious, flighty, giddy, fickle, and above all unbearably vain. But, what! This person is lovable for all that, and I predict in advance that you will love this person all the way to your grave.

VALERE.

You consent to it then?

ANGELIQUE.

Yes.

VALERE.

That will not make you angry?

ANGELIQUE.

No.

VALERE, *aside.*

Her indifference makes me despair. (*Aloud.*) Shall I dare to flatter myself that you would like to make your union with her even closer for my sake?

ANGELIQUE.

That's all I ask.

VALERE, *furious.*

You say all that with a calmness that charms me.

ANGELIQUE.

What then? You were just complaining about my playfulness, and at present you are getting angry over my coolness. I don't know what tone to take with you any more.

VALERE, *softly.*

I am bursting with vexation. (*Aloud.*) Will Mademoiselle grant me the favor of making me acquainted with her?

ANGELIQUE.

That, for example, is a sort of service that I am very sure you do not expect from me: but I wish to go beyond your hope, and I promise to do so.

VALERE.

It will be soon, at least?

ANGELIQUE.

Perhaps as early as today.

VALERE.

I can't stand this any more.

He wants to leave.

ANGELIQUE, *aside.*

All this begins to augur well for me; he is too much vexed to be no longer in love. (*Aloud.*) Where are you going, Valére?

VALERE.

I see that my presence bothers you, and I am going to yield the place to you.

ANGELIQUE.

Ah! Not at all. I am going to depart myself: it is not just that I chase you away from your own home.

VALERE.

Go, go; remember that the one who loves nothing does not deserve to be loved.

ANGELIQUE.

It would still be better to love nothing than to be in love with oneself.

SCENE X.

VALERE.

In love with oneself! Is it a crime to have a bit of feeling for what one is worth? Nevertheless, I am really piqued. Is it possible for anyone to lose a lover like me without suffering? One would say that she looks upon me as an ordinary man. Alas! I conceal my heart's agitation from myself in vain, and I tremble at still loving her after her inconstancy. But no; my entire heart belongs only to this charming object. Let's rush to try some new searches, and let's combine the effort of providing for my happiness with that of exciting Angélique's jealousy. But here is Frontin.

SCENE XI.
VALERE, FRONTIN, *drunk.*

FRONTIN.

What the devil! I don't know why I can't keep myself upright; yet I have done my best to fortify myself.

VALERE.

Well then, Frontin, have you found . . .

FRONTIN.

Oh! Yes, Sir.

VALERE.

Ah! Heavens! Could it be?

FRONTIN.

Also I had a lot of trouble.

VALERE.
Hurry up then and tell me . . .

FRONTIN.
I had to go round to all the taverns in the neighborhood.

VALERE.
Taverns!

FRONTIN.
But I succeeded beyond my hopes.

VALERE.
Tell me then . . .

FRONTIN.
It was a fire . . . a froth . . .

VALERE.
What the devil is this animal muttering?

FRONTIN.
Wait for me to straighten things out.

VALERE.
Shut up, drunkard, knave; or answer me about the orders I gave you on the subject of the original for the portrait.

FRONTIN.
Ah! Yes, the original; precisely. Rejoice, rejoice, I tell you.

VALERE.
Well then?

FRONTIN.
It was not at the White Cross, nor at the Golden Lion, nor the Pineapple,[8] nor . . .

VALERE.
Torturer, will you come to a conclusion?

FRONTIN.

Patience. Since it wasn't there, it must be somewhere else; and . . . oh, I shall find it, I shall find it . . .

VALERE.

He's giving me an itch to knock him down; let's go.

SCENE XII.

FRONTIN.

Here I am, in fact, a rather pretty boy. . . . This floor is devilishly rough. Where was I? By my faith, I'm at a loss. Ah! Done . . .

SCENE XIII.
LUCINDE, FRONTIN.

LUCINDE.

Frontin, where is your master?

FRONTIN.

But, I believe that he is looking for himself right now.

LUCINDE.

What do you mean, he is looking for himself?

FRONTIN.

Yes, he is looking for himself so as to get married.

LUCINDE.

What does this gibberish mean?

FRONTIN.

This gibberish! You don't understand any of it then?

LUCINDE.

No, in truth.

FRONTIN.

By my faith, neither do I: yet I am going to explain it to you, if you want.

LUCINDE.
How will you explain to me something you don't understand?

FRONTIN.
Oh! indeed, I have been studying, I have.

LUCINDE.
I believe he is drunk. Eh! Frontin, I beg you, summon up a little of your good sense; try to make yourself understood.

FRONTIN.
By God nothing is easier. Wait. It is a portrait . . . metamor . . . no, metaphor . . . yes, metaphorized. It is my master, it is a girl. . . . You have made a certain mixture. . . . For I guessed all that, I did. Well then, can one speak any more clearly?

LUCINDE.
No, that is not possible.

FRONTIN.
My master is the only one who doesn't understand any of it. For he has fallen in love with his resemblance.

LUCINDE.
What! Without recognizing himself?

FRONTIN.
Yes, and that's what is extraordinary about it.

LUCINDE.
Ah! I understand all the rest. And who could have foreseen that? Run fast, my poor Frontin, hurry to look for your master, and tell him that I have the most pressing things to communicate to him. Be careful, above all, not so speak to him about your divinations. Wait, here's for . . .

FRONTIN.
For drinking, right?

LUCINDE.
Oh no, you don't need that.

FRONTIN.
It will be only as a precaution.

SCENE XIV.

LUCINDE.

Let's not hesitate for a moment, let's admit everything; and whatever might happen, let's not put up with such a dear brother making himself ridiculous by the very means I had used to cure him of it. How unlucky I am! I have offended my brother; my father, irritated at my resistance, is only more absolute because of it; my absent lover is in no condition to help me; I fear the betrayal of a friend, and the measures of a man I cannot put up with: for I certainly hate him, and I feel that I would prefer death to Léandre.

SCENE XV.
ANGELIQUE, LUCINDE, MARTON.

ANGELIQUE.

Console yourself, Lucinde, Léandre does not want to cause you to die. I admit to you, however, that he did want to see you without you knowing it.

LUCINDE.

Alas, so much the worse.

ANGELIQUE.

But do you know that that is a "so much the worse" that is not excessively modest?

MARTON.

It's a little vein of fraternal blood.

LUCINDE.

My God, how mean you are! What did he say after he saw me?

ANGELIQUE.

He told me that he would be in despair at obtaining you against your will.

MARTON.

He even added that your resistance gave him pleasure in some manner. But he said that with a certain air. . . . Do you know that judging from your feelings for him, I would wager that he is hardly indebted to you? Go on hating him just the same, he will pay you back pretty well.

LUCINDE.

That's not a terribly polite way of obeying me.

MARTON.

To be polite with us women, one must not always be so obedient.

ANGELIQUE.

The only condition he put on his renunciation is that you receive his farewell visit.

LUCINDE.

Oh, as for that, no; I give him a dispensation from it.

ANGELIQUE.

Ah! You cannot refuse him that. Moreover I promised it to him. I even warn you confidently that he counts very much on the success of this interview, and that he dares to hope that, after he has appeared to your eyes, you will no longer resist this alliance.

LUCINDE.

Then he has a great deal of vanity.

MARTON.

He flatters himself that he will tame you.

ANGELIQUE.

And it is only on this hope that he has consented to the treaty that I proposed to him.

MARTON.

I guarantee you that he accepts the bargain only because he is very sure that you will not take him at his word.

LUCINDE.

He must be unbearably conceited. Very well, he has only to appear: I shall be curious to see how he sets about deploying his charms; and I give you my word that he will be received with an air . . . have him come. He needs a lesson; count on him receiving one that is . . . instructive.

ANGELIQUE.

You see, my dear Lucinde, one does not always keep to what one proposes for oneself; I wager that you will be softened.

MARTON.

Men are awfully skillful; you will see that you will be appeased.

LUCINDE.

Be at ease on that point.

ANGELIQUE.

Watch out, at least; don't say that we didn't warn you.

MARTON.

It won't be our fault if you let yourself be taken by surprise.

LUCINDE.

In truth, I believe that you want to drive me crazy.

ANGELIQUE, *aside to Marton.*

Now she's ready. (*Aloud.*) Since you wish it then, Marton is going to bring him to you.

LUCINDE.

What?

MARTON.

We left him in the antechamber; he will be here right away.

LUCINDE.

Oh, dear Cléonte! Why can't you see the manner in which I receive your rivals?

SCENE XVI.
ANGELIQUE, LUCINDE, MARTON, LEANDRE.

ANGELIQUE.

Approach, Léandre, come to teach Lucinde how to become better acquainted with her own heart; she believes she hates you, and is going to make every effort to receive you badly: but I answer to you, myself, that all these apparent marks of hatred are in fact so many real proofs of her love for you.

LUCINDE, *still without looking at Léandre.*

On that footing, he must regard himself as very favored, I assure you; the poor half-wit!

ANGELIQUE.
Come, Lucinde, must anger keep you from looking at people?

LEANDRE.
If my love excites your hatred, know how criminal I am.

He throws himself at Lucinde's feet.

LUCINDE.
Ah! Cléonte! Ah! Wicked Angélique!

LEANDRE.
Léandre displeased you too much for me to dare, under that name, to avail myself of the favors I have received under that of Cléonte. But if the motive for my disguise can justify its result, you will pardon it as the scruple of a heart whose weak point is to want to be loved for itself.

LUCINDE.
Get up, Léandre; an excess of scruples offends only those hearts that lack them, and mine is as satisfied with the test as yours must be with success. But you, Angélique! My dear Angélique was cruel enough to amuse herself with my troubles?

ANGELIQUE.
Truly, it's a fine thing for you to complain! Alas! You are both happy, while I am prey to alarms.

LEANDRE.
What! My dear sister, you have been considering my happiness, even while you have anxieties about your own? Ah! This is a kindness that I shall never forget.

He kisses her hand.

SCENE XVII.
LEANDRE, VALERE, ANGELIQUE, LUCINDE, MARTON.

VALERE.
Don't let my presence bother you at all. What, Mademoiselle? I did not know all your conquests nor the lucky object of your preference, and, out of humility, I shall take care to remind myself that after having sighed the most constantly, Valére has been treated the worst.

ANGELIQUE.

That would be better done than you think, and indeed you need some lessons in modesty.

VALERE.

What! You dare to join raillery to insult, and you have the effrontery to applaud yourself when you ought to be dying of shame?

ANGELIQUE.

Ah! You are getting angry; I leave you; I do not like insults.

VALERE.

No, you will stay; I must enjoy all your shame.

ANGELIQUE.

Well then, enjoy.

VALERE.

For, I hope that you will not have the boldness to attempt your justification.

ANGELIQUE.

Don't be afraid of that.

VALERE.

And that you don't flatter yourself that I still preserve the slightest feelings in your favor.

ANGELIQUE.

My opinion about that will not change the thing at all.

VALERE.

I declare to you that I do not want to have anything but hatred for you.

ANGELIQUE.

That's extremely well done.

VALERE, *taking out the portrait.*

And henceforth this is the sole object of all my love.

ANGELIQUE.

You are right. And I, I declare that I have for this Gentleman (*Showing her brother.*) an attachment that is hardly inferior to yours for the original of that portrait.

VALERE.

Ungrateful one! Alas, there is nothing left for me to do but die!

ANGELIQUE.

Valére, listen. I pity the condition in which I see you. You ought to admit that you are the most unjust of men to get worked up over an appearance of infidelity the example of which you yourself have set for me; but today my kindness wants very much to overlook your failings.

VALERE.

Let someone try to do me the favor of forgiving me!

ANGELIQUE.

In truth, you hardly deserve it. Nevertheless I am going to teach you at what price I can resolve to do it. Formerly you have shown me feelings that I have repaid with a return too tender for an ingrate. In spite of that, you have shamefully insulted me with a preposterous love conceived on a simple portrait with all the flightiness and, I dare to say, all the giddiness of your age and your character. It is not time to examine whether I ought to have imitated you, and it would not be fitting for you—the guilty one—to blame my behavior.

VALERE.

It is not fitting for me, great gods! But let's see where these fine speeches are leading.

ANGELIQUE.

Here. I have told you that I am acquainted with the object of your new love, and that is true. I added that I loved it tenderly, and that is still only too true. By admitting its merit to you, I have not at all disguised its faults from you. I did more, I promised you to make you acquainted with it, and now I give you my word to do so as early as today, as early as this very hour: for I warn you that it is closer to you than you think.

VALERE.

What do I hear? What, the . . .

ANGELIQUE.

Don't interrupt me at all, I beg you. Finally, the truth forces me again to repeat to you that this person loves you ardently, and I can answer to you for this person's attachment as for my own. Now it is up to you to choose between her and me, the one for whom you destine all your tenderness: choose, Knight; but choose from this instant and irreversibly.

MARTON.

My faith, see how perplexed he is. The choice is pleasant. Believe me, Sir, choose the portrait; that is the way to be protected from rivals.

LUCINDE.

Ah! Valére, must you[9] hesitate so long to follow the impressions of the heart?

VALERE, *at Angélique's feet and casting aside the portrait.*

It is done; you have won, beautiful Angélique, and I feel how inferior the feelings born out of caprice are to those that you inspire in me. (*Marton picks up the portrait.*) But, alas! When all my heart returns to you, can I flatter myself that it will bring back yours to me?

ANGELIQUE.

You will be able to judge my acknowledgment by the sacrifice you just made to me. Get up, Valére, and consider these features well.

LEANDRE, *also looking.*

Wait a minute! But I believe I recognize this object . . . it is . . . yes, by my faith, it's him . . .

VALERE.

What do you mean, him? Say, rather, her. It is a woman whom I renounce as I do all the women of the universe, over whom Angélique will always prevail.

ANGELIQUE.

Yes, Valére; it was a woman up to now: but I hope that it will be a man from now on, superior to these little weaknesses that degraded his sex and his character.

VALERE.

Into what a strange state of surprise you are throwing me!

ANGELIQUE

You should be all the less unacquainted with this object as you have
had the most intimate commerce with it, and as assuredly you will not
be accused of having neglected it. Remove from this head that alien
attire that your sister had added to it . . .

VALERE.

Ah! What am I seeing?

MARTON.

Isn't the thing clear? You see the portrait and here is the original.

VALERE.

Oh heavens! and I am not dying of shame!

MARTON.

Ah, Sir, you are perhaps the only one of your order who knows what
shame is.

ANGELIQUE.

Ingrate! Was I wrong to tell you that I loved the original of this
portrait?

VALERE.

And I don't want to love it any more except because it adores you.

ANGELIQUE.

To solidify our reconciliation, please let me present to you my brother
Léandre.

LEANDRE.

Allow, Sir . . .

VALERE.

Gods! What height of felicity! What! Even when I was an ingrate,
Angélique was not unfaithful?

LUCINDE.

How much do I share your happiness! And how much my own is
even increased by it!

SCENE XVIII.
LISIMON, *the Actors of the preceding scene.*

LISIMON.

Ah! Here you are very conveniently gathered together. Because Valére and Lucinde both resisted their marriages, I had at first resolved to constrain them. But I have reflected that sometimes one must be a good father, and that violence does not always make for happy marriages. I have, then, made the decision to break off today everything that had been resolved; and here are the new arrangements that I am substituting for them. Angélique will marry me; Lucinde will enter a convent; Valére will be disinherited; and as for you, Léandre, you will have to be patient, if you please.

MARTON.

Extremely well done, by my faith! That's measuring it out; one could not do better.

LISIMON.

What's the matter, then? You are all taken aback! Doesn't this plan suit you?

MARTON.

See whether any one of them can unclench his teeth! A plague on foolish lovers and foolish young people whose useless babble never dries up, and who cannot find a word in a necessary occasion!

LISIMON.

Come then, you all know my intentions; you have only to comply with them.

LEANDRE.

Ah, Sir! Deign to suspend your wrath. Don't you read the repentance of the guilty ones in their eyes and in their perplexity, and do you want to mix up the innocent ones in the same punishment?

LISIMON.

Now then, I don't mind being weak enough to test their obedience one more time. Let's have a try. Well then, M. Valére, are you still making reflections?

VALERE.

Yes, father; but in place of the pains of marriage, they no longer offer me anything but the pleasures.

LISIMON.

Oh, oh! You have very much changed your tune! And you, Lucinde, do you still love your liberty very much?

LUCINDE.

I feel, father, that it can be sweet to lose it under the laws of duty.

LISIMON.

Ah! Now they are all reasonable. I am charmed by it. Embrace me, my children, and let's go conclude these happy weddings. What a thing is a stroke of authority at the right moment!

VALERE.

Come, fair Angélique, you have cured me of a ridiculousness that was the shame of my youth, and from now on I am going to experience near you that when one loves well, one no longer considers oneself.

CHAPTER TWO

Queen Whimsical[1]

Bookseller's Foreword[2]

This little Tale, written long ago and on a sort of dare,* had not yet been printed at all as far as I know. Seven or eight years ago several of M. Rousseau's friends had copies which multiplied in Paris and the provinces; one of the less disfigured ones fell into my hands. I do not believe that the author will be annoyed with me for publishing a folly already well-known and which he turned over to the public a long time ago.

Queen Whimsical[3]
A Tale

"Once upon a time there was a King who loved his people. . . ."

"That begins like a Fairy Tale," interrupted the Druid. "It is one too," answered Jalamir. "There was, then, a King who loved his people, and who consequently was adored by them. He had made every effort to find ministers who would enter into his views: but having finally recognized the folly of such a search, he made the decision to do by himself everything he could rescue from their seething activity. Obstinate about the bizarre project of making his subjects happy, he acted consistently with that idea, and such peculiar conduct held him up to an indelible ridicule among the Great: the people blessed him, but at Court he passed for a madman. Aside from that he did not lack merit; also he was named Phoenix.

"If that Prince was extraordinary, he had a wife who was less so.

SOURCE: Jean-Jacques Rousseau, *Autobiographical, Scientific, Religious, Moral, and Literary Writings. Collected Writings of Rousseau* XII, trans. and ed. Christopher Kelly (Hanover, N.H.: University Press of New England, 2007).

* It was a question of trying to write a tolerable and even merry Tale, without intrigue, without love, without marriage, and without anything risqué.

Lively, giddy, changeable, mad by her head, wise by her heart, good by temperament, wicked by capriciousness—there in a few words is the Queen's portrait. Whimsical was her name; a famous name that she had received from her ancestors in the feminine line, and the honor of which she worthily upheld. This person, so illustrious and so reasonable, was the charm and the torture of her dear husband; for she also loved him most sincerely, perhaps because of the ease that she had in tormenting him. In spite of the reciprocal love that reigned between them, they passed several years without being able to obtain any fruit from their union. The King was pierced by sorrow at this, and the Queen would have bouts of irritation about it which that good Prince was not the only one to feel: she took it out on everyone because she did not have any children; there was not a courtier whom she did not giddily ask for some secret for having one, and whom she did not hold responsible for its poor success.

"The Doctors were not at all forgotten; for the Queen was uncommonly docile toward them, and there was not a drug that they prescribed that she did not have prepared very carefully in order to have the pleasure of throwing it in their faces the moment that it was necessary to take it. The Dervishes had their turn; it was necessary to have recourse to novenas, to vows, above all to offerings; and woe to the priests in charge of the temples where Her Majesty went on pilgrimage: she rummaged through everything, and under the pretext of going to breathe a prolific air, she never failed to turn the monks' cells upside down. She also wore their relics, and decked herself out alternately in all their different outfits: sometimes it was a white cord, sometimes a leather belt, sometimes a long hood, sometimes a scapular; there was no sort of monastic masquerade that her devotion did not take into its head; and as she had a little sprightly air, which made her charming in all these disguises, she did not leave any of them without taking care to have her picture painted in it.

"Finally by dint of devotions so well performed, by dint of medicines so wisely employed, heaven and earth heard the Queen's prayers; she became pregnant at the moment that they were beginning to despair of it. I leave the joy of the King and that of the people to be guessed: as for her own, as in all her passions she went to the point of extravagance: in her raptures she broke and shattered everything; she embraced everyone she met indiscriminately; men, women, courtiers, valets, to find oneself in her path was to risk being smothered. She did not know, she said, any rapture comparable to the one of having a child to whom she could give a flogging entirely at her ease in her moments of ill humor.

"Because the Queen's pregnancy had been vainly awaited for a long time, it passed for one of those extraordinary events, for which all the world wants to have the honor. The doctors attributed it to their drugs, the monks to their relics, the people to their prayers, and the King to his love. Each took an interest in the child that was to be born as if it were his own, and all made sincere wishes for the fortunate birth of the Prince: for they wanted one, and the people, the Great, and the King united their desires on this point. The Queen strongly disapproved of them taking it into their heads to prescribe to her whom she was to give birth to, and declared that she aspired to have a daughter, adding that it appeared rather singular to her that anyone might dare to dispute with her the right of disposing of a possession that incontestably belonged only to her alone.

"In vain did Phoenix wish to make her listen to reason, she told him clearly that this was none of his business, and closed herself up in her dressing room in order to sulk; a cherished occupation, for which she regularly used at least six months of the year.[4]

"The King understood extremely well that the mother's caprices would not determine the child's sex; but he was in despair that she might thus give her eccentricities as a spectacle to the whole Court. He would have sacrificed everything in the world for universal esteem to justify the love he had for her, and the commotion that he made inappropriately on that occasion was not the only folly that the ridiculous hope of making his wife reasonable would have caused him to commit.

"Being at his wit's end,[5] he had recourse to the Fairy Discreet, his friend and the protectress of his kingdom. The Fairy advised him to take the routes of gentleness, that is to say, to ask the Queen for forgiveness. 'The sole end,' she told him, 'of all women's whims is to disorient masculine pomposity a bit, and to accustom men to the obedience that suits them. The best way that you may have for curing your wife's extravagances is to extravagate along with her. As soon as you stop contradicting her caprices, rest assured that she will stop having them, and that, in order to become wise, she is waiting for nothing but to have made you completely mad. Thus do things with good grace, and give way on this occasion so as to obtain what you will want on another.' The King believed the Fairy, and, to comply with her advice, having returned to the Queen's Circle, he took her aside, whispered to her that he was sorry for having inappropriately disputed, and that in the future he would try by his compliance to make up for the temper he might have put into his speeches in disputing against her impolitely.

"Whimsical, who feared that Phoenix's gentleness might cover her alone with ridicule for this business, hastened to answer him, that under this ironic excuse she saw even more pride than in the preceding disputes, but that, because the wrongs of a husband did not at all authorize those of a wife, she was hastening to give way on this occasion as she had always done. 'My Prince and my spouse,' she added aloud, 'orders me to give birth to a boy, and I know my duty too well to fail to obey. I am not unaware that, when His Majesty honors me with marks of his tenderness, it is less for love of me than for that of his people, whose interest occupies him hardly less at night than during the day. I ought to imitate such a noble disinterestedness and I am going to ask the Divan[6] for an instructive memorandum about the number and the sex of the children that suit the royal family; a memorandum important to the happiness of the State, and upon which every Queen must learn to regulate her behavior during the night.'

"This fine soliloquy was listened to very attentively by the whole Circle, and I leave it to you to think how many outbursts of laughter were rather maladroitly stifled. 'Ah!' said the King sadly, while shrugging his shoulders, 'I see very well that when one has a mad wife, one cannot avoid being a fool.'

"The Fairy Discreet, whose sex and name sometimes pleasantly contrasted in her character, found this quarrel so entertaining that she resolved to amuse herself with it to the end. She publicly told the King, that she had consulted the comets that preside over the birth of Princes, and that she could answer for it to him that the child who would be born of him would be a boy; but in secret she assured the Queen that she would have a girl.

"This notice suddenly made Whimsical as reasonable as she had been capricious up to then. It was with an infinite gentleness and compliance that she took all possible measures to distress the King and the whole Court. She hastened to have the most splendid baby linen made, affecting to make it so suited to a boy that it might become ridiculous for a girl; in this plan it was necessary to change several fashions, but all that cost her nothing. She had a fine collar of the Order prepared, shining with precious stones, and absolutely wanted the King to name in advance the governor and the preceptor of the young Prince.

"As soon as she was certain of having a girl, she spoke only of her son, and omitted none of the useless precautions that could cause those that should have been taken to be forgotten. She laughed uproariously when she depicted for herself the astonished and stupid countenance that the Great and the magistrates who were to adorn her delivery with their presence would have. 'It seems to me,' she said to the Fairy, 'I see on the one side our venerable Chancellor sporting large glasses to verify the child's sex, and on the other His Holy Majesty lowering his eyes and saying in a stutter: 'I believed . . . the Fairy nevertheless told me . . . Gentlemen, it is not my fault . . .' and other equally witty apothegms gathered together by the learned men of the Court, and soon carried to the extremities of the Indies.

"She represented to herself with a mischievous pleasure the disorder and confusion into which this marvelous event was going to throw the entire assembly. She imagined in advance the disputes, the agitation of all the Ladies of the palace to lay claim to, to adjust, to reconcile the rights of their important charges at this unforeseen moment, and the entire Court set into motion for a baby bonnet.

"It was also on this occasion that she invented the decent and witty custom of having the newborn Prince harangued by Magistrates in robes. Phoenix wanted to point out to her that this was to debase the Magistracy at a pure loss, and to cast an extravagant humor over the whole ceremony of the Court to go in great array to display Pretentious Nonsense to a little Brat before he could understand it, or at least respond to it.

"'And so much the better!' chided the Queen in a lively manner, 'so much the better for your son! If only he were lucky enough to have the stupid things they had to say to him exhausted before he understood them, and do you want them to save until the age of reason speeches suited to making him mad? For God's sake, let them harangue him to their delight, while one is sure that he understands none of it and he has the less boredom from it.' You ought to know, moreover, that they did not always get off so lightly. It was necessary to go through that, and by the express order of His Majesty, the Presidents of the Senate and the Academies began to compose, study, scratch out, and leaf through their Vaumoriere[7] and their Demosthenes in order to learn how to speak to an embryo.

"Finally the critical moment arrived. The Queen felt the first pains with transports of joy, which one hardly takes into one's head on such an occasion. She complained with such a good grace, and wept with such a laughing air, that one might have believed that the greatest of her pleasures was that of giving birth.

"At once there was a frightful din throughout the palace. Some ran to look for the King, others the Princes, others the Ministers, others the Senate: the greatest number and the most in a hurry were moving in order to move, and rolling their barrel like Diogenes,[8] had nothing to do but to make themselves look alarmed. In the eagerness to assemble so many necessary people, the last person they thought of was the obstetrician; and the King, who was beside himself with agitation, having by an oversight asked for a midwife, this inadvertence stirred up immoderate laughter among the Ladies,[9] which, joined to the Queen's good humor, made the delivery the most merry one that anyone had ever heard of.

"Although Whimsical had kept the Fairy's secret the best she could, it had not failed to leak out among the ladies of her house, and these kept it so faithfully themselves, that the rumor took more than three days to be spread throughout the city; so that for a long time the King was the only one who did not know anything about it. Thus everyone was attentive to the scene that was looming; as the public interest provided a pretext for all the curious to amuse themselves at the expense of the royal family, they made an event of spying out their Majesties' countenance, and of seeing how, with two contradictory promises, the Fairy could extricate herself from the affair and preserve her influence.

"Oh now, Your Lordship," said Jalimir to the Druid while breaking off, "admit that it is entirely up to me to provoke you within the rules: for you are well aware that this is the moment for digressions, reflections, portraits, and those multitudes of fine things, that every author who is a witty man never fails to employ appropriately in the most interesting spot in order to exasperate his readers." "What, by God!" said the Druid, "do you imagine that anyone is foolish enough to read all that wit? Learn that one always has the wit to do without it and that in spite of Monsieur the Author one has soon covered over one's display case with the pages of his book. And you who are playing the reasoner here, do you think that in order to avoid the imputation of a stupidity, it is enough to say that it would be only up to you to commit it? Truly, you only had to say it to prove it: and unfortunately I do not have the resort of turning the pages." "Console yourself," Jalamir said to him softly, "others will turn them for you, if this is ever written down. Nevertheless, consider that there is the entire Court assembled in the Queen's room, that this is the finest occasion that I shall ever have to depict to you so many illustrious people who are originals, and perhaps the only one that you will have to be acquainted with them." "May God hear you!" retorted the Druid jokingly, "I will be only too well acquainted with them from their actions: make them act, then, if your story needs them, and don't say a word about them if they are useless: I want no other portraits than the facts." "As there is no way," said Jalamir, "to enliven my narrative by a little metaphysics, I am quite simply going to take up its thread again. But to tell for the sake of telling is so flat . . . you do not know how many fine things you are going to lose! Help me, I beg you, to find my bearings, because Philosophy has carried me away so much that I no longer know where I was in the Tale."

"At that Queen," said the exasperated Druid, "whom you are having so much trouble in making give birth, and with whom you have been holding me in labor for an hour." "Oh, oh," responded Jalamir, "do you believe that the children of Kings are laid like a thrush's eggs? You are going to see whether it was not worth the trouble to hold forth. Thus after many cries and laughs the Queen finally removed the curious from pain and the Fairy from intrigue, by giving birth to a girl and a boy more beautiful than the sun and the moon, and who resembled each other so strongly that one could hardly distinguish them, which made it so that in their childhood people were pleased to dress them the same way.

"At this so much desired moment the King, departing from Majesty in order to return to nature, committed extravagances that he would not have allowed the Queen to commit at other times, and the pleasure of having children made him so much of a child himself, that he ran onto his balcony to shout to the people as loud as he could: 'my friends, rejoice all of you, a son was just born to me, to you a father, and a daughter to my wife.' The Queen who found herself for the first time in her life at such a festival, did not notice at all the work she had done; and the Fairy who knew her whimsical mind, was content at first to announce a girl to her, in conformity to what she had desired. The Queen had her brought to her, and, what extremely surprised the spectators, she embraced her tenderly in truth, but with tears in her eyes and with an air of sadness, that squared badly with the one she had had until then. I have already said that she sincerely loved her husband: she had been touched by the anxiety and the tenderness she had read in his glances during her suffering. Indeed at a singularly chosen time she had made reflections about how cruel it was to distress such a good husband, and when her daughter was presented to her, she considered only the regret that the King would have at not having a son. Discreet, to whom the mind of her sex and the gift of fairyhood taught to read easily in hearts, penetrated on the spot what was passing in the Queen's and, no longer having any reason to disguise the truth from her, she had the young Prince brought. Having recovered from her surprise, the Queen found the expedient so funny, that she gave forth peals of laughter about it that were dangerous in the condition she was in. She felt ill, they had a lot of trouble in making her recover, and if the Fairy had not answered for her life, the keenest pain was going to take the place of transports of joy in the heart of the King and upon the faces of the courtiers.

"But here is what might have been most singular in this whole adventure. The sincere regret that the Queen had for having tormented her Husband caused her to acquire a more lively affection for the young Prince than for his sister, and on his side the King, who adored the Queen, marked the same preference toward the daughter for whom she had wished. The indirect caresses that these two unique spouses gave to each other this way soon became a very decided taste, and the Queen could not do without her son any more than the King could without his daughter.

"This double event gave a great pleasure to all the people, and at least for a time reassured them over the fear of lacking a master. The freethinkers, who had made fun of the Fairy's promises, were made fun of in their turn. But they did not regard themselves as beaten; saying that they did not grant even to the Fairy the infallibility of her lie, nor to her predictions the virtue of making the things that she proclaimed impossible. Others, based on the predilection that was beginning to declare itself, pushed impudence to the point of maintaining that by giving a son to the Queen, and a daughter to the King, the event had given the lie to the prophecy at every point.

"While everything was being disposed for the pomp of the baptism of the two newborns, and while human pride was preparing to shine humbly at the altars of the Gods . . ." "One moment," interrupted the Druid, "you are confusing me in a terrible manner: inform me, I beg you, in what place we are. First, in order to make the Queen pregnant you promenaded her among relics and hoods. After that, you suddenly made us pass into the Indies. At present you just spoke to me about baptism, and then the altars of the Gods. By the great Tharamis, I no longer know whether in the ceremony you are preparing we are going to worship Jupiter, the holy Virgin, or Mohammed. It is not that it matters very much to me as a Druid whether these two kiddies are baptized or circumcised, but still one must observe the uniform, and not expose me to taking a Bishop for the Mufti and the Missal for the Koran." "How terrible!" said Jalamir to him, "some as subtle as you would be completely deceived by it. God keep from evil all those Prelates who have seraglios and take the Latin of the breviary for Arabic. God grant peace to all those honest Sanctimonious People who follow the intolerance of the Prophet of Mecca, always ready to massacre the human race in a holy manner for the glory of the Creator. But you ought to remember that we are in a country of Fairies, where no one is sent to hell for the benefit of his soul, where one does not at all take it into one's head to look at people's foreskin in order to damn or absolve them, and where the Miter and the green Turban equally cover sacred heads in order to serve as an indicator in the eyes of the wise and as adornment in those of the fools.

"I know very well that the laws of Geography, which rule all the Religions of the World, want the two newborns to be Moslems, but they only circumcise the males, and I need both of my twins to be ministered to. Thus find it good that I baptize them." "Go ahead, go ahead," said the Druid, "That, faith of a Priest, is the best motivated choice I have heard spoken of in my life." Jalamir continued.

"The Queen who was pleased to overturn all protocol wanted to get up at the end of six days and to go out on the seventh under the pretext that she was well. Indeed, she was nursing her children. An odious example, the consequences of which all the women represented to her in a very lively fashion. But Whimsical, who feared the ravages of spilt milk, maintained that there was no time more lost for the pleasure of life than that which comes after death, and that the bosom of a dead woman shriveled up even more than that of a nurse, adding in the tone of a Duenna, that there was no more beautiful bosom in the eyes of a Husband than that of a woman who nursed her children. This intervention of Husbands in cares that regarded them so little made the Ladies laugh a lot, and after that the Queen, too pretty to be so with impunity, in spite of her caprices, appeared to them almost as ridiculous as her spouse, whom they called derisively the bourgeois of Vaugirard."[10]

"I see you coming," said the Druid right away, "you would like imperceptibly to give me the role of Schahbaham, and make me ask whether there is also a Vaugirard in the Indies, as there is a Madrid in the Bois de Boulogne, an Opera in Paris,[11] and a Philosopher at Court. But go on with your rhapsody and do not set any more of these traps for me; for not being either a husband or a Sultan, it is not worth the trouble to be a fool."

"Finally," said Jalamir, without responding to the Druid, "everything being ready, the day was set for opening the gates of heaven for the two newborns. The Fairy made her way to the Palace early in the morning, and declared to the august couple that she was going to give to each of their children a present worthy of their birth and of her power. 'I want,' she said, 'before the magic water screens them from my protection, to enrich them with my gifts, and to give them names more efficacious than those of all the clods of the Calendar,[12] as they will express the perfections with which I shall take care to endow them at the same time. But because you ought to know better than I do the qualities that conform with the happiness of your family and your peoples, choose yourselves, and accomplish this way upon each of your two children by means of a single act of will what twenty years of education rarely do in youth and what reason does not do any more in an advanced age.'

"Immediately there was a great altercation between the two spouses. The Queen laid sole claim to ordering the whole family's character at her whim, and the good Prince, who felt all the importance of such a choice, was careful not to abandon it to the caprices of a woman whose follies he adored without sharing them. Phoenix wanted children who might someday become reasonable people; Whimsical preferred to have pretty children and, provided that they shone at six years, she troubled herself extremely little over their being fools at thirty. Try as the Fairy might to put their Majesties into agreement, soon the character of the newborns was no longer anything but the pretext for dispute, and it was not a question of being right but of setting out to win the argument against the other.

"Finally Discreet imagined a way to arrange everything without laying the blame on anyone; this was that each might dispose of the child of his own sex to his liking. The King approved an expedient that provided for the essential by sheltering the heir to the crown from the Queen's bizarre wishes, and, seeing the two children on their Governess's knees, he hastened to seize hold of the Prince, not without looking at his sister with a glance of commiseration. But Whimsical, all the more mutinous because she had less reason to be so, rushed like someone carried away to the young Princess and also taking her into her arms, 'You are all uniting,' she said, 'in order to irritate me; but so that the King's caprices might turn to the profit of one of his children in spite of himself, I declare that I ask for the one I am holding exactly the opposite of what he will ask for the other.' 'Choose now,' she said to the King with an air of triumph, 'and since you find so much charm in controlling everything, decide the fate of your entire family with a single word.' The Fairy and the King tried in vain to turn her away from a resolution that put this Prince into a strange perplexity; she never wanted to give in and said that she congratulated herself very much on an expedient that would reflect onto her daughter all the merit that the King would not know how to give to his son. 'Ah!' said this Prince overcome with vexation, 'you have never had anything but aversion for your daughter and you are proving it in the most important occasion of her life.' 'But,' he added in an outburst of rage of which he was not the master, 'in order to make her perfect in spite of you, I ask that this child here resemble you.' 'So much the better for you and for him,' retorted the Queen sharply, 'but I shall be avenged, and your daughter will resemble you.' These words had hardly been blurted out on both sides with an unequaled impetuosity, when the King, despondent over his foolishness, would have very much liked to take them back: but it was done, and without any going back the two children were endowed with the requested characters. The Boy received the name of Prince Caprice, and the girl was called Princess Reason, a bizarre name that she illustrated so well that no other women has dared to bear it since.

"Behold then the future successor to the throne adorned with all the perfections of a pretty woman, and his sister the Princess destined one day to possess all the virtues of a a decent man, and the qualities of a good King; a division that did not appear to be the most thought out, but upon which there was no going back. The amusing thing was that the mutual love of the two spouses, acting at that moment with the whole force that essential occasions always—but often too late— returned to it, and, the predilection not ceasing to act, each found the one of his children that ought to resemble him the more ill endowed of the two, and thought less about congratulating it than about pitying it. The King took his daughter in his arms, and clasping her tenderly, 'Alas,' he said to her, 'what use would the very beauty of your mother be to you, without her talent for setting it off? You will be too reasonable to make anyone's head turn!' Whimsical, more circumspect about her own truths, did not say everything that she was thinking about the wis- dom of the future King, but, from the sad air with which she caressed him, it was easy to doubt that at the bottom of her heart she had a high opinion of his share. Nevertheless the King, looking at her with a sort of confusion, made her several reproaches about what had happened. 'I feel my wrongs,' he said to her, 'but they are your work; our children would have been much more worthy than we are, you are the cause that they will only resemble us.' 'At least,' said she, immediately falling upon her Husband's neck, 'I am sure that they will love each other as much as possible.' Touched by what was tender in this flash of wit, Phoenix consoled himself by this reflection, which he so often had the occasion to make, that in fact natural goodness and a sensitive heart were enough to atone for everything."

"I can guess all the rest so well," said the Druid to Jalamir, interrupt- ing him, "that I would finish the tale for you. Your Prince Caprice will make everyone's head turn, and will be the imitator of his Mother too well not to be her torment. He will turn the Kingdom topsy-turvy while wanting to reform it. In order to make his subjects happy he will put them into despair, always finding fault with others for his own wrongs: unjust for having been imprudent, he will commit new faults in order to atone for the former. Since wisdom will never lead him, the good that he will want to do will aggravate the evil that he will have done. In a word, although at bottom he might be good, generous, sensitive, his very virtues will turn to his harm, and his giddiness alone, united to all his power, will make him more hated than a rational wickedness would have done. On another side, your Princess Reason, new Heroine of the country of the Fairies, will become a prodigy of wisdom and prudence, and, without having adorers, will make herself so much adored by the people, that each will make prayers to be governed by her: her good conduct, advantageous to everyone and to herself, will do wrong only to her brother, to whose foibles her virtues will be ceaselessly opposed, and to whom the public bias will give all the defects that she does not have, even if he does not have them himself. It will be a question of inverting the order of the succession to the throne, of subjecting jester's cap and bells to the distaff and fortune to reason. Scholars will emphatically set forth the consequences of such an example, and will prove that it is better for the people to obey blindly the rabid men that fate can give them as masters, than to choose reasonable leaders for themselves, that although one prohibits to a madman the government of his own possessions, it is good to leave him the supreme disposition of our possessions and of our lives, that the most insane of men is still preferable to the wisest of women, and that, even if the male or the firstborn is a monkey or a wolf, it would be a good policy for a Heroine or an Angel born after him to obey his wishes. Objections and replies on the part of the seditious, in which God knows how one will see your sophistic eloquence shine: for I know you; it is above all in casting aspersions on what is done that your bile gives vent with extreme pleasure, and your bitter frankness seeks to rejoice in men's wickedness by the pleasure it takes in reproaching them for it."

"Zounds, Father Druid, how you do go on," said Jalimir, completely surprised! "What a flood of words! Where the devil did you find such fine tirades? Never in your life have you preached so well in the sacred wood, although you did not speak any more truly there. If I let you do it, you would soon change a Fairy tale into a treatise of politics, and someday one would find in Princes' studies Bluebeard or Donkeyskin[13] instead of Machiavelli. But do not go to such expense to guess the end of my Tale.[14]

"To show you that I am not lacking in denouements as they are needed, in four words I am going to dispatch one of them, not so learned as yours, but at least as natural and surely more unforeseen.

"You will know then that the two twin children, as I remarked, having extremely similar faces, and moreover, dressed the same way, the King, believing he had taken his son, was holding his daughter between his arms at the moment of the influence, and the Queen, deceived by her husband's choice, having also taken her son for her daughter, the Fairy took advantage of this error to endow the two children in the manner that suited them best. Caprice was then the Princess's name, Reason that of her brother the Prince, and in spite of the Queen's peculiarities, everything found itself in the natural order. Having attained the throne after the King's death, Reason caused much good and extremely little commotion; seeking rather to fulfill his duties than to acquire glory for himself, he caused neither war for foreigners, nor violence for his subjects, and received more benedictions than encomiums. All the plans formed under the preceding reign were executed under this one, and by passing from the dominion of the father to that of the son, the peoples—twice happy—believed they had not changed master. The Princess Caprice, after having caused multitudes of tender and lovable lovers to lose their life or reason, was finally married to a neighboring King, whom she preferred because he had the longest moustache and hopped on one foot the best. As for Whimsical, she died of indigestion from a stew of chicken feet, which she wanted to eat before getting into bed where the King was cooling his heels while waiting for her one night when, as a result of flirting, she had induced him to come pass the night with her."

CHAPTER THREE

The Two Sexes

❧❀❧

[*This passage from the* Letter to d'Alembert *occurs in the context of the discussion of actors. After discussing the profession of actor in general and the effect on society of honoring this profession, Rousseau turns his attention to actresses. To prepare for this discussion he examines contemporary prejudices about the proper relations between the two sexes.*]

In every station, in every country, in every condition, the two Sexes have such a strong and such a natural connection between them that the morals of the one always determine those of the other. Not that these morals are always the same, but they always have the same degree of goodness, modified in each Sex by the inclinations that are suited to it. Englishwomen are gentle and timid. Englishmen are harsh and ferocious. Whence this apparent opposition? From the fact that the character of each Sex is reinforced this way and that it is also the national character to take everything to the extreme. Aside from that, everything is similar. The two Sexes love to live separately; both set store by the pleasures of the table; both gather together to drink after the meal, the men wine, the women tea; both abandon themselves to gambling without it being a mania, and make it into an occupation rather than a passion; both have a great respect for decent things; both love the fatherland and the laws; both honor conjugal fidelity, and if they violate it, they in no way make it into an honor to violate it; domestic peace pleases both; both are quiet and taciturn; both hard to move; both carried away in their passions; for both love is terrible and tragic, it settles their life's fate, nothing less is at issue, says Muralt,[1] than to lose one's reason or one's life in it: finally, both take pleasure in the country, and English Ladies wander as willingly in their solitary parks as they go to show themselves at Vauxhall. From this common taste for solitude is also born that for the contemplative readings and Novels with which

England is inundated.* Thus both, concentrated within themselves, abandon themselves less to frivolous imitations, more easily acquire the taste for the true pleasures of life, and think less about appearing happy than about being so.

I have cited the English, out of preference, because they are, of all the nations in the world, the one in which the morals of the two Sexes at first appear the most contrary. From their relation in that country we can conclude for the others. The entire difference consists in the fact that the life of women is a continuous development of their morals, instead of which that of men, being increasingly effaced in the uniformity of business, in order to judge about them it is necessary to wait, to see them in their pleasures. Do you want to know men, then? Study women. This maxim is general, and up to this point everyone will agree with me; but if I add that there are no good morals at all for women outside of a retired and domestic life; if I say that the peaceful concerns of family and household are their share, that the dignity of their Sex is in its modesty, that for them shame and chasteness[3] are inseparable from decency, that to seek out the gazes of men is already to let oneself be corrupted by them, and that every woman who shows herself dishonors herself; at that moment there will be raised against me that philosophy of a day that is born and dies in the corner of a big City, and that wishes to stifle the cry of nature and the unanimous voice of the human race.

"Popular prejudices!" they shout at me; "petty errors of childhood! Deception of laws and education! Chasteness is nothing. It is only the invention of social laws to shelter the rights of Fathers and Husbands, and to maintain some order in families. Why would we blush about needs that nature gave us? Why would we find a motive of shame in an act so indifferent in itself, and so useful in its effects as the one that contributes to perpetuating the species? Why, since the desires are equal on both sides, would their displays be so different? Why would one of the Sexes deprive itself any more than the other of the inclinations that are common to them? Why would man have different laws than the animals on this point?"

Your whys, say the God, would never end.[4]

But it is not to man, it is to his author that they must be addressed. Is it not funny that I must say why I feel shame at a natural sentiment, if that shame is not any less natural than that sentiment? One might

---

* Like the men, they are sublime or detestable. No Novel has ever yet been written in any language whatsoever equal to, or even approaching, *Clarissa*.[2]

as well also ask me why I have this sentiment. Is it up to me to give an account of what nature has done? According to that manner of reasoning, those who do not see why man is in existence ought to deny that he exists.

I am afraid that these great scrutinizers of God's counsels might have weighed his reasons a little lightly. I, who do not pride myself on knowing them, I believe that I see some that have escaped them. Whatever they say about it, the shame that veils the pleasures of love from other people's eyes is something. It is the common safeguard that nature has given to the two Sexes in a condition of weakness and self-forgetting that puts them at the mercy of the first comer: it is this way that it covers their sleep with the shadows of night, so that, during this time of darkness, they might be less exposed to each other's attacks: it is this way that it makes every suffering animal seek out a hiding place and uninhabited places, so that it might suffer and die in peace, away from attacks that it can no longer repel.

With regard to the chasteness of the Female Sex in particular, what gentler weapon could this same nature have given to the one that it destines to protect itself? The desires are equal! What does that mean? Are there the same faculties for satisfying them on both sides? What would become of the human species, if the order of attack and defense were changed? The assailant would choose at random times when victory would be impossible; the assailed would be left in peace when he needed to surrender, and pursued relentlessly when he is too weak to succumb. Finally, power and will—always in disharmony—never letting desires be shared, love would no longer be the support of nature; it would be its destroyer and scourge.

If the two Sexes had equally made and received the advances, empty importunity would not have been avoided at all; ardor, always languishing in a boring freedom, would never have been aroused, the sweetest of all feelings would hardly have brushed against the human heart, and its object would have been poorly fulfilled. The apparent obstacle that seems to move this object farther away is at bottom what draws it nearer. Desires, veiled by shame, only become more seductive for it; by hindering them, chasteness enflames them; its fears, its indirection, its reserves, its timid admissions, its tender and naïve subtlety, say better what it believes it is keeping quiet about than passion would have said without it: it is what gives value to favors and gentleness to refusal. Genuine love possesses in fact what chasteness alone disputes with it; this mixture of weakness and modesty makes it more touching and more tender; the less it obtains, the more the value of what it does obtain increases, and it is this way that it enjoys its privations and its pleasures at the same time.

"Why," they say, "would what is not shameful for man be so for woman? Why would one of the Sexes make into a crime for itself what the other one believes is allowed to it?" As if the consequences were the same on both sides! As if all woman's austere duties did not derive from this alone, that a child must have a Father! Even if these important considerations were lacking to us, we would always have the same answer to make, and it would always be unanswerable. This is the way nature wanted it; it is a crime to stifle its voice. Man can be audacious, that is his purpose:* someone must declare himself. But every woman without chasteness is guilty and depraved, because she crushes underfoot a feeling natural to her Sex.

How can one dispute the truth of this sentiment? If the entire earth did not give striking testimony of it, the comparison of the Sexes alone would be enough to verify it. Is it not nature that adorns young women with those features that are so gentle, that a little shame renders even more touching? Is it not nature that puts into their eyes that timid and tender gaze that one finds so hard to resist? Is it not nature that gives their complexion more radiance, and their skin more delicacy, so that a modest blush allows itself to be better noticed on it? Is it not nature that makes them fearful so that they flee, and weak so that they give way? What good would it be to give them a heart more sensitive to pity, less speed in running, a less robust body, a less tall stature, more delicate muscles, if it did not intend for them to let themselves be overcome?

---

*Let us distinguish this audacity from insolence and brutality; for nothing stems from more opposite feelings and has more contrary effects. I assume innocent and free love, receiving laws only from itself; it belongs to it alone to preside over its mysteries, and to form the union of persons, as well as that of hearts. If a man insults the chasteness of the female sex, and violently attacks the charms of a young object who feels nothing for him; his coarseness is not at all passionate, it is insulting; it proclaims a soul without morals, without delicacy, incapable of both love and decency. The greatest value of the pleasures is in the heart that gives them: a genuine lover would find only suffering, rage, and despair in the very possession of his beloved, if he believed he was not at all loved by her. To want to satisfy one's desires insolently without the permission of the one who causes them to be born, is the audacity of a satyr; that of a man is to know how to give witness to them without displeasing, to make them attractive, to act in such a way that they are shared, to subject the feeling before attacking the person. It is not yet enough to be loved; shared desires do not by themselves give the right to satisfy them; in addition, the consent of the will is needed. The heart grants vainly what the will refuses. The decent man and the lover refrains from it even when he could obtain it. To wrest this tacit consent is to make use of all the violence allowed in love. To read it in the eyes, to see it in the manners, in spite of the mouth's refusal—this is the art of the one who knows how to love. If he then ends by being happy, he is not at all brutal, he is decent; he does not insult chasteness at all, he respects it, he serves it; he leaves it the honor of still defending what it might perhaps have abandoned.

Subject to the inconveniences of pregnancy and to the sufferings of childbirth, does this additional work require a decrease of strength? But in order to reduce them to this painful condition, they had to be strong enough not to succumb except to their will, and weak enough always to have a pretext to surrender. That is precisely the point at which nature has placed them.

Let us pass from reasoning to experience. If chasteness were a prejudice of society and of education, this feeling would increase in the places where education is best tended to, and where they incessantly subtilize social laws; it ought to be weaker everywhere that people have remained closer to the primitive condition. It is exactly the opposite.* In our mountains the women are timid and modest; a word makes them blush; they do not dare raise their eyes to men and keep silent in front of them. In the big cities chasteness is ignoble and base; it is the only thing about which a well-brought-up woman would be ashamed; and the honor of having made a decent man blush belongs only to women of the best tone.

The argument taken from the example of the beasts is inconclusive, and is not true. Man is neither a dog nor a wolf. It is necessary only to establish the first relations of society in his species to give his feelings a morality always unknown to beasts. Animals have a heart and passions; but the holy image of the decent and the beautiful never enters into any heart but man's.

In spite of that, from where does the notion come that instinct never produces in animals effects similar to those that shame produces among men? Every day I see proofs of the opposite. I see some of them hiding themselves at certain needs, in order to conceal from the senses an object of disgust; afterward I see them, instead of fleeing, hurrying to cover up the vestiges. What keeps these efforts from having an air of propriety and decency, other than that they be done by men? In their loves, I see caprices, choices, planned refusals, that derive very closely from the maxim of arousing passion by obstacles. At the very moment that I am writing this, I have under my eyes an example that confirms it. Two young pigeons, in the happy time of their first loves, offer me a very different tableau from the stupid brutality that our so-called wise men lend them. The white pigeon follows her well-beloved step-by-step, and runs away in full flight herself as soon as he turns around. Does he stay inactive? Some light pecks rouse him; if he withdraws, he is pur-

---

* I am expecting the objection. Savage women have no chasteness at all; because they go about naked? I answer that ours have even less, because they get dressed. See the end of this essay, on the subject of the girls of Lacedaemon.

sued; if he resists, a little flight of six feet attracts him again; nature's innocence arranges the coquettish behavior and the feeble resistance with an art that the most skilful coquette would hardly have. No, the playful Galatea did not do any better, and Virgil could have drawn one of his most charming images from a dovecote.

Even if one could deny that a peculiar sentiment of chasteness were natural to women, would it be any less true that in society their share must be a domestic and retired life and that one must bring them up in the principles that relate to it? If the timidity, chasteness, modesty that belong to them are all social inventions, it is important to society that women acquire these qualities; it is important to cultivate them, and every woman who disdains them offends against good morals. Is there in the world a sight as touching, as respectable as that of a Mother of a family surrounded by her children, supervising her servants' labors, procuring a happy life for her husband, and wisely governing the household? It is there that she shows herself in all the dignity of a decent woman; it is there that she truly imposes respect, and that beauty shares with honor the homage rendered to virtue. A household whose mistress is absent is a body without a soul that soon falls into corruption; a woman out of her household loses her greatest luster, and, despoiled of her true ornaments, she shows herself indecently. If she has a husband, what is she looking for among men? If she does not have one, how can she expose herself to repelling by a hardly modest bearing, the one who would be tempted to become her husband? Whatever she might do, one feels that she is not in her place in public, and even her beauty, which pleases without captivating, is only one more wrong for which the heart reproaches her. Whether that impression comes to us from nature or education, it is common to all the peoples of the world; everywhere one gives consideration to women in proportion to their modesty; everywhere one is convinced that by neglecting the manners of their Sex they are neglecting its duties; everywhere one sees then that, turning the manly and firm assurance of man into brazenness, they debase themselves by this odious imitation, and dishonor their sex and ours at the same time.

I know that opposite customs reign in some countries; but see also what morals they have caused to be born! I would not want any other example to confirm my maxims. Let us apply to women's morals what I said above about the honor that they are given. Among all ancient civilized peoples they lived very secluded lives; they showed themselves in public rarely; never with men, they did not walk about with them. They did not have the best place at the theater, they did not put themselves on display;* they were not even allowed to attend all of them, and it is known that there was the death penalty for those who would dare to show themselves at the Olympic Games.

In the house, they had a private apartment where the men did not enter at all. When their husbands had someone over for a meal, they rarely presented themselves at the table; decent women left it before the end of the meal, and the others did not appear at all at the beginning. There was no common gathering for the two Sexes; they did not pass the day together at all. This care not to sate themselves with each other made it so that they saw each other again with more pleasure; it is certain that in general domestic peace was better reinforced, and that more union reigned between spouses** than reigns today.

Such were the practices of the Persians, the Greeks, the Romans, and even the Egyptians, in spite of Herodotus's bad jokes, which refute themselves.[5] If women sometimes went beyond the limits of this modesty, the public outcry showed that this was an exception. What has not been said about the freedom of the Female Sex at Sparta? One can also understand from Aristophanes' *Lysistrata* how shocking the impudence of the Athenian women was to the eyes of the Greeks; and, in Rome already corrupt, with what scandal did they still see the Roman Ladies present themselves at the Tribunal of the Triumvirs.

Everything has changed. Since crowds of barbarians dragging their women with them in their armies, had inundated Europe, the license of the camps, joined to the natural coldness of the northern climates, which makes reserve less necessary, introduced another manner of living, which was favored by the books of chivalry, in which beautiful Ladies passed their lives getting themselves carried away by men, with the most honorable of intentions. Because these books were the schools of gallantry of the time, the ideas of freedom that they inspire were introduced, above all in Courts and big cities, where people prided themselves more on politeness; by the very progress of this politeness, it finally had to degenerate into coarseness. This is how the modesty natural to the Female Sex has disappeared little by little, and the morals of camp followers have been transmitted to women of quality.

But do you want to know how shocking these practices, contrary to natural ideas, are for anyone who is not used to them? Judge about it

---

* At the theater of Athens the women occupied a high Gallery called *Cercys*, not very convenient for seeing and being seen; but, from the adventure of Valeria and Sulla, it appears that at the circus of Rome they were mixed with the men.

** One could attribute the cause of this harmony to the facility of divorce; but the Greeks made little use of it, and Rome survived five hundred years before anyone took advantage of the law that allowed it.

from the surprise and perplexity of Foreigners and Provincials at the sight of these manners that are so new for them. This embarrassment speaks highly of women of their countries, and one can believe that those who cause it would be less proud of it, if its source were better known to them. It is not that they are impressive; it is rather that they make them blush, and that chasteness, dismissed from her speeches and her bearing by the woman, takes refuge in the man's heart.

II

WOMEN

CHAPTER FOUR

"On Women"[1]

[*This fragment dates from an early stage of Rousseau's career, some years before he achieved literary fame with his* Discourse on the Sciences and the Arts. *It probably dates from the period when he was a secretary for the wealthy Dupin family. Mme. Dupin was working on an account of the political influence of women through history.*]

Another subject of admiration for me is the air of confidence with which we make the brilliant enumeration of all the great men that History has celebrated in order to put them into parallel with the small number of Heroines whom it has deigned to remember, and we believe we find our advantage very well in this comparison. Ah, Gentlemen, let the whim of transmitting their annals to posterity come to women, and you will see in what rank you may be placed and whether, perhaps based on reasons that are more just, they will not award themselves the preeminence that you usurp with so much pride.

And after all, if we entered equitably into the details of all the fine actions to which the times have given birth and if we examine the genuine reasons that might have increased or diminished their number, I do not at all doubt that we would find much more proportion there than we find at first and that the scale might stay just about in equilibrium.

Let us first consider women deprived of their freedom by the tyranny of men, and the latter masters of everything. Crowns, offices, employments, command of armies—everything is in their hands; from the earliest times they have taken hold of them by I know not what natural right that I have never been able to understand very well and that might very well have no other foundation than superior force. Let us also consider the character of the human mind, which wants only

SOURCE: Jean-Jacques Rousseau, *Autobiographical, Scientific, Religious, Moral, and Literary Writings. Collected Writings of Rousseau* XII, trans. and ed. Christopher Kelly (Hanover, N.H.: University Press of New England, 2007).

what is brilliant, which admires virtue only in the midst of greatness and majesty, which despises everything greater and more admirable that subject and dependent people can do in their station.

After having speculated about all that, let us enter into the details of the comparison, and, for example, put into parallel Mithridates with Zenobia, Romulus with Dido, Cato of Utica with Lucretia (one of whom gave himself death for the loss of his liberty and the other for that of her honor), the Count de Dunois with Joan of Arc, finally Cornelia, Arria, Artemisia, Fulvia, Elisabeth, the Countess of Thököly, and so many other Heroines of all times with the greatest men;[2] in truth we shall find that the number of the latter outnumber infinitely, but in recompense we shall see in the other sex models as perfect in all sorts of civic and moral virtues. If women had had as great a share as we do in the handling of business, and in the governments of Empires, perhaps they would have pushed Heroism and greatness of courage farther and would have distinguished themselves in greater number. Few of those who have had the good fortune to rule states and command armies have remained in mediocrity; they have almost all distinguished themselves by some brilliant point by which they have deserved our admiration for them. It is far from being the case that one could say as much of so many Monarchs who have governed nations: how many of them are there, as Voltaire also said,[3] whose name deserved to be found anywhere but in chronological tables where they are only to serve as an epoch? I repeat it, all proportions maintained, women would have been able to give greater examples of greatness of soul and love of virtue and in greater number than men have ever done if our injustice had not despoiled, along with their freedom, all the occasions to manifest them to the eyes of the world.

I reserve another time for speaking to you about the women who have had a share in the republic of letters and who have adorned it by their works that are ingenious and full of delicacy.

CHAPTER FIVE

"Sophie; *or, Woman*"

[*This section of Book V of* Emile *forms a self-contained whole within the book. At the end of Book IV the fictional student, Emile, has set out in search for a wife. He and his tutor have discussed what he is looking for and the image they arrive at is given the name, Sophie. The lengthy section that follows discusses the education of Emile's intended wife. It is followed by three short passages from later in Book V that elaborate on details of their courtship up to the day after their wedding.*]

Sophie; *or, Woman*

Sophie must be woman as Emile is man. That is to say, she must have everything that suits the constitution of her species and of her sex in order to fill her place in the physical and moral order. Let us begin, then, by examining the conformities and the differences between her sex and ours.

In everything that does not derive from sex, woman is man: she has the same organs, the same needs, the same faculties. The machine is built in the same way: its parts are the same; the action of the parts is the same in one and the other; the form is similar. According to whatever relation one considers them, they differ only by more or less.

In everything that derives from sex, woman and man are related at every point and differ at every point. The difficulty in comparing them comes from that of determining what in the constitution of one and of the other arises from sex, and what does not. On the basis of comparative anatomy, and even by inspection alone, one finds between them general differences that appear not to derive from sex. They do derive from it nevertheless, but through connections that we are incapable of perceiving. We do not know how far these connections may extend. The only thing we know with certainty is that everything they have in common belongs to the species, and everything in which they differ belongs to sex. According to this double point of view we find between them so many relations and so many oppositions, that it is perhaps one of the marvels of nature to have been able to make two such beings so similar by constituting them so differently.

These relations and these differences must influence what is moral. This consequence is tangible, conforms with experience, and shows the futility of the disputes over whether there is an unequal advantage or equality between the sexes. As if each of the two, proceeding to the ends of nature according to its particular destination, were not more perfect in so doing, than if it resembled the other more! In what they have in common they are equals; in what is different, they are not comparable. A perfect woman and a perfect man must not resemble each other any more in mind than in aspect, and perfection is not susceptible of more or less.

In the union of the sexes each cooperates equally in the common object, but not in the same manner. From this diversity is born the first assignable difference in the moral relations of one and the other. One must be active and strong; the other, passive and weak. It is necessary that one will and be able; it is enough that the other resists little.

This principle once established, it follows that woman is made especially to please man. If man must please her in turn, it arises from a less direct necessity. His merit is in his power; he pleases solely by being strong. This is not the law of love, I agree. But it is that of nature, anterior to love itself.

If woman is made to please and to be subjugated, she must make herself agreeable to man instead of provoking him. Her violence is in her charms. It is by these that she must constrain him to find his force and to use it. The art most sure to animate this force is to make it necessary by resistance. Then amour-propre is joined to desire, and one triumphs in the victory that the other has made him gain. From this are born attack and defense, the audacity of one sex and the timidity of the other, and finally the modesty and shame with which nature armed the weak in order to enslave the strong.

Who can think that it indifferently prescribed the same advances to both, and that the first to form desires must also be the first to give sign of them? What a strange depravity of judgment! Because the enterprise has such different consequences for both sexes, is it natural that they should have the same audacity in yielding to it? With such a great inequality in the common stake, how can one fail to grasp that if reserve did not impose on one the moderation that nature imposes on the other, the ruin of both would soon result, and humankind would perish from the means established to preserve it? With the facility women have of stirring men's senses and of reviving in the bottom of their hearts the remains of an almost extinguished sexual desire, if, especially in warm countries where more women are born than men, there were an unfortunate climate on earth where philosophy had introduced this practice, men tyrannized by them would finally be their victims, and would see themselves dragged to their deaths without ever being able to defend themselves.

If females among animals do not have the same shame, what follows from this? Do they, like women, have the unlimited desires to which this shame serves as a brake? Desire comes for them only with need; the need once satisfied, desire ceases. They no longer feign* to repel the male but really do so. They do exactly the contrary of what Augustus's daughter did: they no longer receive passengers when the ship has its cargo.[1] Even when they are free, their periods of goodwill are short and soon over; instinct impels them and instinct stops them. What will become of the supplement for this negative instinct in women once you have taken away their modesty?[2] To wait until they no longer care for men is to wait until they are no longer good for anything.

The supreme Being wanted to honor the human species in everything. While giving man inclinations beyond measure, he gives him at the same time the law that regulates them, so that he might be free and command himself. In delivering him to immoderate passions, to these passions he joins reason to govern them. In delivering woman to unlimited desires, he joins to these desires modesty to contain them. In addition, he adds yet another actual reward for the good use of one's faculties; namely, the taste one acquires for decent things when one makes them the rule of one's actions. All that, it seems to me, is well worth the instinct of beasts.

Whether, then, the female of man shares his desires or not, and wants to satisfy them or not, she repels him and always defends herself, but not always with the same force, nor consequently with the same success. For the attacker to be victorious, the one attacked has to permit or direct it. For what adroit means does she not have to force the aggressor to use force? The most free and the sweetest of all acts does not admit of real violence. Nature and reason oppose this: nature, in that she has provided the weakest with as much force as needed to resist when it

---

*I have already noted that affected and teasing refusals are common to nearly all females, even among animals, and even when they are most ready to surrender. One has to have never observed their little maneuvers to disagree with this.

pleases her; reason, in that real rape is not only the most brutal of all acts, but most contrary to its end. For either man thereby declares war on his companion and authorizes her to defend her life and her liberty even at the expense of the aggressor's life; or, as woman alone is the judge of her own state, a child would have no father if every man could usurp his rights.

Here then is a third consequence of the constitution of the sexes: the stronger is the master in appearance and depends in fact on the weaker. This is due not to a frivolous practice of gallantry, nor to a protector's proud generosity, but to an unchanging law of nature that, giving woman greater facility in exciting desires than man has in satisfying them, makes the latter, for all he can do, depend on the other's wish. It constrains him to seek to please her in turn, so as to get her to consent to let him be the stronger. Then what is sweetest for the man in his victory is to doubt whether it is weakness that cedes to force, or the will that surrenders. The ordinary ruse of the woman is to keep this in doubt between her and him. In this, women's minds correspond exactly to their constitutions. Far from blushing at their weakness, they glory in it. Their tender muscles are without resistance; they pretend to be unable to lift the lightest burdens; they would be ashamed to be strong. Why is that? It is not only in order to appear delicate. It is due to a more adroit precaution: they are arranging excuses from afar, and the right to be weak as needed.

The progress of the enlightenment acquired through our vices has greatly changed ancient opinions among us on this point. Rapes are hardly spoken of any more, as they are hardly necessary, and as men no longer believe in them.* Conversely, they are very common in early Greek and Jewish antiquities, because these same opinions belong to the simplicity of nature, and because only the experience of libertinism has been able to uproot them. If fewer rapes are alleged in our day, it is surely not because men are more temperate, but because they are less credulous, and because a complaint that would have persuaded simple peoples in days of yore would nowadays only attract the laughter of mockers. One gains more by keeping quiet. In *Deuteronomy* there is a law according to which a girl who had been misused was punished along with the seducer if the offense had been committed in town. If it had been committed in the countryside or in a secluded spot, the man alone was punished: *for,* says the Law, *the girl screamed, and was not*

---

*There can be such a disproportion in age and in force that a real rape occurs, but treating here the relative state of the sexes according to the order of nature, I am considering them both in terms of the common relation that constitutes this state.

heard.[3] This benign interpretation taught the girls not to let themselves be taken by surprise in well-frequented places.

The effect of these differences of opinion regarding morals is palpable. Modern gallantry is their work. Men, finding that their pleasures depended more on the will of the fair sex than they had believed, have captivated that will by obliging attentions for which it has compensated them well.

Observe how the physical leads us imperceptibly to the moral, and how from the crude union of the sexes are born little by little the sweetest laws of love. The empire of women does not belong to them because men willed it, but because thus nature wants it; it belonged to them before they seemed to have it. The same Hercules who believed he raped the fifty daughters of Thespitius was nevertheless constrained to weave by Omphale's side, and the strong Samson was not so strong as Delilah.[4] This empire belongs to women and cannot be taken from them, even when they abuse it. If ever they could lose it, they would have lost it long since.

There is no parity between the sexes when it comes to the consequences of sex. The male is male only at certain moments, the female is female all her life, or at least during her entire youth. Everything ceaselessly recalls her to her sex, and in order to fulfill its functions well, she needs a constitution related to it. She needs attentiveness during her pregnancy; she needs rest when giving birth; she needs a soft and sedentary life to suckle her children; she needs patience and sweetness in order to bring them up, zeal, an affection that nothing rebuffs. She serves as the link between them and their father; she alone makes him love them and gives him the confidence to call them his own. How much tenderness and care she needs to keep the whole family unified! And finally, all these must be not virtues but tastes, without which the human species would soon be extinct.

The inflexibility of the relative duties of the sexes neither is, nor can be, the same. When woman complains on this point of the unjust inequality man sets up in this, she is wrong. This inequality is not a human institution, or at least it is not the work of prejudice, but of reason. It is up to the one of the two whom nature has entrusted with the children to answer for them to the other. Doubtless no one is permitted to break his word, and every unfaithful husband who deprives his wife of the sole reward for the austere duties of her sex is an unjust and barbarous man. The unfaithful wife, however, does more: she dissolves the family, and breaks all the bonds of nature. By giving the man children that are not his, she betrays both him and them; she joins perfidy to infidelity. I can hardly see what disorders and what crimes do not derive from that one. If there is a dreadful condition in the world, it is that of an unhappy father who, without confidence in his wife, does not dare to surrender to the sweetest sentiments of the heart, who has doubts while embracing his child whether he is not embracing the child of another, the token of his dishonor and the plunderer of his own children's goods. What is the family then but a society of secret enemies that a guilty woman arms against one another, while forcing them to feign love for one another?

It is therefore important not only that the wife be faithful, but that she be judged as such by her husband, by her relatives, by everyone. It is important that she be modest, attentive, reserved, and that she presents to the eyes of others, as she does in her own conscience, the evidence of her virtue. If it is important that a father love his children, it is important that he esteem their mother. Such are the reasons that put even appearances among the duties of women, and make honor and reputation no less indispensable for them than chastity. From these principles, along with the moral difference between the sexes, issues a new motive for duty and for propriety that especially prescribes to women the most scrupulous attention to their conduct, their manners, and their bearing. To maintain vaguely that both sexes are equal and that their duties are the same, is to lose oneself in vain declamations. It is to say nothing so long as one does not respond to these reasons.

Is that not a very sound way to reason, to cite exceptions in response to such well-founded general laws? Women, you say, do not always have children? No, but they are particularly destined to have them. What! Because in the universe there are a hundred large cities where women living in license have few children, you claim that the condition of women is to have few! And what would become of your cities, if the remote countryside, where women live more simply and more chastely, did not make good the sterility of your Ladies? In how many provinces are the women who have only four or five children reputed to be not very fertile!* After all, what does it matter that this or that woman has few children? Is the condition of woman any less to be a mother, and is it not by general laws that nature and morals must provide for this condition?

Even if there were as long intervals between pregnancies as are supposed, will a woman so suddenly and alternately change her way of life

---

*Without this the species would necessarily decline. For the species to preserve itself, each woman, when all things are balanced, has to have about four children. For of the children that are born, nearly half die before they can have others, and two must remain in order to represent the father and mother. Consider whether the cities will furnish you with that population.

without peril and without risk? Will she be wet nurse today, and warrior tomorrow? Will she change her temperament and her tastes as a chameleon does its colors? Will she suddenly pass from shade, enclosure, and domestic cares to the ravages of the open air, to the labors, fatigues, and perils of war? Will she be sometimes fearful,* sometimes brave, sometimes delicate, and sometimes robust? If young people brought up in Paris find it hard to bear the profession of arms, will women who have never braved the sun, and who barely know how to walk, bear it after fifty years of softness? Will they take up this hard profession at the age when men leave it?

There are countries where women give birth almost without pain and nurse their children almost without cares. I admit it. But in these same countries men go half-naked in any weather, overpower ferocious beasts, carry a canoe like a knapsack, go on hunting expeditions of seven or eight hundred leagues, sleep in the open air on the ground, bear incredible fatigues, and pass several days without eating.[5] When women become robust, men become even more so; when men become soft, women become even softer. When the two terms change equally, the difference between them remains the same.

Plato in his *Republic* gives women the same exercises as men. I can well believe it! Having removed private families from his form of government, and no longer knowing what to do with women, he found himself forced to make men of them.[6] This fine genius had planned everything, foreseen everything. He was forestalling a difficulty that perhaps no one would have thought of raising, but he resolved badly the one that is raised against him. I am not speaking of this alleged communism of women. The oft-repeated censure about this proves that those who make it have never read him. I am speaking of that civil promiscuity that everywhere confounds both sexes in the same occupations, in the same labors, and cannot fail to engender the most intolerable abuses. I am speaking of that subversion of the sweetest sentiments of nature, immolated to an artificial sentiment that can subsist only through them. As if there were no need for a natural hold on the emotions from which to form conventional bonds; as if the love one has for those near us were not the principle of the love one owes the State; as if it were not through the little fatherland that is the family that the heart attaches itself to the great one; as if it were not the good son, the good husband, the good father who make the good citizen!

---

*The timidity of women is yet another instinct of nature against the double risk that they run during pregnancy.

As soon as it is once demonstrated that man and woman neither are, nor should be, constituted in the same way, neither in character nor in temperament, it follows that they must not have the same education. In following the directions of nature they must act in concert, but they must not do the same things. The goal of the labors is common, but the labors are different and, as a consequence, so are the tastes that direct them. After having attempted to form the natural man, in order not to leave our work imperfect, let us see how the woman that suits this man must also be formed.

Do you want always to be well guided? Always follow the indications of nature. Everything that characterizes the sex must be respected as established by it. You say incessantly that women have this and that defect that we do not have. Your pride deceives you. They would be defects in you; in them they are good qualities. All would go less well if they did not have them. Prevent these supposed defects from degenerating, but be careful not to destroy them.

Women, for their part, incessantly proclaim that we bring them up to be vain and coquettish, that we incessantly beguile them with puerilities in order to remain more easily their masters. They attack us for the defects for which we reproach them. What folly! And since when is it men who meddle with the education of girls? Who prevents mothers from bringing them up as they please? They do not have Colleges. How terrible! Ah, would God there were none for boys; they would be more sensibly and decently brought up! Do we force your girls to waste their time with foolishness? Do we make them, in spite of themselves, spend half their lives dressing up, after your example? Do we prevent you from instructing them, or having them instructed, to your liking? Is it our fault if they please us when they are beautiful, if their simpering seduces us, if the art they learn from you attracts and flatters us, if we like to see them dressed with taste, if we let them sharpen at their leisure the weapons they use to subjugate us? Ah! Decide to bring them up like men; men will willingly consent to it! The more women will want to resemble them, the less will women govern them. It is then that men will really be the masters.

All the faculties common to both sexes are not equally shared between them, but taken all together they balance one another. Woman is worth more as woman and less as man. Everywhere that she asserts her rights, she has the advantage. Everywhere that she wants to usurp ours, she remains beneath us. One can respond to this general truth only with exceptions; this is the way the gallant partisans of the female sex constantly argue.

To cultivate in women the qualities of men and to neglect those proper to them, is therefore clearly to work to their detriment. The cunning ones see this too well to be duped by it. In trying to usurp our advantages, they do not abandon theirs. But it follows from this that, not being able to manage both the one and the other, as they are incompatible, they remain below their capacity without being able to reach ours, and lose half of their value. Believe me, judicious mother, do not make of your daughter a decent man, as if to give the lie to nature. Make a decent woman of her, and you can be sure that she will be worth more both for herself and for us.

Does it follow from this that she must be brought up in ignorance of everything, and limited to the sole functions of housekeeping? Will man make his servant out of his companion? Will he deprive himself near her of the greatest charm of society? In order better to enslave her, will he prevent her from feeling anything, knowing anything? Will he make of her a thorough automaton? No, without a doubt. It is not thus that nature has spoken in giving to women such pleasing and nimble minds. On the contrary, she wants them to think, to judge, to love, to know, to cultivate their mind as they do their looks. Those are the weapons that she gives them to compensate for the force they lack, and in order to direct ours. They must learn a great many things, but only those that it suits them to know.

Whether I consider the particular end to which the sex is destined, whether I consider its inclinations, or count its duties—all equally concur to indicate to me the form of education that suits it. Woman and man are made for each other, but their mutual dependence is not equal. Men depend on women because of their desires; women depend on men because of their desires, and because of their needs. We would sooner subsist without them than they without us. For them to have what is necessary, for them to be in the condition proper to them, we have to give it to them, to want to give it to them, to esteem them worthy of it. They depend on our sentiments, on the value we place on their merit, on the importance we attach to their charms and their virtues. By the very law of nature, women, as much for their own sake as for that of their children, are at the mercy of men's judgments. It is not enough that they be estimable; they must be esteemed. It is not enough for them to be beautiful; they must please. It is not enough for them to be chaste; they must be recognized as such. Their honor is not only in their conduct, but in their reputation, and it is not possible that she who would consent to be looked upon as disreputable could ever be decent. When a man acts well, he depends only on himself, and can brave public judgment. But when a woman acts well, she has carried out only half of her task, and what one thinks of her is of no less importance to her than what she actually is. It follows from this that the system of her education must be in this respect contrary to ours: opinion is the tomb of virtue among men, and its throne among women.

The good constitution of children depends first of all on that of mothers. The first education of men depends on the cares given by women: their morals, their passions, their tastes, their pleasures, their happiness itself, also depend on women. Thus all the education of women must be relative to that of men. To please them, to be useful to them, to make themselves loved and honored by them, to bring them up when young, to care for them when grown, to counsel them, to console them, to make their lives agreeable and sweet—those are the duties of women in all times, and what one must teach them from childhood.[7] As long as one does not return to this principle, one will deviate from the goal, and all the precepts given to them will be useless both for their happiness and for ours.

But although every woman wants to please men, and must want to, there is a great difference between wanting to please a man of merit, a truly lovable man, and wanting to please those little fellows who dance attendance, who dishonor both their sex and the one they imitate. Neither nature nor reason can bring woman to love in men what resembles her. Nor is it in assuming their manners that women must seek to make themselves loved by them.

Consequently when, departing from the modest and composed tone of their sex, they assume the airs of these featherbrained fellows; far from following their vocation, they renounce it. They deprive themselves of the rights they think they are usurping. If we were otherwise, they say, we would not please men. They lie. One has to be mad to love madmen; the desire to attract those people reveals the taste of those who yield to it. If there were no frivolous men, they would hasten to produce some. Men's frivolities are much more her work, than hers are theirs. The woman who loves true men, and who wants to please them, uses means that match her design. Woman is coquettish due to her condition, but her coquetry changes in form and in object according to her aims. Let us regulate her aims according to those of nature, and woman will have the education that suits her.

Little girls love adornment almost from birth. Not satisfied with being pretty, they want to be thought to be pretty. One sees in their little airs that this care already occupies them. When they are scarcely able to understand what one says to them, they are governed by talking to them of what will be thought of them. The same motive, very indiscreetly proposed to little boys, is far from having the same empire on them. Provided that they are independent and that they have pleasure, they hardly care what one might think of them. It is only by dint of time and effort that one subjugates them to the same law.

From wherever this first lesson comes for girls, it is a very good one. Because the body is born, so to speak, before the soul, the body must be cultivated first. This order is common to both sexes, but the object of this cultivation is different. For one, this object is the development of forces; for the other, it is the development of attractions. It is not that these qualities must be exclusive in each sex. Only the order is reversed. Women must have enough force to do everything they do with grace, and men need enough adroitness to do all they do with ease.

The extreme softness of women gives rise to that of men. Women must not be robust like them, but for them, so that the men born from them can also be robust. In this the Convents, where the boarders have coarse food, but many diversions, many races and games in the open air and in gardens, are to be preferred to the paternal home where a girl, delicately fed, always caressed or scolded, always sitting in sight of her mother in a tightly closed room, does not dare get up, walk, speak, or breathe. She does not have a moment of liberty to play, jump, run, yell, or to indulge the exuberance natural to her age. Always either dangerous slackness or misunderstood severity; never anything according to reason. That is how one ruins the body and the heart of youth.

The girls of Sparta practiced military games like the boys, not in order to go to war, but in order one day to bear children capable of enduring its fatigues. That is not what I subscribe to. In order to give soldiers to the State, it is not necessary for mothers to have carried a musket and trained in the Prussian style. But I find that, in general, this part of the Greek education was well thought out. Young girls often appeared in public, not mixed with the boys, but gathered by themselves. There was hardly a feast, sacrifice, or ceremony where one did not see bands of the daughters of the first Citizens crowned with flowers, singing hymns, forming dancing choruses, carrying baskets, vases, offerings, and presenting to the depraved senses of the Greeks a charming spectacle able to compensate for the bad effect of their indecent gymnastic. Whatever impression this practice made on the hearts of men, the fact remains that it was an excellent one, giving to the female sex a good constitution in its youth through agreeable, moderate, and beneficial exercises. It sharpened and formed its taste by the continual desire to please, without ever endangering its morals.[8]

As soon as these young persons were married, one no longer saw them in public. Shut up in their houses, they restricted all their cares to their household and to their family. Such is the way of life that nature and reason prescribe to the female sex. Consequently, from these mothers were born the healthiest, most robust, the most well-made men on earth. And despite the ill repute of a few Islands, it is certain that of all the peoples in the world, without even excepting the Romans, none is ever cited where the women were at the same time more chaste and more lovable, where they better united morals and beauty, than in ancient Greece.[9]

It is known that the ease of clothing that did not hinder the body contributed much in both sexes to leaving it with those beautiful proportions that one sees in their statues. They still serve as model for art when disfigured nature has ceased to furnish one for it among us. They did not have a single one of all these gothic shackles, these multitudes of ligatures that squeeze our limbs at every point. Their women were unaware of the use of these whalebone corsets with which ours counterfeit their waists rather than showing them off. I cannot conceive that this abuse, pushed in England to an inconceivable degree, will not in the end cause the species to degenerate. And I even maintain that the attractive object one intends to produce in doing this is in bad taste. It is not pleasant to see a woman cut in two like a wasp; this offends the sight and makes the imagination suffer. The slenderness of the waist, like everything else, has its proportions, its measure, beyond which it is certainly a defect. This defect would even strike the eye in the nude; why would it be beautiful beneath clothing?

I dare not press the reasons why women are obstinate about armoring themselves in this way. A falling bosom, a fatter stomach, etc.; that is very displeasing, I agree, in a twenty-year-old. But this is no longer shocking at thirty. And as we must in spite of ourselves be at all times what nature pleases, and as man's eye is not deceived by it, these defects are less displeasing at any age than the silly affectation of a little girl of forty.

Everything that hinders and constrains nature is in bad taste. This is as true of the adornments of the body as of the ornaments of the mind. Life, health, reason, well-being must come before everything. Grace does not develop without ease. Delicacy is not languor, and one does not need to be unhealthy in order to please. One excites pity when one suffers, but pleasure and desire seek out the freshness of health.

The children of both sexes have many amusements in common, and that must be the case. Do not they have as many in common when grown? They also have tastes proper to them that distinguish them. Boys seek movement and noise: drums, wooden clogs, little carriages. Girls prefer what strikes the eye and serves to ornament oneself: mirrors, jewels, rags, especially dolls. The doll is the special amusement of this sex. There her taste is very evidently determined according to what she is destined for. The physics of the art of pleasing is in adornment; this is all that children can cultivate of this art.

Observe a little girl spending the day near her doll, ceaselessly changing its outfit, dressing it, and undressing it hundreds of times, continuously looking for new combinations of ornaments. It is not important whether they match or not. Her fingers lack adroitness, her taste is not formed, but already the inclination reveals itself. In this eternal occupation time flows without her thinking of it; the hours pass, and she knows nothing of it. She even forgets her meals; she is hungrier for adornment than for food. But, you will say, she is adorning her doll and not her own person. No doubt. She sees her doll and does not see herself. She can do nothing for herself. She is not formed; she has neither talent nor force; she is nothing yet. She is entirely in her doll. She puts all her coquetry into it. She will not always leave it there. She is waiting for the moment when she can be her own doll herself.

Here then is a very definite first taste; you have only to follow and regulate it. It is certain that the little one would like with all her heart to know how to ornament her doll, to make the embroidered rosettes on its sleeves, its neckerchief, its frills, its lace. For all this she is made to depend so painfully on the goodwill of others, that it would be much more convenient to owe everything to her own industry. In this way emerges the reason for the first lessons one gives her. They are not tasks prescribed to her; they are favors one does for her. Actually, nearly all little girls first learn to read and to write with repugnance. But when it comes to holding the needle, this they always learn willingly. They imagine themselves grown in advance, and think with pleasure that these talents may one day serve to adorn them.

Once this first path is opened, it is easy to follow: sewing, embroidery, lace-making come of themselves. Tapestry-making is not so much to their taste. Furnishings are too far from them: they do not derive from one's person, they derive from other opinions. Tapestry is the amusement of women. Young girls will never take very great pleasure in it.

This voluntary progress will easily extend itself to drawing, for this art is not irrelevant to that of attiring oneself with taste. But I would not want them to be made to apply themselves to landscape, still less to figures. Foliage, fruits, flowers, draperies, everything that can serve to give an elegant contour to one's outfit, and to make an embroidery pattern by oneself when one does not find one to one's taste: that is enough for them. In general, if it is important for men to limit their studies to useful knowledge, it is even more important for women. For the lives of the latter, although less laborious, are or ought to be more assiduous about their cares and more interrupted by various cares, and do not permit them to give themselves over by choice to any talent to the detriment of their duties.

Whatever the humorists may say, good sense belongs equally to both sexes. Girls in general are more docile than boys, and one must even exert more authority over them, as I shall discuss presently. But it does not follow from this that one must demand of them anything whose utility they cannot see. The art of mothers is to show it to them in everything they prescribe to them, and that is all the easier because intelligence is more precocious in girls than in boys. This rule banishes, for their sex as for ours, not only all idle studies that end in nothing good, and that do not even make those who have engaged in them more agreeable to others, but also all those whose utility does not belong to that age, and that the child cannot foresee in a more advanced age. If I do not want a boy to be pushed to learn to read, there is all the more reason not to want young girls to be forced to do so before making them well aware what reading is good for. The way that one ordinarily shows them this utility follows one's own idea much more than theirs. After all, where is the necessity for a girl to know how to read and write so early? Will she so soon have a household to govern? There are very few who do not abuse, more than they make use of, this fatal science. All of them are a little too curious not to learn it without one having to force them to, when they will have the leisure and the occasion to do so. Perhaps they should learn to calculate before anything else. For nothing provides a more palpable utility at all times, demands longer practice, and leaves so much opportunity for error than does accounting. If the little one had cherries for her snack only by doing a sum in arithmetic, I can guarantee that she would soon know how to calculate.

I know a young person who learned to write before learning to read, and who began to write with the needle before learning to write with the quill. Of all the letters, she at first wanted to make nothing but Os. She incessantly made Os large and small, Os of every size, Os one inside the other, and always drawn in reverse. Unfortunately one day when she was occupied with this useful exercise, she saw herself in the mirror, and finding that this constrained attitude made her look ungraceful, like another Minerva she threw away her quill and no longer wanted to make Os.[10] Her brother did not like to write any more than did she, but it was the constraint that annoyed him, and not the air it gave him. Another trick was used to bring her back to writing. The little girl was delicate and vain. She did not like to have her linen used by her sisters. It was marked; one no longer wanted to mark it. She had to learn to mark it herself. One can conceive the rest of her progress.

Always justify the cares you impose on young girls, but always impose some on them. Idleness and lack of docility are the two most dangerous defects for them, and those one cures the least once one has contracted them. Girls must be vigilant and industrious. That is not all. They must be constrained early. This misfortune, if it is one for them, is inseparable from their sex. Never do they deliver themselves from it without suffering far more cruel ones. All their lives they will be enslaved to the most continual and most strict hindrance, which is that of propriety. They must first of all be trained in constraint, so that it will never cost them anything to master all their whims in order to submit them to the will of others. If they always wanted to work, one must sometimes force them to do nothing. Dissipation, frivolity, inconstancy are defects that are easily born from their first corrupted and persistently followed tastes. In order to prevent this abuse, teach them above all to conquer themselves. In our insane establishments, the life of a decent woman is a perpetual combat against herself. It is just for this sex to share the pain of the ills that it has caused us.

Prevent girls from being bored by their work and engrossed by their amusements, as always happens in vulgar educations where, as Fenelon says, all the boredom is put on one side and all the pleasure on the other.[11] The first of these two difficulties will occur, if one follows the preceding rules, only when the persons with them displease them. A little girl who loves her mother or her governess will work all day by her side without boredom. Chatter alone will compensate her for all the constraint. But if the one who governs her is unbearable to her, she will acquire the same aversion for everything she does under her gaze. It is very unlikely that those who do not enjoy themselves more with their mothers than with anyone else in the world, can one day turn out well. But to judge their true sentiments, one has to study them, and not trust in what they say. For they are flattering, dissembling, and know early on how to disguise themselves. Nor must one prescribe that they love their mother. Affection does not come from duty, and constraint is of no use here. Attachment, cares, habit alone will make the mother loved by the daughter, if she does nothing to attract hatred to herself. If well directed, even the constraint in which she keeps her will, far from weakening this attachment, only increase it. For dependence being a natural condition for women, girls feel themselves made to obey.

For the same reason that they have, or must have, little liberty, they carry to excess the liberty one leaves them. Extreme in everything, they give themselves over to their games with even more fervor than boys. This is the second difficulty of which I spoke. This fervor must be moderated, for it is the cause of a number of vices particular to women, such as among others the caprice and infatuation by which a woman is in raptures today over an object she will not look at tomorrow. Inconstancy of tastes is as deadly to them as their excess, and both one and the other come from the same source. Do not take from them gaiety, laughter, noise, frolicsome games, but prevent them from sating themselves with one in order to run to the other. Do not allow that for one instant in their lives they no longer experience any curb. Accustom them to find themselves being interrupted in the middle of their games, and brought back to other cares without murmuring. Again, habit alone is enough for this, because it only aids nature.

From this habitual constraint results a docility that women need all their lives, because they never stop being subjected either to a man, or the judgments of men, and they are never allowed to place themselves above these judgments. The first and the most important quality of a woman is gentleness. Made to obey a being as imperfect as man, a being so full of vices and always so full of defects, she must learn early to suffer even injustice, and to bear the wrongs of a husband without complaining. It is not for his sake, it is for her own that she must be gentle. The bitterness and stubbornness of women never does anything but increase their ills and the bad behavior of the husbands. They feel that it is not with weapons like those that women must conquer them. Heaven did not give them such winning and persuasive ways in order for them to become cantankerous; it did not make them weak in order for them to be imperious; it did not give them such a gentle voice in order to utter insults; it did not give them such delicate traits in order for them to disfigure them with anger. When they get angry, they forget themselves. They are often right to complain, but they are always wrong to scold. One must keep to the tone of one's sex. A husband who is too gentle can make a woman impertinent. But, unless a man is a monster, the gentleness of a wife brings him back to himself, and triumphs over him sooner or later.

Let girls always be subjected, but let mothers not always be inexorable. To make a young person docile, one does not have to make her unhappy. To make her modest, one does not have to brutalize her. On the contrary,

I would not be sorry if she were allowed to use a little adroitness, not in eluding the punishment for her disobedience, but in getting herself exempted from obeying. There is no question of making her dependence painful to her; it is enough to make her feel it. Cunning is a talent natural to the female sex, and as I am persuaded that all the natural inclinations are good and right in themselves, I am of the opinion that this one be cultivated like the others. It is only a question of preventing its abuse.

I refer the truth of my remark to any observer of good faith. I do not want women themselves to be examined on this point. Our constraining institutions can force them to sharpen their minds. I want girls to be examined, little girls who are, so to speak, just born. Let them be compared to little boys of the same age, and if the latter do not seem dull-witted, giddy, and stupid compared with them, I will incontestably be wrong. May I be allowed only one example taken in all its puerile innocence.

It is very common to forbid children to ask for anything at table, for their education is thought to be never more successful than when it is overburdened with useless precepts—as if a piece of this or that were not soon granted or refused* without making a poor child constantly die of greed sharpened by hope. Everyone knows about the adroitness of a young boy submitted to this law, who having been forgotten at table took it into his head to ask for salt, etc. I will not say that one could have quibbled with him for having asked directly for salt, and indirectly for meat. The omission was so cruel, that if he had openly transgressed the law and said without any detour that he was hungry, I cannot believe that he would have been punished for it. But here is how, in my presence, a little girl of six went about it, in a much more difficult case. For in addition to the fact that she was rigorously forbidden from ever asking for anything either directly or indirectly, disobedience would not have been pardonable. For she had eaten of every dish save one that they had forgotten to give to her, and which she coveted very much.

Now in order to get this omission made good without being accused of disobedience, she reviewed all of the dishes, pointing with her finger and saying out loud as she showed them: *I ate some of that one, I ate some of that one.* But she so visibly made a display of passing over the one from which she had not eaten without saying anything, that someone noticing this said: and have you eaten some of that? *Oh no*, gently replied the little glutton, lowering her eyes. I will add nothing. Compare: this trick is a girl's ruse; the other is the ruse of a boy.

*A child becomes importunate when he finds that it profits him, but he will never ask twice for the same thing if the first answer is always irrevocable.

What is, is good, and no general law is bad. This particular adroitness given to the female sex is a very equitable compensation for its lesser force, without which woman would not be the companion of man. She would be his slave. It is by this superiority of talent that she maintains herself as his equal, and that she governs him while obeying him. Woman has everything against her: our defects, her timidity, her weakness. She has for her only her art and her beauty. Is it not just that she cultivate one and the other? But beauty is not general; it perishes through a thousand incidents; it disappears with the years; and habit destroys its effect. The mind is the only true resource of the female sex— not that foolish wit that is so prized in the world and that is useless for making life happy, but the intelligence fit for her condition, the art of making use of ours, and of availing herself of our peculiar advantages. One does not realize how useful this adroitness of women is to us, how much charm it adds to the society of both sexes, how useful it is to curb the exuberance of children, how many brutal husbands it contains, how many good households it maintains that, without it, would be troubled by discord. Crafty and wicked women abuse it, I know it well. But what does vice not abuse? Let us not destroy the instruments of happiness because the wicked sometimes use them to do harm.

One can shine by means of adornment, but one pleases only by one's person. We are not our outfits. Often by dint of being elaborate, they spoil the effect. Often those that make the woman who wears them noticed the most are those one notices least. The education of young girls on this point is entirely misdirected. They are promised ornaments as a reward; they are made to love elaborate finery. *How beautiful she is!* they are told when they are heavily adorned. Quite on the contrary, one must make them understand that so much adjustment of one's outfit is engaged in only in order to hide defects, and that the real triumph of beauty is to shine by itself. The love of fashion is in bad taste, because faces do not change along with it, and because, since one's figure stays the same, what suits it once suits it always.

Were I to see a young girl strutting in her finery, I would seem anxious about her figure being thus disguised, and about how it might be thought of. I would say: all these ornaments adorn her too much. That's too bad. Do you think she could have carried off simpler ones? Is she beautiful enough to do without this one, or that one? Perhaps then she will be the first to beg that one remove this ornament and that she be judged. If this takes place, it is a case for applause. I would never praise her more than when she is most simply dressed. When she looks upon adornment only as a supplement to the graces of one's person, and as a

tacit avowal that she needs help in order to please, she will not be proud
of her outfit, she will be humble about it. And if, when she is more
adorned than usual, she hears it said of her: *how beautiful she is!* she will
blush from vexation.

Moreover, there are figures that need adornment, but none requires
rich finery. Ruinously expensive adornments are the vanity of rank and
not of the person. They derive uniquely from prejudice. True coquetry
is sometimes elaborate, but it is never ostentatious, and Juno dressed
herself more superbly than Venus.[12] *Unable to make her beautiful, you
made her rich*, said Apelles to a bad painter, who was painting Helen
heavily laden with finery.[13] I have also noticed that the most pompous
adornment most often heralds ugly women. One could not have a more
maladroit vanity. Give a young girl who has taste and who despises fashion some ribbons, gauze, muslin, and flowers; without diamonds, trimmings, or lace* she will make herself an outfit that will make her a hundred times more charming than all the brilliant rags of la Duchapt.[14]

Because what is good is always good, and one always has to be the
best possible, women who know something about outfits choose good
ones, and keep to them. Because they do not change them every day,
they are less occupied with them than those who do not know what to
settle on. Real attention to adornment requires little dressing up. Young
Ladies rarely engage in the ceremony of dressing. Work and lessons fill
their day. Yet in general they are attired, except for the rouge, with as
much care as the Ladies, and often in better taste. Overindulgence in
dressing is not what one thinks; it arises much more from boredom
than from vanity. A woman who spends six hours at her dressing table
is not unaware that she does not leave it better attired than someone
who spends only half an hour at it. But it is that much gained on the
stupefying length of time, and it is better to be amused with oneself
than to be bored with everything. Without dressing up, what would one
do with one's life from noon until nine o'clock? By gathering women
around, one amuses oneself by making them impatient—that is already
something. One avoids private conversation with a husband one only
sees at that hour—that is much more. And then come the merchants,
secondhand dealers, lightweights, scribblers, verses, songs, tracts. Without the practice of dressing up, these things would never be so well
combined. The only real profit that derives from this is the pretext to
display oneself a little more than when one is dressed. But this profit is

---

*Women whose skin is white enough to do without lace would very much vex the
others if they wore none. It is almost always ugly persons who bring in the fashions to
which the beautiful ones are stupid enough to subject themselves.

perhaps not so great as is thought, and women at their dressing tables do not gain so much by it as they would like to claim. Give without qualms an education for women to women. Arrange it so that they love the cares of their sex, have some modesty, and know how to watch over their households and keep themselves busy in their homes. The grand ceremony of dressing will go out of fashion by itself, and they will be attired in even better taste for it.[15]

The first thing young persons notice, as they grow up, is that all these external attractions are not enough for them, if they do not have some that are truly theirs. One can never give oneself beauty, and one is not immediately in a condition to acquire coquetry. But one can already seek to give a pleasant turn to one's gestures, a flattering accent to one's voice, to compose one's bearing, to walk lightly, to strike gracious poses and to look one's best everywhere. The range of the voice increases, and it becomes firm and acquires timbre; the arms develop, the gait becomes assured, and one notices that, however one is attired, there is an art to getting oneself looked at. From then on, it is no longer only a matter of the needle and industriousness; new talents present themselves, and already make their utility felt.

I know that strict schoolmasters want neither song, nor dance, nor any of the pleasant arts to be taught to young girls. That is amusing! And to whom then do they want them taught? To boys? To whom, men or women, does it belong specially to have these talents? To no one, they will answer. Profane songs are so many crimes; dance is an invention of the Devil; a young girl must have no entertainment other than her work and prayer. Those are strange entertainments for a child of ten years! As for me, I am afraid that all these little saints whom one forces to spend their childhood praying to God will spend their youth doing something else altogether, and once married, will to the best of their ability make up for the time they think they lost as girls. I consider that one must have regard for what suits the age as well as the sex. A young girl must not live like her grandmother. She must be vivacious, playful, frolicsome, sing and dance as much as she wants, and taste all the innocent pleasures of her age. The time to be composed and to assume a more serious bearing will come all too soon.

But is the necessity for even this change indeed real? Is it not again perhaps a fruit of our prejudices? In enslaving decent women only to sad duties, everything that could make marriage pleasant to men has been banished from it. Must one marvel if the taciturnity they see reigning at home chases them from it, or if they are hardly tempted to embrace such an unpleasant condition? By dint of making all duties excessive, Christianity makes them impracticable and vain. By dint of forbidding women song, dance, and all worldly entertainment, it makes them glum, scolds, and unbearable at home. There is no other religion where marriage is subjected to such strict duties, and none other in which an engagement so sacred is so despised. So much has been done to prevent women from being amiable, that husbands have been made indifferent. You say that this should not be the case. I quite understand, but I say that this had to be, because after all, Christians are men. As for me, I would want a young Englishwoman, in order to please the husband she will have, to cultivate the pleasing talents with as much care as a young Albanian cultivates them for the Harem of Ispahan.[16] It will be said that husbands do not care that much for all these talents. Truly I believe it, when these talents, far from being used to please them, serve only as bait to attract to their home young insolents who dishonor them. But do you not think that a lovable and chaste woman, ornamented with such talents, and who consecrated them to the entertainment of her husband, would add to the happiness of his life? Would she not prevent him, when he leaves his study with an exhausted head, from seeking recreation outside of his home? Has no one seen happy families thus gathered together, where each one knows how to furnish his part of the common entertainment? Let them say whether the confidence and familiarity joined to these, whether the innocence and sweetness of the pleasures one tastes there, do not make up for more noisy public pleasures.

The pleasing talents have been too much reduced to an art. They have been overgeneralized; everything has been made into a maxim and a precept. What ought to be only entertainment and frolicsome games for young people has been made very boring for them. I can imagine nothing more ridiculous than to see an old dancing or singing master addressing with a scowling air young people who only want to laugh, and assuming a more pedantic and magisterial air in order to teach his frivolous science than if it were a question of their catechism. For example, does the art of singing derive from written music? Could one not make one's voice flexible and true, learn to sing with taste, and even to accompany oneself, without knowing a single note? Does the same kind of song suit all voices? Does the same method suit all minds? I shall never be made to believe that the same poses, the same steps, the same movements, the same gestures, the same dances suit both a vivacious and piquant little brunette, and a tall beautiful blonde with languishing eyes. When, therefore, I see a master giving exactly the same lessons to both, I say: this man follows his routine, but he understands nothing about his art.

It is asked whether girls need schoolmasters or schoolmistresses? I do not know. I wish that they needed neither one nor the other, that they learned freely what they have so much inclination to want to learn, and that one did not observe ceaselessly wandering in our cities so many harlequin mountebanks. I find it somewhat hard to believe that intercourse with those people is not more damaging to young girls than their lessons are useful to them. Their jargon, their tone, their airs give their students a first taste for the frivolities that are so important to them and that, following their example, young girls will not be long in making their unique occupation.

In the arts that have only pleasure as their object, everything can serve as master to young people. Their fathers, mothers, brothers, sisters, friends, governesses; their mirrors—and above all their own taste. One must not offer to give them lessons; they have to ask for them. One must not make a task of a reward, and it is above all in these kinds of studies that the first success is to want to succeed. Moreover, if they absolutely must have regular lessons, I would not decide on the sex of those who must give them. I do not know if a dancing master has to take a young student by her delicate white hand, if he makes her draw up her skirt, lift her eyes, spread her arms, thrust forward her palpitating bosom, but I do know that I would not want to be that master for anything in the world.

Through industry and talents taste is formed. Through taste the mind insensibly opens itself to the ideas of the beautiful of all kinds, and finally to the moral notions related to it. That is perhaps one of the reasons why the sentiments of propriety and decency insinuate themselves sooner in girls than in boys. For in order to believe that this precocious sentiment is the work of Governesses, one would have to be very badly educated about the bent of their lessons, and about the march of the human mind. The talent for speaking holds the first rank in the art of pleasing. It is by this alone that one can add new charms to those to which habit accustoms the senses. The mind not only vivifies the body, but in a way renews it. By the succession of sentiments and ideas, the mind animates and varies the physiognomy. By speeches it inspires attention, held in suspense, to sustain for a long time the same interest for the same object. It is, I believe, for all these reasons that young girls so soon acquire a pleasant little chatter, that they accent the things they say even before they feel them, and that men divert themselves so soon by listening to them, even before they can understand them. Men spy out the first instance of this intelligence so as to discern that of sentiment.

Women have a flexible tongue. They speak sooner, more easily, and more pleasantly than men. They are also accused of speaking more. That is as it must be. I would willingly transform this reproach into praise. Among them, the mouth and the eyes have the same activity, and for the same reason. Man says what he knows, woman says what pleases. In order to speak, one needs knowledge; the other, taste. One must have as his principal object useful things; the other, pleasant ones. Their speech must have no common forms other than those of the truth.

One must not restrain the chatter of girls, like that of boys, with this harsh question: *What good is that?* But by this other one, which is no easier to answer: *What effect will that produce?* In their infancy, when they are not yet capable of discerning good and ill, they are judges of no one. They must impose on themselves a law never to say anything except what is pleasant to those to whom they are speaking. What makes the practice of this rule more difficult, is that it always remains subordinate to the first, which is never to lie.

I see in this still many other difficulties, but they belong to a more advanced age. For the present, the only cost to young girls in being truthful is to be so without vulgarity. As this vulgarity is naturally repugnant to them, education easily teaches them to avoid it. I notice generally in social relations that the politeness of men is more officious, and that of women more caressing. This difference is not an instituted one; it is natural. Man seems to seek rather to serve you, and woman to please you. It follows from this that, whatever the case may be regarding the character of women, their politeness is less false than ours. They only know how to extend their first instinct. But when a man pretends to prefer my interest to his own, no matter what demonstrations he uses to color this lie, I am very sure that he is telling one. Hence it costs women little to be polite, and consequently costs girls little to learn how to become so. The first lesson comes from nature. Art does nothing more than to follow nature, and to determine, according to our customs, under what form it must show itself. As to politeness among one another, that is an entirely different matter. They make use of such constrained airs and such cold attentions, that in bothering one another they do not take much care to hide how bothered they are. Their lie seems sincere in that they hardly seek to disguise it. Nevertheless, young people sometimes genuinely form more frank friendships. At their age gaiety takes the place of a good disposition, and when they are satisfied with themselves, they are satisfied with everyone. They also unfailingly kiss one another more willingly and caress one another with more grace in front of men, proud to sharpen their lust with impunity, by means of the image of favors they know how to make them envy.

If one must not permit indiscreet questions to young boys, with even more reason must one forbid them to young girls.[17] Their curiosity, when satisfied or badly eluded, has altogether different consequences, given their discernment in divining the mysteries one hides from them, and their adroitness at uncovering them. But without permitting their questions, I would like that one often questioned them, that one took care to make them talk, that one provoke them in order to excite them to speak easily, to make them prompt with a retort, to loosen their minds and their tongues while one can without danger. These conversations, always turned into gaiety, but managed with art and well directed, would make a charming entertainment for this age. They could convey into the innocent hearts of these young people the first and perhaps the most useful lessons of morality they will learn in their lives, by teaching them, under cover of the attractions of pleasure and vanity, the qualities to which men truly accord their esteem, and in what consist the glories and the happiness of a decent woman.

One easily understands that if male children are not in a condition to form any true idea of religion, with all the more reason is the same idea above the conception of girls. It is for this very reason that I would like to speak about it to girls earlier. For if one had to wait until they are in a condition methodically to discuss these profound questions, one would run the risk of never speaking about them. Women's reason is a practical reason that causes them very skillfully to find the means to arrive at a known end, but that does not cause them to find this end. The social relation of the sexes is admirable. From this society results a moral person of which the woman is the eye and the man the arm, but with such a dependence upon each other that it is from the man that the woman learns what has to be seen, and from the woman that the man learns what has to be done. If woman could ascend to principles as well as man, and if man had as good a mind as she for details, as they would always be independent of one another, they would live in eternal discord. Society could not subsist between them. But in the harmony that reigns between them, everything tends toward the common end. One does not know who contributes more. Each follows the other's impulsion; each obeys, and both are the masters.

By the very fact that the conduct of woman is enslaved to public opinion, her belief is enslaved to authority. Every girl must have the religion of her mother, and every woman that of her husband. Were this religion false, the docility that submits the mother and the daughter to the order of nature erases the sin of error before God. Because they are not in a condition to be judges themselves, they must receive the decision of fathers and husbands like that of the Church.[18]

Not being able to derive the rule of their faith from themselves alone, women cannot set its limits at those of evidence and reason. Letting themselves be carried along by a thousand foreign impulses, they always either fall short of the truth, or go beyond it. Always extreme, they are all either libertines or bigots. None can be observed who knows how to unite wisdom with piety. The source of the ill is not only the extravagant character of their sex, but also the badly regulated authority of ours. The libertinism of morals leads authority to be despised, and the dread of repentance makes it tyrannical. That is how one always does too much or too little.

Because authority must regulate the religion of women, it is not so much a matter of explaining the reasons one has for belief, as of clearly explaining to them what one believes. For the faith one grants to obscure ideas is the first source of fanaticism, and the faith one is required to have in absurd things leads to folly, or incredulity. I do not know to what our catechisms incline us more, whether to be impious or fanatical. But I do know that they necessarily make us one or the other.

First, in order to teach religion to young girls, never make it an object of sadness or bother for them, never a task nor a duty. Consequently, never make them learn by heart anything related to it, not even prayers. Be satisfied with regularly saying yours in front of them, yet without forcing them to join in. Make them short, according to the instruction of Jesus Christ.[19] Always recite them with suitable introspection and respect. Keep in mind that when we ask the supreme Being to pay attention in order to listen to us, it is worth paying some attention to what one is going to say to him.

It is less important that young girls learn their religion early as it is important that they know it well, and especially that they love it. When you make it onerous to them, when you portray God always angry with them, when you impose on them in his name a thousand painful duties that they never see you fulfill, what can they think, except that knowing one's catechism and praying to God are the duties of little girls? And what can they desire, except to be grown up so that they can exempt themselves like you from all this subjection? Example, example! Without this one never succeeds at anything with children.

When you explain articles of faith to them, let your instruction take the form of direct instruction, and not of questions and answers. They must never answer anything except what they think, and not what has been dictated to them. All the answers in the catechism are contrary to sense: the schoolchild instructs the master. They are even lies in the mouths of children, because they explain what they do not understand, and they affirm what they are not in a condition to believe. Among the most intelligent men, show me those who are not lying in saying their catechism?

The first question that I see in ours is this one: *Who created you and brought you into the world?* To which the little girl, believing full well that it is her mother, says nevertheless without hesitation that it is God. The only thing she sees in it is that in response to a question that she hardly understands, she answers something that she does not understand at all.

I would like for a man who knew well the progress of children's minds, to be willing to compose a catechism for them. It would perhaps be the most useful book ever written, and it would not be, in my opinion, the one which would least honor its Author. It is quite certain that if this book were good, it would hardly resemble ours.

Such a catechism will only be good when to the questions alone the child will formulate the responses himself without learning them. Of course, he will sometimes be in a position to ask questions in turn. To make what I want to say understood, a kind of model would be needed, and I thoroughly feel what I lack in order to draw it. I shall try nevertheless to give some slight idea of it.

I therefore imagine that in order to come to the first question of our catechism, it would have to begin more or less like this.

GOVERNESS
Do you remember when your mother was a girl?

LITTLE ONE
No, miss.

GOVERNESS
Why not? You who have such a good memory?

LITTLE ONE
That is because I was not born yet.

GOVERNESS
You have not then always lived?

LITTLE ONE
No.

GOVERNESS
Will you live always?

LITTLE ONE
Yes.

GOVERNESS
Are you young or old?

LITTLE ONE
I am young.

GOVERNESS
And your grandmamma, is she young or old?

LITTLE ONE
She is old.

GOVERNESS
Was she young?

LITTLE ONE
Yes.

GOVERNESS
Why is she no longer young?

LITTLE ONE
It is that she got old.

GOVERNESS
Will you get old like her?

LITTLE ONE
I don't know.*

GOVERNESS
Where are your dresses from last year?

---

* If everywhere that I put down *I don't know*, the little one answers differently, one has to distrust her answer and make her explain it with care.

LITTLE ONE
They were taken apart.

GOVERNESS
And why were they taken apart?

LITTLE ONE
Because they were too small for me.

GOVERNESS
And why were they too small for you?

LITTLE ONE
Because I grew.

GOVERNESS
Will you grow more?

LITTLE ONE
Oh, yes!

GOVERNESS
And what do big girls become?

LITTLE ONE
They become women.

GOVERNESS
And what do women become?

LITTLE ONE
They become mothers.

GOVERNESS
And mothers, what do they become?

LITTLE ONE
They get old.

GOVERNESS
So you will then get old?

LITTLE ONE
When I am a mother.

GOVERNESS
And what do old people become?

LITTLE ONE
I do not know.

GOVERNESS
What became of your granddaddy?

LITTLE ONE
He is dead.*

GOVERNESS
And why is he dead?

LITTLE ONE
Because he was old.

GOVERNESS
What then becomes of old people?

LITTLE ONE
They die.

GOVERNESS
And you, when you are old, what . . .

LITTLE ONE, INTERRUPTING HER
Oh miss, I don't want to die.

GOVERNESS
My child, no one wants to die, and everyone dies.

---

*The little one will say this, because she has heard it said. But one must verify whether she has some clear idea of death, for this idea is not so simple, nor so much within children's comprehension, as one thinks. One can see in the little poem *Abel*[20] an example of the way in which one must give it to them. This charming work radiates a delicious simplicity with which one cannot nourish oneself enough in order to converse with children.

LITTLE ONE
What? Will mommy die too?

GOVERNESS
Like everyone. Women get old like men, and old age leads to death.

LITTLE ONE
What must one do to get old very late?

GOVERNESS
Be good while one is young.

LITTLE ONE
Miss, I will always be good.

GOVERNESS
Good for you. But, in the end, do you believe that you will always live?

LITTLE ONE
When I am very old, very old . . .

GOVERNESS
Well then?

LITTLE ONE
Finally when one is so old, you say that one really has to die.

GOVERNESS
So you will die sometime?

LITTLE ONE
Alas, yes.

GOVERNESS
Who lived before you?

LITTLE ONE
My father and my mother.

GOVERNESS
Who lived before them?

LITTLE ONE
Their fathers and their mothers.

GOVERNESS
Who will live after you?

LITTLE ONE
My children.

GOVERNESS
Who will live after them?

LITTLE ONE
Their children, etc.

By following this road one finds by palpable inductions a beginning and an end to the human race, as there is for all things. That is to say, one finds a father and a mother who had neither father nor mother, and children who will not have children.* It is only after a long series of similar questions that the first question of the catechism is sufficiently prepared for. Only then can one ask it, and can the child understand it. But from there to the second answer, which is, so to speak, the definition of the divine essence, what an immense leap! When will this gap be filled? God is a spirit! And what is a spirit? Shall I launch a child's mind off into this obscure metaphysics from which men have such difficulty extricating themselves? It is not for a little girl to resolve these questions; it is at most up to her to ask them. Then I shall simply respond: you ask me what is God. That is not easy to say. One cannot hear, nor see, nor touch God. He is known only by his works. In order to judge what he is, wait until you know what he has done.

If our dogmas all come from the same truth, they are not for all that equally important. It is highly indifferent to the glory of God that it is known to us in all things. But it is important to human society and to each of its members that every man knows and fulfills the duties toward his fellows and toward himself that the law of God imposes upon him. That is what we must incessantly teach one another, and what fathers and mothers are especially obliged to instruct their children. Whether a virgin is the mother of his creator; whether she gave birth to God, or only to a man to whom God joined himself; whether the substance of

---

*The idea of eternity cannot be applied to the human generations with the mind's consent. Every numerical series reduced to an act is incompatible with this idea.

father and son is the same or only similar; whether the spirit proceeds from one of the two who are the same, or from both jointly: I do not see that the resolution of these questions, which are apparently so essential, matters more to the human species than to know on what lunar day one must celebrate Easter, whether one must say one's rosary, fast, abstain from meat, speak Latin or French in Church, ornament the walls with images, say or listen to mass, and not have a wife of one's own. Let each think as he pleases on these points. I do not see how this can concern others. As for me, it does not concern me in the slightest. But what does concern me, me and all those like me, is that each knows that an arbiter of all human fates exists, whose children we all are; that he orders us all to be just, to love one another, to be benevolent and merciful, and to keep our obligations toward everyone, even toward our enemies and his; and that the apparent happiness of life is nothing, and that there is another one after it, in which this supreme Being will be the remunerator of the good and the judge of the wicked. It is important to teach the young, and to persuade all the citizens of these dogmas, and similar dogmas. Whoever combats them doubtless deserves punishment. He is the disturber of order and the enemy of society. Whoever goes beyond them and wants to subject us to his particular opinions comes to the same point by an opposite road. In order to establish order in his own way, he troubles the peace. In his reckless pride, he makes himself the interpreter of the divinity, he demands in his name that men pay him homage and respects. As much as he can, he makes himself God instead. He must be punished for being sacrilegious, if he were not punished for being intolerant.

Therefore omit all these mysterious dogmas that are for us only words without ideas, all these bizarre doctrines whose vain study takes the place of virtues to those who devote themselves to it, and serves rather to make them mad than good. Keep your children always within the narrow circle of the dogmas related to morality. Thoroughly persuade them that there is nothing useful for us to know except what teaches us to do good. Do not make Theologians and reasoners out of your daughters. Of Heavenly things teach them only those that serve human wisdom. Accustom them always to feel themselves to be under the eyes of God, to have him as witness of all their actions, thoughts, virtue, and pleasures; to do good without ostentation, because they love it; to suffer ill without murmur, because he will compensate them for it; and finally, to be every day of their lives what they will be content to have been when they appear before him. That is the true religion, the only one that is not susceptible either to abuse, impiety, or fanaticism. Let more sublime ones be preached as much as one wants. As for me, I do not recognize any other but that one.

Furthermore, it is good to observe that until the age when reason becomes enlightened and nascent sentiment makes conscience speak, what is good or evil for young people is what the people around them have decided. What they are commanded is good, what they are forbidden is bad. They must not know more than this. By this, one sees how even more important for them than for boys is the choice of persons who must approach them and have some authority over them. At last the moment comes when they begin to judge things by themselves, and then it is time to change the plan of their education.

I have perhaps already said too much up to now. To what will we reduce women if we prescribe only public prejudices as a law for them? Let us not abase to this point the sex that governs us, and that honors us when we have not debased it. There exists for the entire human species a rule anterior to opinion. It is to the inflexible direction of this rule that all the others ought to refer themselves. It judges prejudice itself, and it is only inasmuch as men's esteem accords with it that this esteem ought to have authority over us.

This rule is the inner sentiment. I shall not repeat what has been said about it above.[21] It is enough for me to note that if these two rules do not concur in the education of women, it will always be defective. Sentiment without opinion will not give them that delicacy of soul that clothes good morals with worldly honor. Opinion without sentiment will never make of them anything but false and dishonest women who put appearance in the place of virtue.

It is therefore important for them to cultivate a faculty that serves as arbiter between the two guides, one that does not allow the conscience to lose its way, and that corrects the errors of prejudice. This faculty is reason. But with this word how many questions rear up! Are women capable of solid reasoning? Is it important that they cultivate it? Will they cultivate it with success? Is this culture useful for the functions imposed upon them, and is it compatible with the simplicity suitable to them?

The different ways of envisaging and resolving these questions are such that, tending to contradictory excesses, some limit woman to sewing and spinning in her household with her servants, and thus make of her the first servant of the master. Others, not satisfied with assuring her rights, have her further usurp ours. For to leave her above us in the qualities proper to her sex, and to make her our equal in all the rest: what is this other than to transfer to the woman the primacy that nature has given to the husband?

The reason that leads man to a knowledge of his duties is not very complex; the reason that leads woman to knowledge of hers is even simpler. The obedience and the fidelity she owes her husband, the tenderness and cares that she owes her children, are such natural and palpable consequences of her condition that she cannot without bad faith refuse her consent to the inner sentiment that guides her, nor refuse to recognize the duty in as yet unaltered inclination.

I would not altogether disapprove if a woman were limited to the sole labors of her sex, and left in a profound ignorance of all the rest. But very simple public morals would be needed for this, or a very secluded mode of life. In cities, and amid corrupt men, this woman would be too easy to seduce. Often her virtue would depend only on the occasion. In this philosophical century, she would need one that is proof against attack. She needs to know in advance what can be said to her, and what she must think about it.

In any event, submitted as she is to the judgment of men, she must merit their esteem. She must above all obtain that of her husband. She must not only make him love her person, but make him approve of her conduct. She must justify before the public the choice he has made, and make the husband honored by the honor given to the wife. Now, how will she go about doing all this, if she is ignorant of our institutions, if she knows nothing of our practices, of our proprieties, if she knows neither the source of human judgments, nor the passions that determine them? Because she depends both on her own conscience and on the opinions of others, she must learn to compare these two rules, to reconcile them, and to prefer the first only when they are in opposition. She becomes the judge of her judges. She decides when she ought to submit to them, and when she must repudiate their authority. Before rejecting or admitting their prejudices, she weighs them. She learns to ascend to their source, to anticipate them, to make them favorable to her. She is careful never to attract blame when her duty allows her to avoid it. Nothing of all this can be done well without cultivating her mind and her reason.

I always return to the principle, and it furnishes me with the solution to all my difficulties. I study what is, I seek its cause, and I finally find that what is, is good. I go to receptions where the master and the mistress jointly do the honors. Both have had the same education, both are equally polite, both equally provided with taste and wit, both animated by the same desire to entertain their guests and to send each one home satisfied. The husband omits no effort to be attentive to everything: he comes and goes, he makes a circuit of the room, and makes countless efforts. He would like to be all attentiveness. The wife stays in her place; a little circle gathers around her and seems to hide the rest of the gathering from her. Yet nothing takes place there that she does not perceive, no one leaves to whom she has not spoken. She has omitted nothing that might interest everyone, she has said nothing but what was agreeable to each, and without disturbing anything in the order, the least of the company is no more forgotten than the first. Dinner is served and the company is seated. The man, informed about those who please one another, will seat them according to what he knows. The woman, without knowing anything, will make no mistake about it. She will already have read in their gaze, in their bearing, how everyone is suited, and each will find himself seated as he wants to be. I am not saying that during the course of the dinner no one is forgotten. The master of the house, in sending the food around, may have forgotten no one. But the woman guesses what you look at with pleasure, and offers you some; while speaking to her neighbor she has her eye on the end of the table; she discerns who is not eating because he is not hungry, and who does not dare serve himself or ask because he is clumsy or timid. Upon rising from the table, everyone thinks that she has thought only of him. Everyone thinks that she has not had the time to eat a single bite. But the truth is that she has eaten more than anyone.

When everyone has gone they speak about what happened. The man relates what was said to him, what those he conversed with said and did. If it is not always on this point that the woman is the most exact, on the other hand, she saw what was said in a low voice at the other end of the hall. She knows what so-and-so was thinking, what this remark or that gesture was about. Hardly an expressive movement was made for which she does not have an interpretation ready-made, and one that almost always conforms to the truth.

The same turn of mind, which makes a woman of the world excel in the art of entertaining, makes a coquette excel in the art of beguiling several admirers. The maneuvers of coquetry require even finer discernment than those of politeness. For as long as a polite woman is so toward everyone, she has always done well enough; but the coquette would soon lose her empire with this clumsy uniformity. By dint of wanting to oblige all her lovers, she would repel them all. In society the manners one adopts toward all men do not fail to please each one. As long as one is treated well, one is not that particular about being preferred. But in love a favor that is not exclusive is an insult. A sensitive man would a hundred times prefer to be the only one who is maltreated, than to be caressed along with all the others. The worst that can happen to him is not to be singled out. A woman who wants to keep several lovers therefore has to persuade each one of them that she prefers him, and to persuade him of this under the gaze of all the others, whom she is persuading of the same thing under his.

Do you want to see an embarrassed fellow? Place a man between two women, with each of whom he has secret liaisons, and then observe what a foolish figure he will cut. Place in the same situation a woman between two men (and surely the example will be no rarer) and you will marvel at the skill with which she will mislead both of them, and will make each one laugh at the other. Now, if this woman showed them the same amount of trust and was as familiar with each of them, how would they be her dupes for an instant? By treating them equally, would she not show that they have the same rights over her? Oh, she goes about it much better than that! Far from treating them in the same manner she affects to put them on an unequal footing. She does so well that the one she flatters believes she does it from tenderness, and the one she maltreats thinks she does it from vexation. Thus each, content with his share, sees her always occupied with him, while in effect she is occupied only with herself.

In the general desire to please, coquetry suggests similar means. Caprices would only repel if they were not wisely managed, and it is by dispensing them artfully that she makes of them the strongest chains of her slaves.

> *Usa ogn' arte la donna, onde sia colto*
> *Nella sua rete alcun novello amante;*
> *Ne con tutti, ne sempre un stesso volto*
> *Serba, ma cangia a tempo atto e sembiante.*[22]

From what does all this art derive, if not from subtle and continual observations that allow her to see at each instant what goes on in the hearts of men, and that prepare her to imbue each secret movement she perceives with the force needed to suspend it or to accelerate it? Now, is this art learned? No, it is born with women. They all have it, and men never have it to the same degree. That is one of the distinctive characteristics of the female sex. Presence of mind, penetration, subtle observations are the science of women, and skill in availing herself of them is their talent.

That is what is, and one has seen why that must be. Women are false, we are told. They become so. The gift proper to them is adroitness, and not falseness. According to the real inclinations of their sex, even when they are lying, they are not false. Why do you consult their mouths, when it is not the mouth that must speak? Consult their eyes, their color, their breathing, their fearful air, their soft resistance: that is the language nature gives them to answer you. The mouth always says no, and must say it. But the accent the mouth joins to it is not always the same, and that accent does not know how to lie. Does not woman have the same needs as man, without having the same right to show them? Her fate would be too cruel if even with legitimate desires, she did not have a language equivalent to the one she does not dare use. Need her modesty make her unhappy? Does she not need an art of communicating her inclinations without revealing them? How much adroitness does she not need to have stolen from her what she is burning to grant? How important it is for her to learn how to touch the man's heart without appearing to think about him! Is not Galatea's apple and her clumsy escape a charming speech?[23] What will she need to add to that? Will she go tell the shepherd who is following her among the willows that she is escaping there only with the intention of enticing him? She would lie, so to speak, for then she would no longer entice him. The more reserve a woman has, the more artful she must be, even with her husband. Yes, I maintain that by containing coquetry within its limits, one makes it modest and true; one makes of it a law of decency.

Virtue is one, as one my adversaries has very well said.[24] One does not take it apart in order to admit one part of it and reject the other. When one loves it, one loves it in its entirety, and one sets one's heart when one can, and always one's mouth, against sentiments one must not have. Moral truth is not what is, but what is good. What is bad ought not to be, and must not be admitted, especially when this admission gives it an effect it would not have had without it. If I were tempted to steal, and in saying so I were to tempt another to be my accomplice, would not declaring my temptation to him be to succumb to it? Why do you say that modesty makes women false? For that matter, are those who most lose it truer than the others? Far from it: they are a thousand times more false. One arrives at this point of depravity only by dint of vices all of which one nurses, and which reign only with the aid of intrigues and lies.* On the contrary, those who still have some shame, who do not pride themselves on their faults, who know how to hide

---

*I know that women who have openly made their decision on a certain point aspire to be valued for this frankness, and swear that apart from this there is nothing estimable that is not found in them. But I also know well that they have never persuaded anyone of this but fools. The greatest curb on their sex once removed, what remains that restrains them, and what honor will they set a high value on after having renounced the one proper to them? Once they have put their passions at their ease, they have no further interest in resisting them: *nec femina amissa pudicitia alia abnuerit*.[25] Has any author ever better known the human heart in the two sexes, than the one who said that?

their desires even from those who inspire them, those from whom men force admissions with the greatest difficulty are moreover the truest, the most sincere, the most constant in all their engagements, and those upon whose faith one can generally count the most.

I know of only Mademoiselle de l'Enclos who could be cited as a known exception to these remarks. Thus Mademoiselle de l'Enclos was reputed to be a prodigy. It was said that in despising the virtues of her sex, she had preserved those of ours. Her frankness, her uprightness, her reliability in her dealings with others, her fidelity in friendship, are highly praised. Finally, in order to complete the portrait of her glory, it is said that she made herself a man. So be it. But with all her eminent reputation, I would not have wanted that man as my friend any more than as my mistress.[26]

All of this is not so besides the point as it seems. I see where the maxims of modern philosophy tend when they deride the modesty of the female sex and its alleged falseness, and I see that the most certain effect of this philosophy will be to strip the women of our century of the bit of honor that is left them.

Based on these considerations I believe that one can determine in general what kind of cultivation is suitable for women's minds, and upon what objects their reflections must be directed from youth.

As I have already said, the duties of their sex are easier to see than to fulfill. The first thing they must learn is to love them through consideration of their advantages. That is the only way to make them easy for them. Each condition and each age has its duties. One soon knows one's duties, provided one loves them. Honor your condition as a woman and in whatever rank Heaven places you, you will always be a good woman. What is essential is to be what nature made us; one is always all too much what men want one to be.

The search for abstract and speculative truths, principles, and axioms in the sciences, everything that tends to generalize ideas, is not within women's competence.[27] Their studies must all be related to practice. It is up to them to apply the principles that man has found, and it is up to them to make the observations that lead man to the establishment of principles. All the reflections of women, regarding what does not immediately derive from their duties, must tend to the study of men or to the pleasing attainments that only have taste as their object. For as to works of genius, they are beyond their reach. Nor do they have enough precision and attention to succeed in the exact sciences. As to physical knowledge, it is up to the one who is most active, most lively, and who sees the most objects, it is up to the one who has the most force and who exercises it more, to judge the relations among sensible beings and the laws of nature. Woman, who is weak and who sees nothing outside, estimates and judges the motive forces that she can set to work in order to supplement her weakness. Those motives are the passions of man. Her science of mechanics is stronger than ours; all her levers unsettle the human heart. Her sex must possess the art to make us want everything that it cannot do by itself, and that is necessary or pleasant to it. She must therefore study the mind of man in depth: not the mind of man in general as an abstraction, but the minds of the men who surround her, the mind of the men to whom she is subjected, either by law or by opinion. She has to learn to penetrate their sentiments through their speeches, their actions, their looks, and their gestures. By her speeches, her actions, her looks, and her gestures she has to know how to give them the sentiments that please her, without even seeming to think about it. They will philosophize better than she about the human heart; but she will read better than they into the hearts of men. It is up to women, so to speak, to find experimental morality, and up to us to reduce it to a system. Woman has more wit, and man more genius; woman observes and man reasons. From this cooperation results the clearest enlightenment and the most complete science that the human mind could acquire by itself, the surest knowledge, in a word, of oneself and others that is within the reach of our species. And that is how art can tend incessantly to perfect the instrument given by nature.

The world is the book of women. When they read it badly, it is their fault, or some passion blinds them. Yet the true mother of a family, far from being a woman of the world, is hardly less a recluse in her house than is a nun in her cloister. What is done or ought to be done for the young persons placed in convents would therefore have to be done for those one marries off. They would have to be shown the pleasures they leave before allowing them to renounce them, for fear that the false image of these unknown pleasures does not one day come to lead their hearts astray and trouble the happiness of their retreat. In France, girls live in convents and women gad about in society.[28] Among the ancients it was entirely the opposite. As I have said, the girls had many games and public festivals. Women lived secluded. This practice was more reasonable and maintained morals better. A sort of coquetry is permitted to marriageable girls; entertaining themselves is their chief concern. Women have other cares at home and no longer have husbands to look for. But they would not find this reform to be to their advantage, and unfortunately, they set the tone. Mothers, at least make of your daughters your companions. Give them good sense and a decent soul, and then hide nothing from them that a chaste eye can look at. The ball, feasts, games, even the theater: everything that, when incorrectly seen, is the charm of imprudent youth, can be offered without risk to healthy eyes. The better they see these noisy pleasures, the sooner they will be disgusted by them.

I hear the clamor raised against me. What girl resists this dangerous example? No sooner have they seen society than all their heads are turned; not one of them wants to leave it. That may be. But before presenting them with this misleading picture, did you prepare them well to see it without emotion? Did you thoroughly make known to them the objects that it represents? Did you accurately depict these objects for them as they are? Did you arm them well against the illusions of vanity? Did you incline their young hearts toward the taste for real pleasures that are not found in this tumult? What precautions, what measures did you take to preserve them from the false taste that leads them astray? Far from in any way opposing in their minds the empire of public prejudices, you nourished them on it! You have made them love in advance all the frivolous amusements they find there. You make them love them more as they indulge in them. Young people entering the world have no other governess than their mother, often more foolish than they, and who cannot show them objects otherwise than how she sees them. Her example, stronger than reason itself, justifies them in their own eyes, and the authority of the mother is for the daughter an excuse without reply. When I want a mother to introduce her daughter into the world, I am supposing that she will make her see it as it is.

The evil begins even earlier. Convents are genuine schools of coquetry—not of this decent coquetry of which I spoke, but of the one that produces all women's foibles, and produces the most extravagantly pretentious women of fashion. Upon leaving these suddenly to enter into the noisiest societies, young women at first feel they are in their place. They were brought up to live there. Must one be astonished that they are comfortable there? I would not advance what I am going to say without fear of taking a prejudice for an observation. But it seems to me that, in general, in protestant countries there is more family attachment, more worthy spouses and more tender mothers than in catholic countries. If this is so, one cannot doubt that this difference is due in part to convent education.

In order to love peaceful and domestic life one must know it. One must have felt its sweetness since childhood. Only in the paternal household does one acquire a taste for one's own home, and every woman not brought up by her mother will not like to bring up her children. Unfortunately, there is no longer any private education in big cities. Society is so general and so mixed, that no haven remains in which to retreat, and one is in public even in one's home. By dint of living with everybody one no longer has a family. One hardly knows one's parents; one sees them as strangers, and the simplicity of domestic morals is extinguished along with the sweet familiarity that constituted their charm. This is how one suckles the taste for the pleasures of this century, and for the maxims one sees reigning in it, along with one's milk.

An ostensible constraint is imposed upon girls so as to find dupes who will marry them based on their bearing. But study these young persons for a moment. Under cover of a constrained air they disguise badly the lust that devours them, and already one reads in their eyes the ardent desire to imitate their mothers. It is not a husband they lust for, but the license of marriage. Who needs a husband with so many resources for doing without one? But one needs a husband in order to cover over these resources.* Modesty is on their faces, and libertinism is at the bottom of their hearts. This feigned modesty is in itself a sign of this; they only affect it in order to get rid of it sooner. Women of Paris and London, forgive me, I beg you. No abode excludes miracles, but as for me I know of none. If a single one among you has a truly decent soul, I understand nothing of our institutions.

All these diverse educations equally abandon young persons to the taste for the pleasures of high society, and to the passions that are soon born from this taste. In big cities depravity begins with life, and in the small ones it begins with reason. Young provincial women, taught to despise the happy simplicity of their morals, are eager to come to Paris to share in the corruption of ours. Vices ornamented with the beautiful name of talents are the unique object of their trip, and upon arriving, ashamed to find themselves so far from the noble license of the local women, they lose no time in also deserving to be from the capital. Where does the evil begin, in your opinion? In the places where one plans it, or in those in which one carries it out?

I do not want a sensible mother to bring her daughter from the province to Paris to show her these spectacles that are so pernicious for others. But I say that if she were to do so, either this girl is badly brought up, or these pictures will hardly pose a danger to her. With taste, with sense, and the love of decent things, they are not found to be so attractive as they are to those who let themselves be charmed by them. One

---

*The way of man in his youth is one of the four things that the Wise Man could not understand: the fifth was the impudence of the adulterous woman, *quae comedit, et tergens os suum dicit: non sum operata malum.*[29] Proverbs 30:20.

notes in Paris the young scatterbrains who come hastening to adopt the local tone and to make themselves fashionable for six months, only to get themselves hissed at for the rest of their lives. But who notes those who, repelled by all this commotion, return to their provinces satisfied with their lot, after having compared it to the one the others envy? How many young women have I seen who, brought to the capital by complaisant husbands who are free to establish themselves there, themselves make their husbands renounce it, go back more willingly than they had come, and say with emotion on the eve of their departure: ah! Let us go back to our cottage! One lives more happily there than in the palaces here. It is not known how many good people are still left who have not knelt before the idol, and who despise its insane cult. Only madwomen are noisy; wise women do not make a stir.

If despite the general corruption, despite universal prejudices, despite the bad education of girls, a number of them still have judgment that is proof against attack, what will be the case when this judgment has been nourished by suitable instructions—or, to say it better, when it has not have been degraded by vicious instructions? For everything always consists in preserving or reestablishing the natural sentiments. It is not for all that a matter of boring young girls with your long sermons, or of reciting your dry moralisms at them. For the two sexes, moralisms are the death of all good education. Sad lessons are good only for making those who give them, and everything they say, hated. When speaking to young persons, it is not a matter of making them fear their duties, or of aggravating the yoke imposed upon them by nature. In exposing these duties to them, be precise and mild, do not let them believe that one is sad when one fulfills them.[30] No angry air, no pompous countenance. Everything that must pass into the heart must come from it. Their moral catechism must be as short and as clear as their religious catechism, but it must not be so grave. Show them in the same duties both the source of their pleasures and the foundation of their rights. Is it so hard to love in order to be loved, to make oneself lovable in order to be happy, to make oneself estimable in order to be obeyed, to honor oneself in order to be honored? How beautiful these rights are! How respectable they are! How dear they are to the heart of man when the woman knows how to make them valued! One does not have to wait for years to go by or for old age in order to enjoy them. Her empire begins with her virtues. Hardly have her attractions developed but she already reigns by the sweetness of her character, and makes her modesty imposing. What insensitive and barbarous man does not soften his pride and does not take on more attentive manners near a young girl of sixteen who is lovable and chaste, who speaks little, who listens, whose bearing is decorous and whose conversation is decent, whose beauty makes her forget neither her sex nor her youth, who knows how to interest others even by her timidity, and attract to herself the respect she shows everyone?

Even though these testimonies are external, they are not frivolous. They are not founded upon the attraction of the senses. They spring from the intimate sentiment we all have, that women are the natural judges of men's merit. Who wants to be despised by women? No one in the world, not even the man who no longer wants to love them. And as for me, who tell them such harsh truths, do you think that their judgments are indifferent to me? No, their approbation is dearer to me than yours, readers, often more women than they are. In despising their morals, I still want to honor their justice. It matters little to me that they hate me, if I force them to esteem me.

What great things one would accomplish with this spring of action if one knew how to put it into motion! Woe to the century when women lose their ascendancy, and when their judgment no longer affects men! That is the last degree of depravity. All the peoples who had morals respected women. Consider Sparta, consider the Germans, consider Rome, Rome the seat of glory and of virtue if ever they had one on earth. It is there that women honored the exploits of great Generals, that they publicly wept for the fathers of the fatherland, that their vows or their mourning were consecrated as the most solemn judgment of the Republic. All the great revolutions there came from women. Through a woman Rome acquired liberty, through a woman the plebeians gained the consulate, through a woman the tyranny of the Decemvirs ended, through women Rome under siege was saved from the hands of an outlaw.[31] Gallant Frenchmen, what would you have said if you had seen pass this procession, so ridiculous to your mocking eyes? You would have accompanied it with your jeers. How we see the same objects with a different eye! And perhaps we are all correct. Form this procession of beautiful French Ladies; I know of none more indecent. But compose it of Roman women; you will have upon you the eyes of all the Volscians, and the heart of Coriolanus.

I shall say more, and I maintain that virtue is no less favorable to love than it is to the other rights of nature, and that the authority of mistresses gains no less from it than does that of wives and mothers. There is no genuine love without enthusiasm, and no enthusiasm without an object of perfection, either real or chimerical, but always existing in the imagination. What will inflame lovers for whom this perfection is no longer anything, and who see in what they love only the object of the pleasure of the senses? No, this is not how the soul becomes carried away, and delivers itself to those sublime raptures that are the delirium of lovers and the charm of their passion. Everything is illusion in love, I admit it. But what is real are the sentiments for the truly beautiful that love animates in us, and makes us love. This beautiful is not in the object we love; it is the work of our errors. Ah! What does it matter? Because of this, does one sacrifice any less all one's low sentiments to this imaginary model? Does one fill one's heart any less with the virtues one confers upon what it cherishes? Does one detach oneself any less from the baseness of the human I? Where is the genuine lover who is not ready to immolate his life for his mistress, and where is the sensual and coarse passion in a man who is willing to die? We mock the Paladins![32] That is because they knew love, and we no longer know anything except debauchery. When these romantic maxims began to become ridiculous, this change was less the work of reason than that of bad morals.

Whatever century it may be, natural relations do not change. The suitability or unsuitability that results from them remains the same; prejudices under the vain name of reason only change their appearance. It will always be great and beautiful to reign over oneself, even to obey fantastical opinions. The true motives of honor will always speak to the heart of every woman of judgment who will know how to seek life's happiness within her condition. Chastity must be a delightful virtue for a beautiful woman who has some loftiness in her soul. While she sees all the earth at her feet, she triumphs over everything and over herself. She raises in her own heart a throne to which everything comes to give homage. The tender, or jealous, but always respectful sentiments of the two sexes, universal esteem, and her own esteem ceaselessly pay her a tribute of glory for a few moments of combat. The privations are temporary, but the prize is permanent. What enjoyment for a noble soul is the pride of virtue joined to beauty! Bring to life a heroine from a Novel: she will taste voluptuous delights more exquisite than the Laïses and the Cleopatras.[33] When her beauty will cease to be, her glory and her pleasures will still remain. She alone will know how to enjoy the past.

The greater and more painful duties are, the more palpable and strong must be the reasons upon which they are founded. There is a certain devout language on the gravest of subjects that is dinned into young persons' ears, without producing persuasion. From this language, which is too disproportionate to their ideas, and from the little account they make of it in secret, arises the ease with which they cede to their inclinations, for lack of reasons to resist them derived from the things themselves. A girl brought up modestly and piously no doubt has strong weapons against temptations, but those whose hearts—or rather, ears—are nourished uniquely with mystical jargon infallibly become the prey of the first adroit seducer who undertakes the task. Never will a young and beautiful person despise her body; never will she in good faith afflict herself for the great sins that her beauty causes to be committed; never will she sincerely weep before God for being an object one covets; never will she be able to believe within herself that the sweetest sentiment of the heart is an invention of Satan. Give her other reasons within and for herself, for those will not penetrate. It will be worse yet if, as one rarely fails to do, one sets her ideas in contradiction, and after having humiliated her by debasing her body and her charms as the stain of sin, one then has her respect as the temple of Jesus Christ this same body that one has made so despicable to her. Ideas that are too sublime and too base are equally insufficient, and cannot be combined. A reason within the reach of the sex and of the age is needed. Regard for duty has force only insofar as one joins to it motives that carry us to fulfill it:

Quae quia non liceat non facit, illa facit.[34]

One would not suspect that it is Ovid who passes such a severe judgment.

Do you then want to inspire the love of good morals in young persons? Without saying to them incessantly, be chaste, give them a great interest in being so. Make them feel all the reward of chastity, and you will make them love it. It is not enough to lay hold of this interest far away in the future: show it to them at this very moment, in the relationships of their age, in the character of their lovers. Depict for them the good man, the man of merit. Teach them to recognize him, to love him, and to love him for their own sakes. Prove to them that whether as friends, wives, or mistresses, this man alone can make them happy. Lead virtue in by means of reason. Make them feel that the empire of their sex and all of its advantages depend not only upon her good conduct and morals, but also on those of men, that they have little hold upon vile and base souls, and that one knows how to serve one's mistress only as one knows how to serve virtue. After that, you can be sure that when you depict for them the morals of our day, you will inspire a sincere disgust for them. In showing them those who are in fashion, you will make them despised. You will cause them to be estranged from their maxims, to have aversion for their sentiments, and disdain for their vain compliments. You will cause to be born in them a more noble ambition, that of reigning over great and strong souls, that of the women of Sparta, which was to command men.[35] A bold, shameless, intriguing woman, who does not know how to attract her lovers except by coquetry nor how to keep them except by means of favors, makes them obey like valets in common and servile matters. In important and serious matters she is without authority over them. But the woman who is at once decent, lovable, and chaste, who forces her lovers to respect her, who is reserved and modest, she who, in a word, sustains love through esteem, sends them with a sign to the ends of the earth, to combat, to glory, to death, where it pleases her. This empire is beautiful, it seems to me, and is well worth the purchase.*

That is the spirit in which Sophie has been brought up with more care than effort, and rather by following her taste than by constraining it. Let us now say a word about her person according to the portrait that I drew of her for Emile, and according to which he himself imagines the spouse who can make him happy.

I shall never repeat too often that I am leaving aside prodigies. Emile is not one; Sophie is not one either. Emile is man and Sophie is woman: that is all their glory. In the mingling of the sexes that reigns among us, it is almost a marvel if one belong to one's own.

Sophie is wellborn; she has a good disposition. She has a very sensitive heart, and this extreme sensitivity sometimes throws her imagination into an activity that is hard to moderate. She has a mind that is less precise than penetrating, an easy and yet changeable temper, a common but pleasant face, a physiognomy that promises a soul and does not lie. One can approach her with indifference, but not leave her without emotion. Others have good qualities that she lacks; others have those she has to a greater degree; but none has qualities more suitable to make up a happy character. She knows how to turn even her defects to account, and if she were more perfect, she would please much less.

Sophie is not beautiful, but near her, men forget beautiful women, and beautiful women are displeased with themselves. At first sight she is hardly pretty, but the more one sees her, the more beautiful she becomes. She gains where so many others lose, and what she gains she

---

* Brantôme says that in the time of François I, a young person who had a chattering lover imposed upon him an absolute and unlimited silence that he kept so faithfully for two whole years that it was thought he had become dumb from illness. One day right in the midst of company, his mistress who, in those days when love was made with mystery, was not known as such, boasted that she could cure him on the spot, and did so with this single word: *speak*. Is there not something great and heroic in that love? What more could the philosophy of Pythagoras in full display have done?[36] Would one not imagine a divine being, with a single word, giving a mortal the organ of speech? What woman today could count upon a like silence for a single day, were she to pay for it with the highest reward she can give for it?[37]

never loses. One can have more beautiful eyes, a more beautiful mouth, a more commanding figure; but one could not have a neater waist, a more beautiful complexion, a whiter hand, a daintier foot, a gentler glance, a more touching physiognomy. Without dazzling, she captivates, she charms, and one could not say why.

Sophie likes adornment and is expert at it; her mother has no other maid than her. Dressing to advantage is a good deal to her taste, but she hates expensive clothing. In hers one always sees simplicity joined to elegance. She does not like what is brilliant, but what suits. She is unaware what colors are in fashion, but she knows marvelously well those that become her. There is no young person who seems dressed with less refinement, and whose attire is more refined than hers; not an article of hers is taken at random, and art appears in none. Her adornment is very modest in appearance, and very coquette in effect. She does not display her charms, she covers them; but in covering them she knows how to make them imagined. Seeing her, one says: there is a modest and chaste girl. But as long as one remains near her, eyes and heart rove over her entire person, without one's being able to look away. It is as if all this so simple attire is put on only to be taken off piece by piece with the imagination.

Sophie has natural talents; she is aware of them and has not neglected them. But as it was not within her reach to invest much art into their cultivation, she contented herself with training her pretty voice to sing accurately and with taste; her little feet to walk lightly, easily, and with grace; and to curtsy in every kind of situation without embarrassment and awkwardness. For that matter, she has had no other singing master than her father, no other dancing mistress than her mother, and an organist from the neighborhood has given her a few lessons in accompaniment on the harpsichord, which she has since cultivated alone. At first she thought only of making her hand appear to advantage against its black keys. Then she found that the shrill and dry sound of the harpsichord made her voice sound sweeter. Little by little she became aware of harmony. Finally as she grew she began to feel the charms of expression, and to love music for itself. But it is a taste rather than a talent. She does not know how to decipher one air from sheet music.

What Sophie knows best, and what she has been made to learn with the greatest care, are the labors of her sex, even those one does not think of, such as cutting and sewing her dresses. There is no needlework that she does not know how to do, and that she does not do with pleasure. But the work she prefers to any other is lacework, because there is none that affords one a more agreeable pose, and in which the fingers exert themselves with more grace and lightness. She has also applied herself to all the details of housekeeping. She knows her way around the kitchen and the pantry: she knows the price of foodstuffs; she knows their qualities; and she knows quite well how to keep the accounts. She serves as a butler to her mother. Made to be the mother of a family herself one day, by governing the paternal household she learns how to govern her own. She can supplement the functions of the domestics, and always does this willingly. One never knows how to command anything except what one knows how to execute oneself; that is her mother's reason for occupying her in this way. As for Sophie, she does not go that far. Her first duty is that of a daughter, and it is now the only one she thinks of fulfilling. Her unique aim is to serve her mother and to relieve her of a portion of her cares. Nevertheless, it is true that she does not fulfill them all with an equal pleasure. For example, even though she is gluttonous, she does not like cooking. There is something in its details that disgusts her; she never finds it clean enough. On that point she is extremely delicate, and this delicacy, pushed to excess, has become one of her defects. She would rather let all the dinner fall into the fire than to stain her cuff. For the same reason, she has never wanted to oversee the garden. Earth seems dirty to her; as soon as she sees some manure, she believes she smells it.

She owes this defect to her mother's lessons. According to her, one of the first of woman's duties, a special, indispensable duty imposed by nature, is cleanliness. There is no object in the world more disgusting than an unclean woman, and the husband who is disgusted by her is never wrong. She has so often preached this duty to her daughter since her childhood; she has so often required cleanliness of her person, as well as of her clothing, of her rooms, in her work, and in her dress, that all these attentions, changed into habit, take up a rather good part of her time. They still preside over the rest, such that to do well what she does is only the second of her cares; the first is always to do it cleanly.

Nevertheless, all this has not degenerated into vain affectation or into softness; the refinements of luxury do not enter into it. Never has anything entered her rooms but plain water. She knows no other perfume than that of flowers, and her husband will never breathe a sweeter one than her breath. Finally, the attention she pays to externals does not make her forget that she owes her life and her time to more noble cares. She does not know or disdains the excessive cleanliness of body that soils the soul. Sophie is much more than clean; she is pure.

I said that Sophie was a glutton. She was naturally so, but she became temperate by habit, and now she is temperate by virtue. It is not the case for girls as it is for boys, whom one can up to a certain point govern through gluttony. This inclination is not without consequence for the female sex; it is too dangerous to leave them with it. When little Sophie as a child went alone into her mother's chamber, she did not always return from it empty, and her trustworthiness was not proof against sugared almonds and candies. Her mother took her by surprise, admonished her, punished her, and made her fast. She finally managed to persuade her that candies spoil one's teeth and that eating too much fattens one's waist. So Sophie corrected herself. As she grew she has acquired other tastes that turned her away from this base sensuality. In women as in men, as soon as the heart is animated, gluttony is no longer a dominant vice. Sophie has preserved the taste proper to her sex. She likes dairy products and sweets, pastries and desserts, but does not like meat very much. She has never tasted either wine or strong liquors. What is more, she eats very moderately of everything; her sex, which labors less than ours, needs less restoration. In everything, she likes what is good, and knows how to appreciate it. She also knows how to make do with what is not, without this privation costing her anything,

Sophie has a mind that is pleasant without being brilliant, solid without being profound, a mind about which one says nothing because one never finds that she has more or less of it than one does oneself. She always has one that pleases the people who speak to her, although it is not very adorned according to the idea we have of the cultivation of the minds of women. For hers was not formed by reading; but only by the conversations of her father and mother, by her own reflections, and by the observations she has made among the few people she has seen. Naturally, Sophie is gay. She was even frolicsome during her childhood. But little by little her mother took care to keep in check her giddy airs, for fear that too sudden a change would instruct her about the moment that made it necessary. She has therefore become modest and reserved even before the time to be so, and now that this time has come it is easier for her to keep the tone she has taken than it would be for her to take it without one indicating the reason for this change. It is pleasant to see her sometimes, by the remains of habit, yielding to childhood vivacity, then all of a sudden return to herself, fall quiet, lower her eyes, and blush. The intermediary term between the two ages must share a little of the two.

Sophie's sensitivity is too great for her to preserve a perfect evenness of temper, but she is too gentle for this sensitivity greatly to importune others. She only harms herself. Let one word be said that wounds her: she does not pout, but her heart swells; she tries to escape in order to go cry. If in the middle of her tears her father or her mother calls her back and says one word, she comes instantly to play and laugh, while adroitly wiping her eyes and trying to stifle her sobs.

Neither is she altogether free of caprice. Her temper, which is a little finicky, degenerates into obstinacy, and then she is liable to forget herself. But let her have the time to come back to herself, and her way of wiping away her fault is almost a merit. If she is punished, she is docile and obedient, and her shame can be seen to arise not so much from the punishment, as from the fault. If nothing is said to her, she never fails to correct it herself, but so frankly and with such good grace that it is not possible to hold a grudge against her. She would kiss the dirt before the least servant without this abasement causing her the least pain, and as soon as she is forgiven, her joy and her caresses show how great a burden is lifted from her good heart. In a word, she patiently suffers the wrongs of others, and mends her own with pleasure. Such is the lovable nature of her sex before we have spoiled it. Woman is made to give in to man and to bear even his injustice; you will never reduce young boys to this same degree. The inner sentiment rears up and revolts in them against injustice; nature did not make them to tolerate it.

> *gravem*
> *Pelidae stomachum cedere nescii.*[38]

Sophie is religious, but with a reasonable and simple religion. It has few dogmas and fewer devout practices—or, rather, knowing no other essential practice than morality, she devotes her entire life to serving God by doing good.[39] In all the instruction her parents gave her on this subject, they accustomed her to respectful obedience by always saying to her: "My daughter, this knowledge does not belong to your age. Your husband will teach you when it is time." Moreover, instead of long discourses on piety, they are satisfied to preach it to her by example, and this example is engraved in her heart.

Sophie loves virtue. This love has become her dominant passion. She loves it because there is nothing so beautiful as virtue. She loves it because virtue is the glory of woman, and because a virtuous woman seems to her almost equal to the angels. She loves it as the only road to true happiness, and because she sees nothing but misery, abandonment, unhappiness, and ignominy in the life of a dishonest woman. Finally, she loves it because it is dear to her respectable father and to her tender and worthy mother. Not satisfied with being happy because of their own virtue, they also want to be happy because of hers, and her own first happiness is the hope of making theirs. All these sentiments inspire in her an enthusiasm that elevates her soul, and keeps all her little tendencies subject to such a noble passion. Sophie will be chaste and decent until her last breath. She has sworn it at the bottom of her soul, and she swore it at a time when she already felt everything that it costs to keep such an oath. She swore it when she must have revoked the engagement, if her senses were made to reign over her.

Sophie does not have the good fortune to be an amiable Frenchwoman who is cold by temperament and coquette by vanity, who wants to shine rather than please, who seeks amusement and not pleasure. The need to love alone devours her. It comes to distract and trouble her heart during festivities. She has lost her old gaiety. Frolicsome games are no longer made for her. Far from fearing the boredom of solitude she seeks it: in it she thinks of the one who must make it sweet for her. Everyone indifferent to her importunes her; she does not want a court but a lover. She prefers to please one decent man, and always to please him, than to raise in her favor the cry of fashion that lasts for one day and turns into jeers the next day.

The judgment of women is formed sooner than that of men. On the defensive almost since childhood, and charged to hold in trust something that is difficult to guard, good and evil are necessarily sooner known to them. Sophie, precocious in everything because her temperament inclines her to be, has also had her judgment formed sooner than that of other girls her age. There is nothing very extraordinary in this: maturity is not everywhere the same at the same time.

Sophie has been instructed in the duties and the rights of her sex and of ours. She knows the defects of men and the vices of women. She also knows the qualities and the contrary virtues, and has imprinted them all in the bottom of her heart. One cannot have a higher idea of the decent woman than the one she has conceived, and this idea does not terrify her. But she thinks more obligingly of the decent man, the man of merit. She feels that she is made for that man, that she is worthy of him, that she can give him back the happiness she will receive from him. She feels that she will know how to recognize him; she has only to find him.

Women are the natural judges of men's merit, as men are of women's merit. This belongs to their reciprocal right, and neither one nor the other is unaware of it. Sophie knows this right and uses it, but with the modesty that is suitable to her youth, to her inexperience, to her condition. She judges only things that are within her reach, and she judges them only when this serves to develop some useful maxim. She speaks of those who are absent only with the greatest circumspection, especially.

if they are women. She thinks that what makes them slanderous and satirical is to speak about their sex. As long as they limit themselves to speaking about ours, they are only equitable. Sophie therefore limits herself to this. As to women, she never speaks about them except to say the good that she knows of them. It is an honor she believes she owes her sex. As to those about whom she knows nothing good to say, she says nothing at all, and that is readily understood.

Sophie is not very experienced in the ways of society; but she is obliging, and does everything she does with grace. A fortunate disposition serves her better than a great deal of art. She has a certain politeness of her own that is not derived from formulas, is not subject to fashions, does not change with them, and does nothing by custom, but that comes from a real desire to please, and does please. She does not know the trivial compliments, and does not invent any more elaborate ones. She does not say that she is very much obliged, that one honors her very much, that one should not bother, etc. She thinks even less of turning phrases. For an attention or a conventional politeness, she responds with a curtsy or a simple *thank you*, but these words from her mouth are as good as any others. For a genuine service she lets her heart speak, and it is not a compliment it finds. She has never allowed the French custom to subject her to the yoke of affectation, such as that of stretching out her hand in going from one room to another on the arm of a sexagenarian whom she would very much like to support. When a musk-scented gallant offers her this impertinent service, she leaves the officious arm on the stairs and springs in two bounds into the room, saying that she is not lame. As a matter of fact, even though she is not tall, she has never wanted high-heeled shoes. Her feet are small enough to do without them.

Not only does she remain silent and respectful with women, but even with men who are married, or much older than she. She will never accept a place above them except from obedience, and will take her place again below them as soon as she can. For she knows that the rights of age come before those of sex, as they have on their side the prejudice of wisdom, which must be honored before all else.

With young people of her age, it is another matter. She needs a different tone to command respect from them, and she knows how to assume it without departing from the modest air suitable to her. If they are modest and reserved themselves, she will willingly maintain with them the amiable familiarity of youth. Their conversations, full of innocence, will be jocular but decent. If they become serious, she wants them to be useful; if they degenerate into insipid flattery, she will soon make them stop, for she especially despises the petty jargon of gallantry as very offensive to her sex. She knows very well that the man she is looking for does not use that jargon, and she never willingly suffers from another what is not suitable to the one whose character she has imprinted at the bottom of her heart. The high opinion she has of the rights of her sex, the lofty pride that the purity of her sentiments gives her, the energy of virtue that she feels in herself and that makes her respectable in her own eyes, cause her to listen with indignation to the syrupy remarks with which they affect to amuse her. She does not receive them with obvious anger, but with an ironic ovation that disconcerts, or with a cold tone that one is not prepared for. Let a handsome Phoebus reel off his pleasantries, praise her with wit for hers, for her beauty, for her charms, on what a reward it is to be happy enough to please her, she is the kind of girl who will interrupt him while saying politely: "Sir, I am terribly afraid that I know those things better than you do. If we have nothing more unusual to say to one another, I think we can finish the conversation here."[40] To accompany these words with a big curtsy and to find herself twenty feet from him is for her the work of an instant. Ask those fellows who dance attendance if it is easy to display one's prattle before a mind as contrary as that one.

Yet it is not that she does not very much like praise, as long as it is for real, and she can believe that one really thinks the good one says of her. In order to appear touched by her merit, one has to begin by showing some. Homage founded upon esteem can flatter her haughty heart, but any gallant persiflage is always rebuffed. Sophie is not made to exercise the little talents of a buffoon.

With such great maturity of judgment, and formed in every respect like a girl of twenty, Sophie at fifteen will not be treated like a child by her parents. Hardly will they perceive in her the first disquiet of youth but they will hasten to provide for it before it progresses. They will speak to her tenderly and sensibly. Tender and sensible speeches belong to her age and character. If this character is such as I imagine it, why would not her father speak to her more or less like this:

"Sophie, you are now a big girl, and one does not become one in order always to be one. We want you to be happy. It is for our sake that we want it, because our happiness depends on yours. The happiness of a decent girl is to make the happiness of a decent man. You must therefore think of marrying. One has to think of it soon, for upon marriage depends one's fate in life, and one never has enough time to think about it.

"Nothing is more difficult than the choice of a good husband, unless perhaps it is that of a good wife. Sophie, you will be that rare woman, you will be the glory of our lives and the happiness of our old age. But with whatever merit you have been provided, the earth does not lack men who have even more than you. There is not one who ought not to consider himself honored to win you; there are many who would honor you even more. Among this number, it is a matter of finding one who suits you, of knowing him, and of making yourself known to him.

"The greatest happiness of marriage depends on so many kinds of suitability that it is folly to want to gather them all. One must first assure oneself of the most important ones. When the others are found, one avails oneself of them; when they are lacking one does without them. Perfect happiness is not of this earth, but the greatest of miseries, and the one we can always avoid, is to be unhappy through one's own fault.

"There are kinds of suitability that are natural, some that are instituted, and some that derive only from opinion. Parents are the judges of the last two kinds; children alone are the judges of the first. Marriages made through the authority of fathers conform uniquely to what is suitable according to institution and opinion. Persons are not married, but ranks and goods. But all that can change. Only persons always remain, and carry themselves everywhere with them. Despite fortune, it is only though personal relations that a marriage can be happy or unhappy.

"Your mother had rank, and I was rich. Those are the only considerations that induced our parents to unite us. I lost my goods, she lost her name. Forgotten by her family, what good does it do her today to have been born a Lady? In the midst of our disasters, the union of our hearts consoled us for everything. The conformity in our tastes made us choose this retreat. We live here happily in poverty; we take the place of everything for one another. Sophie is our common treasure. We bless heaven for having given us that one, and for having taken away everything else. Consider, my child, where providence has brought us! The conformities that made us marry have vanished; we are happy only through those that counted for nothing.

"It is up to spouses to match one another. Mutual inclination must be their first bond; their eyes, their hearts must be their first guides. For as their first duty, once united, is to love one another, and as to love or not to love does not depend on us, this duty necessarily involves another, which is to begin by loving one another before uniting. That is the right of nature that nothing can abrogate. Those who have constrained it by so many civil laws have had greater regard for apparent order than for the happiness of marriage and the morals of citizens. You see, my Sophie, that we do not preach a difficult morality. It aims only to make you your own mistress, and to have us depend upon you for the choice of your husband.

"After having told you our reasons for leaving you entirely at liberty, it is just to speak to you also about your reasons for using it wisely. My daughter, you are good and reasonable, you possess rectitude and piety, you have the talents suitable to decent women, and you are not without attractions. But you are poor. You have the most estimable goods, and you lack those that are most esteemed. Aspire therefore only to what you can obtain, and regulate your ambition, not according to your judgments, nor ours, but according to men's opinion. Were it only a question of an equality of merit, I do not know to what I should limit your hopes. But do not raise them above your fortune, and do not forget that it belongs to the lowest rank. Even though a man worthy of you will not count this inequality as an obstacle, you will then have to do what he does not. Sophie must imitate her mother, and enter only into a family that considers itself honored by her. You did not see our opulence; you were born during our poverty. You make it sweet for us, and share it without difficulty. Believe me, Sophie, do not seek goods from which we bless Heaven for having delivered us. We tasted happiness only after having lost wealth.

"You are too lovable to please no one, and your misery is not such that a decent man will be embarrassed by you. You will be sought after, and you may be by people who will not be worthy of you. If they showed themselves to you such as they are, you would esteem them for what they are worth. All their display would not impose upon you for long. But although you have good judgment, and you are knowledgeable about merit, you lack experience, and you do not know to what point men can counterfeit themselves. A skillful cheat can study your tastes in order to seduce you, and feign near you virtues he does not have. He would cause your ruin, Sophie, before you had perceived it, and you would know your error only to weep over it. The most dangerous of all traps, and the only one that reason cannot avoid, is that of the senses. If ever you have the misfortune of falling into it, you will no longer see anything but illusions and chimeras, your eyes will be fascinated, your judgment clouded, your will corrupted. Your error itself will be dear to you, and were you in a state to know it, you would not want to recover from it. My daughter, it is to Sophie's reason that I deliver you; I do not deliver you to the inclination of her heart. As long as you remain in control of yourself, remain your own judge. But as soon as you love, put yourself back in your mother's care.

"I propose to you an agreement that shows you our esteem, and reestablishes between us the natural order. Parents choose their daughter's spouse, and consult her only as a matter of form. That is the custom. Between us we will do entirely the contrary. You will choose, and we will be consulted. Use your right, Sophie, use it freely and wisely. The spouse who is suitable to you must be your choice, and not ours. But it is up to us to judge whether you are mistaken regarding what is suitable, and whether you are unknowingly doing something other than what you want. Birth, goods, rank, opinion will not enter into our reasons. Take a decent man whose person pleases you, and whose character is suitable to you. Whatever else he may be, we accept him as our son-in-law. His possessions will always be great enough if he has a pair of arms, morals, and loves his family. His rank will always be illustrious enough if he ennobles it by virtue. If everyone on earth blamed us, who cares? We are not seeking public approbation. Your happiness is enough for us."

Readers, I do not know what effect such a speech would have on girls brought up according to your manner. As to Sophie, she may not respond to it with words. Shame and emotion would not easily let her express herself. But I am quite sure that it will remain engraved on her heart for the rest of her life, and that if one can count on any human resolution, it is on the one of being worthy of the esteem of her parents that this speech will cause her to make.

Let us look at things in the worst possible light, and let us give her an ardent temperament that will make a long wait painful for her. I say that her judgment, her knowledge, her taste, her delicacy, and especially the sentiments with which her heart has been nourished during her childhood, will oppose to the impetuosity of the senses a counterweight that will be enough for her to vanquish them, or at least to resist them for a long time. She would rather die a martyr to her condition than afflict her parents, marry a man without merit, and expose herself to the miseries of an ill-matched marriage. Even the liberty she has received only gives her a new elevation of soul, and makes her more particular in choosing her master. With the temperament of an Italian woman and the sensibility of an Englishwoman, she has in order to contain her heart and her senses the pride of a Spaniard who, even in seeking a lover, does not easily find the one she esteems worthy of her.

Not everyone is suited to feel what energy the love of decent things can give the soul, and what force one can find within oneself when one wants to be sincerely virtuous. There are people for whom everything great appears chimerical, and who within the limits of their base and vile reason will never know what even the folly of virtue can do over the human passions. One has to speak to people like that only through examples; too bad for them if they persist in denying them. If I told them that Sophie is not an imaginary being, that only her name is my invention, that her education, her morals, her character, even her face have really existed, and that her memory still costs tears to an entire honest family, no doubt they would believe none of it. But in the end what shall I risk by straightforwardly finishing the story of a girl so similar to Sophie, that this story could be hers without occasioning surprise? Whether it is believed to be true or not, it little matters to me. If you wish, I shall have told tales, but in any case I shall have explained my method, and shall continue to pursue my ends.

The young person with the temperament that I have just imputed to Sophie, as a matter of fact, resembled her in all the ways that could have made her merit the name, and I leave it to her. After the conversation that I have related, her father and mother, judging that matches were not going to come and offer themselves in the hamlet where they lived, sent her to pass a winter in town with an aunt who was instructed in secret as to the reason for the trip. For the proud Sophie carried in the bottom of her heart the noble pride of knowing how to triumph over herself, and whatever need she might have for a husband, she would have died a virgin rather than resolve to go look for one.

In order to satisfy the aims of her parents, her aunt presented her among the families, brought her into societies, to festivities. She had her see society—or, rather, had her seen by it, for Sophie cared little for all this commotion. It was noted, however, that she did not flee young people with an agreeable figure who seemed decent and modest. She even had in her reserve a certain art of attracting them that seemed enough like coquetry. But after conversing with them two or three times, she would lose interest. Soon, to that air of authority that seems to accept respects paid to it, she substituted a more humble manner and a more repelling politeness. Always attentive toward herself, she no longer left them the occasion to render her the least service. That was enough to say that she did not want to be their beloved.

Never have sensitive hearts loved loud pleasures, which are the vain and sterile happiness of people who feel nothing, and who believe that to stupefy life is to enjoy it. Not finding what she was looking for, and despairing of finding it this way, Sophie was bored with town. She tenderly loved her parents. Nothing compensated her for them; nothing was able to make her forget them. She returned to join them long before the time fixed for her return.

She had hardly taken up again her functions in the paternal house than it became apparent that while she kept to the same conduct, her temper had changed. She was distracted, impatient, sad, and dreamy. She hid in order to cry. It was thought at first that she loved and was ashamed of it. She was spoken to; she denied it. She protested that she had seen no one who could touch her heart, and Sophie did not lie.

Yet her languor ceaselessly increased, and her health was beginning to be affected. Her mother, worried by this change, finally resolved to know its cause. She took her aside and set to work with her that winning language and those invincible caresses that only maternal tenderness knows how to employ. My daughter, you whom I carried in my womb and carry incessantly in my heart, pour out the secrets of yours into your mother's bosom. What then are these secrets that a mother cannot know? Who pities your pains? Who shares them? Who wants to relieve them, if not your father and I? Ah, my child, do you want me to die of your pain without knowing it?

Far from hiding her sorrows from her mother, the young girl wanted nothing more than to have her as a consoler and confidant. But shame prevented her from speaking, and her modesty did not find the language to describe a condition so unworthy of her as the emotion that troubled her senses despite all she could do. Finally, her shame itself serving as an indication to her mother, she tore from her these humiliating avowals. Far from afflicting her with unjust reprimands, she consoled her, she pitied her, wept for her. She was too wise to make a crime of an ill that only her virtue made so cruel for her. But why bear without necessity an ill whose remedy was so easy and so legitimate? Why did she not use the liberty she had been given! Why did she not accept a husband, why did she not choose one! Did she not know that her fate depended upon her alone, and that whatever her choice, it would be confirmed, as she could not make one that would not be decent? She had been sent to town, and she had not wanted to stay there. Several matches had presented themselves, and she had rebuffed them all. What then was she waiting for? What did she want? What an inexplicable contradiction!

The answer was simple. If it were only a matter of an aid for youth, the choice would soon be made. But a master for the whole of life is not so easy to choose. As one cannot separate these two choices, there is nothing to do but wait, and often lose one's youth, before finding the man with whom one wants to spend one's days. That was Sophie's case. She needed a lover, but this lover had to be a husband, and as for the heart that hers needed, one was almost as hard to find as the other. All these so brilliant young people were suitable to her only in age; they were always unsuitable in the other ways. Their superficial minds, their vanity, their jargon, their unprincipled morals, their frivolous imitations disgusted her with them. She was looking for a man and found only monkeys. She was looking for a soul and did not find one.

How unhappy I am! She said to her mother. I need to love, and see nothing that pleases me. My heart repels all those whom my senses attract. I do not see one of them who does not excite my desires, and not one who does not repress them. A taste without esteem cannot last. Ah, that is not the man your Sophie needs! His charming model is imprinted too much beforehand in her soul. She can love only him, she can make only him happy, she can be happy with him alone. She would rather consume herself and combat without end, she would rather die unhappy and free, than despairing near a man she would not love, and whom she would make unhappy. It is better no longer to be, than to be only in order to suffer.

Struck by these singularities, her mother found them too bizarre not to suspect some mystery. Sophie was neither overly delicate nor ridiculous. How could this excessive delicacy have been suited to her, who had been taught nothing so much since her childhood as to accommodate herself to the people with whom she had to live, and to make virtue of necessity? This model of a lovable man with which she was so enchanted, and that returned so often in her conversations, made her mother conjecture that this caprice had some other foundation of which she was yet still ignorant, and that Sophie had not said everything. The unfortunate, overburdened by her secret pain, sought only to confide in someone. Her mother urges her. She hesitates, she finally surrenders, and leaving without saying anything, she returns a moment later with a book in her hand. Pity your unhappy daughter, her sadness is without remedy, her tears cannot dry. You want to know their cause. Well then, here it is, she said, throwing the book on the table. The mother takes the book and opens it: it was the *Adventures of Telemachus*. At first she understands nothing of this enigma. By dint of questions and obscure answers, she finally sees with a surprise that is easily conceived that her daughter is the rival of Eucharis.[41]

Sophie loved Telemachus, and loved him with a passion of which nothing could cure her. As soon as her mother and father knew about her mania, they laughed at it, and thought they could bring her back by reasoning. They were mistaken. Reason was not entirely on their side. Sophie also had hers, and knew how to turn it to account. How many times she reduced them to silence by using their own reasoning against them, by showing them that they had done all the evil themselves. They had not molded her for a man of her century. She would necessarily have to adopt her husband's way of thinking, or give him hers. They had made the first means impossible by the manner in which they had brought her up, and the other was precisely what she was looking for.

Give me, she said, a man imbued with my maxims, or one I can win over to them, and I marry him. But until then, why do you scold me? Pity me. I am unhappy, and not mad. Does the heart depend on the will? Did not my father tell me this himself? Is it my fault if I love what is not? I am not a visionary. I do not want a prince; I am not looking for Telemachus. I know that he is only a fiction. I am looking for someone who resembles him. Why can this someone not exist, as I exist, I who feel in myself a heart so similar to his? No, let us not thus dishonor humanity. Let us not think that a lovable and virtuous man is only a chimera. He exists, he lives, perhaps he is looking for me; he is looking for a soul who knows how to love him. But what is he? Where is he? I don't know. He is none of those I have seen; no doubt he is not one of those I shall see. O mother! Why did you make virtue too lovable for me? If I can love only virtue, the wrong is less mine than yours.

Shall I bring this sad story to its catastrophe? Shall I report the long debates that preceded it? Shall I represent a mother made impatient, exchanging her first caresses for severity? Shall I show an irritated father, forgetting his first engagements, and treating the most virtuous of girls as a madwoman? Shall I finally depict the unfortunate, even more attached to her chimera by the persecution it makes her suffer, walking with slow steps toward death and descending into the tomb at the moment it is believed she is being dragged to the altar? No, I set aside these baneful objects. I do not need to go so far to show by a rather striking example, it seems to me, that despite the prejudices that arise from this century's morals, enthusiasm for the decent and the beautiful is no more foreign to women than to men, and that there is nothing under the guidance of nature that one cannot obtain from them, as from us.

One stops me here to ask me whether it is nature that prescribes taking so many pains to repress immoderate desires. I answer that it does not, but also that it is not nature that gives us so many immoderate desires. Now, everything that is not from nature is against it; I have proved that a thousand times.

Let us give his Sophie back to our Emile. Let us resuscitate this lovable girl in order to give her a less vivid imagination and a happier destiny. I wanted to depict an ordinary woman, and by dint of elevating her soul I have unsettled her reason. I went astray myself. Let us retrace our steps. Sophie has only a good disposition in a common soul; everything more that she has than others is the effect of her education.

*   *   *

[*This passage is a part of Rousseau's discussion of the search for a wife for Emile.*]

It is also very different for the order of marriage whether the man allies himself above or below himself. The first case is entirely contrary to reason, the second is more conformable with it. As the family is attached to society only through its head, the condition of this head rules that of the entire family. When he connects himself within a lower rank he does not descend, he elevates his spouse. On the contrary, by taking a wife above him, he lowers her without raising himself. So in the first case there is good without ill, and in the second, ill without good. Furthermore, it is according to the order of nature that the woman obey the man. When, therefore, he takes her from an inferior rank, the natural order and the civil order are in accord, and everything is well. The contrary occurs when, connecting himself to a higher rank, the man places himself in the position of offending against either his right or his gratitude, and of being either an ingrate, or despised. Then the woman, aspiring to authority, makes herself tyrant over the head of the family, and the master, become slave, finds himself the most ridiculous and the most miserable of creatures. Such are the unhappy favorites whom the Kings of Asia honor and torment with a relationship by marriage, and who, it is said, dare to enter the bed only by its foot in order to sleep with their wives.

I expect that many readers, remembering that I give woman a natural talent for governing man, will accuse me here of contradiction. However, they will be wrong. There is a great deal of difference between arrogating to oneself the right to command, and governing the one who commands. The empire of woman is an empire of gentleness, skill, and obligingness. Her orders are caresses; her threats are tears. She must reign in the house like a minister in the State, by getting herself commanded to do what she wants to do. In this sense it is always the case that the best households are those in which the woman has most authority. But when she does not recognize the voice of the head of the family, when she wants to usurp his rights and command by herself, nothing ever results from this disorder but misery, scandal, and dishonor.

There remains the choice between one's equals and one's inferiors, and I think there is still some restriction to be applied to the latter. For it is difficult to find in the dregs of the people a spouse able to make a decent man happy. It is not that those among the lowest ranks are more vicious than those among the first, but because there are few ideas of the beautiful and the decent among the former, and because the injustice of the other conditions makes this one see justice even in its own vices.

Naturally, man hardly thinks. Thinking is an art he learns like all the others, and even with greater difficulty. I know, for the two sexes, of only two really distinctive classes: one of the people who think; the other of the people who do not think. This distinction arises almost uniquely from education. A man from the first of these two classes must not connect himself within the other. For the greatest charm of society is lacking when, even though he has a wife, he is reduced to thinking alone. People who spend precisely their whole lives working to live have no other idea than those belonging to their work or their interests, and their whole mind seems to be at the end of their arms. This ignorance harms neither probity, nor morals. Often it even serves them; for one often makes compromises about one's duties by dint of thinking about them, and one ends by putting jargon in the place of things. The conscience is the most enlightened of philosophers. One does not need to know Cicero's *On Duties* to be a good man, and the most decent woman in the world perhaps knows least what decency is.[42] But it is nonetheless true that a cultivated mind alone makes intercourse enjoyable, and it is a sad thing for the father of a family who enjoys himself at home to be forced to withdraw into himself, and not to be able to make himself understood there by anyone.

*   *   *

[*Emile and Sophie meet, apparently by accident, and have begun to fall in love with each other.*]

If genuine love could make use of coquetry, I would even believe that I see some traces of it in the manner in which Sophie acts with others in her lover's presence. One would say that, not satisfied with the ardent passion with which she inflames him by an exquisite mixture of reserve and caresses, she is not sorry to inflame this same passion more by means of a little anxiety. One would say that, making her young guests cheerful on purpose, she intends to torment Emile by the charms of a playfulness she does not dare show toward him. But Sophie is too attentive, too good, too judicious really to torment him. In order to temper this dangerous stimulant, love and decency take the place of prudence in her. She knows how to alarm him and to reassure him precisely when she has to, and if sometimes she makes him anxious, she never makes him sad. Let us forgive the worry she causes to what she loves for the sake of the fear she feels that he will never be sufficiently entwined.

But what effect will these little maneuvers have on Emile? Will he be jealous, or not? That is what has to be examined. For digressions such as these also form a part of the object of my book, and hardly distance me from my subject.

I showed before how in the things that derive only from opinion, this passion introduces itself into man's heart.[43] But in love, it is something else. Jealousy then seems to be derived so closely from nature that one has a great deal of difficulty in believing that it does not come from it. Even the example of animals, some of whom are jealous to the point of fury, seems to establish the opposing sentiment as unanswerable. Is it men's opinion that teaches roosters to tear each other to pieces, and bulls to battle to the death?

Aversion to everything that troubles and combats our pleasures is a natural motion. That is incontestable. Up to a certain point the desire to possess exclusively what pleases us still belongs to the same case. But when this desire, having become passion, transforms itself into fury, or into a stormy and fretful whim called jealousy, then it is something else. This passion can be natural or not; one must distinguish.

The example taken from animals has been examined formerly in the *Discourse on Inequality*, and now that I think of it anew, this examination seems to me solid enough to dare send readers back to it.[44] I shall only add to the distinctions that I drew in this writing that the jealousy that comes from nature derives a great deal from the power of the female sex, and when this power is, or seems to be, unlimited, this jealousy is at its height. For the male, then measuring his rights according to his needs, can never see another male except as an importunate competitor. In these same species the females, always obeying the first comer, belong to the males only by the right of conquest, and cause eternal combats among them.

On the contrary, in species where one unites to one, where coupling produces a kind of moral bond, a kind of marriage, the female, belonging by her choice to the male she gave herself, commonly refuses herself to any other. The male, having as a guarantee of her fidelity this preferential affection, is consequently less anxious at the sight of other males, and lives more peaceably with them. In these species the male shares the care of the little ones, and by one of those laws of nature that one does not observe without emotion, it seems that the female gives back to the male the attachment he has for the children.

Now, to consider the human species in its primitive simplicity, it is easy to see on the basis of the limited power of the male, and the moderation of his desires, that he is destined by nature to content himself with a single female. This is confirmed by the numerical equality of individuals of the two sexes, at least in our climates. This equality does not arise by far in the species where the greater force of the males unites several females to one alone. Further, although man does not sit on eggs like a pigeon, and although, as he does not have breasts to give milk, he is in this respect in the class of quadrupeds, the children are crawling and weak for so long that the mother and they would with difficulty do without the attachment of the father, and without the cares that are its effect.

All observations therefore concur to prove that the jealous furor of males in some animal species is not conclusive at all regarding man. Even the exception of southern climates, where polygamy is established, only better confirms the principle, as it is from the plurality of women that the tyrannical precautions of the husbands come. The sentiment of his own weakness brings man to have recourse to constraint in order to elude the laws of nature.

Among us where these same laws, eluded less on this point, are eluded in a contrary and more odious sense, jealousy has its motive in the social passions more than in primitive instinct. In most liaisons of gallantry, the lover hates his rivals much more than he loves his mistress. If he is afraid of not being the only one to obtain a hearing, that is the effect of this amour-propre whose origin I have shown, and in him vanity suffers much more than love does. Besides, our clumsy institutions have made women so secretive,* and have so strongly aroused their appetites, that one can hardly even count on their most proven attachment, and they can no longer show preferences that reassure one against the fear of competitors.

As to genuine love, it is something else. I showed in the writing already cited that this sentiment is not so natural as one thinks. There is a great deal of difference between the sweet habit that makes a man affectionate toward his companion, and this unbridled ardor that inebriates him with the chimerical attractions of an object he no longer sees as it is. This passion, which yearns for exclusions and preferences, differs from vanity only in this: vanity, requiring everything and according

---

*The kind of dissimulation that I have in mind here is opposed to that which is suitable to them and that they have from nature. One consists of disguising the sentiments they have, and the other of feigning those they do not have. All women in society spend their lives in making a trophy of their pretended sensibility, and never love anything except themselves.

nothing, is always iniquitous, while love, giving as much as it requires, is in itself a sentiment full of equity. Besides, the more exigent it is, the more credulous. The same illusion that causes it makes it easy to persuade. If love is anxious, esteem is trusting, and never has love without esteem existed in a decent heart, because no one loves anything in what he loves but the qualities by which he sets great store.

*   *   *

[*On the wedding day of Emile and Sophie, the tutor brought the young couple together and explained to them that, in order to prolong the happiness of love in marriage as much as possible, and in order to try to assure one another's fidelity, Emile must agree that Sophie will always be the one to determine whether or not she should give herself to him. The tutor suggests that desire remains only for an object one cannot fully command. Sophie exercises her authority over Emile on their wedding night and the next day the tutor has the following conversation with the couple.*]

"My dear child, I have to explain my aims in the conversation we three all had yesterday. You perhaps saw in it only an art for husbanding your pleasures in order to make them durable. O Sophie! It had another object much more worthy of my cares. In becoming your Spouse, Emile has become the head of your house. It is up to you to obey; this is how nature wanted it. When the woman resembles Sophie, however, it is good that the man to be guided by her. That is also a law of nature. It is to give you as much authority over his heart as his sex gives him over your person, that I made you the arbiter of his pleasures. It will cost you some painful privations, but you will reign over him if you know how to reign over yourself. What has already happened shows me that this difficult art is not above your courage. You will reign a long time through love if you make your favors rare and precious, if you know how to make them valued. Do you want to see your husband ceaselessly at your feet? Always keep him at some distance from your person. But in your very severity, make use not of capriciousness, but of some modesty. Let him see you reserved, not whimsical. Be careful that in husbanding his love you do not make him doubt yours. Make yourself cherished for your favors, and respected for your refusals. Let him honor the chastity of his wife without having cause to complain of her coldness.

"It is in this way, my child, that he will give you his trust, listen to your advice, consult you in his affairs, and resolve nothing without deliberating over it with you. It is in this way that you can recall him to wisdom when he goes astray, bring him back by gentle persuasion, make yourself lovable so as to make yourself useful, use coquetry in the interests of virtue, and love for the profit of reason.

"Do not believe, with all of this, that even this art can always serve you. Whatever precaution one can take, enjoyment uses the pleasures, and love even more than others. But when love has lasted a long time, a sweet habit fills the void, and the attraction of trust succeeds the transports of passion. Children form between those who gave them being a bond no less sweet, and often stronger than love itself. When you cease to be Emile's mistress, you will be his wife and his friend. You will be the mother of his children. Then, instead of your first reserve, establish the greatest intimacy between you: no more separate beds, no more refusals, no more capriciousness. Become so much half of him that he can no longer do without you, and that as soon as he leaves you he feels far away from himself. You, who made the charms of domestic life reign so well in the paternal household, make them also reign in yours. Every man who pleases himself in his house loves his wife. Remember that if your Spouse lives happily at home, you will be a happy woman.

"As to the present, do not be so severe with your lover. He has deserved more obligingness. He would be offended by your anxieties. Do not husband his health so much at the expense of his happiness, and enjoy yours. One must not wait for lack of appetite, nor rebuff desire. One must not refuse in order to refuse, but in order to make what one accords valued."

Then, uniting them, I say in front of her to her young Spouse: One has to bear the yoke one has imposed on oneself. Deserve that it be made light for you. Above all, sacrifice to the graces, and do not imagine that you make yourself more lovable by sulking. It is not difficult to make peace, and it is easy to guess the terms. The treaty is signed with a kiss. After that I say to my Pupil: dear Emile, a man needs a counselor and guide all of his life. I have done my best until now to fulfill this duty toward you. Here ends my long task, and begins that of another. Today I abdicate the authority that you entrusted to me, and here is your governor from now on.

CHAPTER SIX

Women of Paris (from Julie)

[*At the end of part I of Rousseau's novel, Julie's father has declared his firm opposition to her proposed marriage to her tutor, who is known as Saint Preux. Saint Preux leaves in order to make his fortune and arrives in Paris from where he writes to his beloved in part II.*]

LETTER XXI
To Julie

You asked for it, Julie, I must then portray for you these fetching Parisian women? Proud woman! This homage your charms had not yet received. With all your feigned jealousy, with your modesty and love, I see more vanity than fear lurking behind this curiosity. However that may be, I shall be truthful; I can afford to be; I would more gladly be so if I had more to praise. I wish they were a hundredfold more charming! I wish their appeal were sufficient to pay a new tribute to yours!

You complained of my silence? Ah dear God, what would I have told you? By reading this letter you will sense why I enjoyed telling you about your neighbors the Valaisan women, and why I did not mention the women of this country. It was that the former constantly called me back to you, and the latter . . . read on, and then you shall judge me. And yet few people share my opinion of French Ladies, if indeed I am not completely alone in my judgment of them. On this point fairness obliges me to forewarn you, so you may know that I describe them to you, perhaps not as they are, but as I see them. Despite that, if I am unfair to them, you will not fail to criticize me again, and you will be more unfair than I; for all the fault in this is yours alone.

SOURCE: Jean-Jacques Rousseau, *Julie; or, The New Heloise. Collected Writings of Rousseau* VI, trans. and ed. Philip Stewart and Jean Vaché (Hanover, N.H.: University Press of New England, 1997).

Let us begin with the outside. That is as deep as most observers go. If I followed them in this, the women of this country would have great cause for complaint; they have an outside of character as well as of countenance, and as the one is hardly more to their advantage than the other, to judge them only by that is to do them wrong. In appearance they are passable at best and on the whole rather plain than pretty; I leave aside the exceptions. Smallish rather than well built, they are not slim at the waist, and so they willingly favor fashions that disguise it; in which respect women of other countries seem to me fairly foolish, trying to imitate fashions made for hiding flaws they do not have.

Their gait is easy and common. Their bearing is devoid of affectation because they do not like constraint: but they naturally have a certain *disinvoltura*[1] that is not lacking in grace, and that they often insist on pushing to the point of foolishness. Their complexion is middling white, and they are commonly a bit skinny, which does not help to make their skin more attractive. As far as the bust is concerned, it is the other extreme from the Valaisans. With tightly laced corsets they attempt to give a misleading notion of its firmness; there are other means to give a misleading notion of its coloration. Although I have perceived these objects only from very far off, they are so available for inspection that little remains to be guessed at. These Ladies in this respect seem ill to understand their own interests; for provided the face is agreeable, the observer's imagination would moreover serve them much better than his eyes, and according to the Gascon Philosopher, total hunger is far more acute than hunger that has already been sated by at least one of the senses.[2]

Their features are not very regular, but though they are not beautiful, they have something about their looks that compensates for beauty, and sometimes eclipses it. Their bright and lively eyes however are neither piercing nor soft: although they attempt to brighten them with rouge, the expression they impart to them by this means is closer to the fire of anger than to that of love; naturally they express only gaiety, or, if they sometimes seem to solicit a tender sentiment, they never promise any.*

They dress so well, or at least, such is their reputation, that in this as in all else they serve as model to the rest of Europe. Indeed, it is not possible to make use with more taste of a costume so curious. They are, of all women, the least subservient to their own fashions. Fashion rules provincial ladies, but Parisian ladies rule fashion, and they can make it bend each to her own advantage. The former are like ignorant and ser-

---

*Let us speak for ourselves, my dear philosopher; why should others not be more fortunate? Only a coquette promises to everybody what she should keep to only one.

vile copyists who copy everything right down to the spelling mistakes; the latter are authors who copy as masters, and know how to correct misreadings.[3]

Their finery is more studied than sumptuous; it is more characterized by elegance than elaborateness. The quick succession of fashions that dates everything from one year to the next, a tidiness that makes them like to change their attire often, protects them from ridiculous sumptuousness; they spend no less for that, but their spending is more shrewd; instead of threadbare and grandiose dresses as in Italy, here you see dresses that are simpler but always new. The two sexes in that regard manifest the same moderation, the same refinement, and this taste gives me great pleasure: I am very pleased to see neither patches nor stains.[4] Among no people except ours do women in particular wear less gold. You see the same fabrics across all estates, and it would be difficult to tell a Duchess from a bourgeoise if the former did not possess the art of inventing distinctions the other would not dare imitate. Now a difficulty seems to arise from this; for whatever fashion is adopted at Court, that fashion is instantly followed in town, and Parisian Bourgeoises are not like provincial and foreign women, who are never more up to date than the previous fashion. Nor is it as in other countries where, the highest ranking being also the richest, the ladies are distinguishable by a degree of luxury the others cannot match. If the ladies of the Court followed that example here, they would soon be outshone by the wives of the Financiers.

So what have they done? They have chosen surer, more clever means, which reflect more thought. They know that the notions of decency and modesty are deeply etched into the minds of the people. It is that which suggested to them fashions that cannot be imitated. They saw that the people had an aversion to rouge, which they insist on coarsely calling fard;[5] they have put on four fingers deep[6] not of fard, but of rouge; for the word being changed, the thing is no longer the same. They saw that an uncovered bust is a scandal to the public; they have considerably lowered their necklines. They saw . . . oh many things, that my Julie will surely never see, Demoiselle that she is![7] They have incorporated into their manners the same spirit that governs their attire. That charming modesty that distinguishes, honors, and beautifies your sex, to them appeared base and lowborn; they have breathed into their gesture and speech a noble impudence, and there is not an honorable man who would not lower his eyes at their bold gaze. So it is that ceasing to be women, for fear of being indistinguishable from other women, they prefer their rank to their sex, and imitate whores, so as not to be imitated.[8]

I do not know how far this imitation on their part goes, but I know they have been unsuccessful in avoiding completely the imitation they were trying to prevent. As for the rouge and the lowered necklines, they have gone as far as they possibly could. The women of the town thought it better to give up their natural colors and the charms that the *amoroso pensier*[9] of lovers could lend them, than to stay done up like Bourgeoises, and if this example did not spread to the lower estates, it is because a woman on foot in such attire is none too secure against the insults of the crowd. These insults are the cry of outraged decency, and in this situation as in many others, the brutishness of the people, more honest than the decorum of polite society, perhaps keeps a hundred thousand women here within the bounds of modesty; such is precisely what the clever women who invented these fashions were after.

As for the soldier-like demeanor and grenadier tone of voice, it is less noticeable, given that it is more universal, and is hardly perceptible except to new arrivals. From the Faubourg Saint Germain to the market place[10] there are few women in Paris whose approach, whose gaze is not sufficiently brazen to disconcert anyone who has seen nothing of that sort in his own country; and from the surprise provoked by these novel manners comes the awkward air that foreigners are faulted for. It is even worse the minute these women open their mouths. The tone is not the sweet and dainty one of our Vaudoises.[11] It is a certain hard, acid, interrogative, imperious, mocking accent, and stronger than a man's. If in their tone there remains something of their sex's grace, their intrepid and inquisitive manner of staring at people utterly eclipses it. It seems that they enjoy relishing the embarrassment they give to those who see them for the first time; but it is to be supposed that the embarrassment would please them less if they had more of an inkling of its cause.

However, whether because of my partiality in favor of beauty, or because of beauty's own instinct to set itself off, beautiful women seem to me in general a bit more modest, and I discern more decency in their comportment. This reserve comes easily to them, they are well aware of their advantages, they know they have no need to tease in order to attract us. Perhaps also effrontery is more perceptible and shocking when combined with ugliness, and it is certain that one would rather cover a shameless ugly face with slaps than with kisses, whereas with modesty it can inspire a tender compassion that sometimes leads to love. But although in general one notices here something gentler in the comportment of pretty persons, there is still so much simpering in their manners, and they are always so visibly preoccupied with themselves, that one is never exposed in this country to the temptation that Monsieur de Muralt sometimes experienced in the company of English women, to tell one she is beautiful for the pleasure of letting her know.[12]

Neither the jollity natural to this nation, nor the desire to imitate pretentious manners are the sole causes of this freedom of expression and comportment one observes here in women. It seems to have a deeper root in their manners, through the indiscreet and continual mixing of the two sexes, which leads each of them to adopt the air, language, and manners of the other. Our Swiss women rather like to gather together;* they spend their time in sweet familiarity, and although evidently they do not despise the society of men, it is certain that their presence introduces a sort of strain into this little gynecocracy. In Paris, it is just the opposite; women like spending their time only with men, only in their presence are they at ease. In each society the mistress of the house is almost always alone in the middle of a circle of men. One can hardly conceive whence come enough men to spread themselves everywhere; but Paris is full of adventurers and bachelors who spend their lives running from house to house, and men like money seem to multiply by circulating. So that is where a woman learns to speak, act, and think like them, and they like her. That is where, sole recipient of their petty gallantries, she placidly enjoys those insulting compliments to which they trouble not to lend even an appearance of good faith. But so what? Seriously or in jest, they pay attention to her and that is all she wants. Should another woman come forth, instantly a ceremonious tone takes the place of familiarity, pretentious manners set in, the men's attention is divided, and the two women hold each other in a concealed unease that can be relieved only by separating.

The ladies of Paris like to see plays, that is to say to be seen at plays, but every time they want to go their problem is to find another lady to accompany them; for the custom allows no woman to go alone to a grand loge,[13] not even with her husband, not even with another man. It would be hard to express how difficult these parties are to arrange in this most sociable country; of ten that are planned, nine fall through; the desire to go to the play causes them to be set up, the annoyance of going together causes them to be broken. I believe women could easily abrogate this awkward custom; for what is the reason a lady cannot be seen alone in public? But it is perhaps this lack of a reason that keeps it alive. It is ideal to focus rules of propriety as much as one can on matters where it would serve no purpose to do without. What would a

---

*All this has much changed. The circumstances make these letters appear to have been written only about twenty years ago. From the manners, the style, one would think they were from another century.

woman gain by the right to go without a lady-friend to the Opera? Is it not preferable to reserve this right for receiving her men-friends alone?

It is certain that a thousand secret liaisons must be the fruit of their manner of living dispersed and isolated among so many men. Everyone now admits this, and experience has destroyed the absurd maxim about overcoming temptations by multiplying them. So it is no longer said that this custom is more honest, but that it is more agreeable, and this is something I do not find any truer; for what can love obtain where modesty is derided, and what charm can a life hold that is deprived at once of love and honesty? And so since the great scourge of all these dissipated people is boredom, the women are less concerned with being loved than being amused, to them being courted and served is more important than love, and provided a man is assiduous, it matters little that he be passionate. The very words love and lover are banished from the inner circles of both sexes and relegated along with the likes of *chain* and *flame* to Novels that are no longer read.[14]

It seems that the whole order of natural sentiments is reversed here. The heart contracts no bonds, maidens are not allowed to have one. That right is reserved to married women, and excludes no one from their choice except their own husbands. It would be better for a mother to have twenty lovers than her daughter even one. Adultery causes no revulsion, nothing about it goes against propriety; the most proper of Novels, those which everyone reads for instruction are full of it, and license is no longer blameworthy, the minute it is combined with infidelity. O Julie! A woman who has not feared to defile the marriage bed a hundred times would dare with her impure mouth to denounce our chaste embraces, and condemn the union of two sincere hearts that never were capable of breaking faith. One would say that marriage in Paris is not of the same nature as everywhere else. It is a sacrament, at least that is what they pretend, and this sacrament lacks the force of the most minor civil contracts: it seems to be no more than the consent of two free persons who agree to live together, to bear the same name, to recognize the same children; but who have, other than that, no sort of claim to each other; and a husband who ventured to criticize his wife's misconduct here would provoke no less grumbling than one who in our country would suffer his wife's public disorderliness.[15] Wives, for their part, do not treat husbands with rigidity, and there has been no instance of having them punished for copying their infidelities. Besides, how can one expect from either party a more honest outcome of a bond about which the heart was not consulted? Anyone who marries only fortune or station owes nothing to the person.

Love itself, even love has lost its rights and is no less denatured than marriage. Given that Spouses here are bachelors and maidens who live together in order to enjoy greater freedom, lovers are passing acquaintances who get together for amusement, for show, out of habit, or for the needs of the moment. The heart has nothing to do with these liaisons, only convenience and certain surface formalities are considered. They consist, if you will, in knowing each other, being together, making arrangements, meeting, even less if that is possible.[16] A liaison of the gallant type lasts a little longer than a social call; it is a collection of pretty conversations and pretty Letters filled with portraits, maxims, philosophy, and wit. With respect to the physical, nothing so mysterious is called for; they have very cleverly discovered the need to make the moment of desire coincide with the means of satisfying it: the first woman, the first man to pass by, one's lover or another, a man is after all a man, they are all almost equally good, and there is at least consistency in that, for why should one be more faithful to a lover than to a husband? And then at a certain age all men are practically the same man, all women the same woman; all these dolls come from the same milliner, and there is scarcely any other choice to be made than of what falls most readily to hand.[17]

Inasmuch as I myself know nothing of this, the manner in which I was told about it was so extraordinary that I was unable to understand what I was being told. What I could make out was that for most women the lover is like one of the house staff: if he does not perform his duty, he is fired and another is found; if he finds a better offer or gets bored with the job, he leaves and another is found. Some women, it is said, are capricious enough even to give the master of the house a try, for after all, he is still a sort of man. This whim does not last; when it is over he is dismissed and another is found, or if he insists, he is kept on and another is found.

But, I would say to the person explaining these strange customs to me, how does a woman then get along subsequently with all those others,[18] who have thus taken or been given their leave? Well! he replied, she doesn't. They no longer see each other; no longer know each other. If ever they took a fancy to start over, they would have a new acquaintance to make, and it would be surprising if they even remembered having met. I see, said I, but even when I scale down these exaggerations, I cannot conceive how after such a tender union they can see each other dispassionately; how it is that the heart no longer pounds at the name of one who was once loved; how one can fail to thrill when encountering that person! You make me laugh, he interrupted, with your thrills! Do you want all our women then to do nothing but fall into spasms?

Discount a portion of this doubtlessly exaggerated tableau; put Julie alongside the rest, and remember my heart; I have nothing more to tell you. Yet it must be admitted: several of these disagreeable impressions fade by force of habit. If the bad is more readily perceived than the good, that does not prevent the good from manifesting itself in turn; the charms of mind and disposition bring out those of the person. The first antipathy overcome soon changes into an opposite sentiment. That is the other vantage point of the tableau, and fairness does not allow exhibiting only its most unfavorable side.

The main objection to large cities is that there men become other than what they are, and society imparts to them, as it were, a being other than their own. This is true, especially in Paris, and especially with respect to women, who derive from the way others look at them the only existence that matters to them. Accosting a Lady in a gathering, instead of the Parisian you think you see, you are seeing only the simulacrum of fashion. Her height, her size, her gait, her waist, her bust, her colorations, her air, her look, her talk, her manners, nothing of all that is hers, and if you saw her in her natural state, you could not recognize her. Now this trade-off is rarely favorable to those women who make it, and in general there is nothing to be gained from all that is substituted for nature. But nature is never completely obliterated; it always shows through somewhere, and the observer's art consists in a certain skill in spotting it. This art is not a difficult one when it comes to the women of this country; for as they have more naturalness than they think, no more is required than to frequent them assiduously, than to detach them from that perpetual posturing they like so much, in order to see them quickly as they are, and it is then that all the aversion they first inspired changes into esteem and friendship.

This I had occasion to observe last week on a country outing to which a few women had foolishly invited me and several other recent arrivals, without paying too much attention to whether we suited them, or perhaps to have the pleasure of laughing at us at their leisure. That did not fail to happen the first day. First they showered us with amusing and malicious quips, which always falling flat soon exhausted their quiver.[19] After that they submitted graciously and, unable to bring us around to using their style, were reduced to adopting ours. I do not know whether they found themselves better off with this trade, for my part I found myself marvelously better off; I was surprised to see that I obtained more enlightenment from them than I would from many men.

Their cleverness so adorned common sense that I regretted they had put so much of it into distorting it, and I deplored, doing better justice to the women of this country, that so many amiable persons lacked reason only because they wanted none. I also perceived that familiar and natural graces insensibly superseded the stiff airs of the city; for one adopts unawares manners that match the things one says, and there is no way to put the grimaces of coquetry[20] on intelligent thoughts. I found them prettier once they were not trying so hard to be pretty, and I felt that in order to please they needed but not to disguise themselves. I ventured to suspect on this basis that Paris, that supposed seat of good taste, is perhaps in all the world the place where there is the least of it, since all the efforts expended there in pleasing distort true beauty.

Thus we remained four or five days together, content with each other and ourselves. Instead of rehearsing Paris and its follies, we forgot it. We had no other care than to enjoy amongst ourselves an agreeable and pleasant society. We needed neither satires nor jests to put ourselves in a good humor, and our laughter, like your Cousin's, was not in mockery but in jollity.

Another thing finally changed my mind on their account. Often in the middle of our liveliest discussions, someone would come utter a word in the hostess's ear. She would go out, close herself in to write, and not return for a long while. It was a simple matter to attribute these disappearances to some sentimental correspondence, or what is thus called. Another woman slipped in a hint to this effect, which was rather ill received, which gave me to understand that if the absentee lacked lovers, at least she had friends. However curiosity having sharpened my perception, what was my surprise when I learned that these supposed Parisian messengers were peasants of the parish, who came in their calamities to implore their Lady's protection! The one, overcharged with taxes[21] to the benefit of someone richer; another, enlisted in the militia without regard to his age and his children;* another, oppressed by a powerful neighbor's unjust lawsuit; another, wiped out by hail, and whose lease had to be promptly paid up. So all had some kind of mercy to ask, all were patiently heard, none was rebuffed, the time attributed to love letters was being employed writing in support of these wretches.[23] I can hardly tell you how astonished I was to learn, both of the pleasure such a young and frivolous woman took in fulfilling these amiable duties, and of how little ostentation she put into it. What? I said, quite moved; if she were Julie, she would be no different! From

---

*We saw that in the other war;[22] but not in this one, so far as I know. Married men are spared, and many thus are induced to marry.

that instant I have regarded her only with respect, and in my eyes all her flaws are blotted out.

Ever since my quest took this turn, I have learned a thousand things advantageous to these same women whom I had first found so unbearable. All foreigners unanimously agree that, aside from fashionable ways of talking, there is no country on earth where women are more enlightened, speak in general more sensibly, more judiciously and know how to give the better advice when needed. If we take away the jargon of gallantry and witticism, what profit will we derive from the conversation of a Spanish, Italian, or German woman? None, and you know, Julie, what our Swiss women are usually like in this respect. But if you dare appear ungallant and entice French women out of that fortress, which in truth they are hardly willing to forsake, you can still find a worthy opponent in the open field, and it is like wrestling with a man, so well does she know how to brandish reason and make a virtue out of necessity. With regard to good character, I shall not attest the zeal with which they serve their friends, for what governs in this may be a certain intensity of amour-propre common to all countries; but whereas ordinarily they love only themselves, a lengthy habituation, when they have enough constancy to acquire it, takes the place of a fairly warm sentiment. Those who can sustain a ten-year attachment ordinarily maintain it for life, and they love their old friends more tenderly, more certainly at least than their young lovers.

A rather common remark that seems to tax women is that they do everything in this country, and consequently more evil than good; but what justifies them is that they do evil impelled by men, and good on their own initiative. This in no way contradicts what I was saying above, that the heart has nothing to do with the commerce of the two sexes: for French gallantry has given women a universal power that requires no tender sentiment to perdure. Everything depends on them; nothing is done that is not by or for them; Olympus and Parnassus, glory and fortune are equally under their power. Books have only as much value, authors have only as much admiration as it pleases women to grant them; they decide sovereignly about the highest knowledge, as well as the most agreeable. Poetry, Literature, history, philosophy, even politics, one can notice right away by the style of all books that they are written to amuse pretty women, and the Bible has just been recast in the form of gallant stories.[24] In business matters, they have a natural influence even over their husbands for obtaining what they ask for, not because they are their husbands, but because they are men and the convention is that a man shall refuse nothing to any woman, were she his own wife.

Furthermore, this domination is founded on neither attachment nor respect, but only politeness and knowledge of the ways of the world; for besides, it is no less essential in French gallantry to scorn women than to serve them. This scorn is a sort of authority that impresses them; it testifies that one has spent enough time among them to know them. Anyone who respected them would pass for a novice in their eyes, a knight-errant, a man who has known women only in Novels. They judge themselves with such equity that to honor them would make a man unworthy of pleasing them, and the principal quality of a man of good fortunes is to be supremely impertinent.

However that may be, it is no use for them to take pride in meanness; they are good in spite of themselves, and this above all is how their goodness of heart serves a purpose. In any country people in charge of much business are always repugnant and short on commiseration, and Paris being the business center of Europe's largest people, those who conduct it are also the hardest of men. So it is to women one turns to obtain favors; they are the recourse of the wretched; they are not deaf to their cries; they listen to them, console and serve them. In the midst of the frivolous life they lead, they know how to take moments away from their pleasures to give over to their good natural disposition, and though a few make a vile traffic of the services they render, thousands of others attend every day to aiding the poor with their purse and the oppressed with their influence. It is true that their attentions are often indiscreet, and that they do unscrupulous harm to the wretched they do not know, in order to serve the ones they know: but how can one know everyone in such a large country, and what more can goodness of soul do separated from true virtue, whose most sublime accomplishment is less to do good than never to do wrong? With that qualification, it is certain that they have some inclination for the good, that they do a great deal of good, do it wholeheartedly, that they alone maintain in Paris the little bit of humanity that still prevails there, and that without them one would see greedy and insatiable men devouring each other like wolves.

I would never have learnt all that if I had kept to the depictions furnished by those who spin out Novels and Comedies, who are inclined to see in women ridiculous traits they themselves share rather than the good qualities they do not possess, or who paint masterpieces of virtue that women exempt themselves from imitating by styling them fantasies, instead of urging them to do good by praising the good they really do. Novels are perhaps the ultimate kind of instruction remaining to be offered to a people so corrupt that any other is useless; then I would wish that the composition of these sorts of books be permitted only to honest but sensible persons whose hearts would depict themselves in their writings, to authors who would not be above human frailties, who would not from the very start display virtue in Heaven beyond the reach of men, but induce us to love it by depicting it at first less austere, and then from the lap of vice know the art of leading men imperceptibly toward it.[25]

I forewarned you, I in no way share the common opinion concerning this country's women. They are unanimously found to possess the most enchanting manner of engaging conversation, the most seductive graces, the most refined coquetry, sublimity in gallantry, and the art of pleasing to the supreme degree. For my part, I find their way of accosting you shocking, their coquetry repulsive, their manners immodest. I imagine that the heart must close itself to all their advances, and I shall never be persuaded that they could for a moment speak of love without revealing themselves at the same time as incapable of inspiring and of feeling any.

On the other hand, renown teaches us to mistrust their character, it depicts them as frivolous, devious, wily, foolish, fickle, speaking well, but not thinking, feeling even less, and thus expending all their merit in empty prattle. All this seems to me to be external to them like their hoops and their rouge. These are vices just for show, which one must possess in Paris, and which ultimately conceal their sense, reason, humanity, natural goodness; they are less indiscreet, less meddlesome than in our country, less perhaps than anywhere else. They are more solidly instructed and their instruction contributes more to their judgment. In a word, if I dislike them for all that characterizes the sex they have disfigured, I respect them for relations with ours that do us honor, and I find that they make a hundred times finer men of merit than appealing women.

Conclusion: if Julie had not existed, if my heart could have endured some attachment other than the one for which it was born, never would I have taken my wife in Paris, still less my mistress; but I would willingly have made a lady friend here, and that treasure would have consoled me, perhaps, for not finding here the other two.*

---

*I shall take care not to pronounce on this letter; but I doubt that a judgment that liberally grants to the women in question qualities they scorn, and denies them the only ones they deem important, is likely to be welcomed by them.

CHAPTER SEVEN

Women of Geneva

[*At this point of the* Letter to d'Alembert *Rousseau is discussing Geneva's political and social institutions. He defends the existence of men's clubs or "circles," claiming that they will be undermined by the establishment of a theater. He introduces the section below by saying that he is taking particular care to write it for a nonphilosophic, general audience.*]

Let us follow the indications of nature; let us consult the good of Society; we shall find that the two sexes must sometimes gather together, and usually live separately. I have said this before in relation to women, I am now saying it in relation to men. They feel as much as and even more than women do the effects of their too intimate commerce; women lose only their morals from it, and we lose our morals and our constitution from it at the same time: for this weaker sex, in no condition to take on our manner of living, which is too hard for them, forces us to take on theirs which is too soft for us; and no longer wanting to endure separation, for lack of being able to make themselves into men, women make us into women.

This inconvenience, which degrades man, is very great everywhere; but above all it is in States like ours that it is important to prevent it. Whether a Monarch governs men or women, must be rather indifferent to him provided that he is obeyed; but in a Republic, men are necessary.*

The ancients passed almost their whole lives in the open air, either

---

* I shall be told that they are necessary for Kings for war. Not at all. Instead of thirty thousand men, they need only, for example, raise a hundred thousand women. Women are not lacking in courage; they prefer honor to life; when they fight, they fight well. The inconvenience of their sex is not to be able to bear the fatigues of war, and the extremes of the seasons. The secret, then, is always to have three times as many as are necessary for fighting, so as to sacrifice the other two-thirds to illness and mortality. Who would believe that this joke, the application of which is seen clearly enough, was taken literally in France by some intelligent people![1]

attending to their business, or regulating that of the State in the public square, or taking a walk in the Country, in gardens, at the seaside, in the rain, in the sun, and almost always bareheaded.* In all that, no women at all; but they knew very well how to find them at need, and we do not see at all from their Writings and from the samples of their conversations that we have left, that either mind or taste, or even love, lost anything from this reserve. As for us, we have taken on completely opposite manners; devoted in a cowardly way to the wishes of the sex that we ought to protect and not serve, we have learned to despise it while obeying it, to insult it by means of our mocking cares; and each woman of Paris gathers in her apartment a seraglio of men more women than she is, who know how to render to beauty every sort of homage, aside from that of the heart which it deserves. But look at these same men, always constrained in these voluntary prisons, get up, sit down again, go and come ceaselessly to the fireplace, to the window, pick up and put down a fan a hundred times, leaf through some books, glance at some pictures, turn, pirouette around the room, while the idol, stretched out motionless in her lounge chair, has nothing active except her tongue and her eyes. Whence this difference, if it is not because nature, which imposes this sedentary and stay-at-home life on women, prescribes a completely opposite one to men, and because this uneasiness indicates a true need in them? If the orientals, whom the heat of the climate causes to sweat quite a bit, do little exercise and do not walk around at all, at least they do sit down in the open air and breathe at their ease; while here the women are very careful to stifle their male friends in good, well-closed-up rooms.

If one compares the strength of ancient men to that of the men of today, one does not find any sort of equality in it. Our exercises at the riding academy are child's play next to those of ancient Gymnastics; tennis has been left off as too tiring; one can no longer travel on horseback. I say nothing about our troops. The marches of the Greek and Roman armies are now inconceivable; the distance traveled, the labor, the burden of the Roman soldier tires us out merely reading about it, and overwhelms the imagination. A horse was not allowed to infantry Officers. Often the Generals made on foot the same journeys as their troops. Never did the two Catos travel any other way either alone, or with their armies. Otho himself, the effeminate Otho, marched in armor at the

*After the battle won by Cambyses over Psammeticus, among the dead they distinguished the Egyptians who were always bareheaded, by the extreme hardness of their skulls; as opposed to which, the Persians, always wearing their large tiaras, had such tender skulls, that they were broken effortlessly. Herodotus was himself a witness of this difference a long time afterward.[2]

head of his, going to confront Vitellius. Try to find at present a single warrior capable of doing as much. We are diminished in everything. Our Painters and our Sculptors complain about no longer finding models comparable to those of antiquity. Why is that? Has man degenerated? Has the species a physical decrepitude, as well as the individual? On the contrary; the barbarians of the north who have, so to speak, populated Europe with a new race, were taller and stronger than the Romans, whom they conquered and subjugated. We should, then, be stronger ourselves, who, for the most part, are descended from these newcomers; but the first Romans lived as men,* and found in their continuous exercises the vigor that nature had refused them, instead of which we lose ours in the indolent and cowardly life into which dependency on the Female Sex reduces us. If the Barbarians about whom I was just speaking lived with women, they nonetheless did not live like them; they were the ones who had the courage to live as the men did, as did also those of Sparta. The woman made herself robust and the man did not enervate himself.

If this effort to contradict nature is harmful to the body, it is even more so to the mind. Imagine what the caliber of the soul might be of a man occupied solely with the important business of amusing women, and who passes his entire life in doing for them what they should be doing for us when, exhausted by labors of which they are incapable, our minds need relaxation. Having abandoned ourselves to these puerile habits, what great thing could we ever raise ourselves up to? Our talents, our writings show the traces of our frivolous occupations:** pleasant if you wish, but petty and cold like our feelings; their entire merit consists in that facile turn that it is not difficult to give to trifles. Those crowds of ephemeral works that are born every day, being made only to

---

*The Romans were the smallest and weakest men of all the peoples of Italy, and this difference was so great, says Titus Livius, that it was noticed at first glance in the troops of each. Nevertheless, exercise and discipline so prevailed over nature, that the weak did what the strong could not do, and conquered them.

**Women in general do not love any art, are not knowledgeable in any, and have no Genius. They can succeed in little works that require only lightness of mind, taste, grace, sometimes even philosophy and reasoning. They can acquire science, erudition, talents, and everything that is acquired by virtue of labor. But that celestial fire that heats up and sets afire the soul, that genius that consumes and devours, that burning eloquence, those sublime raptures that carry their ecstasies all the way to the depths of the heart, will always be lacking in women's writings; all of them are cold and pretty just as they are; they will have as much wit as you would like, never a soul; they would be a hundred times more sensible than passionate. They know neither how to describe nor to feel even love itself. Only Sappho as far as I know, and one other, deserve to be excepted. I would bet anything in the world that the *Portuguese Letters* were written by a man.[3] Now everywhere that women dominate, their taste must also dominate: and that is what determines the taste of our Century.

amuse women, and having neither force nor profundity—all fly from the dressing table to the shop counter. That is the way to rewrite the same things over and over again, and to make them ever new. Two or three will be cited to me that will serve as exceptions; but I, I shall cite a hundred thousand that will confirm the rule: it is for that reason that the majority of the productions of our age will pass away along with it, and posterity will believe that people wrote very few books in this very Century in which so many have been written.

It would not be difficult to show that, instead of gaining by these practices, women lose by them. They are flattered without being loved; they are served without being honored; they are surrounded by fellows who dance attendance, but they no longer have any lovers; and the worst is that the former, without having the others' feelings, do not usurp all their rights any less. Having become too common and too easy, the society of the two sexes has produced these two effects, and this is how the general spirit of gallantry stifles genius and love at the same time.

As for me, I hardly conceive how one gives so little honor to women as to dare to address to them those vapid gallant speeches, those insulting and mocking compliments, to which one does not even deign to give an air of good faith; to insult them by those obvious lies: is this not to declare to them rather clearly that one does not find any obliging truth to tell them? That love deludes itself about the qualities of what one loves happens only too often—but is it a question of love in all this paltry jargon? Don't even those who make use of it, make use of it equally for all women? And wouldn't they be in despair if one believed them to be seriously in love with a single one? Let them not be uneasy about it. It would be necessary to have strange ideas of love to believe them to be capable of it, and nothing is farther from its tone than that of gallantry. From the manner in which I conceive this terrible passion, its turmoil, its wanderings, its palpitations, its raptures, its burning expressions, its more energetic silence, its inexpressible gazes that their timidity renders reckless, and that show desires by means of fear—it seems to me that after such a vehement language, if the lover happened to say a single time, *I love you*, the indignant lover would say to him, *you don't love me any more*, and would not see him again in her life.

Our circles still preserve among us some image of ancient morals. Among themselves the men, dispensed from lowering their ideas to the reach of women and from gallantly dressing up reason, can indulge in grave and serious speeches without fear of ridicule. One dares to speak about fatherland and virtue without passing for a sermonizer; one dares to be Oneself without submitting to a Chattering Woman's maxims. If